We Were the Lucky Ones

By Georgia Hunter

We Were the Lucky Ones

a&b

We Were the Lucky Ones

GEORGIA HUNTER

Allison & Busby Limited
12 Fitzroy Mews
London W1T 6DW
allisonandbusby.com

This edition published by Allison & Busby in 2017.

A CIP catalogue record for this book is available from
the British Library.

First Edition

ISBN 978-0-7490-2156-6

Typeset in 11/16 pt Adobe Garamond Pro by
Allison & Busby Ltd.

The paper used for this Allison & Busby publication
has been produced from trees that have been legally sourced
from well-managed and credibly certified forests.

Printed and bound by
CPI Group (UK) Ltd, Croydon, CR0 4YY

To my husband, Robert Farinholt, with all of my heart. And to my grandfather, with love and wonderment

The Kurc Family

March 1939

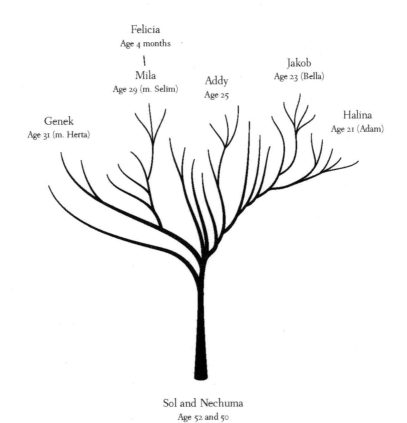

Felicia
Age 4 months

Mila
Age 29 (m. Selim)

Addy
Age 25

Jakob
Age 23 (Bella)

Genek
Age 31 (m. Herta)

Halina
Age 21 (Adam)

Sol and Nechuma
Age 52 and 50

Based on true events

By the end of the Holocaust, ninety per cent of Poland's three million Jews were annihilated; of the more than thirty thousand Jews who lived in Radom, fewer than three hundred survived.

Part I

CHAPTER ONE

Addy
Paris, France ~ Early March 1939

It wasn't his plan to stay up all night. His plan was to leave the Grand Duc around midnight and catch a few hours of sleep at the Gare du Nord before his train ride back to Toulouse. Now – he glances at his watch – it's nearly six in the morning.

Montmartre has this effect on him. The jazz clubs and cabarets, the throngs of Parisians, young and defiant, unwilling to let anything, even the threat of war, dampen their spirits – it's intoxicating. He finishes his cognac and stands, fighting the temptation to stay for one last set; surely there is a later train he can take. But he thinks of the letter tucked into his coat pocket and his breath catches. He should go. Gathering his overcoat, scarf, and cap, he bids his companions *adieu* and weaves his way between the club's dozen or so tables, still half full of patrons smoking Gitanes and swaying to Billie Holiday's 'Time on My Hands'.

As the door swings closed behind him, Addy inhales deeply, savouring the fresh air, raw and cool in his lungs. The frost on Rue Pigalle has begun to melt and the cobblestone street shimmers, a kaleidoscope of greys beneath the late-winter sky. He'll have to walk quickly to make his train, he realises. Turning, he steals a glimpse at his reflection in the club's window, relieved to find the young man peering back at him presentable, despite the sleepless night. His posture is square, his trousers cinched high on his waist, still sharply cuffed and creased, his dark hair combed back the way he prefers it, neat, without a part. Looping his scarf around his neck, he sets off toward the station.

Elsewhere in the city, Addy presumes, the streets are quiet, deserted. Most iron-gated storefronts won't open until noon. Some, whose owners have fled to the countryside, won't open at all – FERMÉ INDÉFINIMENT, the signs in the windows read. But here in Montmartre, Saturday has faded seamlessly to Sunday and the streets are alive with artists and dancers, musicians and students. They stumble from the clubs and cabarets, laughing and carrying on as if they hadn't a worry in the world. Addy tucks his chin into his coat collar as he walks, looking up just in time to sidestep a young woman in a silver lamé gown, striding in his direction. 'Excusez-moi, Monsieur,' she smiles, blushing from beneath a yellow plumed cap. A singer, Addy surmises. A week ago he might have engaged her in conversation. 'Bonjour, Mademoiselle,' he nods, continuing on.

A whiff of fried chicken triggers a rumble in his stomach as Addy rounds the corner onto Rue Victor Masse, where a line has already begun to form outside Mitchell's all-night diner. Through the restaurant's glass door he can see customers chatting over mugs of steaming coffee, their dishes heaped with American-style breakfasts. *Another time*, he tells himself, continuing east toward the station.

His train has barely left the terminal when Addy pulls the letter from his coat pocket. Since it arrived yesterday he's read it twice and thought of little else. He runs his fingers over the return address. *Warszawska 14, Radom, Poland.*

He can picture his mother perfectly, perched at her satinwood writing table, pen in hand, the sun catching the soft, plump curve of her jaw. He misses her more than he ever imagined he would when he left Poland six years ago for France. He was nineteen at the time and had thought hard about staying in Radom, where he'd be near his family, and where he hoped he could make a career of his music – he'd been composing since he was a teenager and couldn't imagine anything more fulfilling than spending his days at a keyboard, writing songs. It was his mother who had urged him to apply to the prestigious *Institut Polytechnique* in Grenoble – and who had insisted that he attend once he was accepted. 'Addy, you are a born engineer,' she said, reminding him of the time when, at seven years old, he'd dismantled the family's broken radio, strewn its parts across the dining-room table, then put it back together again like new.

'It's not so easy to make a living in music,' she said. 'I know it's your passion. You have a gift for it, and you should pursue it. But first, Addy, your degree.'

Addy knew his mother was right. And so, he set off for university, promising that he would return home when he graduated. But as soon as he'd left behind the provincial confines of Radom, a whole new life opened up for him. Four years later, diploma in hand, he was offered a job in Toulouse that paid well. He had friends from all over the world – from Paris, Budapest, London, New Orleans. He had a new taste for art and culture, for *paté de foie gras* and the buttery perfection of a freshly baked croissant. He had a place of his own (albeit a tiny one) in the heart of Toulouse and the luxury of returning to Poland whenever he pleased, which he did at least twice a year, for Rosh Hashanah and Passover. And he had his weekends in Montmartre, a neighbourhood so steeped in musical talent that it was not uncommon for the locals to share a drink at the Hot Club with Cole Porter, to take in an impromptu performance by Django Reinhardt at Bricktop's, or, if you were Addy, to watch in awe as Josephine Baker fox-trotted across the stage at Zelli's with her diamond-collared pet cheetah in tow. Addy couldn't remember a time in his life when he'd been more inspired to put notes to paper – so much so that he'd begun to wonder what it might feel like to move to the United States, the home of the greats, the birthplace of jazz. Maybe in America, he dreamt, he could try his luck at adding his own compositions to the contemporary canon. It was tempting, if it didn't mean putting an even greater distance between him and his family.

As he slips his mother's letter from its envelope, a tiny shock runs down Addy's spine.

Dearest Addy,

Thank you for your letter. Your father and I loved your description of the opera at the Palais Garnier. We're fine here, although Genek is still furious about his demotion, and I don't blame him. Halina is the same as ever, so hotheaded I often wonder if she might implode. We are awaiting an announcement from Jakob that he and Bella are engaged, but you know your brother, he can't be rushed! I've been cherishing my afternoons spent with baby Felicia. I can't wait for you to meet her, Addy. Her hair has begun

15

to grow in – cinnamon red! One of these days she'll sleep through the night. Poor Mila is exhausted. I keep reminding her it will get easier.

Addy flips the letter over, shifts in his seat. It is here that his mother's mood darkens.

I should tell you, darling, that some things have changed here in the last month. Rotsztajn has closed his doors to the ironworks – hard to believe, after nearly fifty years in the business. Kosman, too, has moved his family and the watch trade to Palestine, after his store was vandalised one too many times. I'm not relaying this news to worry you, Addy, I just didn't feel right keeping it from you. Which brings me to the main purpose of this letter: your father and I feel that you should stay in France for Passover and wait until summer to visit us. We'll miss you terribly, but it seems dangerous to travel right now, especially across German borders. Please, Addy, think about it. Home is home – we'll be here. In the meantime, send us news when you can. How is the new composition coming along?

With love, Mother

Addy sighs, trying once again to make sense of it all. He's heard of shops closing, of Jewish families leaving for Palestine. His mother's news doesn't come as a surprise. It's her tone that unsettles him. She's mentioned in the past how things have begun to change around her – she'd been livid when Genek was stripped of his law degree – but mostly Nechuma's letters are cheerful, upbeat. Just last month, she'd asked if he would join her for a Moniusko performance at the Grand Theatre in Warsaw and had told him of the anniversary dinner she and Sol enjoyed at Wierzbicki's, of how Wierzbicki himself had greeted them at the door, offered to prepare something special for them, off the menu.

This letter is different. His mother, Addy realises, is afraid.

He shakes his head. Not once in his twenty-five years has he ever known Nechuma to express fear of any kind. Nor has he or any of his brothers and sisters ever missed a Passover together in Radom. Nothing is more important to his mother than her family – and now she is asking him to stay in Toulouse for the holiday. At first, Addy had convinced himself that she was being overly anxious. But was she?

He stares out the window at the familiar French countryside. The sun is visible from behind the clouds; there are hints of spring colour in the fields. The world looks benign, the same as it always has. And yet these cautionary words from his mother have shifted his equilibrium, thrown him off-balance.

Dizzy, Addy closes his eyes, thinking back to his last visit home in September, searching for a clue, something he might have missed. His father, he recalls, had played his weekly game of cards with a group of fellow merchants – Jews and Poles – beneath the white-eagle fresco on the ceiling of Podworski's Pharmacy; Father Krol, a priest at the Church of Saint Bernardine and an admirer of Mila's virtuosity at the piano, had stopped by for a recital. For Rosh Hashanah, the cook had made honey-glazed challah, and Addy had stayed up listening to Benny Goodman, drinking Côte de Nuits and laughing with his brothers late into the night. Even Jakob, reserved as he usually was, had set down his camera and joined in the camaraderie. Things had seemed relatively normal.

And then Addy's throat goes dry as he considers a thought: what if the clues were there but he hadn't been paying enough attention? Or worse, what if he'd missed them simply because he didn't want to see them?

His mind flashes to the freshly painted swastika he'd come across on the wall of the Jardin Goudouli in Toulouse. To the day he'd overheard his bosses at the engineering firm whispering about whether they should consider him a liability – they'd thought he was out of earshot. To the shops closed all over Paris. To the photographs in the French papers of the aftermath of November's *Kristallnacht*: smashed storefronts, synagogues burnt to the ground, thousands of Jews fleeing Germany, rolling their bedside lamps and potatoes and elderly along with them in wheelbarrows.

The signs were there, for sure. But Addy had downplayed them, brushed them off. He'd told himself that there was no harm in a little graffiti; that if he were to lose his job, he'd find a new one; that the events unfolding in Germany, though disturbing, were happening across the border and would be contained. Now, though, with his mother's letter in hand, he sees with alarming clarity the warnings he'd chosen to ignore.

Addy opens his eyes, nauseated suddenly by a single notion: *you should have returned home months ago.*

He folds the letter into its envelope and slides it back into his coat pocket. He'll write to his mother, he resolves. As soon as he gets to his flat in Toulouse. He'll tell her not to worry, that he will be returning to Radom as planned, that he wants to be with the family now more than ever. He'll tell her that the new composition is coming along well, and that he looks forward to playing it for her. This thought brings a trace of comfort, as he imagines himself at the keys of his parents' Steinway, his family gathered around.

Addy lets his gaze fall once again to the placid countryside. Tomorrow, he decides, he'll buy a train ticket, line up his travel documents, pack his belongings. He won't wait for Passover. His boss will be angry with him for leaving sooner than expected, but Addy doesn't care. All that matters is that in a few short days, he'll be on his way home.

MARCH 15, 1939: *A year after annexing Austria, Germany invades Czechoslovakia. Meeting little resistance, Hitler establishes the Protectorate of Bohemia and Moravia from Prague the next day. With this occupation, the Reich gains not only territory but also skilled labour and massive firepower in the form of weaponry manufactured in those regions – enough to arm nearly half of the Wehrmacht at the time.*

CHAPTER TWO

Genek
Radom, Poland ~ March 18, 1939

Genek lifts his chin and a plume of smoke snakes from a part in his lips toward the grey-tiled ceiling of the bar. 'Last hand,' he declares.

Across the table, Rafal catches his eye. 'So soon?' He takes a drag from his own cigarette. 'Did your wife promise you something special if you got home at a decent hour?' Rafal winks, exhaling. Herta had joined the group for dinner but had left early.

Genek laughs. He and Rafal have been friends since grade school, when much of their time was spent huddled over lunch trays discussing which of their classmates to ask to the year-end *studniówka* ball, or whom they'd rather see naked, Evelyn Brent or Renée Adorée. Rafal knows Herta isn't like the girls Genek used to date, but he likes to give him hell when Herta isn't around. Genek can hardly blame him. Until he met Herta, women were his weakness (cards and cigarettes, too, if he's being honest). With his blue eyes, a dimple on each cheek, and an irresistible Hollywood charm, he'd spent most of his twenties basking in the role of one of Radom's most sought-after bachelors. At the time, he hadn't minded the attention in the least. But then Herta came along and all of that changed. It's different now. *She's* different.

Under the table, something brushes Genek's calf. He glances at the young woman sitting beside him. 'Wish you would stay,' she says, her eyes catching his. Genek had just met the girl that night – Klara. No, Kara. He can't remember. She is a friend of Rafal's wife, visiting from Lublin. She curls a corner of her mouth into a coy smile, the toe of her oxford still pressed against his leg.

In his former life he might have stayed. But Genek no longer has any interest in flirting. He smiles at the girl, feeling a little sorry for her. 'Matter of fact, I think I'm out,' he says, setting his cards down on the table. He stubs out his Murad, leaving the butt to stick up like a crooked tooth in the crowded ashtray, and stands. 'Gentlemen, ladies – it's always a pleasure. I'll see you. Ivona,' he adds, addressing Rafal's wife and nodding toward his friend, 'it's on you to keep that one out of trouble.' Ivona laughs. Rafal winks again. Genek throws up a two-fingered salute and heads for the door.

The March night is unusually cold. He buries his hands in his coat pockets and sets off at a hurried clip toward Zielona Street, relishing the prospect of returning home to the woman he loves. Somehow, he'd known Herta was his girl the instant he laid eyes on her, two years ago. The weekend is still sharp in his memory. They were skiing in Zakopane, a resort town tucked amid the peaks of Poland's Tatra Mountains. He was twenty-nine, Herta twenty-five. They'd happened to share a chair lift, and on the ten-minute ride to the summit, Genek had fallen for her. For her lips, to start, because they were full and heart-shaped, and about all he could see of her behind the cream-white wool of her hat and scarf. But there was also her German accent, which forced him to listen to her in a way that he wasn't used to, and her smile, so uninhibited, and the way, halfway up the mountain, she'd tipped her head back, closed her eyes, and said, 'Don't you just love the smell of pine in the wintertime?' He'd laughed, thinking for a moment that she was joking before realising she wasn't; her sincerity was a trait he would grow to admire, along with her unabashed love of the outdoors and her propensity for finding beauty in the simplest of things. He'd followed her down the slope, trying not to think too much of the fact that she was twice the skier he would ever be, then slid up next to her in the lift line and asked her to dinner. When she hesitated, he smiled and told her that he'd already booked a horse-drawn sleigh. She laughed and, to Genek's delight, agreed to the date. Six months later, he proposed.

Inside his apartment, Genek is glad to see a glow emanating from beneath the bedroom door. He finds Herta in bed with a favourite collection of Rilke poems propped on her knees. Herta is originally from Bielsko, a largely German-speaking town in western Poland. In conversation, she rarely uses the language she grew up with any more, but she enjoys reading in her native tongue, poetry especially. She doesn't appear to notice as Genek enters the room.

'That must be one engaging verse,' Genek teases.

'Oh!' Herta says, looking up. 'I didn't hear you come in.'

'I was worried you'd be asleep,' Genek grins. He slips out of his coat, and tosses it over the back of a chair, blowing into his hands to warm them.

Herta smiles and sets her book down on her chest, using a finger to keep her place. 'You're home far earlier than I thought you'd be. Have you lost all of our money at the table? Did they kick you out?'

Genek removes his shoes and his blazer, unbuttons his shirt cuffs. 'I'm ahead, actually. It was a good night. Just a bore without you.' Against the white sheets, in her pale yellow gown with her deep-set eyes and perfect lips and chestnut hair spilling in waves over her shoulders, Herta looks like something out of a dream, and once again Genek is reminded how immensely lucky he is to have found her. He undresses down to his underwear and crawls into bed beside her. 'I missed you,' he says, propping himself on an elbow and kissing her.

Herta licks her lips. 'Your last drink, let me guess – Bichat.'

Genek nods, laughs. He kisses her again, his tongue finding hers.

'Love, we should be careful,' Herta whispers, pulling away.

'Aren't we always careful?'

'It's just – about that time.'

'Oh,' Genek says, savoring her warmth, the sweet floral residue of shampoo in her hair.

'It would be foolish to let it happen now,' Herta adds, 'don't you think?'

Hours before, over dinner, they'd talked with their friends about the threat of war, about how easily Austria and Czechoslovakia had fallen into the hands of the Reich, and of how things had begun to change in Radom. Genek had ranted about his demotion to assistant at the law firm and had threatened to move to France. 'At least there,' he'd fumed, 'I could use my degree.'

'I'm not so sure you'd be better off in France,' Ivona had said. 'The Führer isn't just targeting German-speaking territories any more. What if this is just the beginning? What if Poland is next?'

The table had quieted for a moment before Rafal broke the silence. 'Impossible,' he claimed, with a dismissive shake of his head. 'He might try, but he'll be stopped.'

Genek had agreed. 'The Polish Army would never let it happen,' he said. Genek recalls now that it was during this conversation that Herta had stood to excuse herself.

She's right, of course. They should be careful. To bring a child into a world that has begun to feel disturbingly close to the brink of collapse would be imprudent and irresponsible. But lying so close, Genek can think of nothing but her skin, the curve of her thigh against his. Her words, like the tiny bubbles in his last flute of champagne, float from her mouth, dissolving somewhere in the back of his throat.

Genek kisses her a third time, and as he does Herta closes her eyes. *She only half means it*, he thinks. He reaches over her for the light, feeling her soften beneath him. The room goes dark, and he slips a hand under her gown.

'Cold!' Herta shrieks.

'Sorry,' he whispers.

'No, you're not. Genek . . .'

'The war, the war, the war.' He kisses her cheekbone, her earlobe. 'I'm tired of it already and it hasn't even begun,' he says, marching his fingers from her ribs down to her waistline.

Herta sighs, then giggles.

'Here's a thought,' Genek adds, his eyes widening as if he's just had a revelation. 'What if there *is* no war?' He shakes his head, incredulous. 'We'll have deprived ourselves for *nothing*. And Hitler, the little prick, will have won.' He flashes a smile.

Herta runs a finger along the hollow of his cheek. 'These dimples are the death of me,' she says, shaking her head. Genek grins harder, and Herta nods. 'You're right,' she acquiesces. 'It would be tragic.' Her book meets the floor with a thud as she rolls to her side to face him. '*Bumsen der krieg.*'

Genek can't help but laugh. 'I agree. *Fuck the war*,' he says, pulling the blanket up over their heads.

CHAPTER THREE

Nechuma
Radom, Poland ~ April 4, 1939 – First day of Passover

Nechuma has arranged the table with her finest china and crockery, setting each place just so, atop a white lace tablecloth. Sol sits at the head, his worn, leatherbound Haggadah in one hand, a polished silver kiddush cup in the other. He clears his throat. 'Today . . .' he begins, lifting his gaze to the familiar faces around the table, 'we honour what matters most – our family, and our tradition.' His eyes, normally flanked with laugh lines, are serious, his voice a sober baritone. 'Today,' he continues, 'we celebrate the Festival of Matzahs, the time of our liberation.' He glances down at his text. 'Amen.'

'Amen,' the others echo, sipping their wine. A bottle is passed and glasses are refilled.

The room is quiet as Nechuma stands to light the candles. Making her way to the middle of the table, she strikes a match and cups a palm around it, bringing it quickly to each wick, hoping the others won't notice the flame shivering between her fingers. When the candles are lit, she circles a hand over them three times and then shields her eyes as she recites the opening blessing. Taking her place at the end of the table opposite her husband, she folds her hands over her lap and her eyes meet Sol's. She nods, an indication for him to begin.

As Sol's voice once again fills the room, Nechuma's gaze slips to the chair she's left empty for Addy, and her chest grows heavy with a familiar ache. His absence consumes her.

Addy's letter had arrived a week ago. In it, he'd thanked Nechuma for her candor, and asked her please not to worry. He would return home as soon as he could collect his travel documents, he wrote. This news brought Nechuma both relief and concern. She had no greater wish than to have her son home for Passover, except, of course, to know that he was safe in France. She'd tried to be honest, had hoped he would understand that Radom was a dismal place right now, that travelling through German-occupied regions wasn't worth the risk, but perhaps she'd held back too much. It wasn't just the Kosmans, after all, who had left. There were half a dozen others. She hadn't told him about the Polish customers they'd recently lost at the shop, or about the bloody brawl that had broken out the week before between two of Radom's soccer teams, one Polish, the other Jewish, and how young men from each team still walked around with split lips and black eyes, glaring at one other. She'd left it all unsaid to spare him pain and worry, but perhaps in doing so, she'd exposed him to a greater danger.

Nechuma had replied to Addy's letter, imploring him to be safe in his travels, and then assumed he was en route. Every day since, she's jumped at the sound of footsteps in the foyer, her heart thrumming at the thought of finding Addy at the door, a smile spread across his handsome face, his valise in hand. But the footsteps are never his. Addy has not come.

'Maybe he had to wrap up some things at the firm,' Jakob offered earlier in the week, sensing her growing concern. 'I can't imagine his boss would let him leave without a couple of weeks' notice.'

But all Nechuma can think is: *what if he's been held up at the border? Or worse?* To reach Radom, Addy would have to travel north through Germany, or south through Austria and Czechoslovakia, both of which have fallen under Nazi rule. The possibility of her son in the hands of the Germans – a fate that might have been avoided had she been more forthright with him, had she been more adamant in asking him to remain in France – has kept her lying awake at night for days.

As tears prick at her eyes, Nechuma's thoughts cartwheel back in time to another April day, during the Great War, a quarter century ago, when she and Sol were forced to spend Passover huddled in the building's basement. They'd been evicted from their apartment and, like so many of their friends at the time, had nowhere else to go. She remembers the suffocating stench of human waste, the air thick with incessant moans of empty stomachs, the thunder of distant cannons, the rhythmic scrape of Sol's blade against wood as he whittled away at a log of old firewood with a paring knife, sculpting figurines for the children to play with and picking splinters from his fingers. The holiday had come and gone without acknowledgement, never mind a traditional Seder. Somehow, they lived three years in that basement, the children surviving on her breast milk while Hungarian officers bivouacked in their apartment upstairs.

Nechuma looks across the table at Sol. Those three years, though they nearly broke her, are now as far behind her as possible, almost as if they'd happened to someone else entirely. Her husband never speaks of that time; her children, thankfully, do not recall the experience in any palpable way. There have been pogroms since – there will always be pogroms – but Nechuma refuses to contemplate a return to a life in hiding, a life without sunlight, without rain, without music and art and philosophical debate, the simple, nourishing riches she's grown to cherish. No, she will not go back underground like some kind of feral creature; she will not live like that ever again.

It couldn't possibly come to that.

Her mind turns once more, to her own childhood, to the sound of her mother's voice telling her how it was common when she herself was growing up in Radom for little Polish boys to hurl stones at her kerchiefed head at the park, how riots had erupted all over the city when the town synagogue was first built. Nechuma's mother had shrugged it off. 'We just learnt to keep our heads down, and our children close,' she said. And sure enough, the attacks, the pogroms, they passed. Life went on, as it did before. As it always does.

Nechuma knows that the German threat, like the threats that came before it, will also pass. And anyway, their situation now is far different than it was during the Great War. She and Sol have worked tirelessly to earn a living, to establish themselves among the city's top-tier professionals. They speak Polish, even at home, while many of the city's Jews converse only in Yiddish, and rather than live in the Old Quarter as the majority of Radom's less affluent Jews do, they own a stately apartment in the centre of town, complete with a cook and a maid and the luxuries of indoor plumbing, a bathtub they imported themselves from Berlin, a refrigerator, and – their most prized possession – a Steinway baby grand piano. Their fabric shop is thriving; Nechuma takes great care on her buying trips to collect the highest-quality textiles, and their clients, both Polish and Jewish, come from as far as Kraków to purchase their ladies' wear and silk. When their children were of school-age, Sol and Nechuma sent them to elite private academies, where, thanks to their tailored shirts and perfect Polish, they fit in seamlessly with the majority of the students, who were Catholic. In addition to providing them with the best possible education, Sol and Nechuma hoped to give their children a chance to sidestep the undertones of anti-Semitism that had defined Jewish life in Radom since before any of them could remember. Though the family was proudly rooted in its Jewish heritage and very much a part of the local Jewish community, for her children Nechuma chose a path she hoped would steer them toward opportunity – and away from persecution. It is a path she stands by, even when now and then at the synagogue, or while shopping at one of the Jewish bakeries in the Old Quarter, she catches one of Radom's more orthodox Jews glancing at her with a look of disapproval – as if her decision to mix with the Poles has somehow diminished her faith as a Jew. She refuses to be bothered by these encounters. She knows her faith – and besides, religion, to Nechuma, is a private matter.

Pinching her shoulder blades down her back, she feels the weight of her bosom lift from her ribs. It's not like her to be so inundated with worry, so distracted. *Pull yourself together*, she chides. *The family will be fine*, she reminds herself. *They have a healthy savings. They have connections. Addy will turn up. The mail has been unreliable; in all likelihood, a letter explaining his absence will arrive any day. It will all be* fine.

As Sol recites the blessing of the *karpas*, Nechuma dips a sprig of parsley into a bowl of salt water and her fingers brush Jakob's. She sighs, feeling the tension begin to drain from her jaw. Sweet Jakob. He catches her eye and smiles, and Nechuma's heart fills with gratitude for the fact that he is still living under her roof. She adores his company, his calm. He's different from the others. Unlike his siblings, who entered the world red-faced and wailing, Jakob arrived as white as her hospital bedsheets and silent, as if mimicking the giant snowflakes falling peacefully to the earth outside her window on that wintery February morning, twenty-three years ago. Nechuma would never forget the harrowing moments before he finally cried – she was sure at the time that he wouldn't survive the day – or how, when she held him in her arms and looked into his inky eyes, he'd stared up at her, the skin over his brow creased with a small fold, as if he were deep in thought. It was then that she understood who he was. Quiet, yes, but astute. Like his brothers and sisters born before and after him, a tiny version of the person he would grow up to be.

She watches as Jakob leans to whisper something in Bella's ear. Bella brings a napkin to her lips, stifling a smile. On her collar, a pin catches the candlelight – a gold rose-shaped brooch with an ivory pearl at its center, a gift from Jakob. He'd given it to her a few months after they met at gymnasium. He was fifteen at the time, she fourteen. Back then, all Nechuma knew of Bella was that she took her studies seriously, that she came from a family of modest means (according to Jakob, her father, a dentist, was still settling the loans he'd taken on to pay for his daughters' education), and that she sewed many of her own clothes, a revelation that impressed Nechuma and prompted her to wonder which of Bella's smartest blouses were store-bought and which were handmade. It was shortly after Jakob gave Bella the brooch that he declared her his soulmate.

'Jakob, love, you're *fifteen* . . . and you've just met!' Nechuma had exclaimed. But Jakob wasn't one to exaggerate, and here they are, eight years later, inseparable. It's only a matter of time before they are married, Nechuma figures. Perhaps Jakob will propose when the talk of war has subsided. Or maybe he's waiting until he's saved enough to afford his own place. Bella lives with her parents, too – just a few blocks west on Witolda Boulevard. Whatever the case, Nechuma has no doubt that Jakob has a plan.

At the head of the table, Sol breaks a piece of matzah gently in two. He sets one half of the matzah on a plate and wraps the other in a napkin. When the children were younger, Sol would spend weeks plotting the perfect hiding spot for the matzah, and when the time came in the ceremony to unearth the hidden *afikomen*, the kids would scamper like mice through the apartment in search of it. Whoever was lucky enough to find it would barter ruthlessly until inevitably walking away with a proud smile and enough zloty in his or her palm to purchase a sack of fudge *krówki* at Pomianowski's candy store. Sol was a businessman and played hard – the King Negotiator, they called him – but his children knew well that deep down he was as soft as a mound of freshly churned butter, and that with enough patience and charm, they could milk him for every zloty in his pocket. He hasn't actually hidden the matzah in years, of course; his children, as teenagers, finally boycotted the ritual – 'We're a bit old for it, don't you think, Father?' they said – but Nechuma knows that the moment his granddaughter Felicia has learnt to walk, he'll resume the tradition.

It's Adam's turn to read aloud. He lifts his Haggadah and peers at it through thick-rimmed eyeglasses. With his narrow nose, high, sharp cheekbones, and flawless skin accentuated in the candlelight, he appears almost regal. Adam Eichenwald had arrived in the Kurc household several months ago, when Nechuma set a room for let sign in the window of the fabric store. Her uncle had recently died, leaving the family with an empty bedroom, and her home, even with her two youngest still there, had begun to feel empty. Nechuma loved nothing more than a crowded dinner table. When Adam had stepped into the shop to enquire, she was delighted; she offered him the room immediately.

'What a fine-looking young man!' Sol's sister Terza had exclaimed, after he left. 'He's thirty-two? He looks a decade younger.'

'He's Jewish, *and* he's smart,' Nechuma added. What are the odds, the women had whispered about the boy – a graduate in architecture at the Polytechnic National University in Lvov – leaving 14 Warszawska Street unwed? And sure enough, a few weeks later, Adam and Halina were an item.

Halina. Nechuma sighs. Born with an inexplicable mop of honey-blonde hair and incandescent green eyes, Halina is the youngest and the most petite of her children. What she lacks in stature, however, she makes up tenfold in personality. Nechuma has never met a child so obstinate, so capable of talking her way into (or out of) practically anything. She recalls the time when, at fifteen, Halina charmed her mathematics professor out of giving her a demerit when he discovered she'd skipped class to see the matinee of *Trouble in Paradise* on opening day, and the time when, at sixteen, she convinced Addy to take a last-minute overnight train with her to Prague so they could wake up in the City of a Hundred Spires on the birthday they shared. Adam, bless his heart, is clearly allured by her. Thankfully, he's proven nothing but respectful in Sol and Nechuma's presence.

When Adam has finished reading, Sol offers a prayer over the remaining matzah, breaks off a piece, and passes the plate. Nechuma listens as the soft *crack* of unleavened bread makes its way around the table. '*Baruch a-tah A-do-nai,*' Sol sings, but stops short when he's interrupted by a high-pitched cry. Felicia. Blushing, Mila apologises and slips from her seat to scoop Felicia from her bassinet in the corner of the room. Tap-dancing her feet, she shushes softly into Felicia's ear to soothe her. As Sol begins again, Felicia squirms beneath the folds of her swaddle, her face contorting, reddening. When she wails a second time, Mila excuses herself, hurrying down the hallway to Halina's bedroom. Nechuma follows.

'What's wrong, love?' Mila whispers, rubbing a finger along Felicia's top gum as she's seen Nechuma do, trying to pacify her. Felicia turns her head, arches her back, cries harder.

'Do you think she's hungry?' Nechuma asks.

'I fed her not too long ago. I think she's just tired.'

'Here,' Nechuma says, taking Felicia from Mila's arms. Felicia's eyes are pinched shut, her hands curled tight into fists. Her bawls come in short, shrill bursts.

Mila sits down heavily at the foot of Halina's bed. 'I'm so sorry, Mother,' she says, straining not to yell over Felicia's cries. 'I hate that we're causing a fuss.' She rubs her eyes with the heels of her hands. 'I can barely even hear myself *think.*'

'No one minds,' Nechuma says, holding Felicia close to her chest, rocking her gently. After a few minutes, Felicia's cries wane to whimpers and soon she is quiet again, her expression peaceful. *It's mesmerising, the joy of holding a baby in your arms*, Nechuma thinks, breathing in Felicia's sweet almond scent.

'I'm such a fool for assuming this would be easy,' Mila says. When she looks up her eyes are bloodshot, the skin beneath them translucent purple, as if the lack of sleep has left a bruise. She's trying – Nechuma can see that. But it's tough being a new mother. The transition has left her reeling.

Nechuma shakes her head. 'Don't be so hard on yourself, Mila. It's not what you thought it would be, but that's to be expected. With children it's never what you think it's going to be.' Mila looks at her hands and Nechuma recalls how, when she was younger, her eldest daughter wanted nothing more than to be a mother – how she would tend to her dolls, cradling them in the crook of her arm, singing to them, even pretending to nurse them; how she took great pride in caring for her younger siblings, offering to tie their shoes, wrap gauze around their bloodied knees, read to them before bed. Now that she has a child of her own, however, Mila seems overwhelmed by it, as if it were the first time she'd held a baby in her arms.

'I wish I knew what I was doing wrong,' Mila says.

Nechuma sits down at the foot of the bed by her daughter. 'You're doing fine, Mila. I told you, babies are difficult. Especially the first. I nearly lost my mind when Genek was born, trying to figure it out. It just takes some time.'

'It's been five months.'

'Give it a few more.'

Mila is quiet for a moment. 'Thank you,' she finally whispers, looking over at Felicia sleeping peacefully in Nechuma's arms. 'I feel like a wretched failure.'

'You're not. You're just tired. Why don't you call for Estia. She's all done in the kitchen; she can help while we finish our meal.'

'That's a good idea.' Mila sighs, relieved. She leaves Felicia with Nechuma while she goes off to find the maid. When she and Nechuma return to their seats, Mila glances at Selim. 'Okay?' he mouths, and she nods.

Sol spoons a mound of horseradish onto a piece of matzah, and the others do the same. Soon, he is singing again. When the blessing of the *korekh* is complete, it's time, finally, to eat. Platters are passed, and the dining room is filled with the murmur of conversation and the scrape of silver spoons on china as dishes are piled high with salted herring, roasted chicken, potato kugel, and sweet apple *charoset*. The family sips wine and talks quietly, gingerly avoiding the subject of war, and wondering aloud of Addy's whereabouts.

At the sound of Addy's name, the ache creeps back into Nechuma's chest, bringing with it an orchestra of worries. He has been arrested. Incarcerated. Deported. He is hurt. Afraid. He hasn't a way to contact her. She glances again at her son's empty seat. *Where are you, Addy?* She bites her lip. *Don't,* she admonishes, but it's too late. She's been drinking her wine too quickly and has lost her edge. Her throat closes and the table melts into a blurry swath of white. Her tears are poised to flow when she feels a hand over hers, beneath the table. Jakob's. 'It's the horseradish root,' she whispers, waving her free hand in front of her face, blinking. 'Gets me every time.' She dabs discreetly at the corners of her eyes with her napkin. Jakob nods knowingly and squeezes her hand.

Months later, in a different world, Nechuma will look back on this evening, the last Passover when they were nearly all together, and wish with every cell in her body that she could relive it. She will remember the familiar smell of the gefilte, the chink of silver on porcelain, the taste of parsley, briny and bitter on her tongue. She will long for the touch of Felicia's baby-soft skin, the weight of Jakob's hand on hers beneath the table, the wine-induced warmth in the pit of her belly that begged her to believe that everything might actually turn out all right in the end. She will remember how happy Halina had looked at the piano after their meal, how they had danced together, how they all spoke of missing Addy, assuring each other that he'd be home soon. She will replay it all, over and over again, every beautiful moment of it, and savour it, like the last perfect *klapsa* pears of the season.

AUGUST 23, 1939: *Nazi Germany and the Soviet Union sign the Molotov–Ribbentrop Nonaggression Pact, a secret agreement outlining specific boundaries for the future division of much of Northern and Eastern Europe between German and Soviet powers.*

SEPTEMBER 1, 1939: *Germany invades Poland. Two days later, in response, Britain, France, Australia, and New Zealand declare war on Germany. World War II in Europe begins.*

CHAPTER FOUR

Bella
Radom, Poland ~ September 7, 1939

Bella sits upright, knees pulled to her chest, a handkerchief balled in her fist. She can just make out the square-cornered silhouette of a leather suitcase by her bedroom door. Jakob is perched on the edge of the bed by her feet, the cold night-time air still clinging to the tweed of his overcoat. She wonders if her parents had heard him climbing the stairs to their second-storey flat, tiptoeing down the hallway to her room. She had given Jakob a key to the flat years ago so he could visit when he pleased, but he'd never been so bold as to come at this hour. She pushes her toes into the space between the mattress and his thigh.

'They're sending us to Lvov to fight,' Jakob says, out of breath. 'If anything should happen, let's meet there.' Bella searches for Jakob's face in the shadows, but all she can see is the oval of his jawline, the dim whites of his eyes.

'Lvov,' she whispers, nodding. Bella's younger sister Anna and her new husband, Daniel, live in Lvov, a city 350 kilometres south-east of Radom. Anna had been begging Bella to consider moving closer to her, but Bella knew she couldn't leave Jakob. In the eight years that they've known each other, they've never lived more than four hundred metres apart.

Jakob reaches for her hands, laces his fingers between hers. He brings them to his mouth and kisses them. The gesture reminds Bella of the day he first told her he loved her. They'd held hands, fingers entwined as they sat facing each other on a blanket spread across the grass in Kościuszki Park. She was sixteen.

'You're it, beautiful,' Jakob had said softly. His words were so pure, the expression in his hazel eyes so unadulterated, she'd wanted to cry, even though back then she'd wondered what a boy so young thought he knew about love. Today, at twenty-two, she isn't surer of anything. Jakob is the

34

man she'll spend her life with. And now he's leaving Radom, without her.

'How – how will you get there?' Her voice is soft. She's afraid that if she raises it, it will crack, and the sob percolating at the base of her throat will escape. The clock in the corner sounds a single toll and she and Jakob flinch, as if stung by a pair of invisible wasps.

'We've been told to meet at the train station at a quarter past one,' Jakob says, glancing toward the door, letting his hands slip from hers. He cups his palms over her knees. His touch is cool through the cotton of her nightgown. 'I have to go.' He leans his chest against her shins, rests his forehead on hers. 'I love you,' he breathes, the tips of their noses touching. 'More than anything.' She closes her eyes as he kisses her. It's over too quickly. When she opens her eyes, Jakob is gone, and her cheeks are wet.

Bella climbs out of bed and walks to the window, the wooden floorboards cold and smooth beneath her bare feet. Pulling the curtain aside a touch, she stares down at Witolda Boulevard two stories below, scanning for a sign of life – the flicker of a flashlight, anything – but the city has been blacked out for weeks; even the street lamps are extinguished. She can see nothing. It's as if she's staring into an abyss. She jiggles the window open, this time closing her eyes for a moment as she listens for footsteps, for the far-off whine of a German dive-bomber. But the street, like the sky above, is empty, the silence heavy.

So much has happened in a week. It was just six days ago, on the first of September, that the Germans invaded Poland. The very next day, before dawn, bombs began to fall on the outskirts of Radom. The makeshift airstrip was destroyed, along with dozens of tanneries and shoe factories. Her father had boarded up the windows and they'd taken refuge in the basement. When the explosions let up, Radom's men dug trenches – shovel-wielding Poles and Jews shoulder to shoulder – in a last-minute effort to defend the city. But the trenches were useless. Bella and her parents were forced back into hiding as more bombs were dropped, this time in broad daylight from low-flying Stukas and Heinkels, mostly on the Old Quarter, some fifty metres or so from Bella's flat. The aerial attack kept up for days, until the town of Kielce, sixty-five kilometres south-west of Radom, was captured. That was when rumours spread that the Wehrmacht, one of the armed forces of the Third Reich, would soon arrive –

and when radios began blaring from street corners, ordering the young and able to enlist. Men left Radom by the thousands, heading east in haste to join up with the Polish Army, their hearts filled with patriotism and uncertainty.

Bella pictures Jakob, Genek, Selim, and Adam making their way past the city's garment shops and iron foundries, treading silently to the train station, which had somehow been spared in the bombings, a few meagre belongings stashed in their suitcases. A division of the Polish infantry, Jakob had said, awaited in Lvov. But did it really? Why had Poland waited so long to mobilise its men? It's been only a week since the invasion and already reports are disheartening – Hitler's army is too vast, moving too quickly, the Poles are outnumbered more than two to one. Britain and France have promised to help, but so far Poland has seen no sign of military support.

Bella's stomach turns. This wasn't supposed to have happened. They were supposed to be in France by now. That was their plan – to move when Jakob finished law school. He'd find a position at a firm in Paris, or Toulouse, close to Addy; he'd work on the side as a photographer, just as his brother composed music in his spare time. She and Jakob had been charmed by Addy's tales of France and its freedoms. There, they'd marry and start a family. If only they'd had the foresight to go before travel to France became too dangerous, before the thought of leaving their families behind was too unnerving. Bella tries to picture Jakob with his fingers wrapped around the wooden stock of an assault rifle. Could he shoot a man? Impossible, she realises. He's *Jakob*. He isn't cut out for war; there isn't a drop of hostile blood in his body. The only trigger he's meant to press is the one on his camera.

She slides the window gently closed. *Just let the boys make it safely to Lvov,* she prays, over and over, staring into the velvet blackness below.

Three weeks later, Bella is stretched out along a narrow wooden bench running the length of a horse-drawn wagon, exhausted but unable to sleep. *What time is it?* Early afternoon, she'd guess. Beneath the wagon's canvas cover, there isn't enough light to see the hands of her wristwatch. Even outside it's nearly impossible to tell. When the rain lets up, the sky, dense with clouds, remains cloaked in gunmetal grey. How her driver can manage up front, exposed to the elements for so many hours, Bella has no idea. Yesterday it rained so long and hard the road disappeared beneath a river of mud, and the horses had to scramble to keep their balance. Twice the wagon had nearly turned over.

Bella tracks the days by counting the eggs remaining in the provisions basket. They began their journey in Radom with a dozen, and this morning they are down to their last, which makes it the twenty-ninth of September. Normally, to ride by wagon to Lvov would take a week at most. But with the incessant rain, the going has been arduous. Inside the wagon the air is damp and smells of mould; Bella has grown used to the feel of sticky skin, clothes that are perpetually damp.

Listening to the creak of the wagon beneath her, she closes her eyes and thinks about Jakob, remembering the night he'd come to say goodbye, the cool of his hands on her knees, the warmth of his breath on her fingers when he'd kissed them.

It was the eighth of September, just a day after he set off for Lvov, when the Wehrmacht arrived in Radom. The Germans sent a single plane first, and Bella and her father tracked it as it flew low over the city, circling once before dropping an orange flare.

'What does it mean?' Bella asked as the plane receded and then disappeared into a grey expanse of swollen, low-hanging clouds. Her father was silent. 'Father, I'm a grown woman. Just tell me,' Bella had said flatly.

Henry looked away. 'It means they're coming,' he answered, and in his expression, the tight downward curve of his mouth, the pleat of skin between his eyes, she saw something she'd never seen before – her father was scared. An hour later, just as the rain began to fall, Bella watched from the window of her family's flat as rows upon rows of ground forces marched into Radom, unopposed. She heard them before she saw them, their tanks and horses and motorcycles rumbling in through the mud from the west. She held her breath as they came into view, at once afraid to watch and afraid to look away, her eyes glued to them as they rolled down Witolda Boulevard in bottle-green uniforms and rain-speckled goggles, so powerful, so *many* of them. They swarmed the city's empty streets, and by nightfall they occupied the government buildings, proclaiming the city theirs with emphatic *Heil Hitlers* as they hoisted their swastika flags. It was a sight Bella would never forget.

Once the city was officially occupied, everyone was wary, Jews and Poles alike, but it was obvious from the start that the Jews were the Nazis' primary targets. Those who ventured out risked being harassed, humiliated, beaten. Radomers learnt quickly to abandon the safety of their homes only to run the most pressing errands. Bella left only once, to collect some bread and milk, detouring to the nearest Polish grocery when she discovered that the Jewish market she used to frequent in the Old Quarter had been ransacked and closed. She kept to the backstreets and walked with a quick, purposeful stride, but on her return she had to step around a scene that haunted her for weeks – a rabbi, surrounded by Wehrmacht soldiers, his arms pinned behind his back, the soldiers laughing as the old man struggled in vain to free himself, his head thrashing violently from side to side. It wasn't until Bella passed him by that she realised with a sickening start that the rabbi's beard was on fire.

A few days after the Germans took Radom, a letter arrived from Jakob. *My love,* he wrote in hurried script, *come to Lvov as soon as you can. They've put us up in apartments. Mine is just big enough for two. I hate that you are so far away. I need you here. Please, come.* Jakob included an address. Her parents, to her surprise, agreed to let her go. They knew how badly Bella missed Jakob. And at least in Lvov, Henry and Gustava reasoned, Bella and her sister Anna could look after one another. Pressing her father's hand to her cheek in gratitude, Bella was overcome with relief. The next day, she brought the letter to Jakob's father, Sol. Her parents didn't have the money to hire a driver. The Kurcs, on the other hand, had the means and the connections, and she was sure they would be willing to help.

At first, though, Sol opposed the idea. 'Absolutely not. It's far too dangerous to travel alone,' he said. 'I cannot permit it. If anything happened to you, Jakob would never forgive me.' Lvov hadn't fallen, but there was speculation that the Germans had the city surrounded.

'Please,' Bella begged. 'It can't be any worse than it is here. Jakob wouldn't have asked me to come if he didn't feel it was safe. I need to be with him. My parents have agreed to it . . . Please, *Pan* Kurc. *Proszę.*' For three days Bella petitioned her case to Sol, and for three days he refused. Finally, on the fourth day, he acquiesced.

'I'll hire a wagon,' he said, shaking his head as if disappointed in his decision. 'I hope I don't regret it.'

Less than a week later, the arrangements were made. Sol had found a pair of horses, a wagon, and a driver – a lithe old gentleman named Tomek, with bowed legs and a greying beard, who had worked for him over the summer and who knew the route well. Tomek was trustworthy, Sol said, and good with horses. Sol promised him that if he brought Bella safely to Lvov, he could keep the horses and wagon. Tomek was out of work and jumped at the offer.

'Wear the things you want to take,' Sol had said. 'It will be less conspicuous.' Civilian travel was still allowed in what was once Poland, but the Nazis issued new restrictions by the day.

Bella wrote immediately to Jakob, telling him of her plans, and left the following day, wearing two pairs of silk stockings, a navy knee-length fluted skirt (a favourite of Jakob's), four cotton blouses, a wool sweater, her yellow silk scarf – a birthday gift from Anna – a flannel coat, and her gold brooch, which she hung on a chain around her neck and tucked into her shirt so the Germans wouldn't see it. She slipped a small sewing kit, a comb, and a family photo into her coat pocket beside the forty zloty Sol insisted she bring. Instead of a suitcase, she carried Jakob's winter jacket and a hollowed loaf of peasant bread with his Rolleiflex camera hidden inside.

They've crossed four German checkpoints since leaving Radom. At each, Bella tucked the bread loaf beneath her coat and feigned pregnancy. 'Please,' she begged, one hand resting on her belly, the other on the small of her back, 'I must reach my husband in Lvov before the baby arrives.' So far, the Wehrmacht has taken pity on her, and waved the wagon on.

Bella's head rocks gently on the bench as they plod eastward. *Eleven days.* They have no radio and thus no access to the news, but they have grown accustomed to the menacing growl of Luftwaffe planes, the distant clap of explosives detonating over what they could only presume was Lvov. A few days ago, it sounded as if the city were under siege. Even more disconcerting, though, was the silence that followed. Had the city fallen? Or were the Poles able to keep the Germans at bay?

Bella wonders constantly if Jakob is safe. Surely he's been called upon to defend the city. Twice Tomek has asked Bella if she would like to turn back, to attempt the journey at a later date. But Bella insists they continue on. She'd told Jakob in her letter that she was coming. She must keep her promise. To quit now, despite the uncertainty ahead, would feel cowardly.

'Whoa,' Tomek calls from the jockey box, and in an instant his voice is swallowed by shouts.

'Halt! *Halt sofort!*'

Bella sits up and swings her feet to the floor. Slipping the bread loaf into her coat, she pulls the wagon's canvas door aside. Outside, a swampy meadow teems with men in belted green tunics. Wehrmacht. There are soldiers everywhere. This is no checkpoint, Bella realises. It must be the German front. A chill tiptoes up her vertebrae as three block-jawed soldiers with grey peaked caps and wood-stocked karabiners approach. Everything about them – their charged expressions, their rigid gait, their sharply creased uniforms – is unforgiving.

Bella climbs out of the wagon and waits, willing herself to remain calm.

The head soldier, gripping his rifle, raises his free hand and thrusts his palm in her direction. '*Ausweis!*' he orders. He turns his palm up to the sky. '*Papiere!*'

Bella freezes. She knows very little German.

Tomek whispers, 'Your papers, Bella.'

A second soldier approaches the jockey box and Tomek hands him his papers, glancing over his shoulder at Bella. She is hesitant to hand over her ID, for it states clearly that she is Jewish, a truth that will likely do her more harm than good – but she has no other choice. She offers her identification card at arm's length and waits, holding her breath as the soldier scrutinises it. Unsure of where to look, her eyes dart from the insignia on his collar to the six black buttons running down the length of his tunic to the words GOTT MIT UNS inscribed across his belt buckle. These words Bella understands: GOD WITH US.

Finally, the soldier looks up, his eyes as grey and merciless as the clouds overhead, and purses his lips. '*Keine Zivilisten von diesem Punkt!*' he snaps, handing her back her card. Something about civilians. Tomek slips his own papers into his pocket and gathers his reins.

'Wait!' Bella breathes, a hand on her belly, but the head soldier cocks his rifle and juts his chin west, in the direction from which they'd come.

'*Keine Zivilisten! Nach Hause gehen!*'

As Bella opens her mouth to protest, Tomek shakes his head quickly, subtly. *Don't.* He's right. Whether or not they believe she's pregnant, these soldiers aren't about to bend any rules. Bella turns and heaves herself back into the wagon, defeated.

Tomek pivots the horses on their haunches and they begin to retrace their footsteps, plodding west, away from Lvov, away from Jakob. Bella's mind spins. She fidgets, too vexed to be still. Extracting the bread from her coat, she sets it on the bench and crawls to the rear door flap, opening it just enough to see out. The men in the meadow appear small, like toy soldiers, dwarfed by the colossal clouds looming above. She lets the heavy canvas fall and is enveloped again in shadows.

They've come so far. They're so close! Bella presses her fingertips into the soft skin of her temples, searching for a solution. They could come back the next day, hope for better luck, a more lenient group of Germans. *No.* She shakes her head. They're at the *front*. What are the chances, really, that they'd be allowed through? Suddenly claustrophobic beneath all of her layers, she tugs off her flannel coat and scoots back up the bench to the front of the wagon, where another flap of canvas separates her from Tomek. Lifting it, she squints up at the jockey box. It's begun to drizzle.

'Can we try again tomorrow?' Bella yells over the muted clop of hooves on the soggy road.

Tomek shakes his head. 'It won't work,' he says.

Bella can feel heat rising in her, crawling up her neck toward her ears. 'But we can't go back!' She glances at the provisions box at her feet. 'We don't have enough food for another eleven days on the road!' She watches Tomek's shoulders rock back and forth, absorbing the sway of the wagon, his head bobbing as if he were drunk. He doesn't answer.

Bella lets the canvas flap fall and slumps back onto the bench. She and Tomek haven't spoken much since leaving Radom; Bella had tried to make small talk at the start of the journey, but it felt odd conversing with someone she barely knew, and besides, there wasn't much to say. Surely Tomek must want to get to Lvov as badly as she. He's but a few kilometres from holding up his end of Sol's bargain. She'll remind him of this, she decides, but when she reaches again for the flap, the horses veer suddenly off-road. Gripping the bench beneath her, Bella braces herself as the wagon pitches and bucks over uneven ground. *What's happening? Where are we going?* Twigs snap like firecrackers beneath the wheels and branches claw at the wagon's cover from above. They must be in the woods. Her mind turns a dark corner: *Tomek wouldn't* leave *her here, alone in the woods?* A simple lie would assure Sol he'd delivered her safely to Lvov. Bella's heart sets off at a gallop. No, she decides. Tomek wouldn't dare. But as the wagon lurches on, she can't help but wonder – *or would he?*

Finally, the horses slow to a halt and Bella steps quickly out of the wagon. The sky has dimmed by several shades; soon it will match the colour of the horses' slick, black coats. Tomek climbs from the driver's bench. In his black hat and dark trench coat, he is barely visible in the shadows. Bella stares at him, her pulse still racing, as he begins unbridling the horses.

'Sorry for the silence,' he says, slipping the bits from the horses' mouths. 'You never know who might be listening.' Bella nods, waiting. 'We're about three kilometres from a back road that leads to Lvov,' Tomek continues. 'There's a clearing up ahead. A meadow. I imagine it's unmanned, but you'll have to crawl across it to be safe. The grass should be tall enough to keep you out of sight.' Bella squints in the direction of the clearing but it's too dark to see anything. Tomek nods, as if reassuring himself his plan will work. 'Once you cross the meadow, you'll have to walk south-east through the forest for about an hour, and then you'll reach the road. By then I believe you'll have skirted the front . . .' He pauses. 'Unless the Germans have the city surrounded . . . in which case you'll have to wait for them to move ahead, or cross the front line on your own. Either way,' he says, finally looking her in the eye, 'I think you're better off without me.'

Bella stares at Tomek, digesting the implication of his plan. To travel alone, and on foot – it sounded outrageous. She would be mad to consider it. She can hear herself explaining the idea to Jakob, to his father; their responses would be the same: *Don't do it.*

'Alternatively we turn around and return as quickly as we can, and search for some food along the way,' Tomek says quietly.

It would be the safer thing, to go home – but Bella knows she can't. Her mind churns. She tries to swallow, but the back of her throat is like sandpaper and instead she coughs. *Tomek is right.* Without the wagon she'll be less conspicuous. And if she *did* run into Germans, they'd be more likely to let her by than they would an old man, a young woman, and a two-horse wagon. She bites the inside corner of her bottom lip, silent for a minute.

'*Tak,*' she says finally, looking in the direction of the clearing. Yes, she resolves. What other choice does she have? She's just a few hours from Lvov. From Jakob. Her *ukochany,* her love. She can't turn back now. She rests a hand on the wagon's frame, her limbs suddenly heavy with the weight of her decision. If there are soldiers patrolling the meadow, she doubts she can make it across unnoticed. And if she *does* reach the other side . . . there's no telling who or what may be lurking beneath the forest canopy. *Enough,* she scolds silently. *You've come this far. You can do this.*

'*Tak,*' she breathes, nodding. 'Yes, this will work. It has to work.'

'All right then,' Tomek says, quietly.

'All right then.' Bella runs a hand over her auburn hair, thick as wool from so many days without a wash; she'd given up trying to pull a comb through it. She clears her throat. 'I'll leave now.'

'You'll be better leaving in the morning,' Tomek says, 'when it's not so dark. I'll stay with you until dawn.'

Of course. She'll need the daylight to find her way. 'Thank you,' Bella whispers, realising that Tomek, too, has a treacherous journey ahead. She climbs back into the wagon, rummaging around the provisions box for the last of their hard-boiled eggs. When she finds it she peels it, and returns to Tomek. 'Here,' she says, breaking it in half.

Tomek hesitates before taking it. 'Thank you.'

'Tell *Pan* Kurc you did everything you could to get me to Lvov. If –' she straightens, 'when I make it, I'll write to let him know I'm safe.'

'I will.'

Bella nods, and there is a silence between them as she contemplates what she has just agreed to. Would Tomek wake up and come to his senses, realising that the plan was too risky? Would he try to talk her out of it in the morning?

'Get some rest,' Tomek offers as he turns back to the horses.

Bella forces a smile. 'I'll try.' As she steps back up into the wagon, she pauses. 'Tomek,' she calls, feeling guilty for questioning his intentions. Tomek looks up. 'Thank you – for getting us this far.'

Tomek nods.

'Goodnight, then,' Bella says.

Inside the wagon, Bella flattens Jakob's overcoat out on the floor and climbs on top, stretching out onto her back. Bringing a palm to her heart and the other to her abdomen, she inhales and exhales slowly, willing herself to relax. *It's the right decision*, she tells herself, blinking into the darkness.

The next morning, Bella awakens at daybreak from a light, restless sleep. Rubbing her eyes, she fumbles for the wagon's side door flap. Outside, a few dense rays of light have begun to sift through the clouds, just barely illuminating the spaces between the tree limbs overhead. Tomek has already rolled up his tent and sleeping mat and harnessed the horses. He nods in her direction, then returns to his work. Apparently, he hasn't had a change of heart. Bella slips a boiled potato into her pocket, leaving three for Tomek. After buttoning her coat, and then Jakob's over hers, she reaches for the bread loaf and climbs out of the wagon. As onerous as the journey ahead may be, she won't mind leaving behind the cramped, mildewed space she's called home for the better part of two weeks.

Tomek is tinkering with one of the horse's bridles. As Bella approaches, she finds herself wishing she knew him better, well enough at least to part with a hug – an embrace of some kind that would boost her strength, fill her with the courage she'd need to go through with the plan. But she doesn't. She barely knows him at all.

'I want to tell you how much I appreciate what you've done for me,' she says, extending a hand. It's important to her all of a sudden to acknowledge

44

the small but immeasureably important role Tomek has played in her life. He takes her hand. His grip is surprisingly strong. Beside them, the horses grow restless. One of them shakes his head and his bit jingles; the other snorts, paws the ground. They, too, are ready to reach the end of their journey. 'Oh, Tomek, I nearly forgot,' Bella adds, fishing a ten-zloty bill from her pocket. 'You'll need some food – a couple of potatoes won't do.' She holds the zloty out for him. 'Take it. Please.'

Tomek glances at his feet and then back up at Bella. He takes the note.

'Good luck to you,' Bella offers.

'Same to you. God bless.'

Bella nods and then turns and begins making her way under the cover of the forest toward the meadow.

After a few minutes, she reaches the edge of the clearing and pauses, scanning the open space for a sign of life. The meadow, as far as she can tell, is empty. She glances over her shoulder to see if Tomek is watching – but beneath the oak trees there are only empty shadows. Has he already left? She shivers as she realises just how alone she is. *You agreed to this,* she reminds herself. *You're better off alone.*

She hikes her skirt up over her knees, ties it in a loose knot at her thigh, and then tucks the bread loaf under Jakob's coat and adjusts it so the loaf rests on her back. There. Now she can move more easily. Squatting, she brings her palms and then her knees silently to the ground.

The earth beneath her squishes as she crawls, the cold mud curling between her fingers, painting her extremities tar black. The grass is long and sharp and damp with dew; it slices relentlessly at her face and neck. Within minutes, one of her cheeks is bleeding and she is soaked all the way through to her undergarments. Ignoring the mud and the wet and the sting on her cheek, she kneels for a moment to scan the tree line a hundred metres ahead, and then glances over her shoulder. *Still no sign of Germans. Good.* She lowers herself back onto her hands, wishing she'd worn trousers, realising now what a pointless vanity it was to want to look nice for Jakob.

As she sloshes her way across the meadow, she thinks of her parents, and the meal they'd shared the night before she left. Her mother had prepared boiled pierogi stuffed with mushrooms and cabbage, Bella's favourite, which she and her father had devoured. Gustava, however, had barely touched the food on her plate. Bella's chest tightens as she pictures her mother with an uneaten pierogi before her. She'd always been thin, but since the Germans arrived she'd grown gaunt. Bella had blamed it on the stress of war, and it had pained her to leave, seeing her mother so frail. She recalls how, the following day, as she boarded Tomek's wagon, she glanced up at the flat and saw her parents standing at the window – her father with an arm wrapped around her mother's slight frame, her mother with her palms pressed up against the glass. All she could make out were their silhouettes, but she could tell from the way Gustava's shoulders shook that she was crying. She'd wanted badly to wave, to leave her parents with a smile that said she'd be fine, she'd be back, not to worry. But Witolda Boulevard was crawling with Wehrmacht; she couldn't risk revealing her departure with a wave. Instead she turned away, pulled the wagon's door flap aside, and climbed in.

Bella winces as her knee strikes something hard, a rock. She breathes through the pain and crawls on, realising just how quickly the events of the past two weeks have unfolded. Jakob's departure, the German invasion, the letter, the arrangement with Tomek. She'd been frantic when she left Radom, thinking solely of getting to Lvov to be with Jakob. But what about her parents? Will they be all right on their own? What if something happens to them while she's away? How will she help them? What if something happens to *her*? What if she never makes it to Lvov? *Stop,* she scolds. *You will be fine. Your parents will be fine.* She recites the sentiment over and over again, until the possibility of any other scenario is removed from her consciousness.

Bella tries to listen for signs of danger as she crawls, but her ears are filled with the thunder of her pulse. She'd have never guessed that walking on her hands and knees would require such work. Everything is heavy: her arms, her legs, her head. It's as if she's anchored to the earth, weighed down by her appendages, by her countless layers of clothing, by Jakob's camera, by the muscle that clings to her bones and the sweat that coats her skin despite the morning chill. Her joints hurt, every one of them, her hips, her elbows, her knees, her knuckles; they grow stiffer by the minute. *Damn the mud.* Pausing, she wipes her forehead with the back of her hand and peers over the tips of the grass; she's halfway to the tree line. Fifty metres to go. *You're nearly there,* she tells herself, resisting the urge to lie down for a few minutes, to rest. *Can't stop now. Rest when you reach the forest.*

Focusing on the cadence of her breath – two beats in through her nose, three beats out through her mouth – Bella is lost in delirious rhythm when a sharp *crack* catapults through the morning sky, splintering the silence. She drops quickly to her stomach and flattens her body to the ground, shielding the back of her head with her hands. There is no mistaking what the sound was. A gunshot. Would there be another? Where had it come from? Are they onto her? She waits, every muscle in her body flexed, contemplating what to do – run? Or remain hidden? Her instinct tells her to play dead. And so she lies, her nose a centimetre from the mud, breathing in the smell of fear and wet earth, counting the seconds as they pass. A minute ticks by, then two as she listens, straining, the meadow playing tricks on her – was that the wind rustling the grass? Or was it footsteps?

Finally, when she can't stand it any longer, Bella presses her palms into the mud and, in slow motion, lifts her torso. Through the grass, she scans the horizon. From what she can see, it's clear. Maybe the shot had sounded closer than it was. Ignoring the likelihood that it had come from the direction in which she is headed, she starts crawling again, faster now, her muscles no longer heavy with fatigue but spiked with a terrifying sense of urgency.

You can do this. You're not far. Just be there when I arrive, Jakob. At the address you sent. Wait for me. With each breath, she repeats the words. *Please, Jakob. Just be there.*

SEPTEMBER 12, 1939 — BATTLE OF LVOV: *The battle for control of the city begins with clashes between Polish and surrounding German forces, which greatly outnumber the Poles in both infantry and weaponry. The Poles sustain nearly two weeks of ground fighting, shelling, and bombing by the Luftwaffe.*

SEPTEMBER 17, 1939: *The Soviet Union cancels all pacts with Poland and invades the country from the east. The Red Army begins marching at full tilt toward Lvov. The Poles push back, but by the nineteenth of September, the Soviets and the Germans have the city surrounded.*

CHAPTER FIVE

Mila
Radom, Poland ~ September 20, 1939

The moment Mila opens her eyes she can sense it – something isn't right. The apartment is too still, too quiet. Taking a sharp breath, she sits up, her spine straight. *Felicia.* She climbs out of bed and hurries barefoot down the hall to the nursery.

The door swings open without a sound and Mila blinks into the darkness, realising that she'd forgotten to check the clock. She pads silently to the window, and as she draws the thick damask curtain aside, a shaft of soft, powdery light fills the room. It must be dawn. Through the wooden bars of Felicia's crib she can vaguely make out the lump of a silhouette. She tiptoes to the crib rail.

Felicia lies on her side, motionless, her face obscured by the pink *koc* draped over her ear. Mila reaches down, lifts the small cotton blanket, and rests her palm gently on the back of Felicia's head, waiting intently for a breath, a rustle, anything. Why is it, Mila wonders, that even when her daughter is sleeping, she worries that something dreadful has happened to her? Finally, Felicia flinches, sighs, and rolls to her other side; within seconds, she is still again. Mila exhales. She slips out of the room, leaving the door ajar.

Running her fingers along the wall, she makes her way quietly to the kitchen, glancing at the clock at the end of the hallway. It's just before six in the morning.

'Dorota?' Mila calls softly. On most mornings, she awakens to the whistle of the kettle as Dorota prepares her tea. But it's still early. Dorota, who stays during the week in the small maid's quarters off the kitchen, doesn't typically start her day until six-thirty. She must be asleep.

'Dorota?' Mila calls again, knowing she shouldn't wake her, but she can't shake the sensation that something is wrong. Perhaps, Mila rationalises, she's still adjusting to the feeling of waking up without Selim by her side. It's been nearly two weeks since her husband, along with Genek, Jakob, and Adam, was sent off to Lvov to join the Polish Army. Selim promised he would write as soon as he arrived, but she hasn't received a letter yet.

Mila follows the news in Lvov obsessively. The city, from what the papers report, is under siege. And as if the Germans weren't enough of a threat, two days ago radios blared news of the Soviet Union allying with Nazi Germany. What peace pacts they'd established with Poland have been broken and now Stalin's Red Army is said to be approaching Lvov from the east. Surely the Poles will soon be forced to surrender. Secretly, she hopes they do; then, perhaps, her husband will come home.

When Selim first left Radom, Mila fought sleep, for when she succumbed to it, she awoke in a cold sweat, shaking with fear, convinced that her bloody nightmares were real. One night it was Selim, the next it was one of her brothers – their bodies mangled, their uniforms soaked in gore. Mila was on the brink of unravelling when Dorota, whose son had also been called up, rescued her from her downward spiral. 'You mustn't think like that,' she scolded one morning as Mila picked at her breakfast after another fitful night. 'Your husband is a medic; he won't be at the front. And your brothers are smart. They'll take care of one another. Be positive. For your sake, and for hers,' she said, nodding toward the nursery.

'Dorota?' Mila calls a third time, switching on the light to the kitchen, noticing the kettle resting cold on the stove top. She knocks softly on Dorota's door. But the *tap-tap* of her knuckles against wood is met with silence. She rattles the knob and nudges the door open, peers inside.

The room is empty. Dorota's sheets and blanket are folded and stacked into a neat pile at the foot of her bed. A lone nail protrudes from the far wall where a beveled crucifix once hung, and the small shelves Selim had installed are bare, except for one, which holds a slip of paper folded in half and propped up in the shape of a tent. Mila rests a hand on the doorway, her legs suddenly weak. After a minute, she forces herself to pick up the note and unfold it. Dorota has left her with two words: *Przykro mi.* I'm sorry.

Mila claps a hand to her mouth. 'What have you done?' she whispers, as if Dorota were beside her, wrapped in her food-stained apron, her silver-streaked hair pulled tight into a pincushion bun. Mila has heard rumours of other maids leaving – some to flee the country before it fell into the hands of the Germans, some simply because the families they worked for were Jewish – but she hadn't considered the possibility that Dorota would abandon her. Selim paid her well, and she seemed genuinely happy in her job. There has never been a cross word between them. And she adores Felicia. More than all of that, though, was the fact that in the past ten months, as Mila struggled with new motherhood, Dorota had become not simply a maid to her; she'd become a friend.

As Mila lowers herself slowly to sit, Dorota's mattress coils moan beneath her. *But what will I do without you?* she wonders, her eyes filling slowly with tears. Radom is in shambles; she needs an ally now more than ever. She rests her palms on her knees and drops her chin, feeling the weight of her head tugging at the muscles between her shoulder blades. First Selim, her brothers, Adam, now Dorota. Gone. A seed of panic sprouts somewhere deep in her gut, and her pulse quickens. How will she manage, fending for herself? The Wehrmacht's men have proved to be brutes, and they've shown no sign of leaving anytime soon. They've desecrated the beautiful brick synagogue on Podwalna Street, robbed it clean, and converted it to stables; they've closed each of the Jewish schools; they've frozen Jewish bank accounts and forbidden Poles from conducting business with Jews. Every day another shop is boycotted – first it was Friedman's bakery, then Bergman's toy store, then Fogelman's shoe repair. Everywhere she looks, there are massive red swastika banners; *Judaism Is Criminality* billboards depicting hideous caricatures of hook-nosed Jews; windows painted over with the same four-letter word, as if *Jude* were some kind of curse rather than part of a person's identity. Part of *her* identity. Before, she would have called herself a mother, a wife, an accomplished pianist. But now she is nothing more than, simply, *Jude*. She can't go out any more without seeing someone being harassed on the street, or pulled from their home and robbed and beaten, for no apparent reason. Things she had taken for granted, like walking to the park with Felicia in tow – leaving the apartment at all for that matter – are unsafe. It has been Dorota lately who has ventured out for food and supplies, Dorota who has retrieved her mail from the post office, Dorota who has delivered notes to and from her parents' house on Warszawska Street.

Mila stares at the floor, listening to the faint tick of the clock in the hallway, the sound of seconds passing. In three days it will be Yom Kippur. Not that it matters – the Germans have dropped leaflets throughout the city with a statement forbidding the Jews from holding services. They'd done the same at Rosh Hashanah, although Mila had ignored the mandate and snuck after dark to her parents' home; she regretted it later when she heard stories of others who'd done the same and been discovered: one man her father's age was made to run through the city centre carrying a heavy stone over his head; others were forced to haul metal bed frames from one end of town to the other while being flogged with metre-long clubs; one young man was trampled to death. This Yom Kippur, Mila had decided, she and Felicia would atone in the safety of their apartment, alone.

What now? Tears spill down her cheeks. She sobs silently, too paralyzed to wipe her eyes, her nose. Looking around the empty room, she knows she should be furious – Dorota has *left* her. But she isn't angry. She's terrified. She's lost the one person under her roof she can trust, confide in, rely upon. A person who seemed to understand far better than she how to care for her child. Mila wishes she could ask Selim what to do. It was Selim, after all, who insisted that they hire Dorota when Felicia was a newborn and Mila was at her wits' end. Mila had resisted at first, her pride too great to submit to relying on a stranger to help parent her child, but in the end Selim had been right – Dorota was her saviour. And now Mila is once again in crisis, but without her husband's steady hand to guide her. The reality of her situation washes over her swiftly and Mila shivers: her safety, and with it, Felicia's, now rests entirely in her own hands.

Bile rises up in her throat and she can taste it, sharp and acrid. Her stomach constricts as a pair of images flashes before her – the first, a photo she'd seen in the *Tribune* taken shortly after Czechoslovakia fell, of a Moravian woman weeping, one arm dutifully raised in a Nazi salute; the second, a scene from one of her nightmares – a soldier in green, tearing Felicia from her arms. *Oh, dear God, please don't let them take her away from me.* Mila gags. Her vomit lands on the linoleum between her feet with a wet slap. Pinching her eyes shut, she coughs, fighting another wave of nausea, and with it, a pang of regret. *What were you thinking, being in such a hurry to start a family?* She and Selim were married for less than three months when they discovered that she was pregnant. She was so confident at the time – there was nothing she wanted more than to raise a child. Multiple children. An *orchestra* of children, she used to joke. And then Felicia was such a fussy baby, and motherhood took so much more out of her than she was expecting. And now there is war. Had she known that before Felicia's first birthday Poland might *no longer exist* . . . she gags again, and in that awful, noxious moment she knows what she has to do. Her parents had asked her to move back to Warszawska Street when Selim left for Lvov. But Mila had opted to stay put. This apartment was her home now. And besides, she didn't want to be a burden. The war would be over soon, she said. Selim would return, and they'd pick up where they left off. She and Felicia could manage on their own, she'd argued, and besides, she had Dorota. But now . . .

Felicia's cry shatters the silence and Mila jumps. Mopping her mouth with the sleeve of her gown, she tucks Dorota's note into her pocket and stands, reaching for the wall to steady herself when the room begins to spin. *Breathe, Mila.* She'll clean up later, she decides, stepping carefully over the puddle on the floor. In the kitchen she rinses her mouth and splashes cold water over her face. 'Coming, love!' she calls when Felicia wails again.

Felicia is standing at the crib rail, gripping it tightly with both hands, her *koc* resting on the floor below her. When she sees her mother she smiles brightly, revealing four tiny tooth buds – two each in her top and bottom gums.

Mila's shoulders soften. 'Good morning, sweet girl,' she whispers, handing Felicia her blanket and lifting her from the crib. Two months ago, when Mila weaned her from her breast, Felicia had begun sleeping through the night. With the extra rest, mother and daughter both had turned a corner; Felicia was a happier baby and Mila no longer felt as if she were teetering on the edge of insanity. Felicia wraps her arms around her mother's neck and Mila relishes the weight of her daughter's cheek, warm against her chest. *This is what I was thinking*, she reminds herself. *This.* 'I've got you,' she whispers, one hand on Felicia's back.

Lifting her head, Felicia turns toward the window and points a tiny index finger. 'Eh?' she intones – the sound she makes when she's curious about something.

Mila follows her gaze. '*Tam*,' she says. 'Outside?'

'*Ta*,' Felicia imitates.

Mila walks to the window to play her usual game of pointing out all the things she can see: four speckled pigeons, perched by a chimney; the opaque white globe of a street lantern; across the way, three arched stone doorways and, above them, three large wrought-iron balconies; a pair of horses pulling a carriage. Mila ignores the swastika flag hanging from an open window, the grafittied storefronts, the newly repainted street sign (she no longer lives on *Żeromskiego* but on *Reichsstrasse*). As Felicia watches the horses plod by below her, Mila kisses the top of her forehead, letting the down of Felicia's cinnamon hair, what there is of it, tickle her nose. 'Your papa must miss you so much,' she whispers, thinking of how Selim could make Felicia laugh by nuzzling his nose into her hair and pretending to sneeze. 'He'll come home to us soon. Until then, it's you and me,' she adds, trying to ignore the tang of bile, still sharp in her throat, as she processes the enormity of her words. Felicia looks up at her, wide eyed, almost as if she understands, then brings her *koc* to her ear and rests her cheek once again on Mila's chest.

Later today, Mila decides, she'll pack up some clothes and her toothbrush, Felicia's *koc* and a pile of diapers, and walk the six blocks to her parents' house at 14 Warszawska. It's time.

CHAPTER SIX

Addy
Toulouse, France ~ September 21, 1939

Addy is tucked away at a cafe overlooking the Place du Capitole's giant square, a spiral-bound pad of music paper open before him. He sets his pencil down and massages a cramp from the muscle between his thumb and forefinger.

It's become his routine to spend his weekends parked at a bistro table, writing. He no longer travels to Paris – it feels too frivolous to get lost in the revelry of Montmartre's nightlife with his homeland at war. Instead he devotes himself to his music and to his weekly trips to the Polish consulate in Toulouse, where he's been trying for months to secure a travel visa – the paperwork required for him to return to Poland. So far, the effort has been exasperatingly fruitless. On his first visit in March, three weeks before Passover, the clerk took one look at Addy's passport and shook his head, pushing a map across his desk and pointing to the countries separating Addy from Poland: Germany, Austria, Czechoslovakia. 'You will not make it past the checkpoints,' he said, tapping his finger on the line of Addy's passport marked RELIGIA. ZYD, the designation read, short for ZYDOWSKI. Jewish. His mother had been right, Addy realised, hating himself for doubting her. Not only was it too dangerous for him to travel across German borders, it was, apparently, illegal. Even so, Addy had returned to the consulate time after time, hoping to convince the clerk to grant him some sort of exemption, to wear him down with persistence. But at each visit, he was told the same. Not possible. And so, for the first time in his twenty-five years, he'd missed Passover in Radom. Rosh Hashanah had come and gone as well.

When he isn't at work or writing home or composing his music or badgering the secretaries at the consulate, Addy pores over the headlines of *La Dépêche de Toulouse*. Every day, as the war escalates, his anxiety heightens. This morning he'd read that the Soviet Red Army was rolling through Poland from the east and had made an attempt to seise Lvov. His brothers are in Lvov; according to his mother, they'd been conscripted along with the rest of Radom's young men into the army. Any day now, it seems, the city will fall. Poland will fall. What will become of Genek and Jakob? Of Adam and Selim? What will become of Poland?

Addy is stuck. His life, his decisions, his future – none of it is in his control. It's a feeling to which he is unaccustomed, and he hates it. Hates the fact that he has no way of getting home, no way of reaching his brothers. At least, thankfully, he is in contact with his mother. They write each other often. In her last letter, which she'd sent just days after Radom fell, she'd described the heartbreak of bidding Genek and Jakob goodbye on the night they left for Lvov, how painful it was to see Halina and Mila do the same for Adam and Selim, and what it was like, a week later, to watch the Germans march into Radom. The city was occupied within hours, she said. *There are Wehrmacht soldiers everywhere.*

Addy thumbs through his pages, skimming his work, grateful for the distraction of his music. This, at least, is his. No one can take it from him. Since Poland went to war, he has written doggedly, nearly completing a new composition for piano, clarinet, and double bass. Closing his eyes, he taps out a chord on an imaginary keyboard resting on his lap, wondering whether it has potential. He's had one commercial success already – a piece recorded by the talented Vera Gran that tells the story of a young man writing home to a loved one. 'List', the letter. Addy composed 'List' just before leaving Poland for university and will never forget how it felt to hear the song for the first time on the air, how he'd closed his eyes and listened to the melody he'd created as it spilt from his radio's speakers, how his chest had swelled with pride when his name was announced afterward, crediting him as composer. Perhaps 'List', he'd fantasised at the time, was the piece that would eventually lead to a vocation in music.

'List' was a hit in Poland – so much so that Addy had come to be something of a celebrity in Radom, which of course provoked constant teasing from his siblings. 'Brother, an autograph please!' Genek would call after him when Addy was home for a visit. At the time, Addy didn't mind the attention, or the fact that in his handsome older brother's ribbing he sensed a hint of envy. His siblings were happy for him, no doubt. Proud of him, too; they'd watched him compose since his toes barely reached the pedals of his parents' baby grand. They understood how much this first break meant for him. It was Addy's big-city life, he knew, that his brother secretly coveted. Genek had visited Toulouse, had met Addy once in Paris; each time, he'd left mumbling about how glamorous Addy's life in France seemed in comparison with his own. Now, of course, things are different. Now, there is nothing glamorous about living in a country where Addy is virtually imprisoned. Even with his hometown overrun by Germans, Addy would do anything to return.

In the square, the last few bits of daylight cast a rose-coloured glow over the marble-columned facade of the Capitole. Addy watches a flock of pigeons take flight as an old woman makes her way toward a series of roofed arcades to the west, and he is reminded of an evening last summer when he and his friends had sat at sundown at a cafe in a similar square in Montmartre, sipping glasses of Sémillon. Addy replays the conversation from that evening, recalling how, when the subject of war arose, his friends had rolled their eyes. 'Hitler is *un bouffon*,' they'd said. 'All this talk of war is just a fuss, *une agitation*. Nothing will come of it. *Le dictateur déteste le jazz!*' one friend had professed. 'He hates jazz even more than he hates the Jews! Can't you just see him walking around Place de Clichy with his hands over his ears?' The table had erupted in laughter. Addy had laughed along with them.

Reaching for his pencil, he returns to his pad of paper. He plots a melodic phrase, and then another, writing quickly, willing his pencil to keep up with the music in his head. Two hours pass. Around him, tables begin to fill with men and women settling in for their evening meal, but Addy hardly notices. When he finally looks up, the sky has darkened to a deep periwinkle blue. It's getting late. He pays his bill, folds his pad of paper under his arm, and walks across the square to his apartment on Rue de Rémusat.

He enters the courtyard of his building, unlocks his mailbox, and rifles quickly through a small sheaf of letters. Nothing from home. Disappointed, he climbs four flights of stairs, hangs up his cap, and removes his shoes, arranging them neatly on a straw mat by the door. He drops his mail on the table, flips on the radio, and fills a kettle with water, setting it on the stove top to boil.

His place is small and tidy, with only two rooms – a tiny bedroom and a kitchen just big enough for a bistro table – but it suits him; he's the only one of his four siblings who is still single, despite his mother's prodding. Opening his icebox, he peruses its contents: an ounce of creamy Camembert, a half litre of goat's milk, two speckled eggs, a red Malus apple – the kind his mother used to set out for a snack when he was little, sliced and drizzled with honey (Addy likes to keep one, always, within reach) – a sliver of steamed cow tongue wrapped in butcher paper, a half-eaten bar of dark Swiss chocolate. He reaches for the chocolate. Careful not to tear it, he peels back the silver foil and breaks off a square of the bittersweet cocoa, letting it melt for a moment in his mouth. '*Merci, la Suisse,*' he whispers as he sits down at the table.

At the top of his pile of mail is the latest *Jazz Hot* review. Addy skims the headlines. STRAYHORN JOINS ELLINGTON IN COMPOSITION PARTNERSHIP, one of them reads. Two of his favourite jazz composers. He makes a mental note to keep an eye out for their work. Beneath *Jazz Hot* is a pale blue slip of paper he'd missed earlier. When he sees it, his heart skips, and the remnants of chocolate suddenly taste sharp on his tongue. He picks it up, turns it over. Typed across the top are three words: COMMANDE DE CONSCRIPTION. It is a military conscription order.

Addy reads the slip twice. He has been ordered to join a Polish column of the French Army. He is to report immediately to L'hopital de La Grave to complete his medical exam and paperwork; his duty will begin in Parthenay, France, on November 6th. Addy sets the order on the table and stares at it for a long while. *The army.* And to think that this morning he was lamenting for his brothers, grappling with the thought of them in uniform, terrified of their fate. Now, his circumstances are no different from theirs.

Addy's ears start to ring and it takes him a moment to realise that the water has begun to boil. He rises to switch off the burner, running a hand through his hair. As the kettle's whistle grows faint, Addy is struck by how quickly things can change in this new realm of his. How, in an instant, his future can be decided for him. Retrieving the conscription notice, he makes his way to the kitchen window overlooking the corner of the Place du Capitole, presses his forehead against the glass. Sidney Bechet's clarinet sings softly through his radio's speakers, but he is oblivious. *The army.* Several of his friends have been called up, but they are all French. He'd hoped that as a foreigner he might be exempt. Perhaps, he thinks, there is a way out of this. But the small print at the bottom of the slip suggests otherwise. FAILURE TO REPORT TO DUTY WILL RESULT IN ARREST AND INCARCERATION. *Merde.* He is in good health. Of fighting age. No, there is no way out. *Merde. Merde. Merde.*

Four stories below, Moretti's Occitan cross, inlaid on the paving stones, reflects beneath the street lamps like a giant granite tattoo. Overhead, a half moon is on the rise. How is it possible, Addy wonders, that amid such serenity a war is being waged across the border? Where are Genek and Jakob now? Are they awaiting orders? Are they in combat, at this very moment? Addy glances up at the sky, picturing his brothers pressed shoulder to shoulder in a trench, oblivious of the rising moon, thinking only of the mortars flying overhead.

Addy's eyes begin to water. He slips a hand into his trouser pocket and retrieves his handkerchief, a gift from his mother. She'd given it to him a year ago, when he was home last for Rosh Hashanah. She'd found the fabric in Milan, she said, on one of her buying trips – a soft, white linen to which she'd hand-stitched a small border and embroidered his initials in the corner, AAIK. *Addy Abraham Israel Kurc.* 'It's beautiful,' Addy had declared when his mother handed him the handkerchief. 'Oh, it's nothing,' Nechuma had replied, but Addy knew how much care she'd put into making it, how much pride she took in her craft. He rubs his thumb over the embroidery, imagining his mother at work in the back room of the shop, a bolt of cloth laid out before her, her tape measure, scissors, and red silk pincushion at her side. He can see her measuring her thread, twisting an end between her fingers and bringing it to her lips to wet it before guiding it through the impossibly small eye of a needle.

Addy breathes deeply, feeling the rise and fall of his chest. *It's going to be all right*, he tells himself. Hitler will be stopped. France hasn't seen any fighting yet; for all one knows, the war will be over before it does. Perhaps his friends in Toulouse, who had begun to call it the *drôle de guerre* – the phony war – were right, and it is only a matter of time before he'll be able to return to Poland, to his family, to the life he'd left behind when he moved to France. Addy thinks about how, a year ago, if someone had offered him a job in New York City, he'd have likely jumped at the opportunity. Now, of course, he would do anything – anything – just to be home, sitting at his mother's dining-room table, surrounded by his parents, his siblings. He folds his handkerchief back into his pocket. Home. Family. Nothing is more important. He knows that now.

SEPTEMBER 22, 1939: *The city of Lvov surrenders to the Soviet Red Army.*

SEPTEMBER 27, 1939: *Poland falls. Hitler and Stalin immediately divide the country – Germany occupies the western region (including Radom, Warsaw, Kraków, Lublin), and the Soviet Union occupies the eastern region (including Lvov, Pinsk, Vilna).*

CHAPTER SEVEN

Jakob and Bella
Lvov, Soviet-Occupied Poland ~ September 30, 1939

Bella checks the brass number hanging on the red door. 'Thirty-two,' she whispers under her breath, comparing it twice with the address scrawled in Jakob's handwriting on the letter she'd carried with her from Radom: *19 Kalinina Street. Apartment 32.*

Jakob's camera hangs around her neck, his coat over her forearm, folded to conceal the layers of mud it had collected en route. Never before has she been so filthy. She'd peeled off a pair of ripped stockings, cursing the loss, and tried her best to stomp the mud from the soles of her shoes and to wipe her face clean, licking her thumb and dabbing at her cheeks, but without a mirror the effort was useless. Her hair is as unruly as a thorn bush, and she's still damp beneath her layers. When she lifts her arms the smell is appalling. How she needs a wash! She must look awful. *Never mind. You're here. You've made it. Just knock.*

Her fist hovers a few centimetres from the door. Taking a slow, deep breath, she licks her lips and taps her knuckles softly on the wood, tilting her head forward, listening. Nothing. She knocks again, louder this time. She's about to knock a third time when she hears the faint clip of footsteps. Her heart raps in sync with each step as it grows louder, and for a moment she panics. What if she's greeted, after coming all this way, not by her Jakob but by a stranger?

'Who is it?'

A puff of air escapes her lips – a laugh, her first in weeks – and she realises she's been holding her breath. *It's him.*

'Jakob! Jakob, it's me!' she says to the door, levitating to her toes, suddenly feather-light. Before she can add, 'It's Bella,' there is a quick metallic *click,* a deadbolt sliding in its mount, and the door swings open, forcefully, pulling with it a vacuum of air. And then, there he is, her love, her *ukochany*, looking at her, *into* her, and beneath the layers of grime and sweat and stink, somehow she feels beautiful.

'It's you!' Jakob whispers. 'How did you . . . ? Come in, quickly.' He pulls her inside and locks the door behind them. She sets his coat and camera on the floor, and when she stands his hands are on her shoulders. He holds her gently, his gaze travelling the length of her, studying her. In his eyes Bella sees the worry, the exhaustion, the disbelief. Whatever has happened here in Lvov has left a mark on him. He hasn't slept, it seems, in days.

'Kuba,' she starts, calling him as she sometimes does by his Hebrew name, wanting nothing but to assure him that she's okay, she's here now, he mustn't worry. But he isn't ready yet to talk. He pulls her to him, enveloping her so fully she can hardly breathe, and in that instant she knows she was right to come.

With her arms tucked beneath his, she presses her head into the familiar crook of his neck, running her forearms up the narrow of his back. He smells as he always does – of wood chips and leather and soap. She can feel his heart beating against hers, the weight of his cheek, heavy on her head. Beneath his shirt, his shoulder blades protrude like boomerangs, sharper than she remembers. They stand like this for a full minute, until Jakob leans back, lifting her with him, up and up until her feet float from the ground. He laughs, spinning around, and soon the room melts out of focus and she's laughing, too. As her toes touch the floor, Jakob leans forward. She lets the weight of her torso dissolve into his arms, and as he dips her she tips her head back, feeling the blood rush to her ears. He cradles her there for a moment, dangling in his arms – the final exultant posture of a ballroom dance – before pulling her to her feet.

Jakob stares at her again, holding both her hands, his expression suddenly serious. 'I can't believe you made it,' he says, shaking his head. 'I got your letter just after the fighting started. And then we were mobilised and by the time I returned you still weren't here. Had I known it would be this bad, Bella, I promise I would never have asked you to come. I've been so worried.'

'I know, love. I know.'

'I don't know how you made it.'

'We nearly turned back, on several occasions.'

'You have to tell me everything.'

'I will, but first a bath, please,' Bella smiles.

Jakob sighs, his eyes softening. 'What would I have done if . . .'

'Shhh, *kochanie*. It's okay, darling. I'm here.'

Jakob tucks his chin so his forehead rests gently on Bella's. 'Thank you,' he whispers, closing his eyes, 'for coming.'

They sit at a small square table in the kitchen, their hands wrapped around mugs of hot, black tea. Bella's hair is still wet from her bath, the skin of her neck and cheeks flushed pink – she'd scrubbed herself clean and soaked for all of three minutes before Jakob tapped softly on the washroom door, undressed, and climbed into the tub with her.

'I honestly didn't think it would work,' Bella says. She's just finished explaining Tomek's plan, how petrified she was of being discovered, turned back, or taken captive. Tomek, it turns out, had been right about the German front line – she was able to skirt it by crossing the meadow where he left her. But when she reached the forest on the other side, she lost her sense of direction and veered north, walking for hours until finally stumbling across a pair of train tracks, which she followed to a small station on the outskirts of the city. There, despite her muddy, pathetic state, she talked her way through one last checkpoint, bought a one-way ticket with her remaining zloty, and rode the last several kilometres to Lvov by train.

'I was surprised when I got here,' Bella says, 'I didn't see Wehrmacht on the streets – I expected to find the city swarming.'

Jakob shakes his head. 'The Germans are gone,' he says quietly. 'Lvov is Soviet-occupied now. Hitler pulled his men out a few days before Poland fell.'

'Wait – what?'

'Lvov fell just three days before Warsaw—'

'Poland has – has *fallen*?' The colour has left Bella's cheeks.

Jakob takes her hand. 'You haven't heard?'

'No,' Bella whispers.

Jakob swallows, seeming unsure of where to begin. He clears his throat, and explains as succinctly as he can what Bella has missed, telling her how the Poles in Lvov had waited for days for help from the Red Army, which was stationed just east of the city, how they thought the Soviets had been sent to protect them, and how, after a while, it became clear that wasn't the case. He describes how completely outnumbered they were; how, when the city finally surrendered, General Sikorski, head of the Polish military, negotiated a pact that allowed Polish officers to leave the city – '"Register yourselves with Soviet authorities and go home," the general said.' Jakob pauses, peers for a moment into his mug. 'But just after the Germans left, dozens of Polish officers were arrested by the Soviet police, without explanation. That's when I scrapped my uniform,' Jakob adds, 'and decided I'd be better off hiding out here, waiting for you.'

Bella watches Jakob's Adam's apple travel up and down the length of his throat. She is stunned.

'A few days later,' Jakob continues, 'after Warsaw fell, Hitler and Stalin split Poland in two. Right down the middle. The Nazis took over the west, the Red Army the east. We're on the Soviet side here in Lvov . . . which is why you didn't see any Germans.'

Bella can barely speak. *The Soviets are on the side of the Germans? And Poland has fallen.* 'Did you – did you have to . . .' But she trails off, the words jammed in the roof of her mouth.

'There was fighting,' Jakob says. 'And bombing. The Germans dropped loads of bombs. I saw people die, I saw horrible things . . . but no.' He sighs, looking at his hands, 'I didn't have to . . . I didn't manage to hurt anyone.'

'And what of your brother, Genek? And Selim? And Adam?'

'Genek and Adam are here in Lvov. But Selim . . . we haven't heard from him since the Germans retreated.'

Bella's heart sinks. 'And the officers they arrested?'

'No one's seen them since.'

'My God,' she whispers.

It's dark in the bedroom, but from the sound of Jakob's breathing next to her, Bella can tell that he is awake, too. She'd nearly forgotten how lovely it felt to lie down for a night's sleep on a mattress; it was heaven compared with the wooden floorboards of Tomek's wagon. Rolling to face Jakob, she loops a bare calf over his knee. 'What should we do?' she asks. Jakob sandwiches her leg between his. She can feel him looking at her. He finds her hand, kisses it, and brings her palm to his chest.

'We should get married.'

Bella laughs.

'I missed that sound,' Jakob says, and Bella can tell that he's smiling.

Of course, she'd meant what should they do next – as in, should they stay in Lvov or return to Radom? They haven't discussed yet which option is safest. She presses her nose and then her lips to his, holding the kiss for a few seconds before pulling away.

'Are you serious?' she breathes. 'You can't be serious.' *Jakob.* She wasn't expecting the subject of marriage to come up. Not on their first night together again, at least. The war, it seems, has emboldened him.

'Of course I'm serious.'

Bella closes her eyes, her bones sinking heavily into the mattress beneath her. They can talk about their plan tomorrow, she decides. 'Was that a proposal?' she asks.

Jakob kisses her chin, her cheeks, her forehead. 'I guess that depends on what your answer is,' he says finally.

Bella smiles. 'You know what my answer is, love.' She rolls over and he pushes his knees into the backs of hers, wraps his arms around her, cocooning her in his warmth. They fit perfectly together.

'Then it's a deal,' Jakob says.

Bella smiles. 'It's a deal.'

'I still can't believe you're really here,' Jakob whispers. 'I was so scared you wouldn't make it.'

'I was so scared I wouldn't find you.'

'Let's not do that again.'

'What again?'

'I mean . . . let's not ever be apart, ever again. It was –' His voice fades to a whisper. 'It was awful.'

'Awful,' Bella agrees.

'Together from now on, all right? No matter what.'

'Yes. No matter what.'

CHAPTER EIGHT

Halina
Radom, German-Occupied Poland ~ October 10, 1939

Gripping a knife in her free hand, Halina blows a wisp of blonde hair from her eyes and rocks forward onto her knees. Pressing a clump of pink beet stems against the earth, she flexes her jaw, raises her blade, and brings it down with as much force as she can muster. *Thwack.* Earlier in the day, she learnt that if she put enough muscle into it, she could slice off the stems in one motion instead of having to go at each plant twice. But that was hours ago. Now she's spent. Her arms feel as if they are hewn from oak, as if they may split at any moment from her shoulders. Now it takes two, sometimes three attempts. *Thwack.*

Her brothers had written recently from Lvov, where they reported that the Soviets have assigned them desk jobs. *Desk jobs!* The news has begun to irk her. How is it that she, of all people, has ended up in the fields? Before the war, Halina worked as an assistant to her brother-in-law Selim at his medical lab, where she wore a white coat and latex gloves; her hands, most certainly, were never dirty. She thinks back to her first day at the lab, to how sure she had been that she would find the work tedious, and how, after a week, she discovered that the research – the minutiae of it all, the daily potential for new discoveries – was surprisingly gratifying. She would do anything to return to her old job. But the lab, like her parents' shop, has been confiscated, and if you were a Jew out of a job, the Germans were quick to appoint you with a new one. Her parents have been dispatched to a German cafeteria, her sister Mila to a garment workshop, mending uniforms in from the German front. Halina has no idea why she was given this particular assignment; she'd assumed it was a joke, laughed even, when the clerk at the city's makeshift employment agency handed her a slip of paper with the words BEET FARM written across the top. She hasn't a lick of experience harvesting vegetables. But clearly it doesn't matter. The Germans are hungry, and the plants are ready to come out of the ground.

Glancing down at her hands, Halina frowns, disgusted. She can barely recognise them; the beets have stained them dark fuchsia, and in every crevice there is dirt – beneath her fingernails, in the small folds of skin around her knuckles, stuck between flesh in the open blisters pockmarking her palms. Even worse, though, are her clothes. They're as good as ruined. She doesn't mind as much about the trousers (thank goodness she'd decided to wear slacks, and not a skirt), but she was particularly fond of her chiffon blouse, and her shoes are another story entirely. They are her newest pair, brogue lace-ups with a slightly squared-off toe and a small, flat heel. She'd purchased them over the summer at Fogelman's and worn them today assuming she'd be assigned a task at the farm's business office, perhaps in accounting, and that it wouldn't hurt to look put together to impress her new bosses. Once a beautiful, polished cordovan brown, the toes are now scuffed and discolored, and she can barely see the intricate decorative perforation on the sides. It's tragic. She'll have to spend hours with a sewing needle later, picking them clean. Tomorrow, she's decided, she'll dress in her shabbiest clothes, maybe borrow some things Jakob left behind.

She sits back on her heels, wipes the sweat from her brow with the back of her hand, and pokes out her bottom lip as she blows again at the stubborn lock of hair tickling her face. How long, she wonders, before she's able to get a trim? Radom has been occupied for thirty-three days. Her salon is closed now to Jews, which is a problem as she's desperate for a haircut. Halina sighs. It's her first day at the farm, and already she's sick of it. *Thwack.*

It feels like an eternity since her day began. She was picked up that morning by a Wehrmacht officer who wore a pressed green uniform with a crisp swastika band on his arm and a moustache so thin it appeared to have been drawn over his lip with a charcoal pencil. He'd greeted her with a glance from beneath his visored field cap and a single word, '*Papiere!*' (hellos, apparently, were too good for Jews), then jabbed his thumb over his shoulder. 'Get in.' Halina had climbed gingerly into the bed of the truck and found a seat among eight other workers. She recognised all but one. As they motored beneath the chestnuts flanking Warszawska Street – she refused to call it by its new German name, *Poststrasse* – she kept her head down for fear of being recognised; how embarrassing it would be, she'd thought, for someone from her previous life to see her being carted away like this.

But when the truck paused at the corner of Kościelna Street, she looked up and managed, to her horror, to catch the eye of an old schoolmate standing by the entrance to Pomianowski's candy shop. At gymnasium, Sylvia had desperately wanted to be Halina's friend – she'd followed her around for the good part of a year before they finally grew close. They did their homework together and visited each other on weekends. One year, Sylvia invited Halina to her home for Christmas; on Nechuma's insistence, Halina brought along a tin of her mother's star-shaped almond biscuits. They'd lost touch since graduation; the last Halina knew, Sylvia had taken a job as a nurse's aide at one of the city's hospitals. All of this flashed through her mind as the truck sat idling, as the old friends stared at one another from across the cobblestone. Halina had thought for a moment about waving – as if it were perfectly normal for her to be huddled there, in the back of a truck, she and eight other Jews, on their way to work – but before she could lift a hand, Sylvia narrowed her eyes and looked away; she'd pretended she didn't even *know* her! Halina's blood had boiled with humiliation and fury, and when the truck finally motored on, she spent the next half hour thinking of the things she'd like to say to Sylvia when she ran into her next.

They drove and drove, the cityscape quickly fading, two-laned streets and seventeenth-century brick facades giving way to a patchwork of orchards and pastureland and narrow dirt roads hemmed in by pine and alder trees. Halina had cooled off by the time they arrived at the farm, but her bottom was bruised from all of the jostling, which made her hate the day even more.

When they parked, there wasn't a building in sight, just dirt, and rows upon rows of leafy stems. It was then that Halina realised, looking out over the hectares of farmland, that this was no desk job. The officer lined them up beside the truck and tossed baskets and burlap sacks at their feet. '*Stämme*,' he said, pointing to the sacks. '*Rote rüben*,' he added, kicking a basket. Though she knew enough German to get by, 'stems' and 'beets' weren't yet in her vernacular, but the instructions were easy enough to decipher. Stems in the sack, beets in the basket. After a moment the officer handed each of the Jews a knife with a long, dull blade. He glared at Halina as she took hers. '*Für die stämme*,' he said, resting a hand on the well-worn wooden grip of the pistol strapped to his belt, his moustache morphing along with the curve of his lips into the shape of a talon. *Brave of him giving us knives as big as these,* Halina thought.

And so it went. *Thwack, rip, shake, stuff. Thwack, rip, shake, stuff.*

Perhaps she should pocket a couple of beets to bring home to her mother. Before their food was rationed, Nechuma would grate roasted beets and toss them with horseradish and lemon to make *cwikla,* pairing it with smoked herring and boiled potatoes. Halina's mouth waters; it's been weeks since her last decent meal. But something in her knows that an extra beet at dinner wouldn't be worth the consequence of getting caught stealing.

A whistle shrills and she looks up to see the silhouette of a truck a hundred or so metres away, and beside it, a German officer, presumably the one who brought them, waving his cap over his head. From her plot, she can make out two of the others, already walking in his direction. As she stands, her muscles scream. She's spent far too many hours of the day bent at right angles. She drops the knife on top of the beets in her basket and balances the wicker handle in the crook of her elbow. Wincing, she reaches for the stem-filled sack, loops its twine strap over her opposite shoulder, and begins limping toward the truck.

The sun has dipped behind the tree line, giving the sky a pinkish hue, as if stained by the juice of the plants she'd spent all day harvesting. She'll need a warmer coat soon, she realises. The officer whistles again, motioning for her to pick up her pace, and she curses him under her breath. Her basket is heavy; it must weigh nearly fifteen kilos. She walks as quickly as her joints will allow her, wondering if any of the beets she's pulled will end up in the cafeteria where her parents work. They've been there for a week. 'It's not so bad . . .' her mother said after their first day, '. . . aside from having to prepare such lovely food we'll never taste.'

At the truck, the officer with the flyaway moustache waits with an out-stretched palm. '*Das Messer*,' he says. Halina hands him the knife, then sets her bag and basket on the truck bed before climbing up. The others are already seated, each looking as bedraggled as she. They retrieve a final worker and then hunker down for the ride home, their day's work at their feet, too tired to talk.

'Same time tomorrow,' the German barks, as the truck slows to a stop in front of 14 Warszawska Street. It's nearly dark. He hands Halina her papers through the window of the truck's cab, along with a small, stale, 100-gram wedge of bread, her compensation for the day.

'*Danke*,' Halina says, taking the bread, trying to mask her sarcasm with a smile, but the officer refuses to look at her and speeds off before the word has left her lips. '*Szkop*,' she whispers as she turns and hobbles toward home, fishing for a key in her coat pocket.

Inside, Halina finds Mila in the foyer, hanging up her coat; she has just returned from the uniform workshop. Felicia sits on a Persian rug, waving a silver rattle, smiling at its tinkly sound.

'My goodness,' Mila gasps, taken aback by Halina's appearance. 'What on earth did they put you up to?'

'I've been *farming*,' Halina says. 'Crawling about in the fields all day. Can you believe it?'

'You – on a farm,' Mila quips, suppressing a laugh. 'Now there's a thought.'

'I know. It was dreadful. All I could think,' Halina says, balanced on one foot by the door as she slips out of a shoe, wincing as she reopens a blister, 'was if Adam could only see me, grovelling around on all fours in the dirt, like an animal! What a laugh he'd get. Look at my shoes!' she cries. 'God, what a mess.' She studies her socks, marvelling at the soil they, too, have collected, peeling them off carefully so as not to sully the floor. 'What's that?' she asks, pointing to a loop of fabric draped loosely around Mila's neck.

'Oh,' Mila says, glancing at her chest, 'I forgot I was wearing it. It's something I made – I don't know what you'd call it, a harness I suppose?' She turns, pointing to where the fabric is crisscrossed between her shoulder blades. 'I can tuck Felicia inside here.' She turns again, pats the loop dangling down the length of her torso. 'It keeps her concealed on the way to and from the workshop.'

Mila brings Felicia with her to work every day, even though technically children aren't allowed. *No persons under the age of twelve in the workplace* – it's

70

one of the Germans' many decrees, disregard of which is punishable by death. But Mila can't *not* work – everyone has to work – and it's not as if she can leave Felicia, who's not even a year old, alone all day in the apartment while she's away.

Halina admires her sister's ingenuity, her courage. She wonders if she were in Mila's shoes whether she would have the gall to walk into a workshop with a child strapped illegally to her breast. Mila has changed since Selim left. Halina thinks often about how, when everything was easy, motherhood was hard for Mila – and now that everything is hard, it's a role that seems to come more naturally. It's as if some sort of sixth sense has set in. Halina doesn't worry any longer whether, with one more sleepless night, Mila might come undone.

'Does Felicia like it in there, in her – harness?' Halina asks.

'She doesn't seem to mind it.'

Halina tiptoes to the kitchen as Mila begins arranging the table for dinner. Even though their meals aren't what they used to be, Nechuma still insists that they use their silver and chinaware. 'What does Felicia do while you're sewing all day?' she calls.

'She plays beneath my worktable, mostly. She naps in a basket of fabric scraps. She's been incredibly patient,' Mila adds. The cheerfulness has evaporated from her voice.

Bent over the kitchen sink, Halina runs water over her hands and arms, imagining her eleven-month-old niece playing beneath a table for hours on end. She wishes there were something she could do to help. 'Nothing from Selim today?' she asks.

'No.'

Water splashes against the sink's metal basin, and Halina is quiet for a moment. Genek, Jakob, and Adam have all written to share their new addresses in Lvov, to check in. In their letters, they say that they haven't seen Selim since the Soviets took over. Halina's heart breaks for her sister. It must be impossible not knowing where her husband is, if he's even *alive*. She's tried a few times to console Mila with her own outlook – which is that no news is better than bad news – but even she knows that Selim's disappearance can't be a good thing.

In his last letter, Adam had confirmed what they'd read in the *Tribune* and in the *Radomer Leben* – the papers were their only source of news now, as their radios had been confiscated – that the Polish Army in Lvov had disbanded, and the Germans had pulled out, leaving the city in the hands of the Red Army. *Not terrible,* was how Adam described living under the Soviets. There was plenty of work to be had, he said. He'd found a job, in fact. The pay was pitiful, but it was a job. He could find Halina one, too. And he had news – something he had to share with her in person. He signed his letter *With love,* and added a postscript: *I think you should come to Lvov.*

Despite her apprehension of living under Soviet rule, the idea of moving to Lvov thrills Halina. She misses Adam deeply – his calm, reassuring way, his gentle, confident touch, the touch that made her realise that the boys she'd dated before him were utterly inept compared with the man that he is. She'd do anything to be with him again. Halina wonders whether his *news* might be a proposal. She's twenty-two, he thirty-two. They've been together long enough; marriage seems the logical next step. She thinks about it often, her heart flooding at the idea of him asking for her hand and then wringing itself dry as she realises that to be with Adam would mean leaving Radom. No matter how she spins it, it doesn't feel right to abandon her parents. With Jakob and Genek in Lvov, who else would watch out for them? Mila has Felicia to tend to, and Addy is still stuck in France – in his last letter he said he'd received orders to enlist, that in November he would be joining the army. And so that leaves only her. And anyway, even if she *could* justify going to Lvov for just a short while with the intention of returning, the trip itself would be nearly impossible, as the latest of the Nazi decrees has robbed her of the right to leave her home or ride the train without a special pass. For now, she has no choice. She will stay put.

A lock rattles and Sol's voice echoes a moment later through the apartment as he calls for his granddaughter.

'Where is my peach?'

Felicia grins and pushes herself to a wobbly stand, toddling down the hallway from the dining room, her arms extended in front of her like little magnets, pulling her to her *dziadek*'s arms. Halina and Mila follow behind. Felicia laughs as Sol scoops her up, growling playfully, nibbling on her shoulder until her giggles turn to squeals. Nechuma appears behind him, and Halina and Mila greet their parents, exchanging kisses.

'Oh my,' Nechuma breathes, staring at Halina's clothes. 'What happened?'

'I've been *harvesting*. Have you ever seen me this vile?'

Nechuma studies her youngest child, shakes her head. 'Never.'

'And you? The cafeteria?' Halina asks, hanging up her mother's coat.

Nechuma holds up her thumb, wrapped in a bloodstained bandage. 'Aside from this, it was a bore.'

'Mother!' Halina reaches for Nechuma's hand so she can take a closer look.

'I'm fine. If the Germans would give us decent knives I wouldn't cut myself so often. But you know what? A little blood in their *kartoflanka* won't kill anyone.' She smiles, pleased at her secret.

'You should be more careful,' Halina scolds.

Nechuma pulls her hand away and ignores the comment. 'I have a treat for us,' she says, extracting a handkerchief filled with a handful of potato peelings from under her blouse. 'Just a few,' she says, when she sees Halina's eyebrows jump. 'I've peeled them thick. Look, we've got nearly half a potato here.'

Halina stares. 'You *stole* them? From the cafeteria?'

'No one saw me.'

'But what if they had?' Halina's tone is harsh, probably too harsh. It's not like her to speak like that to her mother and she knows she should apologise, but she doesn't. It was one thing for Mila to sneak an infant into her workplace – she has no alternative but to do so – but another for her mother to steal from the Germans and then shrug it off.

The room is silent. Halina, Mila, and their parents all look at one another, their gazes forming a square. Finally, Mila speaks. 'It's okay, Halina, we need it. Felicia is a skeleton, look at her. Mother, thank you. Come, let's make soup.'

CHAPTER NINE

Jakob and Bella
Lvov, Soviet-Occupied Poland ~ October 24, 1939

Bella steps carefully so as not to clip the backs of Anna's heels. The sisters move slowly, deliberately, talking in whispers. It's nine in the evening, and the streets are empty. There isn't a curfew in Lvov as there is in Radom, but the blackout is still in effect, and with the street lamps extinguished, it's nearly impossible to see.

'I can't believe we didn't bring a flashlight,' Bella whispers. 'I walked the route earlier today,' Anna says. 'Just stay close, I know where I'm going.'

Bella smiles. Slinking through backstreets in the pale blue light of the moon reminds her of the nights she and Jakob used to tiptoe at two in the morning from their apartments to make love in the park under the chestnut trees.

'It's just here,' Anna whispers.

They climb a small flight of stairs, entering the house through a side door. Inside, it's even darker than it is on the street.

'Stay here for a moment while I light a match,' Anna says, rummaging through her handbag.

'Yes, ma'am,' Bella says, laughing. All her life it's been *she* who bosses Anna about, not the other way around. Anna is the baby, the family's sweetheart. But Bella knows that behind the pretty face and quiet facade, her sister is whip-smart, capable of anything she sets her mind to.

Despite being two years younger, Anna was the first to marry. She and her husband, Daniel, live just down the street from Bella and Jakob in Lvov – a circumstance that has softened Bella's pain at leaving her parents behind. The sisters see each other often and talk frequently about how to convince their parents to make the move to Lvov. But in her letters, Gustava insists that she

74

and Henry are getting by on their own in Radom. *Your father's dentistry is still bringing a bit of income,* she wrote in her last correspondence. *He's been treating the Germans. It doesn't make sense for us to move, not yet at least. Just promise to visit when you can, and to write often.*

'How on earth did you find this place?' Bella asks. She'd been given no address, just told to follow. They'd snaked through so many narrow back alleys on their way, she'd lost her sense of direction.

'Adam found it,' Anna says, striking a match over and over without a spark. 'Through the Underground,' she adds. 'Apparently they've used it before, as a sort of safe house. It's abandoned, so we shouldn't have any surprise visitors.' Finally, a match takes, emitting a cloud of sharp-smelling sulphur and an amber halo of light. 'Adam said he left a candle by the faucet,' she mutters, shuffling toward the sink, a hand cupped over the flame. Adam had found the rabbi, too, which Bella knew was no easy task. When Lvov fell, the Soviets stripped the city's rabbis of their titles and banned them from practicing; those who were unable to find new jobs went into hiding. Yoffe was the only rabbi Adam could find, he said, who wasn't afraid to officiate a marriage ceremony, under the condition that the wedding take place in secrecy.

In the match's faint glow, the room begins to take shape. Bella looks around, at the shadow of a kettle resting on a stove top, a bowl of wooden spoons silhouetted on the counter, a blackout curtain hanging in a window over the sink. Whoever lived here left in a hurry, it seems. 'It's incredibly kind of Adam to do this for us,' Bella says, more to herself than to her sister. She'd met Adam a year ago, when he leased a room in the Kurcs' apartment. Mostly she knew him as Halina's boyfriend, calm and cool and rather quiet – oftentimes his voice was barely heard around the dinner table. But since arriving in Lvov, Adam has surprised Bella with his ability to orchestrate the impossible: handcrafting false identification cards for the family. As far as the Russians know, Adam works at an orchard outside the city, harvesting apples – but in the Underground, he has become a prized counterfeiter. By now, hundreds of Jews have pocketed his IDs, which he produces with such a meticulous hand, Bella would swear they are real.

She'd asked him once how he was able to make them look so authentic.

'They *are* authentic. The stamps, at least,' he'd said, explaining how he'd discovered that he could remove official government stamps from existing IDs with a peeled, just-boiled egg. 'I lift the original when the egg is still hot,' Adam said, 'then roll the egg over the new ID. Don't ask why, but it works.'

'Found it!' Darkness envelops them once again as Anna fumbles for another match. A moment later, the candle is lit.

Bella removes her coat, lays it over the back of a chair.

'Cold in here,' Anna whispers. 'Sorry.' Carrying the candle, she makes her way from the sink to stand beside Bella.

'It's okay.' Bella suppresses a shiver. 'Is Jakob already here? And Genek? Herta? It's so quiet.'

'Everyone's here. Getting settled in the foyer, I imagine.'

'So I'm not to be married in the kitchen?' Bella laughs and then sighs, realising that for as many times as she'd told herself she'd marry Jakob anywhere, the idea of wedding him here, in the shadowy, ghostlike home of a family she'll never know, was beginning to make her feel uneasy.

'Please. You're far too classy for a kitchen wedding.'

Bella smiles. 'I didn't think I'd be nervous.'

'It's your *wedding* day – of course you're nervous!'

The words reverberate through her and Bella goes still. 'I wish Mother and Father could be here,' she says finally, and as she hears herself, her eyes well up with tears. She and Jakob had talked about waiting until the war was over to marry, so they could hold a more traditional ceremony in Radom with their families. But there was no telling when the war would end. They'd waited long enough, they decided. The Tatars and the Kurcs had both given their blessings from Radom. They'd practically begged Jakob and Bella to marry. Still, Bella hates that her parents can't be with her – hates that, despite how happy she is now that she's with Jakob, she's also guilty for it. Is it right, she wonders, to celebrate while her country is at war? While her parents are alone in Radom – her parents, who, for all of her life, have given her so much when they had so little? Bella's memory flashes to the day when she and Anna returned home from school to find their father in the living room with a scruffy-looking dog at his feet. The pup was a gift, their father told them, from one of his patients who had fallen on hard times and was unable to pay to have a tooth extracted. Bella and Anna, who had begged for a dog since they were toddlers, had shrieked with joy and rushed to hug their father, who wrapped his arms around them, laughing as the dog nipped playfully at their ankles.

Anna squeezes her hand. 'I know,' she says, 'I wish they could be here, too. But they want this so badly for you. You mustn't worry about them. Not tonight.'

Bella nods. 'It's just so far from what I imagined,' she whispers.

'I know,' Anna says again, her voice soft.

When they were teenagers, Bella and Anna would lie in bed and talk for hours, concocting stories of their wedding days. At the time, Bella could see it perfectly: the sweet-smelling bouquet of white roses her mother would arrange for her to carry; the smile on her father's face as he lifted her veil to kiss her forehead beneath the chuppah; the thrill of Jakob slipping a ring over her index finger, a symbol of their love that she would carry with her for the remainder of her lifetime. Her wedding, had it been in Radom, would have been far from lavish, this she knows. It would have been simple. Beautiful. What it would *not* have been was a secret ceremony, held in the cold carcass of an abandoned, blacked-out house 500 kilometres from her parents. But, Bella reminds herself, she'd chosen to come to Lvov, after all. She and Jakob had decided together to marry here. Her sister is right; her parents have wanted this for her for years. She should focus on what she has, not what she doesn't – on this night, especially.

'No one could have predicted this,' Anna adds. 'But just think,' she says, her voice growing more chipper, 'the next time you see *Mama i Tata*, you will be a married woman! Hard to believe, isn't it?'

Bella smiles, willing away her tears. 'It is, in a way,' she whispers, thinking about her father's letter, which had arrived two days ago. In it, Henry described how overjoyed he and Gustava were upon learning of her intent to marry. *We love you so much, dear Bella. Your Jakob is a good soul, that boy, with a fine family. We will celebrate, all of us, when we are together again.* Rather than show the letter to Jakob right away, Bella had slipped it under her pillow and decided she'd let him read it later that evening, once they'd returned to their apartment, a married couple.

Sucking in her stomach, Bella runs her hands along the lace bodice of her dress. 'I'm so happy it fits,' she says, exhaling. 'It's just as beautiful as I remember it.'

When Anna became engaged to Daniel, their mother, knowing that they couldn't afford the kind of dress Anna would want from a dressmaker, decided to make a gown herself. She, Bella, and Anna had scoured the pages of *McCall's* and *Harper's Bazaar* for the designs they liked. When Anna finally picked her favourite – inspired by film stills of Barbara Stanwyck – the Tatar women spent an entire afternoon at Nechuma's fabric shop, poring over bolts of various satins, silks, and laces, marvelling over how luxurious each felt as they rubbed it between their fingers. Nechuma gave them the materials they finally selected at cost, and it took Gustava nearly a month to finish the gown – a V-neck, with a white lace-trimmed bodice, long gathered Gibson sleeves, buttons down the back, a bell-shaped skirt that fell just to the floor, and a powder-white satin sash tied at her hips. Delighted, Anna deemed it a *masterpiece*. Bella had secretly hoped she'd get to wear it someday.

'I'm just happy I brought it,' Anna says. 'I almost left it with Mother, but I couldn't bear to part with it. Oh, Bella.' Anna stands back to take her in. 'You look so beautiful! Come,' she says, adjusting the gold brooch hanging around Bella's neck so it sits perfectly centred in the hollow between her collarbones, 'before I cry. Are you ready?'

'Almost.' Bella fishes a metal tube from her coat pocket. She removes the lid, then swivels the bottom a half turn and applies a few dabs of Peppercorn Red lipstick carefully to her lips, wishing she had a mirror. 'I'm glad you brought this, too,' she says, rubbing her lips together before dropping the tube back into her pocket. 'And that you were willing to share,' she adds. When lipstick was pulled from the market – the army had better use for petroleum and castor oil – most women they knew clung fiercely to what was left of their supplies.

'Of course,' Anna says. 'So – *gotowa?*'

'Ready.'

Carrying the candle in one hand, Anna guides Bella gently through a doorway.

The foyer is dimly illuminated by two small votives propped on the staircase balusters. Jakob stands at the foot of the stairs. At first, all Bella can make out of him is his silhouette – his narrow torso, the gentle slope of his shoulders.

'We'll save this one for later,' Anna says, snuffing out her candle. She kisses Bella on the cheek. 'I love you,' she says, beaming, and then makes her way to greet the others. Bella can't see them, but she can hear whispers: *Och, jaka piękna! Beautiful!*

A second silhouette stands motionless beside her groom, the candlelight catching the frizz of a long, silver beard. It must be the rabbi, Bella realises. She steps into the flickering glow of the votives, and as she slides her elbow through Jakob's, she feels the tightness between her ribs disappear. She isn't nervous any more, or cold. She's floating.

Jakob's eyes are wet when they meet hers. In her sister's ivory kitten heels, she's nearly as tall as he. He plants a kiss on her cheek.

'Hello, sunshine,' he says, smiling.

'Hi,' Bella replies, grinning. One of the onlookers chuckles.

The rabbi extends a hand. His face is a maze of wrinkles. He must be in his eighties, Bella guesses. 'I am Rabbi Yoffe,' he says. His voice, like his beard, is rough around the edges.

'Pleasure,' Bella says, taking his hand and dipping her chin. His fingers feel frail and knotted between hers, like a cluster of twigs. 'Thank you for this,' she says, knowing what a risk he'd taken to be there.

Yoffe clears his throat. 'Well. Shall we get started?'

Jakob and Bella nod.

'*Yacub*,' Yoffe begins, 'repeat after me.'

Jakob does his best not to bungle Rabbi Yoffe's words, but it's difficult, partly because his Hebrew is rudimentary, but mostly because he's too distracted by his bride to keep a thought in his mind for more than a few seconds. She is spectacular in her gown. But it's not the dress he's taken by. He's never seen her skin so smooth, her eyes so bright, her smile, even in the shadows, such a perfect, radiant cupid's bow. Against the ebony backdrop of the abandoned house, ensconced in the golden glimmer of candlelight, she appears angelic. He can't take his eyes off her. And so he stumbles through his prayers, thinking not about his words but about the image of his soon-to-be wife before him, memorising her every curve, wishing he could snap a photo so he could show her later on just how beautiful she looked.

Yoffe pulls a handkerchief from his breast pocket, places it over Bella's head. 'Walk seven times,' he instructs, drawing an imaginary circle on the floor with his index finger 'around *Yacub*'. Bella extracts her elbow from Jakob's and obeys, her heels clicking softly on the wooden floorboards as she walks a circle, and then two. Each time she passes in front of him, Jakob whispers, 'You are exquisite.' And each time, Bella blushes. When she has returned to Jakob's side, Yoffe offers a short prayer and reaches again into his pocket, this time removing a cloth napkin, folded in two. He opens it, revealing a small light bulb with a broken filament – a functioning light is too precious to break now.

'Don't worry, it no longer works,' he says, wrapping up the bulb and bending slowly to place it at their feet. Something creaks and Jakob wonders whether it's the floorboards or one of the rabbi's joints. 'In the midst of this happy occasion,' Yoffe says, righting himself, 'we should not forget how fragile life truly is. The breaking of glass – a symbol of the destruction of the temple in Jerusalem, of man's short life on earth.' He motions to Jakob, and then to the floor. Jakob brings a foot down gently on the napkin, resisting the urge to stomp for fear that someone might hear.

'Mazel tov!' the others cry softly from the shadows, also straining to subdue their cheers. Jakob takes Bella's hands, weaving his fingers between hers.

'Before we finish,' Yoffe says, pausing to look from Jakob to Bella, 'I would like to add that, even in the darkness, I see your love. Inside, you are full, and through your eyes, it shines.' Jakob tightens his grip on Bella's hand. The rabbi smiles, revealing two missing teeth, then breaks into song as he recites a final blessing:

You are blessed, Lord our God, the sovereign of the world,
who created joy and celebration, bridegroom and bride,
rejoicing, jubilation, pleasure and delight,
love and brotherhood, peace and friendship . . .

The others sing along, clapping softly as Jakob and Bella seal the ceremony with a kiss.

'My wife,' Jakob says, his gaze dancing across Bella's face. The word feels new and wonderful on his lips. He steals a second kiss.

'My *husband*.'

Hand in hand, they turn to greet their guests, who emerge from the shadows of the foyer to embrace the newlyweds.

A few minutes later, the group is assembled in the dining room for a makeshift dinner, a meal smuggled in under their coats. It's nothing fancy, but a treat, nonetheless – horsemeat burgers, boiled potatoes, and homemade beer.

Genek clinks a fork gently against a borrowed glass and clears his throat. 'To *Pan i Pani* Kurc,' he says, his glass lifted. 'Mazel tov!' Jakob can sense how difficult it is for Genek to keep his voice low. 'Mazel tov,' the others echo.

'And it only took nine years!' Genek adds, grinning. Beside him, Herta laughs. 'But seriously. To my little brother, and to his ravishing bride, who we've all adored since the day we met – may your love be everlasting. *L'chaim!*'

'*L'chaim*,' the others repeat in unison.

Jakob raises his glass, smiling at Genek, and wishing as he often does that he'd proposed sooner. Had he asked for Bella's hand a year ago, they would have celebrated with a proper wedding – with parents, siblings, aunts, and uncles by their sides. They'd have danced to Popławski, sipped champagne from tall flutes, and gorged on gingerbread cake. The night, no doubt, would have wrapped with Addy, Halina, and Mila taking turns at the keys of a piano, serenading their guests with a jazz tune, a Chopin nocturne. He glances at Bella. They'd agreed it was the right thing, to marry here in Lvov, and even though she never said it, he knows she must feel a similar longing – for the wedding they thought they'd have. The wedding she deserved. *Let it go,* Jakob tells himself, pushing aside the familiar stitch of regret.

Around the table, glasses touch rims, their cylindrical bottoms catching the candlelight as bride and groom and guests sip their beer. Bella coughs and covers her mouth, her eyebrows arched, and Jakob laughs. It's been months since they've had a drink, and the ale is harsh.

'Potent!' Genek offers, his dimples carving shadows in his cheeks. 'We'll all be drunk before we know it.'

'I think I might already be drunk,' Anna chimes in from the far end of the table.

As the others laugh, Jakob turns, rests his hand on Bella's knee beneath the table. 'Your ring is waiting for you in Radom,' he whispers. 'I'm sorry I didn't give it to you sooner. I was waiting for the perfect moment.'

Bella shakes her head. 'Please,' she says. 'I don't need a ring.'

'I know this isn't—'

'Shush, Jakob,' Bella whispers. 'I know what you're going to say.'

'I'm going to make it up to you, love. I promise.'

'Don't.' Bella smiles. 'Honestly, it's perfect.'

Jakob's heart swells. He leans closer, his lips brushing her ear. 'It's not how we imagined it, but I want you to know – I've never been happier than I am right now,' he whispers.

Bella is blushing again. 'Me either.'

CHAPTER TEN

Nechuma
Radom, German-Occupied Poland ~ October 27, 1939

Nechuma has stockpiled the family's valuables and laid them out into neat rows across the dining-room table. Together, she and Mila take inventory.

'We should bring as much as we can,' Mila says.

'Yes,' Nechuma agrees. 'I'll leave a few things as well with Liliana.' Nechuma's boys grew up playing *kapela* in the building's courtyard with Liliana's children; the Kurcs and the Sobczaks are close.

'I can't believe we're leaving,' Mila whispers.

Nechuma rests her hands on the carved mahogany back of a dining chair. No one has actually said the words yet, not out loud at least. 'I can't either.'

A pair of Wehrmacht soldiers had rapped on their door early that morning with the news. 'You have until the end of the day to collect your personal belongings and get out,' one of them said, thrusting a slip of paper in Sol's direction with their new address stamped across the top. 'You will return to work tomorrow.' Nechuma had glared at the man from beside her husband and he'd glared back, looking at her with his face pinched, as if he'd ingested something rotten. 'The furniture stays,' he added, before turning to leave. Nechuma had thrown a fist in the air and whispered a string of profanities once the door was closed, then huffed down the hall to the kitchen to wrap a cold cloth around her neck.

The soldiers' visit was no surprise, of course. Nechuma had sensed it was only a matter of time before the Nazis came around. There was an influx of Germans in Radom; they needed homes, and the Kurcs' five-bedroom apartment was spacious, their street one of Radom's most desirable. When two Jewish families in the building were evicted the week before, she and Sol had begun to prepare.

They'd counted and polished their silver, tucked a few bolts of fabric behind a false wall in the living room, even contacted the committee that allocated new addresses for evicted Jews in order to request a space that was clean and large enough to fit them all, Halina, Mila, and Felicia included. Still, nothing could truly prepare Nechuma for how it would feel to leave her home of over thirty years at 14 Warszawska.

'Let's pack quickly and get it over with,' she declared, once she'd calmed. While Nechuma and Mila arranged their most precious possessions into piles, Sol and Halina made trips back and forth to their assigned two-bedroom flat on Lubelska Street in the Old Quarter, lugging copper pots and bedside lamps, a Persian rug, a favourite oil on canvas purchased years ago in Paris, a sack full of linens, a sewing kit, a small tin of kitchen spices. With no indication as to when they'd be able to return to their home, they stuffed their suitcases full of clothes for all seasons.

By noon, Sol declared the flat nearly full. 'Once we bring the valuables,' he said, 'we won't have room for much else.' It came as no shock, but still, Nechuma's heart dropped. She knew that the bathtub, her writing table, and the piano would have to stay, as would the antique vanity bench that she'd upholstered in French silk brocade; the brass headboard with its beautiful scalloped castings and rounded posts, a surprise gift from Sol on their tenth anniversary; the mirrored china cabinet that once belonged to her great-grandmother; the wrought-iron basket on the balcony that she filled each spring with geraniums and crocuses – she would miss them, too. But how could they leave behind the portrait of Sol's father, Gerszon, that hung in the living room? The indigo tablecloths and ivory statuettes she'd collected over the years from her travels? The crystal serving bowl filled with blown-glass grapes that she'd placed on the parlour windowsill to catch the morning light?

The afternoon had slipped away as Nechuma wandered around the apartment, running her fingers along the spines of her favourite books and picking through boxes of drawings and assignments she'd saved from her children's school days. Though they wouldn't do them any good in the new flat, these were the things that mattered, Nechuma realised as she turned them over in her hands. These were the things that defined them. In the end, she allowed herself one suitcase of keepsakes with which she simply couldn't part: a collection of Chopin waltzes for the pianoforte, a stack of family photos, a book of Peretz's poetry. She packed the sheet music for a piece Addy learnt when he was five – a Brahms lullaby, with his piano teacher's note scrawled in the margin: *Very good, Addy, keep up the hard work.* A gold-plated picture frame engraved with the year 1911, and inside, a photo of Mila, bald and big-eyed, no bigger than Felicia is now. The tiny red leather shoes that were laced first to Genek's, then Addy's, then Jakob's feet, when they took their first steps. The faded pink hair clip Halina had insisted on wearing every day for years. The rest of her children's things she placed carefully in boxes, which she then pushed to the very back of her deepest closet, praying she would return to them soon.

Now, at the dining-room table, Nechuma sets a silver bowl and ladle aside for the Sobczaks. The rest, she decides, will come with them. 'Let's start with the porcelain,' she says. She lifts a teacup from the table, gold-trimmed, with delicate pink peonies painted beneath its rim. They wrap the cups and saucers individually in linen napkins, nestle them into a box, then move on to the silver – two sets, one passed down from Sol's mother, the other from Nechuma's.

'These I thought I'd cover with fabric and sew onto a shirt, to look like buttons,' Nechuma says, pointing to the two gold coins she'd set atop a substantial pile of zloty bills – the fraction of their savings they were able to withdraw before their bank accounts were frozen.

'Good idea,' Mila says. She picks up a sterling hand mirror and peers at her reflection for a moment, wrinkling her nose at the sight of the dark circles under her eyes. 'This was your mother's, yes?' she asks.

'It was.'

Mila sets the mirror gently into the box, folding a few metres of ivory Italian silk and white French lace into squares on top of it.

Nechuma stacks the zloty and rolls them, along with the gold coins, into a napkin, which she slips into her purse.

The table is bare now, save for a small black velvet pouch. Mila picks it up. 'What's this?' she asks. 'It's heavy.'

Nechuma smiles. 'Here,' she says. 'I'll show you.' Mila hands her the pouch and Nechuma loosens the string cinching the top of it closed. 'Open your hand,' she says, emptying its contents into Mila's palm.

'Oh,' Mila breathes. 'Oh, my.'

Nechuma peers down at the necklace glittering in her daughter's palm. 'It's an amethyst,' she whispers. 'I found it a few years ago, in Vienna. There was something about it . . . I couldn't resist.'

Mila turns the purple stone over, her eyes wide as it catches the light from the chandelier overhead.

'It's beautiful,' she says.

'Isn't it?'

'Why don't you ever wear it?' Mila asks, holding it up to her own neckline, feeling the weight of the stone, the gold chain resting on her collarbone.

'I don't know. Seems a bit ostentatious. I always felt self-conscious wearing it.' Nechuma recalls how, on the day she first saw the necklace, the idea of owning such an extravagance had made her knees weak. It was 1935; she'd been in Vienna on a buying trip and had spotted it in a jeweller's window on her walk back to the train station. She tried it on and decided on an uncharacteristic impulse that she should have it, wondering the instant she left the store whether she would regret her decision. It was an investment, she told herself. And besides, she'd earned it. The shop had been doing well for a number of years by then, and her children were for the most part independent, finishing their final years in university, making a living for themselves. It was exorbitant, yes, but she remembers thinking that it was also the first time in her life that she could easily justify a splurge.

Nechuma starts at the sound of banging on the door. She's lost track of the time. The Wehrmacht soldiers must be back to escort them out. Mila drops the necklace quickly back into its pouch and Nechuma tucks it into her shirt, between her breasts.

'Can you see it?' she asks.

Mila shakes her head no.

'Stay here,' Nechuma whispers. 'Don't take your eyes off of these,' she adds, setting her purse atop the box of valuables at their feet. Mila nods.

Nechuma turns and straightens her back, inhaling deeply, gathering her composure. At the door, she lifts her chin, almost imperceptibly, as she tells the Wehrmacht soldiers in rudimentary German that her husband and daughter will be home soon to help them carry the last of their things. 'We need another fifteen minutes,' she says coolly.

One of the soldiers glances at his watch.

'*Fünf minuten*,' he snaps. '*Schnell.*'

Nechuma says nothing. She turns from the door, resisting the urge to spit on the officer's polished leather jackboots. With her fingers curled around the key to the apartment – she isn't yet ready to hand it over – she pads through her home one last time, stepping quickly into each room, scanning for something she might have forgotten to pack, forcing her eyes to jump over the things she'd decided earlier she couldn't bring; if she looks too long she'll have second thoughts, and leaving them behind will be torture. In her bedroom she adjusts the base of a lamp so it aligns with the front of her dresser and smooths a wrinkle from the bedsheet. She folds and refolds a linen towel in the powder room. She pulls at a curtain in Jakob's room so it's even with the other. She tidies as if she is expecting company.

In the living room, which she's left for last, Nechuma lingers for an extra moment, staring at the space where her children had practised for hours upon hours at the piano, where for so many years they'd gathered after meals with someone at the keys. Making her way to the instrument, she runs her hand along its polished lid. Slowly, soundlessly, she closes the fall over the keys. Turning, she takes in the room's oak-panelled walls, the desk by the window overlooking the courtyard where she loved, more than anything, to sit and write, the blue velvet couch with its matching club chairs, the marble mantle over the fireplace, the floor-to-ceiling shelves stacked with music – Chopin, Mozart, Bach, Beethoven, Tchaikovsky, Mahler, Brahms, Schumann, Schubert – and with the works of their favourite Polish authors: Sienkiewicz, Żeromski, Rabinovitsh, Peretz. Walking quietly to her writing table, Nechuma brushes a bit of dust from the satinwood surface, grateful that she'd remembered to pack her stationery and favourite fountain pen. Tomorrow she will write to Addy in Toulouse, telling him of their circumstances, of their new address.

Addy. The fact that he will be leaving Toulouse soon to join the army troubles Nechuma deeply. Already, she's coped with the stress of two sons in the military. Genek and Jakob's duty, at least, was short; Poland had fallen quickly. France, on the other hand, has yet to join the war. If the French get involved, and it seems only a matter of time before they do, there is no telling how long the fighting will last. Addy could be in uniform for months. Years. Nechuma shudders, praying that she's able to reach him before he leaves for Parthenay. She will need to write to Genek and Jakob in Lvov, too. Her sons will be furious to learn that the family has been evicted from their home.

Nechuma looks up at the ceiling as her eyes fill with tears. *It's just temporary,* she tells herself. Exhaling, she glances at the portrait of her father-in-law; he stares down at her, his gaze austere, penetrating. She swallows, then nods respectfully. 'Watch over our home for us, will you?' she whispers. She touches her fingers to her lips and then to the wall, and makes her way, slowly, toward the door.

CHAPTER ELEVEN

Addy
Outside Poitiers, France ~ April 15, 1940

Beneath the deep green spires of an endless row of cypress trees, a dozen pairs of leather soles crunch the dirt. The men have been walking since dawn; soon, it will be dusk.

Addy has spent the past several hours listening to the synchronised rhythm of footfall behind him, ignoring the blisters on his feet, and thinking of Radom. Six months have passed since he's heard from his mother – it was the end of October, just before he left Toulouse, when he received her last letter. She'd written to tell him that the family was safe – all but Selim, who had gone missing; that his brothers were still in Lvov; that Jakob and Bella were soon to be married. *The shop has been closed. We've been put to work,* Nechuma wrote, detailing their new assignments. There were curfews and rations and the Germans were despicable, but all that mattered, Nechuma had insisted, was that they were in good health and, for the most part, accounted for. Before signing off, she said that two Jewish families in their building had been evicted and forced into tiny flats in the Old Quarter. *I fear,* she wrote, *that we will be next.*

In his reply, Addy had begged his mother to let him know right away if she was forced to move, and to send addresses for Jakob and Genek, but he hadn't received a response before he left Toulouse. Now he's on the move, impossible to reach. A knot has formed in his chest, and as the days and weeks slip by, it tightens. He loathes the unease of feeling so far away, so helplessly removed from his family in Poland.

Addy switches on his headlamp, willing himself to stay positive. It has become easy to think the worst. He mustn't fall into that trap. And so, rather than imagine his parents and sisters evicted from their home and slaving away in some kitchen or factory under the Wehrmacht's watch, he thinks of Radom – the *old* Radom, the one he remembers. He thinks of how springtime in his hometown has always been his favourite time of year, for it is the season of Seder dinners and of birthdays – his and Halina's. Spring is when the Radomka and Mleczna Rivers flanking the city run high, feeding the city's rye fields and orchards, and when the domes of the horse chestnuts bordering Warszawska Street begin to leaf, offering shade to patrons perusing the ground-floor shops for leathers, soaps, and wristwatches. Spring is when the flower boxes adorning the balconies on Malczewskiego Street overflow with crimson-red poppies – a welcome reprieve after the long, grey winters; when Kościuszki Park bustles with vendors selling pickled cucumbers, shredded beets, smoked cheese, and sour rye-meal mash at the Thursday market; when the Kurcs' neighbour Anton invites the children in the building to see his hatchlings, which barely even look like birds, all tiny and dusted in cream-coloured down, unable, even, to hold up their heads. When he was a boy, Addy loved watching as Anton's flock of doves would fly from his window up to the eaves of the building's steepled rooftop, where they'd coo softly, presiding for a few minutes over the courtyard before returning through the window to the wooden crate their keeper had built for them.

Addy smiles at the memories but is jolted back to the present, the images vanishing as a sound filters into his consciousness. A rustle. He stiffens and halts, lifting his elbow to ninety degrees, palm forward, fingertips skyward. In an instant the soldiers behind him freeze. Addy cocks his chin, listening. There it is again, the rustling, coming from a cluster of elder bushes at the base of a cypress a few metres ahead. He toggles his rifle's safety to the off position.

'Ready,' he whispers in Polish, resting his index finger gently on the metal curve of his trigger and aiming its muzzle at the shrubbery. Behind him, the soft *click* of twelve safeties sliding off. The rustle continues. Addy contemplates shooting but decides to wait. What if it's just a raccoon – or a child?

A year ago, he could count on the fingers of one hand the times he'd carried a gun. When Addy was growing up, his uncle occasionally invited him and his brothers to go pheasant hunting, and while Genek seemed to enjoy the sport, Addy and Jakob preferred to stay back, warm by the fire, finding the whole process of flushing a bird from its cover unappealing. Now, to think about the responsibility he assumes every time he points his rifle makes his head spin.

He and his men train their barrels on the cluster of bushes and wait. After a minute, something small appears at the base of one of the bushes, triangular, black, and shiny. A moment later, a pair of lower branches part and a hound dog emerges. He sniffs at the darkening sky, then glances nonchalantly over his shoulder at the men staring at him, at the thirteen muzzles aimed in his direction. Addy exhales, grateful he hadn't been quick to shoot. He lowers his rifle. 'You scared us there, *kapitan*,' he offers, but the hound, uninterested, turns and trots along the road, headed east.

'We have a new guide,' Cyrus jokes, from the rear. 'Captain Paws.' A murmur of laughter.

'Let's go,' Addy calls. Safeties are reset and the men march on, the air around them filled again with the steady lilt of boots meeting the earth.

Overhead, the cloud cover is thick. The air is cool and smells of rain. In another kilometre or two, Addy decides, they'll set up camp, before they lose their light, before the rain comes. In the meantime, he lets his mind slip to Toulouse, thinking of how different his life is now from how it was six months ago.

Addy had reluctantly left his apartment on Rue de Rémusat on the 5th of November and reported for duty in Parthenay with the 2nd Polish Rifle Division of the French Army, the 2DSP, on the sixth as he was ordered. After eight weeks of basic training, he was awarded an official uniform of the French Army and assigned, thanks to his engineering degree and to his fluency in both French and Polish, the rank of *sergent de carrière*, which put him in charge of twelve *sous-officiers*. Addy enjoyed the company of the others in the 2DSP; surrounding himself with a group of young Poles filled a tiny bit of the void that had consumed him since being denied the right to return home – but that was about all he found comforting about the army. While he did his best to mask it, his rifle felt awkward in his hands, and when his captain barked orders in his direction, his instinct was to laugh. During drills, he found himself composing music in his head to distract himself from the monotony of wind sprints and target practice. Despite his distaste for the military, though, he found the days passed more enjoyably if he embraced the routine. After a while, he wore his double chevron stripes with a modicum of pride, and discovered that he was actually quite good at leading his small squad. Good, at least, at the logistics of it all – at getting his men from point *a* to point *b,* and in the meantime, discovering their strengths and delegating jobs. When they were on the move, for example, Bartek started the fires each night at camp. Padlo cooked. Novitski climbed the tallest tree in the vicinity to confirm that the lookout was clear. Sloboda schooled his men on how to safely pull the pin on the WZ-33 grenades they carried on their belts, and on what to do should a bullet get stuck in the barrel of their Berthiers in a squib load malfunction. And Cyrus, the best of the lot if Addy had to choose, called out marching songs to kill time. Thus far the favourites were *'Marsz Pierwszej Brygady'* and, of course, Poland's most patriotic anthem, *'Boże, coś Polskę'*.

A couple of days ago, Addy's platoon, among the others of 2DSP, was ordered to march fifty kilometres east to Poitiers. Addy guesses they've about twenty more kilometres to cover. From Poitiers they'll continue some seven hundred kilometres farther by military convoy to Belfort, on the Swiss border, and from Belfort they are to join up with the French Eighth Army in Colombey-les-Belles, a city not far from the German border that lay on France's Maginot Line of defence. Addy has never been to Poitiers, Belfort, or Colombey-les-Belles, but he's studied them on the map. They're not close.

'Cyrus!' Addy yells over his shoulder, in need of a distraction. 'A tune, please.'

From the back of the line comes a 'Yes, sir!' and after a moment's pause, a whistle. At the sound of the first notes, Addy's ears perk up. He recognises the tune immediately. The piece is called 'List'. It's his. The others recognise it, too, and join in, and the whistling becomes louder.

Addy smiles. He hasn't told anyone about his dream of being a composer, or about the piece he wrote before the war, a big enough success, apparently, for his platoon to know it by heart. Perhaps it's a sign, Addy thinks. Perhaps hearing it now is an indication that it's only a matter of time before he reconnects with his family. It's a song about a letter, after all. The knot in Addy's chest loosens. He hums along with his men, scripting his next letter home as he marches: *You won't believe, Mother, what I heard today in the field . . .*

MAY 10, 1940: *The Nazis invade the Netherlands, Belgium, and France. Despite Allied defences, the Netherlands and Belgium surrender within the month.*

JUNE 3, 1940: *The Nazis bomb Paris.*

JUNE 22, 1940: *The French and German governments reach an armistice, dividing France into a 'free zone' in the south under the puppet leadership of Marshal Petain, based in Vichy, and a German-controlled 'occupied zone' in the north and along the French Atlantic coast.*

CHAPTER TWELVE

Genek and Herta
Lvov, Soviet-Occupied Poland ~ June 28, 1940

The knock comes in the middle of the night. Genek's eyes snap open.

He and Herta sit up in bed, blinking into the darkness. Another knock, and then, an order. '*Otkroitie dveri!*'

Genek kicks himself free of the bedsheet and fumbles in the dark for the chain on his bedside lamp, squinting as his eyes adjust to the light. The air in the small room is hot, stagnant; with the blackout still in effect in Lvov, their curtains are permanently drawn. There is no such thing any more as sleeping with the windows open. He runs the back of his hand across his forehead, wiping away a film of sweat.

'You don't think . . .' Herta whispers, but she's interrupted by more shouting.

'*Narodnyy Komissariat Vnutrennikh Del!*' The voice outside is loud enough to wake the neighbours.

Genek curses. Herta's eyes are wide. It's them. The secret police. They climb out of bed.

In the nine months since they settled in Lvov, Genek and Herta have heard stories of these raids in the middle of the night – of men, women, and children snatched from their homes for money falsely owed, for being perceived resisters, for simply being Polish. Neighbours of the accused said they heard the knocks, the footsteps, a dog barking, and then in the morning, nothing; the homes were empty. The people, whole families, vanished. Where they were taken, no one knew.

'We'd better answer it,' Genek says, convincing himself that he has nothing to fear. What could the secret police have on him? He's done no wrong. He clears his throat. 'Coming,' he calls, reaching for a robe and, at the last minute, his wallet from the dresser. He slips it into his robe pocket. Herta wraps her own robe around her nightgown and follows him down the hallway.

The moment Genek unlocks the door, a gang of rifle-wielding soldiers explodes into the apartment, forming a semicircle around them. Genek feels Herta's elbow loop around his as he counts the hammer-and-sickle patches, the blue and maroon peaked caps – there are eight men in total. Why so many? He stares hard at the intruders, his fingers curled into fists, the hair on the back of his neck electric. The soldiers eye him with locked jaws until one finally steps forward. Genek sizes him up. He's short, with a squat wrestler's build and an obvious swagger – the one in charge. A small red star over his visor bobs up and down as he nods to his men, who turn obediently on their heels and file past them, down the hallway.

'Wait!' Genek protests, scowling at the backs of their tunics. 'What right do you –' he nearly says *cockroaches* but catches himself – 'What right do you have to search my home?' He can feel blood begin to throb in his temples.

The officer in charge extracts a sheet of paper from a breast pocket. He unfolds it carefully and reads.

'Gerszon Kurc?' It sounds like *Gairzon Koork*.

'I am Gerszon.'

'We have warrant to search flat.' The officer's Polish is broken, his accent as thick as his midline. He waves the paper in Genek's face for an instant as if to prove its credibility, then refolds it, returning it to his pocket. Genek can hear the havoc being wreaked in the adjacent rooms – drawers pulled from a dresser, furniture slid across the hardwood floor, papers scattered.

'A warrant?' Genek narrows his eyes. 'On what grounds?' He glances at the officer's rifle, hanging by his side. He had been shown photos of Soviet carbines in the army, but Genek has yet to see one up close. This one looks like an M38. Or perhaps an M91/30. He knows where to look for the safety. It's off. 'What the hell is going on?'

The officer ignores the question. 'Wait here,' he says, tucking his fingers into his Sam Browne belt as he strides down the hall, casually, as if the place were his own.

Left alone in the foyer, Herta frees her elbow from Genek's and wraps her arms around her chest, flinching at the sound of something heavy colliding with the floor.

'Bastards,' Genek whispers under his breath. 'Who do they think—'

Herta meets his eye. 'Don't let them hear you,' she whispers.

Genek bites his tongue, breathing heavily through flared nostrils. It's nearly impossible for him to keep quiet. He paces with his hands on his hips. The lawyer in him screams to demand to see the warrant – it can't be real – but something tells him it will do no good.

After a few minutes, the flock of uniformed men assembles again at the door. They stand with their feet planted at shoulder width, their chests puffed up like roosters, still gripping their weapons. The one in charge points to Genek. 'We take you for interrogation, *Koork*,' he says.

'Why?' Genek asks through his teeth. 'I've done nothing wrong.'

'Just some questions.'

Genek glowers down at the Russian, relishing the fact that he is a full head taller, that the officer must look up to make eye contact. 'And then I'll be free to come home?'

'Yes.'

Herta steps forward. 'I'm coming with you,' she says. It is a statement, her tone definitive. Genek looks at her, contemplates an argument, but she's right – it's better if she comes. What if the NKVD return?

'She comes with me,' Genek says.

'Fine.'

'We need to dress,' Herta says.

The officer looks at his watch and then prongs his middle fingers. 'You have three minutes.'

In the bedroom, Genek steps into trousers and a button-down shirt. Herta zips herself into a skirt and then reaches under the bed for her suitcase. 'Just in case,' she says. 'Who knows when we'll be back.' Genek nods and retrieves his own suitcase. As much as he is reluctant to admit it, Herta may be right to assume the worst. He packs some undergarments, his good-as-new army-issued boots, a photograph of his parents, a pocketknife, his tortoiseshell comb, a deck of cards, his address book. He reaches for his robe, tucks his wallet into his trouser pocket. Herta packs a small pile of hosiery, undergarments, a hairbrush, two pairs of slacks, a wool tunic. At the last minute they decide to bring their winter coats, then hurry down the hallway to the kitchen to collect what's left of a loaf of bread, an apple, and some salted fish from the pantry.

'My pocketbook,' Herta whispers. 'I nearly forgot.' She ducks back into the bedroom. Genek follows, frowning as he remembers that his own wallet is nearly empty.

'Let's go!' the officer barks from the foyer.

'Find it?' Genek asks. But Herta doesn't answer. She stands at the closet door, hands at her head, auburn hair spilling through her fingers.

'It's gone,' she whispers.

Genek brings a fist to his mouth to keep from cursing. 'What was in it?'

'My ID, some money . . . a lot of money.' Herta touches her left wrist. 'My watch is gone, too. It was – on my bedside table, I think.'

'Maggots,' Genek whispers.

The officer yells again, and Genek and Herta make their way silently back to the foyer.

Twenty minutes later, they sit at a small desk across from an officer clad in the same royal blue and maroon peaked cap worn by the men who had brought them in. The room is bare, save for a portrait of Joseph Stalin suspended on the wall behind the desk; Genek can feel the general secretary's thick-browed eyes bearing down on him like a vulture's and fights the urge to rip the photo from the wall and shred it.

'You say you are *Polish*.' The officer opposite them makes no attempt to mask the disgust in his voice. He squints at a piece of paper in his hands. Genek wonders whether it's the so-called warrant.

'Yes. I'm Polish.'

'Where were you born?'

'I was born in Radom, 350 kilometres from here.'

The officer sets the paper on the table and Genek immediately recognises the handwriting as his own. The paper, he realises, is a form – a questionnaire he was made to complete upon signing a lease with the manager of his apartment on Zielona Street, shortly after the Soviets took control of Lvov in September.

The agreement was written on Soviet letterhead; Genek had thought little of it at the time.

'Your family is still in Radom?'

'Yes.'

'Poland surrendered nine months ago. Why haven't you returned?'

'I found a job here,' Genek says, although it's only half true. In all honesty, he is reluctant to return home. His mother's letters painted an awful picture of Radom – of the armbands the Jews were forced to wear at all times, of the citywide curfew, the twelve-hour workdays, the laws banning her from using the sidewalks, from going to the cinema, from walking to the post office without special permission. Nechuma wrote about how they, like thousands of others living in the city centre, had been evicted from their home and made to pay rent for a space a fraction of the size in the Old Quarter. 'How are we to afford rent when they've taken away our business, confiscated our savings, and put us to work like slaves for next to nothing?' she fumed. She had urged him to stay. 'You're better off in Lvov,' she wrote.

'What kind of job?'

'I work for a law firm.'

The officer eyes him suspiciously. 'You're a Jew. Jews aren't fit to be lawyers.'

The words sizzle like drops of water on a hot pan. 'I'm an assistant at the firm,' Genek says.

The officer leans forward in his wooden chair, resting his elbows on the desk. 'You understand, Kurc, that you are now on *Soviet* soil?'

Genek parts his lips, tempted to unleash – *No, sir, you are wrong; you are on* Polish *soil* – but he thinks better of it, and it's in this moment that he understands the reason for his arrest. The questionnaire, he recalls, had a box he was meant to check in order to accept Soviet citizenship. He'd left it blank. It had seemed false, to call himself anything but Polish. How could he? The Soviet Union is – has always been – an enemy to his homeland. And besides, he'd spent every day of his life in Poland, had fought for Poland – he sure as hell wasn't going to give up his nationality just because a border had changed. Genek feels his body temperature rise as he realises now that the questionnaire wasn't just a formality, it was a test of sorts. A way for the Soviets to weed out the prideful from the weak. By refusing citizenship, he'd labelled himself a resister, someone who could be dangerous. Why else would they come for him? He locks his lips, refusing to admit there is truth in the officer's statement, and instead meets the man's eyes with a cold, stubborn stare.

'And yet,' the officer continues, pressing his forefinger to the questionnaire, 'you *still* say you are Polish.'

'I told you. I am from *Poland*.'

The veins in the officer's neck deepen in colour to match the purple of the piping around his collar. 'There's no such *thing* as *Poland* any more!' he bellows, a ball of spit torpedoing from his mouth.

A pair of young soldiers appears, and Genek recognises them as two of the men who searched his flat. Genek glares at them, wondering if it was one of them who had stolen Herta's purse. *Thugs*. And then it's over. The officer dismisses them with a wag of his chin, and Genek and Herta are escorted out of the police quarters, to the train station.

It's dark inside the cattle car, and hot, the air swampy and reeking of human waste. There must be three dozen bodies packed inside, but they can't tell for sure – it's hard to know – and they've lost track of how many have died. The prisoners sit shoulder to shoulder, their heads rocking back and forth in unison as the train clatters along on crooked rails. Genek closes his eyes, but it's impossible to sleep sitting up, and it'll be hours before it's his turn to stretch out. A man squats over a hole cut in the centre of the car and Herta gags. The stench is unbearable.

It is July 23rd. They've been confined to the cattle car for twenty-five days; Genek has carved a small gash in the floor with his pocketknife for each day. On some, the train rolls straight through, into the night, never slowing. On others, it stops and the doors are flung open to reveal a small station with a sign bearing an unrecognisable name. Every so often, a brave soul from a nearby village approaches the tracks, commiserating – *Poor people . . . where are they taking them?* Some come carrying a loaf of bread, a bottle of water, an apple, but the Russian guards are quick to shoo them away, swearing, their M38s cocked. At most stops, a few of the train cars peel off, veering north or south. But

Genek and Herta's car continues on its path. They haven't been told, of course, when or where they'll disembark, but they can tell by pressing their faces to the cracks in the train car's walls that they are headed east.

When they first boarded the car in Lvov, Genek and Herta made a point of getting to know the others. All are Poles, Catholics and Jews alike. Most, like themselves, were sequestered in the middle of the night, their stories similar – arrested for refusing Soviet citizenship as Genek had, or for some made-up crime they had no way of proving they didn't commit. Some are alone, some with a brother or a wife by their side. There are several children on board. For a while, Genek and Herta found comfort in talking with the other prisoners, in sharing stories of the lives and families they'd left behind; it made them feel as if they weren't alone. Whatever was in store for them, it helped the prisoners to know they were in it together. But after a few days, they found they had little left to talk about. The chatter ceased and a funerary silence settled upon the train car, like ash over a dying fire. Some wept, but most slept or simply sat quietly, withdrawing deeper into themselves, encumbered by the fear of the unknown, the reality that wherever they were being sent, it was far, far away from home.

Genek's stomach rumbles as the train screams to a stop. He can't remember what it feels like to not be hungry. After a few minutes, a metal latch lifts, and the car's heavy door slides open, bathing the prisoners in daylight. They rub their eyes and squint at the outside world. Framed in the door, the landscape is bleak: flat, endless tundra, and in the distance, forest. They are the only humans in sight. No one rises. They know better than to try to climb from the train until they are given the order to do so.

A guard in a starred cap climbs into the car, stepping over legs and between lice-ridden bodies. In the far corner he stops, bends down, and prods the shoulder of a prisoner propped against the wall with his chin resting on his chest. The old man is oblivious. The guard nudges him again, and this time the man's torso tips to the left, his forehead landing heavily on the shoulder of the woman next to him, who gasps.

The guard seems annoyed. 'Stepan!' he yells, and soon a comrade in a matching cap appears in the doorway. 'Another one.'

The new guard climbs aboard. 'Move!' he barks, and the Poles in the corner scramble stiffly to their feet. Herta looks away as the Soviets bend to lift the limp body and shuffle toward the open door. Genek glances up as they pass by him, but the man's face is obscured – all he can see is an arm, dangling at an awkward angle, its skin a sickly yellow, the colour of phlegm. At the doorway, the guards count to three, grunting as they heave the corpse from the train.

Herta covers her ears, worried she might scream if she hears the sound of another dead body colliding with the ground. He's the third to be discarded this way in three days. Tossed out like trash, left to rot beside the train tracks. For a while, she'd been able to tune it out, the hideousness of it. She'd let herself go numb. Sometimes, she pretended it was all a farce, something out of a horror film, and she'd let her mind float out of her physical body as she watched herself from above. Other times her mind took her off the train entirely, conjuring up an image of an alternate universe, usually one salvaged from her past, from growing up in Bielsko: the opulent synagogue on Maja Street with its ornate neo-Romanesque facade and its twin Moorish-style turrets; the view of the valley and of the beautiful Bielsko Castle from atop Szyndzielnia Mountain; her favourite shady park, a couple of blocks from the Biala River, where she and her family would picnic when she was little. She would stay there as long as she could, comforted by the memories. But last week, when the baby died, a little girl no older than Genek's niece, she couldn't take it any longer. The child had starved. The mother's milk had gone dry; she didn't say anything for days, just sat in silence, her torso cocooned around the lifeless parcel in her arms. One afternoon, the guards noticed. And when they pulled the infant from her mother, the others erupted in shouts – *Please! It's unfair! Let her be, please!* – but the guards turned their backs and threw the tiny body out of the train as they had the others, and the prisoners' pleas were soon drowned by the desperate howl of a woman whose heart had been severed in two, a woman who would refuse to eat, her grief too overpowering to withstand, and whose own lifeless body would be thrown from the train four days later.

It was the soft thud of the infant's body meeting the earth that broke Herta, causing the numbness to give way to a hate that burnt so deeply within, she wondered if her organs might catch fire.

A third blue cap walks by with a bucket of water and a basket of bread – loaves the size of cigarette cartons, hard as bark. Genek takes one, breaks off a piece, hands the loaf to Herta. She shakes her head, too nauseated to eat.

The door slides closed and it's dark again inside the train car. Genek scratches at his scalp, and Herta reaches for his hand. 'It'll only make it worse,' she whispers. Genek slumps, unsure of what he's sickened by more – the fact that he's trapped in a world of inescapable decay, or the army of lice that has proliferated on his filthy scalp. He adjusts his suitcase beneath his bent knees and breathes through his mouth to avoid the appalling, fetid smell of death and rot. After a moment there is a tap on his shoulder. The communal water tin has reached him. He sighs, dips his bread in the putrid water and passes the tin to Herta. She takes a small sip and hands it to the body to her right.

'It's disgusting,' Herta whispers, wiping her mouth with the back of her hand.

'It's all we've got. We'll die without it.'

'Not the water. The rest of it. All of it.'

Genek reaches for Herta's hand. 'I know. We just need to get off this train, and then we'll manage. We'll be okay.' In the darkness, he can feel Herta's eyes on him.

'Will we?'

A rush of guilt, now familiar, surges through him when Genek considers the fact that it is he who is responsible for their being here. Had he thought for a moment about the potential consequences of denying Soviet citizenship – had he willingly checked the box on the questionnaire that fateful day – things would be different. They would in all likelihood still be in Lvov. He rests his head against the wall of the train car behind him. It seemed so obvious at the time. It would have felt like a betrayal to give up his Polish citizenship. Herta swears that she wouldn't have declared allegiance to the Soviets either, that she'd have done the same had she been in his shoes, but *oh,* if he could only turn back time.

'We will,' Genek nods, swallowing his remorse. Wherever they are headed, it has to be better than the train. 'We will,' he repeats, wishing for some fresh air. Some clarity. He closes his eyes, tormented by the sense of powerlessness that has settled inside him like a fistful of rocks since they boarded the train. He hates it. But what is there to do? His wit, his charm, his looks – the things he's relied upon all of his life to talk his way out of trouble – what good will they do him now? The one time he'd smiled at a guard, thinking he might win him over with niceties, the louse had threatened to punch in his pretty-boy face.

There has to be a way out. Genek's stomach turns and he is struck suddenly by an impulse to pray. He's not a pious person, certainly hasn't spent much time in prayer, hasn't seen the point of it, really. But he's also not used to feeling so vulnerable. If there were ever a time to ask for help, he decides, it's now. It can't hurt.

And so, Genek prays. He prays for their month-long exodus to reach its end; for a livable situation once they are allowed off the train; for his health and for Herta's; for his parents' safety, for his siblings' safety, especially his brother Addy's, whom he hasn't seen in well over a year. He prays for the day when he can be together again with his family. If the war is over soon, he fantasises, perhaps he'll see them in October, for Rosh Hashanah. How sweet it would be to start the Jewish New Year together.

Genek silently repeats his pleas, over and over again, until someone in the car begins to sing. An anthem: '*Boże, coś Polskę*'. God save Poland. Others join, and the singing grows louder. As the words reverberate through the dark, dank car, Genek sings along quietly. *Please, God, protect Poland. Protect us. Protect our families. Please.*

NOVEMBER 1939–JUNE 1941: *Over one million Polish men, women, and children are deported by the Red Army to Siberia, Kazakhstan, and Soviet Asia, where they face hard physical labour, squalid living conditions, harsh climate extremes, disease, and starvation. They die by the thousands.*

SEPTEMBER 7, 1940: *The London Blitz. For fifty-seven consecutive nights, German planes drop bombs on the British capital. The Luftwaffe's aerial attacks extend to fifteen other British cities over thirty-seven weeks. Refusing to capitulate, Churchill orders the Royal Air Force to maintain a relentless counter-attack.*

SEPTEMBER 27, 1940: *Germany, Italy, and Japan sign the Tripartite Pact, forming an Axis alliance.*

OCTOBER 3, 1940: *The Vichy government of France issues a law, the Statut des Juifs, abolishing the civil rights of Jews living in France.*

CHAPTER THIRTEEN

Addy
Vichy, France ~ December 1940

Addy paces along the sidewalk before the stepped entranceway of the Hôtel du Parc. It's not yet eight in the morning but he is charged, every fibre of his body alive with nervous energy. He should have eaten something, he realises, shaking off the cold as he walks. It has already begun to feel like one of the coldest winters ever in France.

A suited man with close-cropped blonde hair emerges from the hotel and Addy pauses for a moment, recalling the most recent photo of Souza Dantas he'd seen in the paper. Not him. Luis Martins de Souza Dantas, Brazil's ambassador to France, is dark haired with broad features. He's heavier set. Addy has spent the past month learning everything he can about him. From what he's gleaned, the ambassador is a popular man. He is especially adored in Paris, where his name carries somewhat of a celebrity status in the city's elite social and political circles. Souza Dantas was relocated from Paris to Vichy when France fell to Germany in June – he and a handful of other ambassadors from Axis-friendly powers: the Soviet Union, Italy, Japan, Hungary, Romania, Slovakia. His new office is on the Boulevard des États-Unis, but Addy has heard rumours that he sleeps at the Hôtel du Parc – and that he's been quietly, and illegally, issuing Jews visas to Brazil.

Addy checks his watch; it's almost eight. The embassy will open soon. He exhales through the corners of his mouth as he contemplates the consequence of his plan not working. What then? As much as it pains him to admit it, returning to Poland is out of the question. With France in the hands of the Nazis, not only is a transit visa impossible to acquire, the idea of staying put seems impossible, too. There is no safe future for him in Axis-controlled Europe.

Addy had thought twice about applying for a Brazilian visa, as Brazil's quasi-fascist dictator, Getúlio Vargas, was said to be sympathetic to the Nazi regime. But he had already been denied visas to Venezuela, to Argentina, and, after waiting for two days in a line that stretched around the American embassy's block, to the United States. He is running out of options.

Of course, fleeing to Brazil would mean putting the distance of an ocean between Addy and his family – the thought of which torments him to no end. It's been thirteen months since he last heard from his mother in Radom. He wonders often if any of his letters have reached her, if she would feel hurt or betrayed to learn of his plan to leave Europe. *No. Of course not,* he assures himself. His mother would want him to get out while he can. And anyway, he will be no less reachable in Brazil than he has been for the past several months in France. Still, to leave without the peace of mind of knowing that his parents and siblings are safe, without their knowing of his plan or how to contact him, feels wrong. To quiet his conscience, Addy reminds himself that if he's able to secure a visa – and thanks to it, a more permanent address – he can put all of his energy into tracking down the family once he's settled somewhere safe.

If only procuring a Brazilian visa were an easier task. His first attempt was a failure. He'd waited at the Brazilian embassy for ten hours in the freezing rain, he and dozens of others desperately seeking permission to sail for Rio, only to be told apologetically by one of Souza Dantas's staffers that there were no visas left to issue. He'd returned to his hostel and spent the next several evenings lying awake, mulling over how he might convince the young woman to make an exception, but he could see it in her eyes – nothing could make her break the rules. He would have to appeal to the person above her, to the ambassador himself.

Addy rehearses his plea, feeling in his pocket for his paperwork – a certificate from the Polish Embassy in Toulouse allowing him permission to emigrate to Brazil, if Brazil deemed him worthy of a visa. '*Monsieur Souza Dantas, je m'appelle Addy Kurc,*' he recites under his breath, wishing he could converse in the ambassador's native Portuguese. '*Plaisir de vous rencontrer.* You are an extremely busy man, but if you would allow me a moment of your time, I'd like to tell you why it is in your best interest to grant me a visa to your beautiful country.' Too forward? No, he must be forward. Otherwise, why would Souza Dantas offer him the time of day? If he could just explain his degree, his experience in electrical engineering, the ambassador would take him seriously. Brazil was a developing country – they must need engineers.

Adjusting his scarf between the lapels of his overcoat, Addy catches his reflection in one of the hotel's ground-floor windows, his trepidation momentarily quelled as he studies himself as if through the ambassador's eyes. He looks sharp, put together, professional. The suit was the right call, he decides. Addy had thought about wearing his army uniform, which he carries with him wherever he goes. Bearing the respectable triple stripes of a *sergent-chef,* a promotion he'd earned shortly after arriving in Colombey-les-Belles, his military attire often comes in handy – he wears it sometimes beneath his civilian attire, on the chance that he might need to change quickly. But he is himself, and more confident, in his suit. Besides, if he'd worn his uniform, he'd have risked Souza Dantas asking how and when he'd been demobilised. And technically, he hadn't been.

For Addy, the process of leaving the army transpired quickly and unconventionally. He got out shortly after France capitulated and Germany ordered all but a few units of the French Army discharged. Those that remained fell under German rule. He would have waited for his official demobilisation papers but discovered that, with the implementation of Hitler's recent *Statut des Juifs,* France's Jews were being stripped of their rights, arrested, and deported by the thousands. And so, rather than await arrest, Addy had borrowed a typewriter and a friend's demobilisation papers as reference and forged a document for himself – a dangerous move, but he'd sensed he was running low on time. So far, thankfully, his papers have worked. No one has taken much care in looking at them – not his platoon leader, not the agent at the Bureau Polonais in Toulouse where he'd requested permission to emigrate from Poland, not the driver of the French military truck aboard which he'd hitched a ride to Vichy. Still, he doesn't have any interest in pressing his luck with Souza Dantas.

Addy snaps to attention at the sound of footsteps on the stairs above him. He turns to see a broad-faced and even broader-shouldered gentleman approaching and can tell in an instant – *it's him.* Souza Dantas. Everything about the man is straightforward and unassuming: his pressed navy slacks and wool overcoat, his leather briefcase, even his stride is efficient, businesslike. Addy's heart floods with adrenaline. He clears his throat. '*Senhor Souza Dantas*,' he calls, greeting the ambassador at the bottom of the stairs with a strong handshake and silencing the voice in his head reminding him that his request for a Brazilian visa has already been turned down. That no one else will take him. That this plan, it *has* to work; it's his only option. *Stay calm*, Addy reminds himself. *This man may be the most important person in your life at the moment, but you mustn't seem desperate. Just be yourself.*

CHAPTER FOURTEEN

Halina
The Bug River,
Between German- and Soviet-Occupied Poland ~ January 1941

Halina gathers up the tail of her woollen overcoat and plunges a stick into the water, inching toward the Bug River's opposite bank. The frigid water purls around her knees and tugs at her trousers. Pausing, she glances over her shoulder. It's past midnight, but the moon, full and round as a *szarlotka* pie, might as well be a spotlight in the cloudless night sky; she can see her cousin Franka perfectly. 'Are you sure you're all right?' she asks, shivering. Franka's freckled face is pinched with concentration. She moves slowly, one arm outstretched for balance, the other hooked through the willow handle of a wicker basket held snug to her side.

'I'm fine.'

Halina had offered to carry the basket, but Franka insisted. 'You go ahead,' she'd said, 'feel for holes.'

It's not the basket itself Halina is worried about. It's the money inside. They'd wrapped their fifty zloty in a panel of waxed canvas and slipped it through a small hole in the basket's lining where they hoped it would remain safe, and hidden, should they be searched. Leaning into the current, Halina thinks about how, before the war, fifty zloty was nothing. A new silk scarf, perhaps. An evening at the Grand Theatre in Warsaw. Now, it's a week's worth of meals, a train ticket, a way out of jail. Now, it's a lifeline. Halina stamps her stick into the riverbed and takes another tentative step, the blue-white reflection of the moon pooling and dancing around her.

In his letters, Adam continued to promise she'd be better off in Lvov, that life under the Soviets wasn't nearly as bad as life in Radom under the Germans as she'd described it. Halina knew he was right. She hated living in the cramped little flat in the Old Quarter, where Mila and Felicia slept in one bedroom, her parents in the other, and she on a too-small settee in the living room. She loathed the fact that there was no icebox, and that they often went days without running water. They were constantly stepping on each other's toes. And to make matters worse, the Wehrmacht had begun roping off sections of the neighbourhood. They hadn't come out and said it yet, but they were building a ghetto. A prison. Soon, the city's Jews would be completely segregated from the non-Jews. According to Isaac, a friend in the Jewish Police, they'd already done the same in Lublin, Kraków, and Łódź. Radom's Jews were still allowed to come and go from the Old Quarter, but everyone knew it was only a matter of time before the ropes would be replaced with walls, and the neighbourhood would be sealed.

'Come to Lvov and we'll start over,' Adam wrote. 'Bella found a way. You will too. And then we'll bring your parents, and Mila.' *Start over.* It sounded promising, even romantic, despite the circumstances. Halina was sure now that she and Adam would soon be married. She was also certain, however, that her conscience wouldn't let her desert her parents and sister in Radom, however uncomfortable the living conditions might be.

For weeks Halina told herself that Lvov was out of the question. But that changed when she received a letter from Adam, asking her to meet a colleague at the steps of Radom Czachowski Mausoleum at a particular time on a particular day. She'd gone with a quiver in her gut, and it was then that she learnt that Adam had been recruited to the Underground. 'He's already earned a reputation as the best counterfeiter in Lvov,' his colleague said – he hadn't offered his name, and Halina never asked. 'He wanted you to know, and asked that you come to Lvov. I think the trip would be worth your while,' he'd added, before disappearing down Kościelna Street. This must have been the 'news' Adam mentioned, which of course he couldn't share in writing. It didn't surprise Halina. Adam was the most meticulous person she'd ever met. *Flawless*, she remembered thinking, when he first showed her one of his architectural drawings – a rendering of a railroad station lobby. His lines were clean and modern, his aesthetic perfectly practical. 'I try to design "free of untruths",' he'd said, quoting the famed modernist, and his idol, Walter Gropius.

With this news, Halina decided she would go to Lvov. She would have made the journey alone, but her cousin Franka wouldn't allow it. 'I'm coming with you,' she declared, 'whether you want me to or not.' Their parents were fearful about the journey, understandably so. According to Jakob's letters, her brother Genek had disappeared from Lvov one night at the end of June. Selim was still nowhere to be found. Radom was miserable, her parents admitted, but at least they were together, and accounted for. And anyway, with Jewish civilian travel illegal – punishable by death according to the decree – it seemed far too risky. But Halina vowed to find a way to get to Lvov safely, and promised she wouldn't stay long. 'Adam says he can get me a job,' she said. 'I'll return to Radom in a few months with enough cash and ID cards to help us breathe a little easier. And with Adam's help,' she added, 'I might be able to find some answers about what's happened to Genek and Herta, and to Selim.' Once Halina had made up her mind to go, Sol and Nechuma acquiesced; there wasn't any point in trying to sway her otherwise.

The water has crawled to her thighs. Halina curses, wishing she'd been blessed with Franka's height. *Damn*, it's cold. If it gets much deeper she'll be forced to swim. She and Franka are good swimmers – they learnt together one summer at the lake, taught by their fathers – but this water is nothing like the beautiful water at Lake Garbatka. This water is January-cold, jet-black, and running fast. To swim it would be treacherous. They'd risk hypothermia. And the basket – would it stay dry? Halina thinks again of the money, of what it had taken for her mother to scrape together the fifty zloty. *All the more reason to get to Lvov, to replenish our savings. The cold is nothing*, she tells herself. *It's all part of the plan.*

They'd stayed the night before in the town of Liski with the Salingers, family friends whom Halina had first met at the fabric shop some ten years ago. Mrs Salinger was the only woman Halina knew who could sit and talk for hours about silk. Nechuma adored her and looked forward to her visits, which Mrs Salinger made twice a year before the shop was closed.

The small town of Liski sits fifteen kilometres from the Bug River, the designated dividing line between German- and Soviet-occupied Poland. Mrs Salinger told Halina and Franka that the bridges over the river were manned on either side by soldiers, and that the safest way to cross was to wade through the water. 'The river is narrow, and we've heard the water is shallowest at Zosin,' Mrs Salinger explained. 'But Zosin is swarming with Nazis,' she warned, 'and the river runs fast. You must be careful not to fall. The water is freezing.' Mrs Salinger's nephew had made the same trip in reverse just the week before, she said. 'According to Jurek, after you cross, you can follow the river south to Ustylluh and hitch a ride to Lvov.'

That morning, Mrs Salinger had filled Halina and Franka's basket with a small loaf of bread, two apples, and a boiled egg – 'a feast!' Halina had exclaimed – and whispered, 'Good luck,' kissing the girls on their cheeks as they left.

Halina and Franka used back roads to walk to Zosin to avoid being spotted and questioned by German soldiers, trying not to think too much about what would happen if they were caught without an ausweis, the special permission slip needed in order to travel outside one's village. The journey took nearly three hours. They arrived in Zosin at dusk and prowled the riverbank for the narrowest stretch of water they could find, then waited until dark to begin the crossing.

The portion of the river they chose is no broader than ten metres; Halina guesses that they are nearly halfway to the far bank. 'Still okay?' she asks, bracing herself with her stick as she turns again to look over her shoulder. Franka has begun to fall behind. She looks up for a moment and nods, the whites of her eyes jerking up and down in the moonlight. As Halina returns her attention to the liquid abyss in front of her, she catches a flash in her periphery. A tiny flash of light. She freezes, staring hard in the direction from which it came. It disappears for a moment, but then she sees it again. A prick. Two pricks. Three! Flashlights. In the trees to the east, lining the field on the opposite side of the river. They must belong to Soviet soldiers. Who else would be out in the cold this time of night? Halina looks to see if Franka has noticed, but her cousin's chin is pinned to her chest as she struggles to navigate the river. Halina listens for voices but can hear only the steady rush of moving water. She waits another minute, deciding at last not to say anything. *It's nothing to panic about,* she tells herself. Franka doesn't need distracting. They'll be across soon, and once on dry land they can lie low, wait for the owners of the flashlights to pass.

Underfoot, the mud of the riverbed gives way to rocks, and after a few steps, it feels as if Halina is walking on marbles. She contemplates turning back, looking for a better, shallower place to cross. Perhaps they could return tomorrow, or on a rainy day, when the clouds are thicker, when they are better camouflaged. But what's the point? It doesn't matter where they cross, for there is no way of knowing how deep the water runs. Plus, they don't have any acquaintances in Zosin. Where would they stay? They'll freeze to death if they try to spend the night outside. Halina scans the tree line. The pinpricks of light, thankfully, have disappeared. They've only four more metres to go, five at the most. *We'll have better luck on the Russian side,* she reassures herself, pressing on.

'We're halfw—' Halina calls, but her words are cut short by a shrill 'Whoop!' and the distinct *plunk* of a body meeting the water behind her. Halina whips her head around in time to see Franka, her mouth curved into a perfect *o*, disappear, her scream muted as she vanishes beneath the river's surface.

'Franka!' Halina gasps, holding her breath. A second ticks by, then two. Nothing.

Only the sound of coursing water, the rippling reflection of the moon and the night sky, a few bubbles where her cousin once stood. Halina scours the river, searching desperately for movement. 'Franka!' she whispers, her eyes frantic.

Finally, several metres downriver, Franka springs up out of the water, spitting, gasping for air, tendrils of hair plastered over her eyes. 'The basket!' Franka yowls, reaching toward a beige orb that has surfaced in front of her. She lunges, grasping at the handle, but the current is too quick. Dipping and weaving in the racing water, the basket disappears.

'Noooooo!' The panic in Halina's voice severs the thin air. Without thinking, she drops her stick, holds her breath, and throws herself, arms outstretched, into the water. The cold is shocking. It slices at her cheeks, wraps itself around her like a suit of armour, and for a moment she's paralyzed, her body frozen, a log caught in the current. Lifting her head, she gulps at the air and paddles fiercely, craning her neck to keep her chin above water. She can barely make out the basket, its handle bobbing like a buoy in rough seas, several metres downriver.

'Stop,' Franka wails from behind her. 'Leave it!' But Halina paddles harder, her cousin's pleas drifting farther and farther into the distance until all she can hear is the sound of her breath and the slap of water against her ears. She paddles desperately, scraping a knee on the riverbed. She could stand, but she knows that if she does the basket will be gone. Frog-kicking her legs, she trains her eyes downriver, fighting the numbness overtaking her body and the impulse to quit, to swim to the bank and rest.

As she rounds a slight bend, the river widens and for a brief moment the current slackens. The basket slows, gliding peacefully along an eddy, the water's surface now as smooth and shiny as the lacquered lid of her parents' old Steinway. Halina begins to close the gap. When the river narrows and the current picks up again, she's within arm's reach. Extracting the last few drops of strength left in her screaming muscles, she rockets her torso out of the water and lunges, one arm thrust forward, fingers spread wide.

When she opens her eyes she's surprised to see the basket in her hand. Her extremities might as well be useless; she can't feel a thing. She lets her feet sink to the riverbed and finds her footing. Standing slowly, keeping her body low to the water to resist the current, she wrestles her way along slippery rocks to the far bank, gripping the handle of the basket so tightly that her fingers, white at the knuckles, begin to cramp and she has to peel them loose with her free hand once she's safely across.

On dry land, Halina collapses on the muddy bank, her shoulders heaving, her heart thrashing against her chest. Crouching, she peers into the basket. The food is gone. She slips her fingers into the slit in the lining, feeling for the panel of waxed canvas. The zloty! 'They're here!' she whispers, forgetting for a moment how terribly cold she is. She removes her coat and beats it against a rock before draping it over her shoulders. Her shivers come in spasms. They'll need to find shelter soon.

Hurrying upriver, it's only a few minutes before she hears Franka's cry. 'I'm here!' Halina calls, waving, her body still laced with adrenaline. Franka has made it across the river as well and is jogging along the bank in Halina's direction. Halina holds the basket up over her head in triumph. 'We lost the food, but the zloty are there!' she beams.

'Thank God!' Franka gushes, panting. She wraps her arms around Halina. 'My foot slipped on a rock. I'm so sorry!' She takes Halina in. 'Look at you, you look like a drowned cat!'

'So do you!' Halina crows, and under the steely blue light of the moon, numb with cold, dripping and shivering from their heads to their feet, they laugh – quietly at first – and then louder, until tears run from their eyes, warm and salty down their cheeks, and they can barely breathe.

'What now?' Franka finally asks, once they've regained their composure.

'Now we walk.' Halina slips her arm through Franka's, blowing warmth into her free hand as they begin making their way east, toward the tree line.

As quickly as they'd set off, Franka stops. 'Look!' she gasps. She is no longer smiling. 'Flashlights!' There are a half dozen, at least.

'Red Army,' Halina whispers. 'Must be. *Kurwa.* I was hoping they'd be gone by now. They must have heard us.'

'You knew they were there?' Franka's eyes are wide.

'I didn't want to scare you.'

'What should we do? Should we run?'

Halina bites down hard on the insides of her cheeks to keep her teeth from chattering. She'd thought about running, too. But then what? No, they've come this far. She pulls her shoulders back, determined to remain strong, outwardly at least, for Franka's sake as much as her own. 'We'll talk to them. Come. We need to find warmth. Maybe they'll help us.' Halina tightens her grip on Franka's elbow, coaxing her on.

'Help us? What if they don't? What if they shoot? We could swim downriver a bit, hide.'

'And freeze to death? Look at us; we won't survive another hour in this cold. Look, they've seen us already. We'll be fine, just be calm.'

They walk on, tentatively, into the constellation of flickering lights.

When they are ten metres from the soldiers, a silhouette from behind one of the lights shouts.

'*Ostanovka!*'

Halina sets the basket down slowly at her feet and she and Franka raise their hands over their heads. 'We are allies!' Halina calls, in Polish. 'We have no weapons!' Her mouth goes dry as she counts ten uniformed bodies advancing. Each holds a long metal flashlight in one hand, a rifle in the other; both are aimed at Halina and Franka. Halina turns a cheek to avoid the burst of white light boring into her eyes. 'I've come to find my fiancé and my brother in Lvov,' she says, willing her voice to remain steady. The soldiers draw closer. Halina looks down at her wet clothes, at Franka, who is shaking with cold. 'Please,' she says, squinting at the soldiers, 'we are hungry, and freezing. Can you help us find something to eat, a blanket, some shelter for the night?' Her breath, caught in the light, escapes her in fleeting grey wisps.

The soldiers form a circle around the young women. One of them picks up the basket, looks inside. Halina holds her breath. *Distract him,* she thinks. *Before he finds the zloty.*

'I would offer *you* something to eat,' Halina continues, 'but by now our lone egg has made its way to Ustylluh.' She shivers dramatically, allowing her teeth to knock together like castanets. The soldier looks up and she smiles as he studies her face, then Franka's, surveying their wet clothes, their mud-soaked shoes. *He is no older than me,* Halina realises. Perhaps even younger. Nineteen, twenty.

'You come to see family. And her?' the young soldier quizzes in rudimentary Polish, aiming his flashlight at Franka.

'She—'

'My mother is in Lvov,' Franka says, before Halina has a chance to answer. 'She is very ill – she has no one to take care of her.' Her tone is so clear, so matter of fact, Halina must make an effort not to look surprised. Franka is an open book; the art of deception has never come easily to her. At least, not until now.

The soldier is silent for a moment. River water drips from the young women's elbows, landing with a *pat* on the earth at their feet. Finally, the soldier shakes his head, and in his expression Halina can sense a hint of sympathy, or perhaps amusement. She can feel the tension dissolving in her neck, a bit of blood returning to her cheeks.

'Come with us,' the soldier orders. 'You peel potatoes, stay night at our camp. In morning we discuss if you free to go.' He hands Halina the basket.

She accepts it casually, loops it over her elbow and then finds Franka's hand as they begin to make their way north, flanked on either side by men in uniform. No one speaks. The air is filled with the cadence of their footsteps only – the thump of heavy boots and the squelch of wet soles on grass. After a few minutes, Halina looks over at Franka, but her cousin stares ahead as she walks, expressionless. It is only because Halina knows her so well that she can detect the slight twitch in her jaw. Franka is terrified. Halina squeezes her hand in a gesture to convey that all will be all right. She hopes it will, at least.

They walk for nearly an hour. As her adrenaline wanes, Halina can think of nothing but the cold – of the pain in her joints, in her hands and feet, and in the tip of her nose, which is no longer numb but searing. Is it possible, she worries, for her blood to freeze while she's moving? Will she have to amputate her nose, if she arrives at camp to find it frostbitten? *Enough,* she tells herself, forcing her mind to turn a corner.

Adam. Think of Adam. She pictures herself at the door of his flat in Lvov, her arms wrapped around his neck as she tells him of Franka's fall, of her own icy paddle down the Bug. It sounds rather demented when she replays it in her mind. What was she thinking, jumping like that into the water? Would Adam understand? Her parents wouldn't, she's sure of that – but he would. He might even admire her for it.

She glances at the soldier to her right. He, too, is young. In his early twenties. And he, too, is cold. He shivers beneath his army-issued coat, looking miserable, as if he would rather be anywhere else but here. Perhaps, Halina thinks, beneath the big guns and important-looking uniforms, these young men are harmless. Perhaps they are just as eager for the war to be over as she. She could have sworn she'd caught one of them, the tallest of the lot, stealing a glance at Franka. She knows the look – part curiosity, part longing; usually it's directed at her. She'll turn up the charm, she decides. She'll compliment the soldiers' patriotism; convince them with a smile that it's in their best interest to let them continue on their way. Maybe Franka can flirt a little with the tall one, promise to write, leave him with a kiss. A kiss! How long it's been since she's felt Adam's lips against hers. Halina's blood warms a degree as she convinces herself that her plan will work. They'll have to keep their guard up, of course, but she will get what she wants – she always has; it's what she's best at.

It is their third night at the makeshift camp. Beneath a wool blanket, Halina listens from her tent as Franka and Yulian whisper by the fire. Halina had left the pair a few minutes before, sitting beside a diminishing flame, Yulian's winter coat draped over Franka's shoulders. Franka has surprised Halina again with her flirtatiousness. Halina has seen her before with boys. Around a crush, or someone she's trying to impress, Franka often flails. Apparently, Halina marvels, she hasn't any trouble leading on a boy when she's faking it. Halina wonders if Yulian will catch on eventually, to the fact that he's nothing more than a tall bump in the road that will, she prays, eventually lead them to Lvov.

She had hoped they'd be well on their way by now. These last few days have been trying. The soldiers have treated them with a brusque courtesy, but Halina is all too aware of the fact that she and Franka are two pretty girls far away from home, surrounded by lonely men; she worries about what could happen should the soldiers decide not to be polite. So far, Yulian, it seems, is content just to talk.

She blows into her fingers, flexes her toes for warmth. The blanket helps, but she's still bitterly cold. Her clothes are finally dry and she doesn't dare take any of them off to sleep; every layer helps. Closing her eyes, she drifts, shivering, into a half sleep, only to be awoken a few minutes later by the sound of someone crawling inside the tent. She sits up quickly, her hands balled reflexively into fists, half expecting to find the silhouette of one of the Soviets coming at her. But it is only Franka. She sighs, lies back down.

'You scared me,' Halina whispers, her heart racing.

'Sorry.' Franka slips beneath the blanket and pulls it up over their heads so they can talk without being heard. 'Yulian told me he's going to get us out of here,' she whispers. 'Tomorrow. Says he's already talked to his captain about letting us go.' Halina can hear the relief in Franka's voice. 'He said he would give us a ride in the morning to the nearest train station.'

'Well done,' Halina whispers.

'I promised I would stay in touch,' Franka says.

Halina smiles. 'Of course you did.'

'You know, he's not so bad,' Franka says, and Halina wonders for a moment if she's joking or if Franka really has softened to him. 'Can you imagine it,' Franka adds, 'me and Yulian? Our children would be giants,' she says, and the thought sends the pair into a fit of muffled laughter.

'I'd rather *not* imagine it,' Halina finally says, pulling the blanket back down to their chins. She rolls over and presses her body close to Franka's.

'I'm only joking,' Franka whispers.

'I know.'

Halina closes her eyes, letting her mind drift, as it tends to in the darkness, to Adam. What would *their* children look like, she wonders? It's premature to think that far ahead, but she can't help it. Hopefully, she and Franka will be on their way tomorrow. Finally. *One more night, Adam. I'm coming to you.*

Part II

CHAPTER FIFTEEN

Addy
The Mediterranean ~ January 15, 1941

The pier is a swarm of bodies. Some shout, gripped with panic as they elbow their way toward the gangplank; others speak only in whispers, as if raising their voices might strip them of the privilege of boarding the ship – one of the last passenger vessels, they've been told, permitted to leave Marseille with refugees on board. Addy moves steadily with the throng, clutching a brown leather satchel in one hand and a one-way, second-class ticket in the other. The January cold is biting, but he's barely noticed it. Every few minutes he cranes his neck, scanning the crowd, praying he might see a familiar face. An impossible wish, but he can't help but hold on to the minute chance that his mother had received his last letter, had made her way with the family to France. *Whatever it takes,* he'd written, *please, just get to Vichy. There is a man there by the name of Souza Dantas. He's the one you need to speak with about visas.* He'd included the details of Souza Dantas's address, both at the hotel and at the embassy. Addy sighs, realising how preposterous the proposition now felt. It's been fifteen months since he last heard from his mother. Even if she *had* received the letter, what were the odds of an entire family making it out of Poland? On the lucky chance that his mother could find a way out, she would never leave the others behind, that much he knows.

With every step closer to the ship, the knot in Addy's chest tightens. He brings a hand to his left-side ribs, to the place where it hurts. Beneath his fingers, he can feel the beat of his heart, his pulse like a timepiece, ticking down the seconds until he disappears from the continent. Until an ocean separates him from the people he loves most. It doesn't help that the handful of Polish refugees he's met on the pier – those lucky enough still to be in contact with family back home – describe what they know of the state of their country in terms Addy can't fathom: overcrowded ghettos, public beatings, Jews dying of cold, hunger, and disease by the thousands. One young woman from Kraków told Addy that her husband, a professor of poetry, had been taken, along with dozens of the city's intellectuals, to the wall of the city's Wawel Castle, where they were lined up and shot. Afterward, she said, with tears streaking her cheeks, their bodies were rolled down the hill and into the Vistula River. Addy had hugged her as she cried into his shoulder, and then tried with all of his might to erase the image from his mind. It was too much for him to bear.

As he inches toward the ship, Addy takes inventory of the languages being spoken around him: French, Spanish, German, Polish, Dutch, Czech. Most of his fellow passengers carry small valises like his own – in them, the handful of belongings with which they hoped to start their new lives. Tucked into Addy's are a roll-necked sweater, a collared shirt, an undershirt, a spare pair of socks, a fine-tooth comb, a small sliver of army-issued soap, some twine, a razor, a toothbrush, a date book, three leather pocket notebooks (already full), his favourite 78 RPM record of Chopin's 'Polonaise, op. 40, no. 1', and a photograph of his parents. In his shirt pocket he carries a half-used notebook, in his trouser pocket a few coins and his mother's linen handkerchief. He has 1,500 zloty and 2,000 francs – his life's savings – stashed in his snakeskin wallet, along with the sixteen documents he's collected in order to talk his way out of the army and into a Brazilian visa.

Addy's encounter with Ambassador Souza Dantas in Vichy had been brief. 'Leave your passport with my secretary,' Souza Dantas told him, when they were far enough from the hotel that no one would overhear. 'Tell her I sent you, and come back for it tomorrow. Your visa will await you in Marseille. It will be good for ninety days. There's a ship leaving for Rio around the 20th January – the *Alsina*, I believe. I don't know when, or if, there will be another. You should get on it. You will need to renew the visa once you arrive in Brazil.'

'Of course,' Addy said, thanking the ambassador profusely and reaching for his wallet. 'What will I owe you?' But Souza Dantas just shook his head, and Addy realised then that it wasn't for the money that the ambassador was risking his job and his reputation.

The next day, Addy retrieved his passport. Across the top, in the ambassador's hand, was written: *Valid for Travel to Brazil.* He kissed the words, along with the hand of Souza Dantas's secretary, shed a few belongings, and hitchhiked south. He wore his army attire, hoping the uniform would help get him a ride; the train would have been faster, but he wanted to steer clear of the station checkpoints.

When he arrived in Marseille, Addy made his way immediately to the embassy, where, amazingly, his visa awaited. It was marked with the number 52. After staring at it for a long moment, he tucked it into his passport and half walked, half jogged to the port. At the sight of the *Alsina*'s huge black hull looming over the harbour, he laughed and cried in the same breath, at once overwhelmed with hope and anticipation of what the free world would bring, and devastated by the notion of leaving Europe, and with it his family, behind.

'Do you know of other ships sailing for Brazil in the coming months?' he'd asked at the maritime office. 'Son,' the agent behind the window said, shaking his head, 'consider yourself lucky to make it out on this one.' The agent was right. There were fewer and fewer passenger ships permitted to sail for the Americas. But Addy refused to give up hope. He'd spent the afternoon huddled in the corner of a cafe near the port, penning a letter to his mother.

10 Jan. '40

Dear Mother,
I pray that my letters have reached you and that you and the others are well. I have secured passage to Brazil on a ship called Alsina. *We leave in five days, on the 15th of January, for Rio de Janeiro. Captain estimates we will reach South America in two weeks. As soon as I arrive I will write again with an address where you can reach me. Remember what I told you about Ambassador Souza Dantas in Vichy. Please be safe. Counting the minutes until I hear from you.*
    Love always,
    Addy

Before he left the cafe, Addy stepped into the washroom, where he changed out of his fatigues and into his suit. But instead of folding his uniform into his satchel as he normally did, he balled it up and slipped it into the waste bin.

* * *

Addy's cabin is pint-sized. He removes his shoes and shuffles in sideways, careful not to graze the rickety shoulder-width berth, whose walnut-veneer headboard and candlewick-yellow bedcover appear a decade past their prime. Opposite the sagging mattress sit a small mahogany bench and some shallow shelves. He sets his shoes on the bottom shelf and his satchel on the bench, hangs his overcoat and fedora on the hook on the back of the washroom door, then peeks inside. The washroom – his reason for splurging on a second-class ticket – is also impossibly small. Inside, a showerhead dangles from a metal hose attached to the wall over the toilet, and a small, round mirror hangs over a tiny porcelain sink. Addy's skin tingles at the thought of a hot shower – it's been nearly a week since his last. He undresses immediately.

After folding his shirt, vest, and pants into a neat pile on his bed, he collects his soap, comb, and razor and steps into the washroom, still clad in his underwear and socks. He slides the showerhead into its wall mount, and turns the metal lever to the hot position. The pressure is dismal, but the water is warm, and as it washes over him he can feel it softening the strain in his shoulders. He hums as he scrubs himself – underwear and all – until he's worked up a satisfying lather, then pivots slowly in a small circle to rinse. When his undergarments are suds-free, he peels them off and hangs them over the sink, then soaps himself once again and lets the water run over his bare skin for a moment before cranking the shower lever to off. He reaches for the sole white towel hanging from a bar on the backside of the washroom door and dries himself, still humming. At the mirror, he brushes his teeth, combs his hair, and shaves, running his fingers along the square of his jaw, examining closely for places he might have missed. Finally, he wrings out his wet clothes and, rigging up a clothesline with his twine, hangs them to dry. Stepping back into spare undergarments and his suit, he smiles; he feels like a new person.

On deck, Addy weaves through a crowd of refugees, nodding hellos and catching snippets of conversations as he makes his way toward the bow of the ship: *Did you hear Zamora's on board?* someone asks as he passes. Addy wonders if he would recognise Zamora if he bumped into him; surely the ex-president of Spain has purchased a ticket in first class, a deck above. Most of the talk

Addy overhears is that of the ingenious planning and relentless effort required to secure visas. *Stood in line for eighteen days straight. Paid off the embassy worker. Just awful, to leave my sisters behind.*

There are several guesses as to how many refugees are aboard – *I heard six hundred . . . ship's built for three hundred . . . no wonder it's so damned crowded . . . those poor folks down in third class must be miserable.* The second-class deck is cramped, but Addy knows it's nothing compared with the quarters below, in steerage.

About half of the refugees Addy meets are Jews, several of whom mention Souza Dantas's name. *If it weren't for the ambassador . . .* The others are a mix of Spaniards fleeing Franco's regime, French socialists and so-called degenerate artists, and other 'undesirables' from across Europe, all seeking safety in Brazil. Most have left behind their families – siblings, parents, cousins, even grown children – and not a soul knows what, exactly, the future will hold. But despite the uncertainty, the underlying mood has shifted, now that everyone has settled on board, to one of giddy anticipation. With the *Alsina* set to sail at 1700 hours, the air suddenly smells of hope, and freedom.

Addy walks the length of the ship until he reaches the bow, where he discovers a navy blue door with a brass placard and laughs at his good luck: SALON DE MUSIQUE, PREMIERE CLASSE. A music lounge! He holds his breath as he reaches for the knob and is saddened to discover it locked. *Perhaps someone will open it,* he tells himself, stepping to the rail, watching as a crush of men and women amble by. Sure enough, after a few minutes, the blue door swings open and a young crewman dressed in white emerges; Addy waits until he has disappeared into the crowd, catching the door with his toe just before it closes. Inside, he faces a stairwell. He climbs the steps in twos.

The lounge is empty. Its cherry floors gleam from beneath a patchwork of soft wool rugs in red, gold, and indigo. Floor-to-ceiling windows along the starboard-facing wall offer a view of the port, and the wall opposite is decked with mirrors, making the room feel larger than it is. There are polished wood columns in the corners and a broad, arched doorway leading to what Addy presumes to be the first-class cabins. A leather sofa, a few round tables, and a dozen chairs are gathered at one end of the lounge, and at the other end, perched in the corner – his heart somersaults when he sees it – a Steinway grand piano.

He sizes up the instrument as he approaches. It was made in the early 1900s, he guesses, before the Great Depression, when manufacturers began downsizing to the baby grand. Addy blows on the hood, blinking as a plume of dust levitates over the instrument, gleaming in the sunlight. Beneath the keys, an elegant round stool with carved walnut legs and cast-iron dolphin feet beckons for him to sit. Addy gives the stool a gentle spin to adjust the height and settles onto the smooth, slightly worn surface. He lifts the fall and rests his hands on the keys, overwhelmed, suddenly, with nostalgia for home. Flexing an ankle, he suspends a toe over the piano's damper pedal. It's been months since he's had the luxury of playing, but he has no doubt which piece he'll play first.

As the opening notes of Chopin's 'Waltz in F minor, op. 70, no. 2' fill the room, Addy tips his head forward and closes his eyes. In an instant, he's twelve years old, perched on a bench beneath the keys of his parents' piano in Radom, where he, Halina, and Mila used to take turns practicing for an hour every day after school. When they were advanced enough, they learnt Chopin, whose name was practically sacred in the Kurc household. Addy can still recall the sense of accomplishment that had filled his heart after he completed his first étude without a single mistake. 'Maestro Chopin would be very proud,' his mother had said quietly, patting his shoulder.

When Addy opens his eyes, he's surprised to find a small crowd gathered around him. The onlookers are all very smartly dressed. The women wear cloche hats and elegant beaver-collared overcoats, the men fedoras, bowler hats, and tailored three-piece suits. There's a hint of cologne in the air, a pleasant reprieve from the rank body odour permeating the common spaces a deck below. A different class of refugee, yes, but Addy knows that beneath the fine furs and tweeds, everyone on the boat is fleeing the same dire fate.

'Bravo! Che bello,' an Italian behind him beams as Addy's last note settles over the lounge. 'Encore!' the woman next to him cries. Addy grins, raising his hands. 'Pourquoi non?' he shrugs. He doesn't need to be asked twice.

When he finishes one piece, he's encouraged to play another, and with each encore Addy's audience grows, along with his gusto. He plays the classics:

Beethoven, Mozart, Scarlatti, working up a sweat. He removes his coat, unbuttons his collar. As the onlookers continue to gather, he transitions to pop melodies by his favourite American jazz composers: Louis Armstrong, George Gershwin, Irving Berlin. He's partway through Duke Ellington's 'Caravan' when the ship's horn sounds.

'We're leaving!' someone shrieks. Addy wraps up 'Caravan' with an improvised cadence and stands, the lounge suddenly full of chatter. He reaches for his coat and follows as the crowd converges on the starboard deck to watch the *Alsina* push back from the dock, her engines growling. The horn sounds again – a long, guttural farewell that hangs in the air for several seconds before floating off to sea.

And then they are moving, barely at first, as if in slow motion toward an orange sun hanging low over the glittery waters of the Mediterranean. A few of the passengers cheer, but most, like Addy, simply stare as they steam west, past Napoleon III's splendid nineteenth-century Palais du Pharo, past the pink stone forts and the lone lighthouse at the mouth of the Vieux Port. By the time the *Alsina* reaches deeper waters, the sun has vanished and the sea is more black than blue. The boat arcs south, and the scenery shifts to an endless expanse of open water. Somewhere beyond the horizon, Addy realises, as the ship picks up speed, is Africa. Beyond that, the Americas. He glances over his shoulder at the long trail of foam dissipating in their wake, at a miniature Marseille. *'Adieu* for now,' he whispers as the city disappears.

They've been at sea for over a week and he is a regular now in the first-class lounge, which has transformed into a concert hall of sorts – a stage where the passengers gather each night to sing, dance, play whatever they play best, a place where they can get lost in the music, the arts, and forget, for the time being at least, about the worlds they've left behind. The piano has been pulled from the corner into the middle of the room, a few rows of chairs arranged in a half circle around it, and various other instruments have surfaced – an African drum, a viola, a saxophone, a flute. The musical talent on board is astounding. Addy just about fell from his stool one evening when he looked up to see not only the Kranz brothers in the crowd – he'd grown up listening to their concert piano on the radio – but beside them, Poland's sterling violinist, Henryk Szeryng. Tonight, Addy guesses, there are more than a hundred people crowded into the lounge.

But he can see only one.

She's seated to his right at two o'clock, in the second row of chairs, next to a woman with the same pale eyes, ivory skin, and square, self-assured posture. A mother–daughter pair, surely. Addy reminds himself not to stare. Clearing his throat, he decides his final piece of the evening will be one of his own, 'List'. He glances at her between stanzas. There are dozens of pretty women on board, but this one is different. She can't be older than eighteen. She wears a white collared blouse and, between her lapels, a gleaming string of pearls. Her finger-waved ash-blonde hair is pinned into a loose bun at the nape of her neck. He wonders where she is from, and how he hadn't noticed her before. He'll introduce himself, he decides, before the night is over.

Addy caps his performance with a bow, and the lounge swells with applause as he leaves the stool. Snaking through the crowded room, he glances again at the girl, and their eyes meet. Addy grins, his heart galloping. She returns his smile.

It's midnight when Ziembiński, a director and actor whom the audience has also come to love, finally clinches the soirée with a theatrical reading from Victor Hugo's *Les Voix Intérieures*. As the crowd begins to dissipate, Addy waits quietly just beyond the arched doorway to the first-class cabins, averting his eyes so as not to get caught in conversation with passersby – no easy task. After a few minutes, the girl and her mother appear. Addy rights his posture, and as they stroll by, he extends a hand to the mother. 'It's what distinguishes the gentlemen from the boys,' Nechuma told him once. 'When a mother approves, *then* you may introduce yourself to her daughter.'

'*Bonsoir, Madame* . . .' Addy ventures, his arm outstretched between them.

The girl's mother stops abruptly, seemingly irked to have been disturbed. The way she carries herself, with her shoulders pinned back and her lips pressed tightly together, reminds Addy of his old piano teacher in Radom – a formidable woman whose rigid standards pushed him to become the musician he is today, but with whom he wouldn't want to share a drink. Reluctantly, she takes his hand.

'Lowbeer,' she says in a slight accent, her ice-blue eyes drifting down the length of Addy's torso. '*De Prague*,' she says, when her gaze finally meets his. Her face is long, her lips painted mauve. They are Czechoslovakian.

'Addy Kurc. *Plaisir de vous rencontrer.*' Addy wonders how much French the pair understands.

'*Plaisir*,' Madame Lowbeer replies. After a moment's silence, the woman turns to her daughter. '*Puis-je vous présenter ma fille, Eliska.*'

Eliska. Her blouse, he can now see, is sewn from a fine linen, her knee-length navy skirt, a rich cashmere. His mother would be impressed, he thinks, and then swallows the familiar pull, the worry that coils around his heart whenever his thoughts turn to his mother. *There is nothing more you can do now*, he tells himself. *You will write to her again in Rio.*

Eliska offers her hand. Her eyes, powder blue like her mother's, once again meet Addy's. '*Votre musique est très belle*,' she says, holding Addy's gaze. Her French is perfect, her handshake firm. Addy finds her confidence at once attractive and startling. There is more to this young woman, he realises, than her lovely face. He lets his hand slide from hers and immediately regrets it. It's been a year since he's felt a woman's touch – he hadn't realised how much he longed for it. His fingertips are electric. His whole body is electric.

'They call you the Master of Ceremonies on the ship, you know?' As Eliska smiles, two small dimples form around the corners of her lips. She brings a hand to the pearls resting on her collarbone.

'So I've heard,' Addy replies, trying desperately not to seem flustered. 'I'm glad you enjoy the piano. Music has always been my passion.' Eliska nods, still smiling. Her cheeks are flushed, although it doesn't appear she's wearing any rouge. 'Prague is an alluring city. You are Czechoslovakian, then,' Addy says, tearing his gaze from Eliska's to address her mother.

'Yes, and you?'

'I am from Poland.' A stab in his gut. Addy doesn't even know if his home country exists any more. Again, he pushes the worry aside, refusing to let it ruin the moment.

Madame Lowbeer's nose twitches, as if she might sneeze. *Poland* is clearly not the answer she was anticipating – or perhaps for which she was hoping.

131

But Addy doesn't care. He looks from mother to daughter, a flurry of questions darting through his mind. *How did you wind up on the* Alsina? *Where is your family? Where is* Monsieur *Lowbeer? What's your favourite song? I'll learn it and play it a hundred times if it means you will sit and watch me again tomorrow!*

'Well,' Madame Lowbeer says, her smile tight, 'it is late. We must sleep. Thank you for the concert; it was lovely.' With a quick nod in Addy's direction, she links elbows with her daughter and they make their way through the arched doorway toward their cabin, the soles of their buffed ankle-strap heels knocking softly on the hardwood floor.

'*Bonne nuit*, Addy Kurc,' Eliska calls over her shoulder.

'*Bonne nuit!*' Addy replies, a bit too loudly. Every part of him wishes Eliska would stay. Should he ask her to? It had felt so *good* to flirt with her. It had felt so – normal. No, he'll wait. *Be patient,* he tells himself. *Another night.*

CHAPTER SIXTEEN

Genek and Herta
Altynay, Siberia ~ February 1941

Nothing could have prepared Genek and Herta for the Siberian winter. Everything is frozen: the dirt floor of the barracks. The straw scattered over their log bed. The hairs on the inside of their noses. Even their spit, long before it hits the ground. It's a wonder that there is still water at the pit of the well.

Genek sleeps fully clothed. Tonight he wears his boots, hat, a pair of gloves he'd purchased when the snow first started falling in October, and his winter coat – it is lucky he'd thought at the last minute to bring it from Lvov – and still, he aches from the cold. The feeling is intense. It's nothing like the dull pain between his shoulder blades after hours spent heaving his axe, but rather a deep, relentless throb that pulses from his heels, up through his leg bones, into his gut and out his arms, triggering spastic involuntary full-body shivers.

Genek curls and uncurls his fingers and wiggles his toes, nauseated by the thought of losing one. Nearly every day since November, someone at the camp has awoken to find an appendage black with frostbite; when it happens, there is often no other choice but for a fellow prisoner to amputate. Genek watched a man once writhing in pain as his small toe was sawed off with the dull blade of a pocketknife; Genek had nearly fainted. He inches his body closer to Herta's. The bricks he'd warmed by the fire and wrapped in a towel to set at their feet have gone cold. He's tempted to burn some more wood but they've already used their two allotted logs, and sneaking out under Romanov's watch to steal an extra from the pile would be reckless.

This godforsaken land has turned on them. Six months ago, when they'd first arrived, the air was so hot they could hardly force it into their lungs. Genek would never forget the day their train finally screeched to a stop and the doors were thrown open to reveal nothing but pine forest. He'd leapt to the ground clutching Herta's fist in one hand and his suitcase in the other, his scalp swarming with lice, the skin over his vertebrae scabbed from leaning against the splintered wooden wall of the train car for forty-two days and nights. *Fine,* he'd thought, looking around at their surroundings. They were alone in the woods, impossibly far from home, but at least here they could stretch their legs and urinate in private.

They'd walked for two days in the blistering August heat, dehydrated and dizzy with hunger, before arriving at a clearing with a long, one-storey log barracks that appeared to have been built in a hurry. When they finally set their suitcases down, their exhausted bodies reeking and sticky with sweat, they were welcomed with a few select words from Romanov, the black-haired, steel-eyed guard assigned to their camp: 'The closest town,' Romanov said, 'is ten kilometres south. The villagers there have been warned of your arrival. They want nothing to do with you. This,' he barked, pointing at the ground, 'is your new home. You will work here, you will live here; you will never again see Poland.'

Genek had refused to believe the words – there was no way Stalin could get away with this, he'd told himself. But as the days turned into weeks and then months, the strain of not knowing their future began to chip away at him. Was this it? Was this how they were destined to live out their lives, felling logs in Siberia? Would they, as Romanov promised, never go home again? If that were the case, Genek wasn't sure if he could live with himself. For not a day passed that he wasn't reminded of the fact that it was his own pride that had put them here in this horrific camp – a truth that weighed on him so heavily that he feared he might soon break.

The worst of it, though, the piece that tormented Genek more than any other, was the fact that it wasn't just his wife for whom he was accountable any more. She didn't realise it at the time, but Herta was newly pregnant when they left Lvov – a surprise, of course, and one they'd have celebrated if they still lived in Poland. By the time they figured it out they'd been cooped up on the train for weeks. Herta had mentioned just before their arrest that she was late, but considering the stress they were under, it didn't strike either of them as strange.

A month later, her period still hadn't arrived. Six weeks after that, her waistline had thickened enough despite the lack of food to announce the baby's arrival. Now, she's weeks from giving birth to their child – in the middle of a Siberian winter.

Genek shivers as a loudspeaker clicks on, spitting static into the frigid air. He groans. All day and into the night the speakers spew propaganda – as if the incessant rants will convince the prisoners that communism is the answer to their problems. Fanatical revolutionary ideology fills their ears all day, and now, nearly fluent in Russian, Genek can understand the majority of the nonsense, making it impossible to tune it out. He drapes an arm gently around his wife and rests a palm on her belly, waiting for a kick – Herta says the baby is most active at night – but there isn't any movement. Her breathing is heavy. How she can sleep through the cold and the roar of the loudspeaker is a mystery. She must be spent. Their days are gruelling. Most involve cutting down trees in the bitter cold, hauling logs from the forest across slippery, frozen bogs and over windswept snow dunes to a clearing, and piling them on sleds for the horses to pull away. Genek is done in to the point of delirium by the end of each twelve-hour shift, and he's not carrying a child. In the past two weeks he's begun begging Herta to stay put in the mornings, fearful that she'll overexert herself on the job, that the baby will arrive while she's stranded in the middle of the woods, knee-deep in snow. But they've already sold every keepsake and article of clothing they can live without for extra food, and they both know that the moment Herta stops working, their rations will be cut in half. 'You don't work, you don't eat,' Romanov reminded them often. Then what?

The loudspeakers finally go silent and Genek exhales, relaxes his jaw. Blinking into the darkness, he makes a silent promise, that this will be the first and last winter they spend in this frozen hellhole. He doesn't have it in him to survive another. *You got us here, you can find a way out.* He will figure a way. Perhaps they can escape. But where would they go? He'll think of *something*. Some means to protect his family. His wife, his unborn child. They are all that matters. And to think that all it would have taken was a check mark – a willingness to feign allegiance to the Soviets until war's end. But no, he was too prideful. Instead, he'd marked himself as a resister. *Fuck* – what has he gotten them into?

Genek clamps his eyes shut, wishing with every part of his being that he could go back in time. That he could transport them to a better place, a safer place. A warmer place. In his mind, he travels to the clear waters of Lake Garbatka, where he and his siblings spent endless afternoons in the summertime swimming and playing hide-and-seek in the nearby apple orchards. He visits the sunny shores of Nice, where he and Herta once spent a week basking on a black pebbled beach, drinking sparkling wine and feasting on generous portions of *moules frites*. Finally, his memory skips to Radom. What he would do to sit down to a lavish dinner at Wierzbicki's, to settle in with his friends for back-to-back pictures at the local movie house.

For a moment, Genek is lost, the memories wrapped around him like blankets, easing the cold. But he is jolted back to his icy barracks when, in the distance, a wolf howls, its sorrowful call echoing through the trees on the outskirts of camp. He opens his eyes. The forest is full of wolves – he sees them every now and then while he's working – and at night the howling has recently grown louder, closer. How hungry would a pack have to get, he wonders, before venturing into camp? The fear of being torn apart and eaten by a wolf seemed childish, like something his father would have threatened in jest when he refused to eat his cabbage as a boy – but here in the woods in snow-smothered Siberia, it feels eerily possible.

As Genek contemplates how, exactly, he would go about staving off a hungry wolf, his heart begins to punch at his ribs, and out of his mind pours a barrage of horrific what-if scenarios: what if he simply isn't strong enough and, in the end, the wolf wins? What if there's a complication in Herta's labour? What if the baby, like the last three born in the camp, doesn't make it? Or worse, what if the baby survives, and Herta doesn't? There is one doctor left living among them. Dembowski. He's promised to help deliver their child. But Herta . . . The odds of survival for the average prisoner at Altynay narrow by the day. Of the three-hundred-some Poles who arrived at the camp in August, over a quarter have died – of starvation, pneumonia, hypothermia, and one he doesn't dwell on, in childbirth – their bodies laid to rest in the forest, exposed to the snow and the wolves, the ground too frozen for a decent burial.

Another howl. Genek lifts his head and glances toward the door. A sliver of moonlight glows beneath it. Overhead, he can make out the shadows of icicles suspended from the beams of the barracks, trained like daggers at the dirt floor. Returning his cheek to the straw mat beneath him, he presses his shivering body tighter to his wife's, willing himself to sleep.

CHAPTER SEVENTEEN

Addy
Dakar, West Africa ~ March 1941

Addy and Eliska sit staring at the sea, watching as a liquid sun sinks toward the horizon. A cool breeze rustles the giant leaves on the coconut trees behind them. This is their third visit to the crescent-shaped Plage de la Voile d'Or. Tucked away between the Parc Zoologique and an ancient Christian cemetery, the beach is an hour-long walk from the port of Dakar. At each visit, they've had it entirely to themselves.

Addy brushes a few silvery flecks of sand from his forearms, which over the past ten weeks have browned to the shade of toasted *baltona* bread. He never imagined when he set sail from Marseille in January that he'd wind up in Africa, with a tan. But since the *Alsina* was detained in Senegal by British authorities – 'This is a French ship, and France is no longer a friend of the Allies,' their captain was told – Addy's skin had grown accustomed to the relentless West African sun.

The *Alsina* has been anchored for two months. The passengers haven't an inkling of when – or if – they'll be allowed to sail again. The only date Addy knows for sure, the date he is acutely aware of, is the one two weeks from now when his visa will expire.

'I'd do anything for a swim,' Eliska says, her shoulder grazing Addy's. They didn't believe it at first, when the locals told them the sea was infested with great whites. But then they saw the headlines in the paper – SHARK ATTACK, DEATH TOLL RISES – and began spotting shadows beneath the water's surface from the bow of the *Alsina,* long and grey like submarines. On the beach, sharp, heart-shaped teeth washed up by the dozens, pricking the soles of their feet if they weren't careful where they stepped.

'Me, too. Shall we *tempt the fate*, as the Americans say?' Addy smiles, thinking of the night, two and a half years ago, that he'd learnt the expression. He'd been at a cabaret in Montmartre, and had taken a seat beside a saxophonist who turned out to be from Harlem. Willie. Addy remembers the conversation well. He'd told Willie that his father had lived for a short stint in the States – an adventure that has always intrigued Addy to no end – and had peppered poor Willie with endless questions about life in New York. Hours later, to Addy's great amusement, Willie offered up a few of his distinctly American idioms, which Addy scribbled in his notebook. *Tempt fate, break a leg,* and *close but no cigar* were among his favourites.

Eliska laughs, shakes her head. '"Tempt the fate"? Did you get that one right?' she asks. Addy is obsessed with his American sayings and is reluctant to admit to butchering them on occasion.

'Probably not. But what do you say, shall we?'

'I will if you will,' Eliska says, narrowing her eyes at him as if daring him to accept the offer.

Addy shakes his head, marvelling at the ease with which Eliska is able to laugh off danger. Aside from complaining about the heat, she hasn't seemed fazed by their two month detour in Dakar. He turns to her, blowing playfully into the blonde hair over her ear and studying her scalp as his mother used to study the skin of the chickens at the market in Radom. 'You look just right,' he says, cupping his hand into the shape of a *c*. 'It's supper time. I bet the sharks are hungry.' He clamps down on Eliska's knee.

'*Netvor!* ' Eliska shrieks, slapping his hand away.

Addy catches her hand. '*Netvor!* This is new.'

'*Tu es un netvor,*' she says. '*Un monstre! Tu comprends?* ' They speak French together, but Eliska has been teaching Addy a dozen or so Czech words a day.

'*Monstre?* ' Addy banters. 'That was nothing, *Bebette!* ' He wraps his arms around her, biting her ear as they roll backward, their heads landing softly on the sand.

They'd discovered the beach two weeks before. The fresh air and seclusion are heavenly. The others from the ship aren't brave enough to venture so far off on their own, and the locals don't seem to have much interest in the beach.

'What with their dark skin and all, why would they?' Eliska once quipped, prompting Addy to ask her if she'd ever seen a black person before. Like many of the others aboard the *Alsina,* until she set foot in Dakar, she hadn't. Most of the *Alsina*'s European refugees refused, in fact, to converse with the West Africans, a behaviour Addy found absurd. Racism, after all – the very root of Nazi ideology – was the reason most of them had fled Europe.

'Why *wouldn't* I want to get know the Africans?' he'd asked, when Eliska questioned why he thought it necessary to mingle with the locals. 'We're no better than them. And besides,' he'd added, 'the people are everything – they're how you come to know a place.' Since they arrived, he'd befriended several of the shopkeepers who manned the stores lining the harbour, even bartered with one – a photo of Judy Garland torn from a magazine left by a passenger in the *Alsina*'s first-class lounge for a colourful string bracelet that Addy had tied around Eliska's wrist.

Addy checks his watch, stands, and pulls Eliska to her feet.

'It's time already?' Eliska pouts.

'*Oui, ma cherie.*'

They carry their shoes as they make their way back down the beach in the direction from which they'd come. 'I hate leaving this place.' Eliska sighs.

'I know. But we can't afford to be late.' They'd talked a sentry into giving special permission to disembark the *Alsina* between noon and six in the evening. If they broke curfew, the privilege would be revoked.

'How is Madame Lowbeer today?' Addy asks as they walk.

Eliska chuckles. 'La Grande Dame! She's . . . how do you say it . . . a *bourru.* A curmudgeon.'

In the past month, Eliska's mother has made it quite clear that there is nothing acceptable about Addy courting her daughter. It hasn't anything to do with the fact that he's Jewish, Eliska assures him – the Lowbeers are Jewish, too, after all – it's that he's a Pole, and in Magdalena's mind, her Swiss boarding-school-educated and bright-futured daughter is far too good for a *Pole.* Addy is determined to win over Madame Lowbeer, though, and has gone out of his way to treat with her nothing but the utmost respect and deference.

'Don't worry about my mother,' Eliska sniffs. 'She doesn't like anyone. She'll come around. Just give it some time. The circumstances are a bit . . . *étrange*, wouldn't you say?'

'I suppose,' Addy says, although he's never met a soul who didn't like him.

They walk slowly, enjoying the open space around them, chatting about music and films and favourite foods. Eliska reminisces about growing up in Czechoslovakia, about her best friend, Lorena, from the international school in Geneva, about her summers in Provence; Addy talks about his favourite cafes in Paris, his dream to visit New York City and the jazz clubs in Harlem, to hear some of the greats in person. It feels good to converse like this, in a way that they might have before their worlds were turned upside down.

'What do you miss the most about life before the war?' Eliska asks, looking up at him as they walk.

Addy doesn't hesitate. 'Chocolate! The dark kind, from Switzerland,' he beams. The *Alsina* had depleted its supply of chocolate weeks ago. Eliska laughs.

'And you?' Addy asks. 'What do you miss the most?'

'I miss my friend Lorena. I could tell her anything. I suppose I still do in my letters, but it's not the same in writing.'

Addy nods. *I miss people, too. I miss my family,* he wants to say, but he doesn't. Eliska's parents are separated, and she isn't close with her father, who is in England now, as are many of her friends, including Lorena. She has an uncle who lives in Brazil, and that's it – that's the extent of her family. Addy knows, too, that despite the daily complaints, Eliska loves her mother dearly. She has no concept of what it might feel like to live *without* la Grande Dame. She's not lying awake at night as Addy is, worried sick about the fate of loved ones left behind. It's different for him. It's unbearable at times. He hasn't a clue as to the whereabouts of his parents, his siblings, his cousins and aunts and uncles, his baby niece – he doesn't even know if they're *alive.* All he knows is what the newspaper reports, none of which is promising. The latest headlines confirm what the Poles on the *Alsina* have told him – that the Nazis have begun rounding up entire communities of Jews, forcing them to live four and five to a single room in roped-off neighbourhoods. Ghettos. Most major cities now have one, some two. The thought of his parents being evicted from their apartment – forced to surrender the home where he'd spent the first nineteen years of his life, the home they'd worked so hard to acquire –

makes Addy's stomach turn. But he can't talk about the headlines with Eliska, or about his family. He's tried a few times, knowing that just hearing their names spoken aloud would help make them feel more present, more *alive*, in his heart at least. But each time he broaches the subject, she's brushed him off. 'You look so sad when you talk of your family,' she says. 'I'm sure they're fine, Addy. Let's talk of only the things that make us happy. The things we have to look forward to.' And so, he's humoured her and – if he's being perfectly honest – let himself be distracted, catching in their frivolous chatter a moment's relief from the crushing weight of the unknown.

As they round a bend, they see the silhouette of the *Alsina*'s cylindrical steam towers jutting up over the horizon. From afar, the ship appears toylike compared with the monstrosity anchored beside it – a 250-metre-long battleship with quadruple turrets that soar four stories into the sky. The *Richelieu* has been detained, along with the *Alsina*, by the British. When either vessel will be able to sail again remains a mystery. 'We should be thankful,' Addy says, when Madame Lowbeer complains about the hopelessness of their situation. 'We have a roof over our heads, food to eat. It could be worse.' In fact, it could be much worse. They could be starving, forced to beg for scraps, to dig for grains of spoilt rice in the gutter, as they'd seen some of the West African children doing the week before. Or they could be stuck in Europe. Here, at least, they have a place to rest their heads at night, an endless supply of chickpeas, and, most important, a visa into a country where they'll be allowed a life of freedom. A fresh start.

At the port, Addy checks his watch again. With a few minutes to spare, they pause at a roadside newsstand. His heart sinks as he reads the headlines. GLASGOW HIT BY LUFTWAFFE, the front page of the *West Africa Journal* reads. Every day, news of the war in Europe worsens. Countries fall, one after the next. First Poland, then Denmark and Norway, parts of Finland, Holland, Belgium, France, and the Baltic states. Italy, Slovakia, Romania, Hungary, and Bulgaria have joined the Axis powers. Addy ponders the whereabouts of Willie and his friends in Montmartre who had poked so much fun at the idea of war. Did they stay in France, or did they flee, as he had?

In a few weeks, Addy realises, it will be Passover – the third Passover that he will be forced to spend away from his home. Will his family try to find a way to celebrate this year? A lump forms in his throat and he turns away, hoping Eliska won't notice the sadness in his eyes. *Eliska*. He is falling in love. *In love!* How can he feel this way, with so much worry consuming him? There is no explanation, other than that he can't help it. It feels good. And with all that is happening around him, that in itself is a gift. He reaches for his mother's handkerchief, dabs discreetly at the tears that have materialised in the corners of his eyes.

Eliska loops her arm through his. 'Ready?' she asks.

Addy nods, forcing a smile as they continue on toward the ship.

APRIL 7, 1941: *The gates to Radoms two ghettos are sealed, confining some 27,000 Jews to the main ghetto on Wałowa Street and another 5,000 to the smaller Glinice ghetto just outside the city. With only 6,500 rooms between the two ghettos, they are drastically overcrowded. Living conditions and food rations deteriorate by the day, and disease spreads quickly.*

CHAPTER EIGHTEEN

Mila and Felicia
Radom, German-Occupied Poland ~ May 1941

The whispers pass swiftly among the workers, like a gust of wind through tall grass. '*Schutzstaffel.*' German military. 'They're coming.' The colour drains from Mila's cheeks. She looks up from her sewing and, in her haste, pricks her forefinger with her needle.

It's been over a month since the gates to Radom's two ghettos were sealed. Most of the city's Jews – those who didn't already reside in the ghetto – were given a ten-day notice at the end of March to leave their homes. A fortunate few were able to trade apartments with Poles whose homes fell within the designated ghetto borders. But the majority scrambled to find a place to live, which was exceptionally challenging as the ghettos were already far too crowded, even before the Jewish refugees began filing in from Przytyk, a nearby village that the Germans had converted into a military camp. The Kurcs, of course, had been forced out of their apartment and into the Old Quarter a year and a half ago. They were lucky in a sense, not to have to take part in the mad rush to find a space to reside. Instead, they stayed in their two-bedroom flat on Lubelska Street, watching from a second-storey window as the others filed in by the thousands.

Soon after the ghetto was sealed in April, however, the Wehrmacht stationed in the city were replaced with Schutzstaffel, who brought along a new era of evil. Easily recognisable by their beetle-black uniforms and lightning-shaped *s* insignia, the SS prided themselves on being the *purest* of all Germans. Rumour spread quickly among the Jews that to become a member of the SS, officers had to prove the racial history of their families dating back to the 1700s. 'These guys are true believers,' Mila's friend Isaac warned. 'We are nothing to them.

Just remember that. We are less than dogs.' As a member of the Jewish Police, Isaac is in the unenviable position of working closely with the SS – he'd seen, up close, what they were capable of.

There have been rumours at the workshop of a raid. It happens often – a swarm of SS will storm unannounced into one of the ghetto workspaces and order the Jews to line up so they can be counted, their permits checked. To live in the ghetto, the Jews must have papers deeming them worthy of work. Most without papers – the elderly, the sick, or the very young – have already been deported. The few who are left remain in hiding; they would rather take the risk of being discovered – and killed on the spot – than be torn from their families, especially now that word has begun to trickle back to Wałowa about the conditions of the slave labour camps where the deported are sent. Trying not to think of what will happen if Felicia is discovered, Mila has spent the past several weeks devising a plan, a way to hide her daughter in the event of a raid – and praying for her sister's return.

Halina had written in February. She and Franka had made it to Lvov, she said, and she'd found work at a hospital; she would come home as soon as she could with some savings and with the 'drawings' Adam promised. Mila hoped that 'soon' meant in the next few weeks. Their monthly rations lasted ten days, at most. Every day their hunger grew; every day Felicia's spine felt sharper as Mila ran her fingertips along her back, coaxing her to sleep. Occasionally Nechuma was able to find an egg or two on the black market, but when she did it cost her fifty zloty, or a tablecloth, or one of her porcelain teacups. They are burning through their savings and have nearly depleted the supplies they'd brought from home – a disturbing reality, considering there is no end in sight to this life in captivity.

It's dreadful, the routine of it all – the hunger, the work, the claustrophobia of living on top of one another. There is no such thing as privacy any more. There is no space to think. Every day the streets grow dirtier, smellier. The only beings that thrive in the ghetto are the lice, which have grown so big the Jews have taken to calling them 'blondies.' When you found one, you burnt it and hoped it wasn't a typhus carrier. Mila and her parents are becoming despondent. They need Halina now more than ever – they need the money and the IDs, but even more they need her conviction. Her will. They need someone who can lift their spirits, who can look them in the eye and declare with confidence that there is a plan. A plan that will get them out of the ghetto.

Mila sets her sewing down, the tunic's buttonhole half complete, and licks a drop of blood from her finger. 'Felicia,' she whispers, pushing her chair away from her workbench and peering between her knees. Beneath the table, Felicia looks up from her spool of thread – she's made a game of trying to roll it from one hand to the other.

'*Tak?*'

'Come.'

Felicia extends her arms and Mila lifts her carefully to her hip, then half walks, half jogs to the far corner of the room, to a wall lined with long bolts of viscose rayon, wool, and recycled shoddy, and beside them, a row of paper sacks, each nearly twice Felicia's size, filled with fabric scraps. Setting Felicia down on the floor, Mila glances over her shoulder at the door in the opposite corner. A few of the others in the room look up from their sewing but go about their business.

Mila squats so her eyes are level with Felicia's and takes Felicia's hands in hers. 'Remember the day we played hide-and-seek?' she asks, steadying her breath and trying not to rush her words. She doesn't have much time, but Felicia must understand exactly what Mila is about to tell her. 'Remember, you hid here, and pretended you were a statue?' Mila glances toward the paper sacks. When they'd first practised the drill, Mila had to act out what it meant to 'be a statue,' and Felicia had giggled watching her mother stand perfectly still, as if she were carved from a block of marble.

Felicia nods, her expression suddenly sober, like that of a child much older than two and a half.

'I need you to hide for me, love.' Mila opens the sack she'd marked at the bottom corner with a tiny *x*, lifts Felicia up again, and gently lowers her inside. 'Sit, darling,' she says.

Inside the sack, Felicia bends her knees to her chest and then feels the ground moving beneath her as her mother pushes the bag so it's flush against the wall. 'Lean back,' Mila instructs from above. Felicia rests her spine tentatively on the

147

cold cement behind her. 'I'm going to wrap you up tight,' her mother says. 'It will be dark, but only for a little while. Stay perfectly still, like we practised. Just like a statue. Don't make a noise, don't move a muscle until I come find you, okay? Do you understand, love?' Her mother's eyes are wide, unblinking. She's talking too fast.

'Yes,' Felicia whispers, although she doesn't understand why her mother would leave her here, in the dark, alone. The last time, it felt like a game. She remembers her mother's impression of a statue, how it had seemed silly. Today, there is nothing to laugh about in the urgency of her mother's voice.

'Good girl. Like a statue,' her mother whispers, holding a finger to her lips and bending down to kiss her on the top of her head. *She's shaking*, Felicia thinks. *Why is she shaking?*

In an instant the paper sack is rolled shut and Felicia's ears are filled with a crunching sound as the world around her goes black. She strains to hold on to the faint tap of her mother's heels retreating across the room, but all she can make out is the whirring of sewing machines, and the subtle rhythmic crinkle of the paper sack, a finger-width from her lips, moving with her breath.

After a moment, though, there are new sounds. A door opening. A sudden commotion – men's voices yelling strange words, chairs scraping the floor. Then there are footsteps, lots of them, passing by her all at once, toward the far side of the room. The people, the workers, are leaving! The men continue to yell until the last of the footsteps have dissipated. A door slams shut. And then all is quiet.

Felicia waits for several heartbeats, her eardrums straining, reaching. Shreds of cotton tickle her elbows and ankles and she wants badly to move, to scratch at the places that itch, to call out. But she can still feel the tremble in her mother's touch and decides she'd better sit quietly as she'd been told. She blinks into the darkness. After a while, just as her bottom has begun to ache, the door clicks open. Again, footsteps. She stiffens, sensing right away that they are not her mother's. Their owners traipse around the room, their boots landing heavily on the floor.

Soon there are voices accompanying the footsteps. More strange words. Felicia's heart knocks hard against her chest, so hard she wonders if the men in the room might hear it. Pressing her eyes shut, she sips delicately at the dark, claustrophobic air, whispering silently to herself to stay *still as a statue, still as a statue, still as a statue.* The footsteps grow closer. The floor throbs beneath her now, with every stomp. Whoever it is must be *centimetres* from her! What will they do if they find her? And then she hears it: a horrible *crunch* – something heavy, a boot maybe, colliding swiftly with the paper sack next to hers. She gasps, then quickly covers her mouth with her hands. Shaking, she's struck by the sensation of something hot and wet between her legs, realising a moment too late that her bladder has given way.

The men begin yelling again, in a singsong voice. 'Come out, come out *wherever* you are!' they taunt. A tear slides down Felicia's cheek. As quietly as she can, she cups her hands over her face, bracing herself for the blow that's sure to come. When it does, she'll be discovered, and they'll snatch her up – where will they take her? Holding her breath, she wishes with every ounce of her two-and-a-half-year-old soul that the men will pass.

CHAPTER NINETEEN

Halina and Adam
Lvov, Soviet-Occupied Poland ~ May 1941

In Halina's half sleep, her brother Genek has escaped from whatever hell he's undoubtedly been subjected to and returned to Lvov. He's at the door to her apartment, knocking, for his flat has been confiscated and he needs a place to stay. Halina rolls to her side, feeling Adam's warmth beside her, and then her stomach clenches as she realises she isn't dreaming. The knocks are real.

Disoriented, she sits up, reaching for Adam's arm. 'What time is it? Did you hear that? Who on earth – who could it be?' A fraction of her still believes, or wants to believe, it's Genek.

Adam reaches for his bedside lamp. 'Franka, maybe?' he offers, rubbing the sleep from his eyes with the heels of his hands.

When Halina and Franka arrived in Lvov in January, Franka had found an apartment two blocks south of Adam's. She visits often, but never in the middle of the night. Halina slips out of bed and into her robe, glancing at the clock – it's half past one in the morning. Standing perfectly still, she waits for another knock. It comes a moment later, this time faster – *thump-thump-thump-thump-thump* – the fleshy outer edge of a fist beating quick and hard against wood. 'NKVD!'

Halina's eyes widen. '*Kurwa,*' she curses under her breath.

It's been months, as far as she knows, since Stalin shipped off his last trainful of 'undesirables' to the east. The NKVD had come for Genek – his neighbours confirmed it, the knock like this one after midnight. Most likely they'd come for Selim, too – she's searched and searched and found no trace of him. Are they here now for her? For Adam?

Halina and Adam had talked at first about living separately, for this exact reason. Adam's work in the Underground is risky – if he were caught, he'd no doubt be deported or killed – but Halina was adamant. 'I didn't hike across a river and nearly die of hypothermia so we could live down the street from one another,' she'd said. 'You have a perfect false ID. If they come for you, use it.' Adam had agreed, and soon after, they were married in a quiet fifteen-minute ceremony, with Jakob and Bella as their witnesses. Now, Halina wonders whether she should have been so stubborn in insisting that she and Adam share an address.

Adam leaps out of bed and pulls a shirt over his head. 'Let me go, see what they—'

'Halina Eichenwald!' a second voice calls through the door, deeper, also in Russian. 'Open up *immediately* – or you will face arrest.'

'Me?' Halina whispers. Since she began work at the hospital, she's learnt to understand and speak Russian. 'What could they want from me?' She smooths her hair behind her ears, her pulse thundering. They had prepared for a knock on the door for Adam, but hadn't thought through what to do if it was for her.

'Let me—' Adam tries again, but this time it's Halina who interrupts.

'I'm coming, just give me a moment!' she calls. She turns to Adam as she knots the cotton belt of her robe around her waist, 'They know I'm here,' she says. 'No use hiding.'

'They do now,' Adam whispers, his cheeks flushed. 'Our IDs – we could have used them.'

Halina realises her mistake. 'I'm sure it's nothing,' she says. 'Let's go.' They hurry together down the hallway.

Thus far, living in Lvov has been relatively painless. They use their real names because as Jews, they're treated much like the city's Poles. They have jobs, Franka as a maid, Adam as a railroad engineer, and Halina as a technician's assistant at the city's military hospital. They live in apartments in the centre of town; unlike Radom, Lvov has no ghetto yet. Their days are simple. They go to work, they return home, they earn enough to get by. Halina saves what little extra she can for when she returns to Radom. And of course Adam works in his spare time on IDs. For the most part, life in Lvov has been uneventful. They've been left alone. Until now.

At the door, Halina gathers up her confidence. Standing as tall as her diminutive frame will allow, she unlocks the deadbolt. Outside, two NKVD officers greet her with quick, stern nods.

'What can I do for you?' Halina asks in Russian, one hand still gripping the doorknob.

'Pani Eichenwald,' one of the officers begins, 'we need you to come with us right away to the hospital.'

'What is this about?' she asks.

'We need your blood. Dr Levenhed is awaiting us at the lab.'

Levenhed is Halina's supervisor. He spends his days examining blood – finding matches for transfusions and testing samples for infectious disease. Halina's job is to help prepare the tests, and to write down the findings as Levenhed stares at a plate through a microscope.

'What do you mean – my *blood*?' Halina asks, incredulous.

'We have a general in. He has lost a lot of blood. Levenhed says you are a match.' It was a requirement for all the hospital staff to have their blood tested when they began work there. Halina hadn't been told what type she was when her labs were run, but apparently the information was on file.

'And no one at the hospital can give blood?'

'No. Let's go.'

'I'm sorry, but this isn't a good time for me. I'm not feeling well,' Halina lies. She's sceptical. What if all of this is just a ruse, a clever excuse to get her out the door, so the NKVD can arrest her and send her away?

'I'm afraid that's not of our concern. You're needed right away. Dress quickly.'

Halina contemplates putting up a fight but knows better. 'Fine,' she whispers. As she makes her way back to the bedroom, Adam follows close behind. *It's not a ploy,* she tells herself. Why would the NKVD concoct such an elaborate story when, from everything she's heard, they needed no pretence to arrest her? And why would they come for just her, and not Adam, if they were to be deported?

'I'm going with you,' Adam declares, once they've reached the bedroom.

'I'm sure they won't allow it,' Halina says. 'Levenhed will be at the hospital. I trust him, Adam. And if they only need my blood, I'll be back by morning.'

Adam shakes his head and Halina can see the fear in his eyes. 'If you're not back in a few hours, I'm coming for you.'

'All right.' Halina wonders about the Russian general, about what he's been responsible for. Would giving him her blood and allowing the man to live make her complicit in his actions? She shakes the thought from her mind, reminding herself that this isn't her choice. She's been able to avoid trouble so far because she's done what's been asked of her. If they need her blood, so be it.

At the hospital, everything happens quickly. She's escorted to the lab, and along the way she learns that the general was brought in earlier that night for an emergency surgery. Once she's seated, a doctor in a white coat instructs her to roll up her sleeves.

'Both of them?' Halina asks.

'*Da.*'

Halina rolls the sleeves of her blouse to just above her elbow and watches as the man in the coat, who she presumes to be a doctor, sets a pair of needles, a rubber tourniquet, a cotton swab, two bandages, a bottle of rubbing alcohol, and a small army of collection tubes – she counts twelve – on a metal tray beside her. A minute later he brings a needle to her arm, bevel up, and pushes the tip into a vein. It hurts, more than it should, she feels, but she locks her jaw, refusing to wince. She is a puppet to these men, but this at least – the strength conveyed in her expression – she can control. Within a few seconds, the first test tube has turned a deep purple-red. The doctor removes the tourniquet from her upper arm with one hand and replaces the full tube with an empty one, the needle still stuck in her arm. A nurse waits behind him, and every time a tube is full, she whisks it away in a hurry. By the sixth tube, Halina's blood moves at a slow drip, and the doctor asks her to flex and unflex her fist until the tube is filled. Finally, he removes the needle and wraps a bandage around her elbow crease, then turns his attention silently to her other arm.

It's three in the morning when Halina is allowed to return home. She has given nearly a litre of her blood. She is light-headed and has no idea if the general survived the night, if the transfusion was successful. But she doesn't care. She just wants to get back to Adam. The doctor scribbles a note and hands it to her as she leaves. 'In case anyone asks why you are out,' he says. The NKVD who had retrieved her had brought her by car to the hospital. She gathers from the note that there will not be a ride home. Just as well, Halina thinks. She's glad to be free of them. She takes the slip and leaves without a word.

Her flat is seven blocks from the hospital. She walks the route daily, knows it well. But in the dead of night, the city feels foreign. The streets are dark, empty.

153

With every tap of her heels on the cobblestones she becomes more convinced that someone is following her, or waiting up ahead, in the shadows. *You are just tired*, she tells herself. *Stop being paranoid.* But she can't help it. In her depleted state, she isn't herself. She's cold, to start – it's May, but the nights are still chilly. She can't stop shivering. On top of that, her head is spinning, and her limbs feel heavy, as if she's drunk. Halfway home, spooked by the sensation of being spied upon, she slips her shoes off and summons what's left of her strength to jog the last three blocks.

Before she can extract a key from her pocket, the door swings open and Adam appears, still clothed.

'Thank God,' he says. 'I was on my way out. Come in, quickly.' He takes her by the arm and she grimaces when his thumb presses up against the bruise in the crease of her elbow. 'Halina, are you all right?'

'I'm fine,' she says. She smiles, a feeble attempt to mask the pain, and her delirium. If he knew how much blood they'd taken out of her he'd be livid, and more livid still at his inability to stop it from happening. 'Just tired,' she adds.

Adam locks the door behind her and pulls her to him, and she can feel his heartbeat through his shirt. 'I was so worried,' he whispers.

The reserve of energy Halina had tapped to jog home has disappeared, and she suddenly feels as though she might faint. 'I'll be fine in the morning,' she says, 'but I need to lie down.'

'Yes, of course.' Adam helps her onto the bed. He adjusts her pillow and pulls a blanket up over her shoulders before fetching a glass of water and a few slices of apple, which he leaves on her bedside table.

'You take good care of me,' Halina whispers. Her eyes are already closed, her breath heavy. 'Of us.'

Adam brushes her hair aside, kisses her forehead. 'I'm just glad you're back,' he says. He undresses, turns out the light, and climbs into bed. 'You had me petrified.'

Halina can feel sleep pulling her into its abyss. 'Adam?' she asks. She is seconds from drifting off.

'Yes, love.'

'Thank you.'

MAY 1941: *Brazil's dictator, Getúlio Vargas, begins issuing restrictions on the number of Jews allowed into the country, calling them 'undesirable and non-assimilable.' Infuriated by the number of visas Souza Dantas has granted without permission in France, Vargas begins turning away refugees seeking freedom in Brazil, and issues Law 3175, forcing Ambassador Souza Dantas to retire.*

CHAPTER TWENTY

Addy
Casablanca, French-Occupied Morocco ~ June 20, 1941

Addy surveys Casablanca's port, the column of buses parked just off the pier, the dark-skinned soldiers who have formed a human tunnel at the foot of the gangplank. The *Alsina*'s captain had told his passengers that the ship was sent north from Dakar to Casablanca 'for repairs.' But the heavily armed men ordering the refugees off the boat don't remotely resemble a repair team.

So this is Morocco, Addy thinks to himself.

In the end, the *Alsina* had spent nearly five sweltering months docked in Dakar. By the time she finally pulled up anchor in June, most of the passengers' ninety-day visas to South America had long since expired. *What are we to do? What if Vargas won't renew our papers? Where will we go?* Retracing their route north toward Europe didn't help the mood on board, which grew increasingly frantic by the day. No one believed that they were going to Casablanca for mechanical reasons. To quell the refugees' hysteria, the *Alsina*'s captain promised to contact the appropriate authorities in order to guarantee passage to Rio – he would wire the Brazilian embassy in Vichy, he said, with the request for passenger visas to be extended to make up for the weeks they'd spent helplessly idle. But whether or not that telegram was ever sent or received, no one knew, for the captain, along with the crew and the refugees on board, were ordered off the boat soon after docking in Casablanca. The few passengers who could pay for a hotel were offered the option to stay in the city centre, but most were to be escorted to a detention camp outside of town to await a decision by Morocco's Axis-friendly government on whether the *Alsina* would be allowed to sail again.

As Addy descends the ship's gangplank, the soldiers wave their rifles toward the buses, shouting at the mob of foreigners spilling out onto the pier: *'Allez!*

Allez!' Addy boards a bus and finds a seat by a window facing the pier, searching for the Lowbeers, who are no doubt among the cluster of first-class passengers gathered in the shadow of the *Alsina*'s bow awaiting transport to the city. He scans the crowd, but it's impossible to see much of anything through the dirt-smudged pane. Kneeling on his seat, he ratchets the window down a few inches, peers through the opening. As the bus pulls away, he spots Eliska – or at least he thinks he sees her, the top of her blonde head; she appears to be standing on her toes, looking in his direction. Pushing his hand through the crack in the window, he waves, wondering if she'll know it's him. A moment later, the bus lurches away, kicking up a cloud of dust and fumes in its wake.

They drive for forty-five minutes before the caravan slows to a stop at a patch of desert hemmed in with barbed wire. As Addy makes his way inside, he glances at the wooden sign over the entrance: KASHA TADLA. The camp is fly infested and cloaked in the inescapable scent of excrement, thanks to several holes dug in the dirt that serve as toilets. Addy lasts two uncomfortable nights sleeping head to toe with a pair of Spaniards in a tent built for one before deciding he's had enough of Kasha Tadla. On the morning of his third day, he sidles up to a guard at the camp's entrance and, in perfect French, offers to go to the city for a few desperately needed supplies for the group. 'We are out of toilet paper, and soap. We are dangerously low on water. Without these things, people will be sick. They will die.' He flips to the page in his pocket notebook where he's scribbled *papier hygiénique, savon, eau embouteillée. 'I* speak your language, and I know what we need. Take me to town; I'll purchase a few provisions.' Addy rattles the change in his pocket, and adds, 'I have some francs; I'll buy what my satchel here can hold, and pay for everything myself.' He smiles, and then shrugs, as if he's just offered up a generous favour – *take it or leave it.* After a moment's pause, the guard acquiesces.

Addy is dropped at the top of Ziraoui Boulevard and told to meet back in the same place in an hour, with supplies. 'One hour!' Addy calls as he sets off, dodging donkey carts and taking in the sharp, unfamiliar aromas of a colourful spice market as he weaves his way through Casablanca's centre. Of course, he won't be returning in an hour. His only intention is to track down the Lowbeers, which fortunately isn't nearly as difficult as he worried it might be. He finds them at an outdoor cafe, sipping French 75s from tall glass flutes; perched among a gaggle of long-faced men in robes cradling mugs of tea, they stand out like a couple of parakeets in a flock of doves. Eliska leaps from her chair when she sees him. After a quick celebratory reunion, Addy suggests they go back to their hotel, where he can keep a low profile. It feels presumptuous to ask for their protection, but surely the guard who is expecting him on Ziraoui Boulevard will soon come looking for him, realising he's been duped. Madame Lowbeer reluctantly agrees, on the condition that Addy sleep on the floor while they await news on the *Alsina*'s fate.

Five days later, Moroccan authorities declare the *Alsina* an enemy ship, claiming they'd discovered contraband on board. Addy and the Lowbeers find this charge hard to believe, but whether or not the ship is, in fact, carrying illegal goods, the authorities have made up their minds. The *Alsina* will not be leaving Casablanca. The detainees at Kasha Tadla are released and, along with those who had been spared the tent camp, are refunded seventy-five per cent of the cost of their tickets. The passengers are left to fend for themselves. Addy and the Lowbeers consider staying in Casablanca, on the chance that the authorities might issue them Moroccan visas, but then think better of it. Casablanca has already seen its fair share of warfare, and Morocco, now under Vichy governance, is likely no safer an option than France.

They have to move quickly. There are six hundred refugees, most of whom are desperate for a way out. They need a plan, and they need one fast. After several days of gathering information from every possible source – expats, government officials, dockhands, journalists – they learn that there are ships sailing for Brazil from Spain. Spain and Portugal, according to the newspapers, are still neutral. Addy and the Lowbeers decide right away to travel north to the Iberian Peninsula, where the only boats headed for South America, they discover after further research, depart from Cádiz, a port in western Spain. To get there, however, will first require finding a way to Tangier, a city on the North African coast, 340 kilometres from Casablanca, and then crossing the Strait of Gibraltar, a narrow stretch of water funnelling virtually all traffic into and out of the Mediterranean from the Atlantic – a stretch of water that had been bombed heavily the year before by the Vichy French Air Force, and which is now under strict surveillance and fortification by the British Navy. If they are able to cross the Strait to Tarifa, they'll have to make their way north another hundred kilometres to Cádiz. It won't be easy. But from what they can tell, it's their only option. They pack quickly and Addy goes about arranging transportation to Tangier.

The port in Tangier is crowded with ships steaming across the Strait, to and from Tarifa. Addy counts three British aircraft carriers, a handful of cargo ships, and dozens of fishing boats. He and the Lowbeers walk the piers, debating which vessel they should approach. There is a ticketing office at the far end of the port, but visas will surely be required to make a purchase. They decide they'll be better off hiring a captain on their own.

'How about him?' Addy points to a fisherman with sun-cracked skin and a shaggy beard sitting at the square stern of his boat, eating his lunch. His skiff is small with a flat bottom and peeling blue paint – just inconspicuous enough, Addy hopes, to cross the Strait unnoticed, and just functional enough to bring them safely to Tarifa. A faded Spanish flag flaps gently from the craft's narrow bow. The fisherman shakes his head, however, at Madame Lowbeer's first offer.

'*Peligroso*,' he says.

Madame Lowbeer removes her watch. '*Esto también*,' she says, surprising Addy with her Spanish.

The fisherman squints down the pier as if trying to decipher whether anyone of authority might be watching, and then looks back up at the threesome again for a moment, considering his options. Addy is grateful for their appearance – they may be refugees, but they are certainly put together well enough to look trustworthy. '*El reloj*,' the fisherman finally huffs.

Madame Lowbeer slips the watch into her purse. '*Primero, Tarifa*,' she says coolly. The fisherman grunts and waves them aboard.

Addy lowers himself into the skiff first to help load their belongings. The Lowbeers, thankfully, had decided in Casablanca to ship their three massive portmanteaux to Madame Lowbeer's brother in Brazil. They travel now with leather valises similar in size to Addy's. When their things are stowed, Addy offers his hand as the women step gingerly into the boat, eyeing a small pool of oily water gathered on the floor of its stern.

The ride is bumpy. Madame Lowbeer vomits twice over the side. Eliska's cheeks turn a ghostly shade of white. No one speaks. Addy holds his breath on multiple occasions when he's sure their small skiff is about to be engulfed in the wake of a passing freighter. He keeps his gaze fixed on Tarifa's rocky coastline, praying they can make their way unnoticed – and afloat – to Spanish soil.

JUNE 22–30, 1941: *In a surprise twist of events, Hitler turns his back on Stalin, breaking the German–Soviet Nonaggression Pact and attacking the entire eastern front, including Russian-occupied Poland. Huge in scope, the invasion is code-named Operation Barbarossa. In Lvov, after a week of bitter fighting, the Soviets are defeated; before retreating, however, the NKVD massacres thousands of Polish, Jewish, and Ukrainian intellectuals, political activists, and criminals held in the city's prisons. The Germans publicly blame the Jews for these massacres, declaring that the victims were mainly Ukrainian. This of course enrages the pro-German Ukrainian militia, who, along with the Einsatzgruppen (SS death squads), take vigilante action against the Jews inhabiting the city. Jewish men and women who haven't found their way into hiding are stripped, beaten, and murdered in the streets by the thousands.*

CHAPTER TWENTY-ONE

Jakob and Bella
Lvov, Soviet-Occupied Poland ~ July 1, 1941

Lvov has come undone. The madness began at the end of June, shortly after Hitler's surprise attack on the Soviet Union, which is when Jakob, Bella, Halina, and Franka went into hiding.

They've been holed up in their building's basement for over a week. A Polish friend named Piotr brings news and food when he can – a one-man makeshift relief organisation. 'The city is swarming with Einsatzgruppen and what appears to be a Ukrainian militia,' Piotr said when he first came by to check on them. 'They are targeting Jews.' When Jakob asked why, Piotr explained that the NKVD had murdered the majority of the inmates at the city's jails before fleeing, thousands of whom were Ukrainian, and that the Jews were being blamed. 'It doesn't make much sense,' he said. 'Hundreds of the inmates were Jewish – but this doesn't seem to matter.'

There is a single knock from upstairs. Piotr. It was no secret that he, too, would be targeted by the Germans should he be discovered aiding Jews. Jakob stands. 'I'll go,' he offers, lighting a candle and tiptoeing to the staircase. Along with news of the pogrom, Piotr often brings food – small parcels of bread and cheese. His knocks usually come once a day, in the evening.

'Be careful,' Bella whispers.

Yesterday, ten days after the pogrom began, Piotr said that the paper estimated the city's Jewish death toll at a horrific thirty-five hundred. Ten, twenty, even a hundred, Bella could believe. But thousands? The statistic is far too gruesome for her to bear, and she can't put out of her mind the fact that she hasn't heard from her sister since the invasion. Again and again she imagines Anna's beautiful body among those strewn in the streets – Piotr says he has to step over corpses just to reach their doorstep. Bella has begged Piotr to visit Anna's flat; he's been twice, and twice he's returned with the news that his knocks have gone unanswered.

She listens as Jakob climbs the stairs. Soon there is another single knock, this one from Jakob, followed by four quick reciprocal taps, Piotr's code indicating it is safe to open the door. The hinges whine, and a storey below, Bella exhales, listening to the faint murmur of conversation.

'It's going to be all right,' Halina says, sitting down next to her.

Bella nods, admiring her sister-in-law's strength. Adam is missing, too. He'd insisted on remaining aboveground during the pogrom, claiming that the resistance needed him now more than ever. Halina has yet to hear from him, and yet here she is offering Bella comfort.

The women sit quietly, listening. After a while, the conversation halts and Bella stiffens. The silence overhead stretches on for two, three, four seconds, then nearly half a minute. 'Something's wrong,' she whispers. She can feel it in the dread blooming within her rib cage; whatever it is, she doesn't want to know. Finally, the door above squeals, the deadbolt snaps shut, and footsteps make their way slowly back to the staircase. By the time Jakob reaches the basement, Bella can barely breathe.

Jakob hands the candle and a loaf of bread to Halina and lowers himself to sit. 'Bella,' he says softly.

Bella looks up, shakes her head. *Please, no.* But in Jakob's face she can see that her instinct is right. *Oh God, no.*

Jakob swallows, staring at the ground for a moment before uncurling his fingers. In his palm is a note. 'Piotr found it, sticking out from under Anna's door. Bella, I'm so sorry.'

Bella stares at the wrinkled slip of paper as if it were a bomb about to detonate. She presses her lower back into the wall behind her, brushing Jakob's hand away when he reaches for her. Jakob and Halina exchange a worried glance, but Bella doesn't notice. She is paralysed by the notion that whatever her husband has, whatever he knows, will destroy her. That in a moment's time, everything will change. Jakob waits patiently, silently, until finally Bella gathers the courage to take the note. Holding the wrinkled paper with both hands, she recognises her sister's handwriting immediately.

They are taking us away. I think they are going to kill us.

Bella braces herself, suddenly unsteady, as if the ground beneath her has given way. She crumples the note, and as the walls begin to spin, her world goes dark. She brings her fist to her forehead and wails.

CHAPTER TWENTY-TWO

Halina
Lvov, German-Occupied Poland ~ July 18, 1941

'Ready?' Wolf asks.

They've paused on a street corner, a block from the work camp. Halina nods, surveying the camp – a shoddy cement structure confined by a barbed-wire-topped fence. At the entrance, a guard with a German shepherd at his heels. If things don't go as planned, she realises, she'll spend the foreseeable future staring at that fence from the inside. But what other choice does she have? She can't sit idle any longer. It will destroy her. And perhaps Adam, too, if it hasn't destroyed him already.

'You'd better go,' Wolf says. 'Before they think we're up to something.'

Halina glances down the street at the tables in front of a cafe two blocks east of them, their designated meeting place.

'Right,' Halina says. She takes a breath and straightens her posture.

'Are you sure you want to do this alone?' Wolf shakes his head, as if willing her to say no.

Halina turns her attention again to the camp. 'Yes. I'm sure.'

Wolf, an acquaintance of Adam's from the Underground, had insisted on walking with her to the camp from the city centre, but Halina was adamant that he hang back once they arrived – at least that way, she reasoned, if her plan failed, he would be able to return to Lvov, recruit some help.

Wolf nods. A Polish couple walks by, arm in arm. He waits for them to pass, then leans in as if to kiss Halina on the cheek. 'Good luck,' he whispers, before righting himself and turning toward the cafe.

Halina swallows. *This is madness.* She should be en route to Radom, she thinks, the summer's heat suddenly stifling in her lungs. Her father had sent a truck. *There are rumours of another pogrom in Lvov,* Sol wrote after hearing of the first one. *Come to Radom. You will be better off here with us.* Jakob, Bella, and Franka had left that morning. Halina had stayed.

She'd been home seven weeks ago, in early June. She'd brought IDs along with some zloty she'd saved – not that either would do her parents and Mila any good in the ghetto; the black market had all but dried up, and there was no use for an Aryan ID inside Wałowa's walls. Halina had thought about staying in Radom, but her job at the hospital provided some income – she'd have been foolish to leave it – and Adam was far too entrenched in Lvov's Underground efforts for him to move back. And anyway, there wasn't room for the two of them in the tiny flat in the ghetto. She'd stayed only briefly, returning to Lvov with travel documents approved by her supervisor at the hospital, and with a set of her grandmother's silver, carefully wrapped in a napkin. 'Take it,' Nechuma had insisted before she left. 'Maybe you can use it to help get us out of here.' And then Hitler broke his pact with Stalin and unleashed his Einsatzgruppen in Lvov; a massacre ensued, and her father sent the truck to retrieve his family. It had pained her, turning down his plea to return home, and she hates to think about what the truck had cost. She knows the family needs her. But she can't leave Lvov without Adam. And Adam is missing.

Halina recalls the day, just over two weeks ago, when the fighting let up in Lvov and it was finally safe to come out of hiding. She'd run the half kilometre to her old apartment only to discover it empty. Adam was gone. He'd left in a hurry, it seemed – had taken his suitcase, some clothes, and his false ID from behind the watercolor painting in the kitchen. Halina had searched the apartment for a note, a hint, anything that might reveal where he'd gone, but had found nothing. Over the next three days she visited each of the spots they'd designated as safe places to meet in an emergency, a dozen times – the arched doorway beneath the steps leading up to Saint George's Cathedral, the stone fountain in front of the university, the back bar of the Scottish cafe – but Adam was nowhere to be found.

It wasn't until Wolf knocked on her door that Halina was able to piece together what had happened. Apparently, Wolf said, the Germans had shown up at Adam's flat one night during the pogrom. He had been taken to a work camp just outside Lvov's city centre – Wolf knew this only because someone in the Underground had managed to bribe a guard in the camp to pass notes through the fence surrounding the property. Adam's note had shown up in Wolf's hands the week before: *Please check on my wife,* it read. He'd signed the note with the name he and Halina used on their false papers – Brzoza. The Underground had been trying to find a way to get him out, but without any luck. Hearing this news was an enormous relief – Adam was alive, at least – but it also made Halina sick, not knowing what the Germans had in store for him. If they knew about his involvement in the Underground, he was a dead man. 'I have some silver,' she told Wolf, 'a set of cutlery.' Wolf had nodded tentatively. 'That could work,' he said. 'It's worth a try.'

Halina wraps her fingers around the leather handles of the purse hanging over her shoulder. *You'll get only one shot at this,* she reminds herself. *Don't botch it.* Her heart beats in double time as she makes her way toward the guard at the camp's entrance, feeling as if she's about to go on stage, to perform in front of an unforgiving audience.

The German shepherd notices her first and barks, straining against his leash, the tan and black fur over his shoulders spiked and angry. Halina doesn't flinch. She keeps her chin high, trying her best to exude a sense of purpose in her stride. With the leash wrapped firmly around his wrist, the guard stands with his feet spread wide for balance. By the time Halina reaches him, the German shepherd is nearly hysterical. Halina offers the guard a tight smile and then waits for the dog to quiet. When the barking ceases, she rifles through her purse for her ID.

'My name is Halina Brzoza,' she says in German. Like Russian, German had come easily to her; she'd perfected it when the Nazis first invaded Radom. She rarely speaks it, but to her surprise, the words flow naturally off of her tongue.

The guard doesn't speak.

'I'm afraid you have mistaken my husband for a Jew,' Halina continues, handing the guard her forged ID. 'He is inside, and I'm here to collect him.' She hugs her purse to her side, feeling the lump of the cutlery against her ribs. The last time she'd used these knives and forks was around her parents' dining table. She'd have laughed then if someone had told her that someday they might be worth her husband's life. She eyes the guard as he examines her ID. Unlike some of the Germans in town, whose necks appear as broad as their skulls, this one is built tall and narrow. Shadows pool in his eye sockets and beneath his cheekbones. Halina wonders if his features have always been this sharp, or if he is as hungry as she. As the rest of Europe.

'And why would I believe you?' the guard finally asks, handing her back her ID.

Sweat has begun to gather on Halina's upper lip. She thinks quickly. '*Please*,' she huffs, shaking her head as if the guard has offended her. 'Do I *look* Jewish?' She stares hard at him, her green eyes unblinking, praying that her assertiveness, which she has grown to rely upon, might help her. 'Clearly there's been a mistake,' she says. 'And anyway, what would a Jew be doing with silver of this quality?' She slips the silver from her purse and unwraps a corner of the napkin to reveal the handle of a spoon. It glints under the sun. 'It's my husband's great-great-grandmother's. Who was German, by the way,' Halina adds. 'She was a Berghorst.' She runs her thumb over the engraved B, silently thanking her mother for insisting she take it when she left Radom, and sending up an apology to her deceased grandmother, who grew up a proud Baumblit.

The guard blinks at the sight of the silver. He looks around, making sure no onlookers have seen what he's seen. Returning his gaze to Halina, he lowers his chin, his silt-grey eyes again meeting hers.

'Listen to me,' he says. His voice has fallen almost to a whisper. 'I don't know who you are, and frankly I don't care if your husband is a Jew or not. But if you say your husband is of German decent,' he pauses, looking down at the silver in Halina's hands, 'I'm certain that the boss can help you out.'

'Then take me to him,' Halina says, without hesitation. The guard shakes his head. 'No visitors. Give me what you have there and I'll bring it to him.'

'No offence, Herr——?'

The German hesitates. 'Richter.'

'Herr Richter. But I'm not parting with this until you've delivered me my husband.' She slips the silver back into her purse, tucks it tightly into the crux of her elbow. Inwardly, she is trembling, but she keeps her knees locked in place and her expression steady.

The guard narrows his eyes, then blinks. It seems he's not used to being told what to do. At least not by a civilian. 'He'll have my head,' Richter says coolly.

'Then keep your head. And keep the silver. For yourself,' Halina counters. 'You look like you could use it.' She holds her breath, wondering if she's gone too far. She hadn't meant the last bit as an insult, but it had sounded like one.

Richter considers her for a moment. 'His name,' he finally says.

Halina feels her shoulders relax a touch. 'Brzoza. Adam Brzoza. Round spectacles, pale skin. He's the one in there who looks nothing like a Jew.'

Richter nods. 'I make no promises,' he says. 'But come back in one hour. Bring your silver.'

Halina nods. 'All right then.' She turns, walking briskly away from the camp.

At the cafe she finds Wolf seated at an outdoor table, a cup of chicory coffee before him, feigning interest in a newspaper. By the time she's seated across from him, Richter has disappeared from his post. 'Can you spare an hour?' Halina asks, gripping the seat of her chair to steady her hands, grateful for the fact that the tables around them are empty.

'Of course,' Wolf says, and then lowers his voice. 'What happened? I couldn't see a thing.'

Halina closes her eyes for a moment and exhales, willing her pulse to slow. When she looks up she sees that Wolf has gone pale, that he is as nervous as she.

'I offered him the silver,' she says. 'He tried to take it right then but I told him he could have it as soon as he delivered me my husband.'

'Did it seem like he would come through?'

'It's hard to tell.'

Wolf shakes his head. 'Adam always said you had guts.'

Halina swallows, suddenly exhausted. 'It's all an act. Let's just hope he believed it.'

As Wolf motions for the waitress, Halina contemplates how the war, until recently, has in many ways felt surreal. For a while, her family got by. Soon enough, she often told herself, life would return to normal. She would be fine. Her family would be fine. Her parents had endured the Great War and made it through. In time, they'd toss the horrible hand of cards they'd been dealt back into the pile, and start anew. But then things started to fall apart. First it was Selim, then Genek and Herta – gone. Vanished. Then it was Bella's sister Anna. And now, Adam. All around her, it seems, Jews were *disappearing*. And suddenly, the consequences of this war were undeniably real – an understanding that sent Halina spiraling as she wrestled with the knowledge she both feared and loathed: she was powerless. Since then she's begun to imagine the worst, picturing Selim and Genek and Herta locked up in Soviet prisons, starving to death, and drumming up a long list of the atrocities Adam had no doubt been subjected to at the work camp, telling herself that if he of all people – with his looks and ID – had not been able to talk himself out of captivity by now, then it must be dire.

And what of Addy? They haven't heard from him since the family moved into the ghetto, nearly two years ago. Had he joined the army as he said he would? France has capitulated. Did the French Army even exist anymore? She racks her memory often for the sound of Addy's voice, but quits when she finds she can't retrieve it. She hopes against hope that wherever he, Genek, Herta, and Selim are, they are safe. That they can sense how much the family misses them.

A waitress brings a second mug of coffee and sets it on a saucer before Halina. She nods in thanks and glances at her watch, discouraged to find that only five minutes have passed. It's going to be a long hour, she realises, removing the watch and setting it under the lip of her saucer so she can check the time more discreetly. And then she waits.

CHAPTER TWENTY-THREE

Genek and Herta
Altynay, Siberia ~ July 19, 1941

Herta drags the limb of a small pine toward a clearing in the forest. Józef, four months old, is tied snug to her breast with a bedsheet. She steps carefully, scouring the ground for sleeping vipers and half-buried scorpions, humming to distract herself from the rumble in her stomach. It'll be hours before she receives her slice of bread and, if she's lucky, a tiny slab of dried fish.

Józef squirms and Herta lowers the log to the ground, running the cotton of her sweat-stained shirtsleeve across her forehead, and squints up at the sky. The sun is directly overhead; Ze, as they've taken to calling the baby, must be hungry. She finds a shady spot beneath a tall larch at the edge of the clearing and lowers herself carefully to sit, cross-legged. From her perch she can see Genek and a handful of others, fifty or so metres away, piling logs by the river. Their figures appear blurry in the July heat, as if they've begun to melt.

Herta extracts Józef carefully from his bedsheet harness and lays him gently to face her in the space between her legs, propping his head on her ankles. Wearing nothing but a cloth diaper, his skin, like hers, is pink and sticky to the touch. 'Hot, aren't you, my love,' she says softly, wishing the sweltering temperatures would break, but knowing it will be another month, at least, before they do, and that the heat of summer, despite its intensity, is far more tolerable than the cold that will envelop them come October. Józef looks up with his father's sky-blue eyes, staring at her in the only way he knows how, without blinking or judgement, and for a moment Herta can do nothing but smile. Unbuttoning her blouse, she follows his gaze as he studies the branches of the larch above. 'Any birds up there?' she asks, smiling.

Though Genek will never admit it (he refers to Altynay as an 'endless swath of Siberian shitscape'), the forest, despite the suffocating heat and hellish circumstances, is undeniably beautiful. Here, seemingly as far removed from civilisation as possible, surrounded by pine, spruce, and larch – every shade of green she can imagine – and by big, open skies and black-water rivers that snake their way through the trees on their journey north, Herta is but a fleck against nature's backdrop. She feels at peace. She closes her eyes as Józef nurses, taking in the soft breeze, the chatter of swallows and wagtails in the branches above, feeling grateful for the blessing of the healthy child at her breast.

Józef was born just before midnight on the 17th of March, on the frozen dirt floor of their barracks. Herta had heaved logs on the day he arrived, breathing through contractions as they came and went every ten, then seven, then five minutes, before finally asking her friend Julia to find Genek, unsure if she could make her way back to camp on her own. 'When you count three minutes between contractions,' Dr Dembowski had said, 'then you know the baby is coming.' Julia had returned alone, explaining that Genek had been sent to the town on an errand and that her husband, Otto, would cover for him as soon as he returned. Julia had helped Herta to her feet and walked with her, slowly, arm in arm, back to camp, where she called for Dembowski.

When Genek arrived two hours later, Herta was barely recognisable. Despite the arctic cold, she was drenched in sweat, her eyes pressed shut as she lay in a fetal tuck, drawing and exhaling breath in quick, heavy bouts through o-shaped lips as if trying to extinguish a stubborn flame. Clumps of wet, dark hair stuck to her forehead. Julia sat by her side, massaging her back between contractions. 'You made it,' Herta breathed when she rolled over to see Genek, wrapping her hands around his and squeezing hard. Julia wished them luck and left, and Herta endured another six hours of pelvis-splitting pain before it was time, finally, mercifully, to push. It was a quarter to midnight when, with Genek at Herta's side and Dembowski crouched between her knees, Józef took his first breath. At the sound of their baby's cry, and at Dembowski's definitive 'to chłopiec' – it's a boy – Herta and Genek beamed at each other with wet, exhausted eyes.

That night, they tucked Józef between them in their straw bed, swaddled in Herta's wool scarf and bundled with two of Genek's extra shirts and a small knit

172

hat that was passed down between the babies born at the camp; all they could see of him were his eyes, which he rarely opened, and the pink of his lips. They worried about whether he was warm enough, or whether they'd roll over onto him in the night. But soon a deep fatigue overcame them, blotting out their fears like blizzard clouds over the sun, and after a few minutes all three Kurcs were sound asleep.

Within days, Józef began to put on weight, Herta went back to work, and she and Genek grew used to sleeping with a lump between them. The only real trouble came in the mornings, when Józef would wake wailing, his eyes frozen shut. Herta learnt to rub warm droplets of breast milk onto his lids to coax them open.

Now, Herta marvels, it's hard for her to believe it's been four months since her son was born. She has marked the passage of time by his first smile, his first tooth, by the day he was able to roll himself over from his belly to his back. What will it be next, she wonders: will he suck his thumb? Start to crawl? Say his first words? Herta has written home at each milestone, aching for news of her family in Bielsko. She hasn't heard from them, though, since before she and Genek left Lvov. The last letter she received had been from her brother Zigmund; his news was disheartening. *There are fewer and fewer Jews left in Bielsko*, he wrote. Some apparently had left at the start of the war to join the Polish Army. Others had been shipped off by train, and never returned. *I've pleaded with the family*, Zigmund wrote, *begged them to leave, or to hide, but Lola is far too pregnant to travel safely*. By now, Herta realises, her sister's baby would be almost a year old. *And our parents*, Zigmund added, *are too stubborn to leave. I suggested we might come to you in Lvov, but they refused*. Herta thinks about the child she has yet to meet, wondering if she's an aunt to a boy or a girl, if the day would come that Ze would get to know his cousin. At the moment it seems unfathomable, separated by such a vast stretch of land, with the world crumbling around them.

Herta prays often for her family. As much as she is able to somehow make the most of her time here in Altynay, there is nothing she wants more than to return to a life of freedom. Part of her wishes she could travel forward in time, and skip to the end of the war. But there is also part of her that prays for time

173

to stop. For there is no telling what the future might bring. What if, at war's end, she returns to Poland to discover her family is no longer there? The idea is impossible to contemplate. It's like staring directly at the sun. She can't do it. She won't. And so instead she puts it out of her mind, finding solace in the fact that, for now, at least at this very moment, she and Genek are healthy, and their son is perfect.

At dusk, Herta finds Genek in their barracks, smiling. 'Some good news?' she asks. She unties Józef from her chest, lays the sheet on the dirt floor, and sets him on it. Standing, she rests a hand on her husband's cheek, realising how lovely it is to see his dimples.

Genek's eyes are bright. 'I think the tides have finally turned,' he says. 'Herta, the Soviets may soon be on our side.'

A month ago, they learnt that Hitler had broken his pact with Stalin and invaded the Soviet Union. The news had apparently stunned the world, but it had done nothing to change their situation in Altynay.

Herta tilts her head at this news. 'We thought so at the start of the war, too, yes?'

'True. But this afternoon Otto and I heard the guards whispering something about moving prisoners south to form an army.'

'An army?'

'Darling, I think Stalin is going to grant us amnesty.'

'Amnesty.' Herta marvels at the word. A pardon. But for what? For being Polish? It's a difficult concept to digest. But if it means they will be freed, Herta decides, then by all means, she will welcome an amnesty. 'Where would we go?' she wonders aloud. From what they've heard, there isn't a Poland to return to.

'Perhaps Stalin is thinking of sending us off to fight.'

Herta looks at her husband, at his gaunt figure, his newly receding hairline, the hollow over his collarbone. He's still handsome despite it all, but they both know he isn't in any shape to fight. She thinks of the others in the camp, too, most of whom are either sick or starving or both. Aside from Otto, born with the natural build of a heavyweight boxer, *none* of the prisoners are fit to go to battle. She opens her mouth to voice the concern, but, seeing the hope in

Genek's eyes, she swallows the thought, kneeling instead by Józef, who is busy practising his new trick of rolling onto his stomach. Herta tries to picture it: Genek, suited up alongside the Soviets, fighting for Stalin – for the man who'd put them in exile, condemned them to a life of labour. It seems backward. She wonders what this would mean for her and Józef – what would become of them if Genek is sent off to battle?

'Do you have a sense of when this *amnesty* might be granted?' she asks, rolling Józef gently to his back. Józef flaps his arms happily, showing off two miniature replicas of his father's dimples.

'No,' Genek says, lowering himself to sit beside her. He squeezes Józef's knee and Józef coos, smitten. Genek smiles. 'But soon, I think. Soon.'

CHAPTER TWENTY-FOUR

Addy
Ilha das Flores, Brazil ~ Late July 1941

It's become Addy's habit to wake early, well before the other detainees are up, and walk the path circumventing the tiny Ilha das Flores. He needs the exercise and even more so the chance to be alone for an hour – together they help preserve his sanity. The scenery helps, too. Guanabara Bay is beautiful at dawn, when it is at its calmest, a mirror image of the sky. By ten in the morning, it's teeming with boat traffic heading to and from Rio de Janeiro's busy port.

This morning Addy awoke before dawn to the shrill cavatina of a kingfisher perched on his windowsill. He was tempted to slip back into sleep, for in his dream he was home in Radom, and his family was just as he'd left them. His father sat at the dining-room table reading the weekend edition of *Radomer Leben,* his mother opposite, humming as she sewed a leather patch onto the elbow of a sweater. In the living room, Genek and Jakob played a game of cards, Felicia toddled about gripping a ragdoll by the ankles, and Mila and Halina shared the bench at the baby grand, taking turns at the keys, Beethoven's 'Moonlight Sonata' spread out on the music rack before them. The only person missing from the dream was him. He didn't mind, though; he could have watched the scene for hours, content just to hover above it, basking in its warmth, in the simple knowledge that all was well. But the kingfisher was persistent, and eventually Addy's dream faded and he rose, sighing as he rubbed the sleep from his eyes, dressed, and set off for his walk.

On the trail, he plucks flowers, each with a name that has become familiar to him over the past three weeks: amaryllis, hibiscus, azalea, and his favourite, the bird of paradise, which, with its fanlike crown of foliage and Technicolor red and blue petals, resembles a bird in flight. There is one species of lily on the island to which he seems to be allergic. When he stumbles upon it he sneezes for the next fifteen minutes into his mother's handkerchief, which he carries with him always, like a talisman.

Back at the cafeteria, Addy props his bouquet into a water glass, setting it at the table where he and the Lowbeers typically meet for breakfast. A staff worker appears, and Addy greets him with a smile and a '*buon dia, tudo bem?* ' – the first Portuguese words he'd learnt upon arrival.

'*Estou bem, si, senhor,*' the staffer offers, handing Addy a cup of yerba mate tea.

Addy carries his tea to the porch, where he turns his chair to face west, toward Rio's coastline. Since their ship arrived in South America, the bitter taste of yerba has grown on him. As he brings the cup to his lips, he takes in the peaceful morning, the smell of the tropics, the ubiquitous birdsong. Under normal circumstances, he might close his eyes and bask in the beauty of it all. But the circumstances, of course, are nowhere near normal. There is far too much at stake for him to truly unwind. And so, instead, he stares at the coastline, reflecting on the past several months – on what had been required of him to get to this island off the coast of Brazil.

As it turns out, the fisherman he'd chosen in Tangier was able, despite his shoddy skiff, to deliver Addy and the Lowbeers safely to Tarifa. From there, they rode north by bus to the port of Cádiz, where they were told a Spanish ship called the *Cabo do Hornos* would depart in a week for Rio. 'I'll sell you tickets,' the agent in Cádiz said, 'but I cannot guarantee they will let you off the boat with expired visas.' This was not what they wanted to hear, but as far as they knew, the *Hornos* was their only hope – a speculation that was confirmed when they began recognising the faces of other *Alsina* passengers at the port, passengers who had also been lucky enough to make their way across the strait to Cádiz. Addy and the Lowbeers didn't waste time in purchasing one-way tickets aboard the *Hornos,* assuring themselves that if they made it as far as South America, they would not be turned away.

When they finally boarded the ship, Addy was forced to acknowledge that he had but a handful of francs left to his name. He would be starting over in Brazil with next to nothing – a truth he grappled with as the *Hornos* steamed south-west toward Rio. The trip took ten days. None of the refugees on board slept much, as they had been warned when they embarked that at least half a dozen ships before them had been sent back to Spain – the thought of which prompted some to threaten suicide. 'I'll jump, I swear it,' one Spaniard told Addy, 'I'll kill myself before I let Franco do the deed.'

Addy, Eliska, and Madame Lowbeer clung to their expired visas, and to the steadfast hope that the captain of the *Alsina* had been able to send a wire as he'd promised to the Brazilian embassy in Vichy. Perhaps if the petition had reached Souza Dantas, the ambassador would help. Even if it hadn't, there was always the chance that Brazil's president, Getúlio Vargas, would understand their circumstances and extend their papers upon arrival. It wasn't their fault, after all, that the journey had taken so long.

It was the 17th of July when the *Cabo do Hornos* finally docked in Rio and, by some stroke of luck, her passengers were allowed to disembark. Addy was overjoyed. The freedom was short-lived, however. Three days later, Addy, the Lowbeers, and the thirty-seven other *Alsina* passengers who'd arrived on the *Hornos* with expired visas were greeted at their doorsteps by Brazilian police and escorted back to the port, where they were loaded onto a freight boat and shipped seven kilometres offshore to Ilha das Flores, where they were now detained.

'We're being held *hostage*,' Madame Lowbeer seethed after their first day on the island. '*C'est absurde.*' They were given no explanation for why they were being held. They could only assume it was due to their expired visas, a hunch that was verified when one of the passengers, fluent in Portuguese, caught a glimpse of a written notice indicating Vargas's intent to send the refugees back to Spain.

Addy takes another sip of tea. He refuses to believe that, after six months, he'll end up where he began, in war-torn Europe. The *Alsina* passengers have come this far. Someone will surely persuade the president to let them stay. Eliska's uncle, perhaps – he'd hosted them those first few days in Rio. He seemed like a good person. He had money. But then again, what access did a civilian have to the president? They will need someone with influence. As Madame Lowbeer often says, 'When the right palms are greased, we'll get our

178

visas.' The Lowbeers have the means to offer a bribe, but to whom those 'right' palms belong, Addy has no clue. He *is* certain that with no contacts in Brazil, no grasp of the language, and no savings, he will be of little help. He's done everything he can to get them this far – the rest, as hard as it is to admit, is beyond his control.

According to the Lowbeers, their hope at the moment lies with Haganauer, an *Alsina* passenger whose grandfather in Rio has a tenuous connection to Brazil's minister of foreign relations. A week ago, Haganauer had bribed a guard on the island to pass along a letter to his grandfather explaining the circumstances, in hopes that his grandfather would then deliver a plea to the minister on the hostages' behalf. The plan, everyone agreed, seemed promising. Until it came to fruition, though, there was nothing to do but wait.

Addy finishes his tea and cradles the ceramic cup in his palms, his mind drifting to Eliska, to the spot at the base of his neck she'd kissed the night before as she excused herself to 'get her beauty rest.' They'd decided in Dakar that they were destined to marry – an idea Madame Lowbeer resented vehemently. But Addy isn't fazed by her disapproval. In time, he assures himself, he'll convince la Grande Dame he's worthy of her daughter's hand.

He watches a barge make its way to Rio's port, wondering as he often does what his family would think of Eliska. She is smart, and she is Jewish. She's passionate and well spoken, capable of a good debate. Surely his siblings would think well of her. His father, too. But would his mother? He can hear Nechuma sometimes, telling him he's in over his head – warning that Eliska is too spoilt to be the kind of wife Addy deserves. She *is* spoilt, he can admit, but he knows that this isn't the real reason his mother would object.

Relationships begin with honesty, Nechuma once told him. *This is the foundation, for to be in love means to be able to share everything – your dreams, your faults, your deepest fears. Without these truths, a relationship will collapse.* Addy has spent hours contemplating his mother's words, ashamed to admit that for all of his and Eliska's talk of Prague and Vienna and Paris – those glamorous snapshots of their lives before the war – he still cannot speak freely with her about his family. Nearly two years have passed since he last heard from his parents and siblings. Two years! On the outside, he maintains his characteristic cheerfulness, but inside the uncertainty is tearing him apart. He is unravelling. Eliska, on the other hand, is bright and sharp and seems so sure of her future. Addy knows instinctively that she would not be able to understand why at night he dreams of Radom and not Rio, why often he wishes he could wake up at home, in his old room on Warszawska Street, despite the circumstances. He runs a thumb along the rim of his cup. Eliska has suffered losses too, he knows. Her father leaving when she was young was hard for her – and perhaps because of this, she's convinced herself it's useless to live in the past. Eliska's world, Addy has begun to realise, does not allow for retrospection, for grief.

You don't need to choose between Radom and Rio, Addy reminds himself. Not at the moment, at least. *You are here now, on a nearly deserted island in South America, with a woman you love.* Addy closes his eyes, trying for a moment to imagine a life *without* Eliska. A life with nothing connecting him to their shared European roots. A life without her smile, her touch, her unwavering ability to find joy in looking ahead, rather than back. But he can't.

CHAPTER TWENTY-FIVE

Jakob and Bella
Outside Radom, German-Occupied Poland ~ Late July 1941

Jakob and Bella crouch behind a wall of supplies in the back of the delivery truck, their knees pulled to their chests, leaning into one another for support. Franka, her parents Moshe and Terza, and her brother Salek are hidden along the opposite wall. Up front, their driver curses. Brakes whine as they begin to slow. Since leaving Lvov, they've stopped only twice, for fuel; otherwise, per Sol's instructions, they've barrelled north-west, toward Radom.

The truck is crawling now. Through the walls there are voices. Germans.

'Anhalten! Stop the vehicle!'

'Don't stop,' Jakob whispers aloud. 'Please don't stop.' What will happen if they are discovered? They are carrying their false papers, but it's obvious they are being transported illegally. Why else would they be hidden?

Beside Jakob, Bella is silent, unflinching. It's as if, since losing Anna, she has become impervious to fear. Jakob has never seen her so inconsolable. He would do anything to help her. If she would just talk to him. But he can see it in her eyes; it's still too painful, too raw. She needs time.

He wraps an arm around her, holding her close as the truck rolls to a stop, weaving a plea together in his mind. He will offer the Germans his camera, he decides, if they will let them continue on. But just as quickly as the truck had stopped, it lurches, engine roaring. They swerve hard and, for a moment, it feels as if they are balanced on two wheels. Succumbing to gravity, boxes begin to topple. Outside, German voices swell, angry, threatening. As the truck picks up speed, a volley of shots is fired and a bullet rips through the wooden walls, inches above Jakob's head, leaving two small holes in its path. Amid the chaos, he and Bella bend their bodies between their knees. Jakob cradles the back of his head with one hand, Bella's with the other, praying as the engine growls and pops in its exertion. *Faster. Drive faster.* The crack of gunfire chases them long after the shouting has dissipated.

At first, Bella had opposed the idea of returning to Radom, clinging to the hope that Anna might still be alive. 'I have to find my sister,' she'd snapped, surprising Jakob with the anger in her tone. When it was safe enough to come out of hiding, they'd discovered that the Germans had set up detention camps around Lvov where anyone 'suspicious' was imprisoned indefinitely; Bella had become fixated on visiting these camps, on the chance that her sister might be confined to one of them. Jakob didn't like the idea of her going anywhere near a German detention camp, but he knew better than to object. And so for a week, Bella made the rounds, risking confinement herself. In the end, she found no record of Anna, nor of her husband, Daniel. It was through a neighbour that Bella finally learnt what, exactly, had happened: Anna and Daniel had been in hiding as well, along with Daniel's brother Simon, when the Germans first invaded Lvov. On the second night of the pogrom, a group of Wehrmacht soldiers broke into their apartment with a warrant to arrest Simon, calling him an 'activist.' Simon wasn't there – he'd ventured out to find some food. 'Then we take you,' the soldiers had said, grabbing Daniel by the arm. He had had no choice but to leave, and Anna insisted she go with him. The neighbour said that there were dozens of others taken as well, that a friend of hers lived on a farm nearby and had seen them being funnelled from a caravan of trucks to the edge of a forest, had heard the shots detonating, like fireworks, late into the night.

Reluctantly, painfully, Bella gave up her search, agreeing, finally, to accept Sol's offer to send a truck. Since then, she's barely spoken.

The truck decelerates slightly and Jakob lifts his head. *Please, not again.* He listens for shots, for shouting, but all he can hear is the rumble of the truck's diesel engine. He closes his eyes, praying they are in the clear. Praying that life in the ghetto will be better than the one they've left behind in Lvov. It's hard to imagine it could be any worse. They would be near family, at least. What's left of it.

Beside him, Bella wonders whether they will make it back to Radom alive. If they do, she'll have to face her parents. Henry and Gustava have been assigned to Radom's smaller Glinice ghetto, several kilometres outside the city. She'll have to tell them what has happened to their youngest daughter.

It's been nearly three weeks since Anna disappeared. Bella closes her eyes, feeling the familiar pain in her chest, deep and hollow, as if a piece of her is missing. *Anna.* For as long as she can remember, Bella has imagined her children growing up alongside Anna's – a fantasy that had felt almost attainable when, just before the pogrom, Anna had hinted that she and Daniel had exciting news to share. Briefly, Bella had pushed the war out of her mind and let the dream of children, of cousins being raised side by side, take over. Now, her sister will never have children, or know hers. Fresh tears run along the curve of Bella's jaw as she swallows this cold, incomprehensible truth.

JULY 25–29, 1941: *A second pogrom engulfs Lvov. Allegedly organised by Ukrainian nationalists and encouraged by the Germans, this pogrom, known as Petlura Days, targets Jews accused of collaborating with the Soviets. An estimated two thousand Jews are murdered.*

CHAPTER TWENTY-SIX

Addy
Ilha das Flores, Brazil ~ August 12, 1941

'What kind of ship is it?' Eliska asks.

Addy had spotted the small grey craft that morning on his walk around the island. As soon as Eliska woke, he'd brought her to the dock where it was moored, to see for herself.

'Looks like a navy ship.'

'Do you think it's for us?'

'Can't imagine who else it would be for.'

Addy and Eliska spin endless scenarios of where the ship might take them. Would it deliver them to Rio, the 'Arrival Destination' stamped on their *Alsina* tickets, beside a date of early February – six months past? Or was the ship simply a means to deliver them to a larger passenger vessel, bound for Europe? If it were the latter, would they be returned to Marseille? Or dropped somewhere else? Would they be able to apply for new visas? And if they did, were there still passenger ships allowed to sail across the Atlantic from Europe?

At noon, the *Alsina* detainees are called to the cafeteria, and Addy and Eliska's questions are finally answered.

'Today is your lucky day,' an officer in white announces, although it's hard to know from his tone whether or not he's joking. Haganauer translates.

'President Vargas,' the officer continues, 'has granted you permission to extend your visas.'

The refugees exhale collectively. Someone whoops.

'Pack your belongings,' the officer orders. 'You leave in an hour.'

Addy grins. He wraps his arms around Eliska, lifts her from her feet.

'Of course, just to be clear,' the officer adds, holding up a palm as if to dampen whatever kind of revelry was about to unfold, 'the president can, at *any time* and for *any reason,* revoke the privilege.'

'There is always a clause,' Madame Lowbeer hisses. But the refugees don't care. They've been allowed to stay. The cafeteria is filled with the emphatic slap of hands meeting backs and the sound of cheeks being kissed as men and women embrace, laughing, crying.

Two hours later, Addy and the Lowbeers stand in a serpentine line winding down the length of the island's dock. Rumours, about who finally persuaded Vargas to allow the group of vagabond, visaless refugees into the country, pass surreptitiously from ear to ear, although no one is brave enough to come out and ask. Best not to bring it up.

Once on board, Addy and Eliska stow their valises, help Madame Lowbeer to find a seat inside, and make their way to the front of the craft. There, gripping a metal bow rail, they watch as one of the crew unloops a rope from a cleat on the dock. An engine purrs to life, and as they push off, Addy takes a last look at the tiny island that's been his home for the past twenty-seven days. A piece of him will miss it, he realises, as the vessel moves slowly in reverse, churning the water beneath it from indigo to white. The island, with its fragrant wildflowers and endless symphony of birdsong, had brought along with it a sense of ease. On Ilha das Flores, there was nothing for Addy to do but walk, sip yerba tea, and wait. The moment he arrives a free man in Rio, his destiny will once again lie in his own hands. He'll need to learn the language, apply for a work permit, find a place to live, a job, a way to support himself. It won't be easy.

The boat completes its half turn and fixes its bow westward, toward the continent. Addy and Eliska breathe in the salt air and lean their torsos over the shimmering sea, squinting at the granite domes of the Pão de Açúcar standing guard over Guanabara Bay. The ride is short – fifteen minutes at most – but the seconds pass slowly.

'This is really happening,' Eliska declares in awe as the vessel docks. 'All the waiting, the anticipation . . . this is where the journey ends. I can't believe it's been seven months since we left Marseille.'

'It's really happening,' Addy echoes, pulling Eliska to him and leaning in for a kiss. Her lips are warm, and when she looks up at him her eyes are a bright, crystalline blue.

As they disembark, the refugees are ushered to a white brick customs building and ordered to wait – a nearly impossible task. Three hours later, when their paperwork is finally complete, Addy, Eliska, and Madame Lowbeer step hastily from the customs building onto Via Elvada da Perimetral. Addy flags a taxi, and before they know it they are speeding south, toward Eliska's uncle's apartment in Ipanema.

The following morning, Addy awakens, stiff from sleeping on the floor, to a tap on his shoulder. 'Let's explore!' Eliska whispers, leaping to her feet to prepare some coffee.

Addy dresses and peers through a window down at the cobblestones of Rua Redentor and then up at the morning sky, jingling a few coins in his pocket. He's nearly broke, and refuses to live off of the Lowbeers' dime. But the day is sunny and they are months overdue for a celebration.

'*Vamos*,' he says.

Eliska writes her mother a note, promising to return by sundown. 'Where to?' she asks as they leave her uncle's building. Addy can tell from the way she bounces beside him how elated she is to learn about her new home.

'How about Copacabana?' he suggests, telling himself it's okay to take part in Eliska's excitement, to share her enthusiasm about what it means to start over. *Go ahead, embrace it. For her, at least.* Tomorrow, he can worry about a job, an apartment, about his family, and how he will go about trying to track them down now that he has made it, finally, to a city with a post office. A city where he hopes he will be allowed to stay, indefinitely.

'Copacabana. *Parfait!*'

They walk south to the waterfront and then east along Ipanema's scalloped coastline, arriving after a few minutes at a massive, helm-shaped rock and at the realisation that neither of them knows where Copacabana is. Eliska suggests that they buy a map, but Addy points to a woman on the beach wearing what appears to be a typical Rio outfit: bathing suit, cotton tunic, and leather sandals. 'Let's ask her,' he says.

The woman smiles at their question and then holds up two fingers, pointing at her index finger.

'*Aqui estamos en Ipanema*,' she explains. '*A próxima praia é Copacabana*,' she says, pointing toward a huge rock at the end of the beach.

'*Obrigado,*' Addy says, nodding to indicate he understands. '*Muito bonita,*' he adds, sweeping an upturned palm along the coastline, and the woman smiles.

Addy and Eliska skirt the rock called Arpoador, and within minutes they arrive at the south end of a long, half-moon cove – a perfect confluence of golden sand and cobalt surf.

'I think we've arrived,' Addy says quietly.

'*Ces montagnes!*' Eliska whispers.

They pause for a moment, taking in a skyline dominated by peak after peak of rolling green crests.

'Look – you can catch a lift up that one,' Addy says, pointing to the tallest of the domes, where a cable car crawls its way toward the summit.

As they walk on, the promenade, a mosaic of stones in black and white, undulates underfoot in a pattern that resembles a giant wave. Addy stares at the mosaic for a while, amazed at the work that must have gone into laying so many stones which, up close, are surprisingly irregular in shape and orientation. It is the places where the black meets the white, the perfect edges, that evoke a sense of harmony. *We are walking on art,* Addy muses, glancing up at the coastline and imagining how the scene would look through the eyes of his mother, his father, his siblings. *They would love it here,* he thinks, and just as quickly as this occurs to him he is flooded with a rush of guilt. How is it that he is here – in paradise! – while his family is being subjected to who-knows-what unfathomable horror? A shadow of melancholy passes over his face, but before it can take over, Eliska points to the beach.

'Apparently we need to work on our suntans,' she says, laughing about how their complexions, bronze by their European standards, are pallid in comparison with those of the brown figures juggling soccer balls in the sand.

Addy swallows, taking in the spectacle and savouring the joy in Eliska's voice. 'Copacabana,' he whispers.

'Copacabana,' Eliska croons, looking up at him, folding his cheeks into her palms and kissing him.

Addy softens. Her kisses have a way of stopping time. When her lips brush his, his thinking mind melts away.

'Thirsty?' Eliska asks.

'Always,' Addy nods.

'I am, too. Let's have a drink.'

They pause along the promenade at a little blue wagon selling refreshments from beneath a red umbrella reading *Bem vindo ao Brasil!* 'Coconuts!' Eliska cries. 'To eat or to drink?' She pantomimes the difference in hopes that the vendor will understand.

The young Brazilian beneath the umbrella laughs, amused by Eliska's enthusiasm. *'Para beber,'* he says.

'Do you take francs?' Addy asks, holding up a coin.

The vendor shrugs.

'Beautiful. We'll take one,' Addy says, and he and Eliska watch in awe as the vendor selects a coconut, lops off its top with a swift swipe of a foot-long machete, drops two straws inside, and hands it to them.

'Agua de coco,' he announces triumphantly.

Addy smiles.

'Primeira vez que visita o Brasil?' the vendor asks. To the average passer-by, it must appear as if they are on holiday.

'Si, primeira visita,' Addy says, mimicking the vendor's accent.

'Bem vindos,' the vendor says, grinning.

'Obrigado,' Addy replies.

Eliska holds the coconut as Addy pays. They thank the vendor again before continuing on down the mosaic promenade. Eliska takes the first sip. 'Different,' she says after a moment, passing the coconut to Addy.

He holds it with two hands – it's furry, and heavier than he'd expected. He brings it tentatively to his nose, taking in its delicate, nutty smell, looking up again at the horizon. *You would love it here,* he thinks, relaying the sentiment across the Atlantic. *It is nothing like home, but you would love it.* He takes a sip, savouring the strangely milky, subtly sweet, and entirely foreign taste of *agua de coco* on his tongue.

JULY 30, 1941: *The Sikorski–Mayski Agreement, a treaty between the Soviet Union and Poland, is signed in London.*

AUGUST 12, 1941: *The Soviets grant amnesty to the surviving Polish citizens who have been detained in work camps throughout Siberia, Kazakhstan, and Soviet Asia, on the condition that they fight for the Soviets, now sided with the Allies. Thousands of Poles begin an exodus to Uzbekistan, where they are told an army is being formed under the new commander in chief of the reformed Polish Army (also known as the Polish II Corps), General Władysław Anders. Anders himself has been recently released from two years of confinement in Moscow's Lubyanka prison.*

CHAPTER TWENTY-SEVEN

Genek and Herta
Aktyubinsk, Kazakhstan ~ September 1941

They left their camp three weeks ago in August, almost a year exactly from when they arrived. For Genek and Herta, the journey from Altynay feels in many ways reminiscent of the one that brought them there, except this time, the top doors of their cattle cars are left open, and the ill outnumber the healthy. Two of the cars at the back have been designated sick cars, for the malaria- and typhus-ridden, and in twenty-one days, over a dozen of them have died. Genek, Herta, and Józef have managed to stave off sickness – they wear handkerchiefs over their mouths and noses and keep Józef, now six months old, tucked into his sling on Herta's breast for as many hours of the day as he'll tolerate. Starving and sleep deprived, they do their best to remain optimistic – they are no longer prisoners, after all.

'Where are we?' one of the exiles wonders aloud as the train slows to a stop.

'The sign says "Ak-ty-ubinsk",' someone replies.

'Where the hell is Aktyubinsk?'

'Kazakhstan, I believe.'

'Kazakhstan,' Genek whispers as he stands to peer from the cattle car at his surroundings – a land as alien to him as the luxury of a toilet, a clean shirt, a decent meal, a comfortable night's sleep. The station looks like the others – nondescript, with a long, wooden platform peppered with the occasional wrought-iron gas-burning lantern.

'Anything to see?' Herta asks. She's seated on the floor, and with Józef asleep in her arms she's reluctant to move.

'Not much.'

Genek is about to return to his spot beside Herta when something catches his eye. Leaning his head out over the car door, he blinks, and then blinks again. *I'll be damned.* Several metres down the platform, two uniformed men roll a cart overflowing with what appears to be freshly baked bread. It's not the bread, however, that excites him. It's the white eagle emblems embroidered on the officers' four-cornered caps. They are Polish soldiers. Poles!

'Herta! You have to see this!'

He helps Herta to her feet and she squeezes in next to him at the door, where half a dozen others have gathered to glimpse what Genek has seen. Sure enough, there are Polish soldiers here in Aktyubinsk. A burst of hope in Genek's chest. Someone behind him cheers, and in an instant the atmosphere in the train car is electric. The door is unlocked and the exiles pile out, feeling more limber than they have in months.

'One loaf per head,' the two-starred lieutenants call in unmistakable Polish as swarms of bodies, bone-thin, envelop their carts. A second pair of soldiers follows behind pushing a gleaming silver urn inscribed in choppy Cyrillic letters: KOFE. Two years ago, Genek would have turned up his nose at the thought of sipping grain coffee. But today, he can't think of a more perfect gift. The brew is hot and sweet and, coupled with the still-warm bread, he and Herta drink it down with enthusiasm.

The exiles are brimming with questions. 'Why are you here? Is there an army camp here? Are we enlisting now?'

The lieutenants behind the carts shake their heads. 'Not here,' they explain. 'There are camps in Wrewskoje and in Tashkent. Our job is just to feed you and to make sure you continue on your way south. The whole Polish Army in the USSR is on the move. We'll reorganise in Central Asia.'

The exiles nod, their faces falling as the train's whistle sounds. They don't want to leave. They climb reluctantly back aboard and lean over the tracks as the train pulls away, waving furiously. One of the lieutenants throws up a two-finger Polish salute, igniting a roar amid the exiles, who return the salute en masse, their hearts racing to the *clack-clack-clack* of the train's wheels as it picks up speed. Genek wraps an arm around Herta, kisses the top of Józef's head, and beams, his spirits fuelled by the sight of his sharply clad countrymen, by the *kofe* warming his blood, the bread in his belly, the wind on his face.

* * *

The bread and coffee at Aktyubinsk station would prove to be the closest thing to a meal they would encounter on their journey. As they clatter on toward Uzbekistan, the exiles go days without eating. Genek and Herta have no concept of when or where the train might stop. When it *does* stop, those with something to trade or a few coins in their pockets barter with the locals, who flank the tracks with baskets of delicacies in their arms – round loaves of *lepyoshka* bread, *katik* yogurt, pumpkin seeds, red onions, and, farther south, sweet melons, watermelons, and dried apricots. Most of the exiles, though, Genek and Herta included, know better than to waste their time looking hungrily at the food they can't afford – instead, when the train stops, they leap from the cars and line up for the toilet and the water tap – or a *kipyatok*, as the Uzbeks call it – waiting as the dry, empty remains of *semyechki* seeds whirl about at their feet, listening intently for the hiss of steam, the first tug of the train's engine, indicating that their ride is leaving, as it often does, without warning. The moment they hear the train stir, it's a race to get back to their car, whether or not they've had a chance to use the toilet or fill their water buckets. No one wants to be left behind.

After another three weeks of travel, Genek finally finds himself in line at a makeshift recruiting centre in Wrewskoje. A young Polish officer mans the desk.

'Next!' the officer calls. Genek steps forward, only two bodies separating him from his future in the Polish II Corps. The line had wrapped twice around the small city block when he took his place that morning, but he hadn't minded. For the first time since he can remember, he is filled with a sense of purpose. Perhaps, he thinks, this was his fate all along, to fight for Poland. If anything, it's a chance for redemption – to make right the poor decision that had cost him and Herta a year of their lives.

Genek has been told nothing yet of when or where accepted recruits will report for duty. He hopes their stay in Uzbekistan won't be long. The single-room flat they've been assigned, while better than the barracks in Altynay, is hot, dirty, and teeming with rodents. He and Herta spent their first few nights being jarred awake by the disconcerting feeling of tiny feet skittering across their chests.

'There must be some kind of mistake,' the recruit at the front of the line says.

'I'm sorry,' the officer behind the desk replies.

Genek leans in to eavesdrop.

'No, it has to be a mistake.'

'No, sir, I'm afraid it isn't,' the officer shakes his head apologetically. 'Anders's Army isn't accepting Jews.'

Genek's stomach turns. *What?*

'But –' the man stammers, 'you mean to tell me I've come all this way . . . but *why?*'

Genek watches as the officer lifts a piece of paper and reads: '"According to Polish law, a person of Jewish heritage belongs not to Poland but to a *Jewish* nation." I'm sorry, sir.' He says this without malice, but with an efficiency that suggests he's eager to move on.

'But what am I supposed to—'

'I'm sorry, sir, it isn't up to me. Next, please.'

With the issue put to rest, the man slinks from the line, muttering under his breath.

No Jews in Anders's Army. Genek shakes his head. He wouldn't put it past the Germans to deprive a Jew the right to fight for his country, but the Poles? If he's unable to enlist, there's no telling how he and Herta will manage. In all likelihood they'll be thrown back to the wolves, to a life of forced labour. To hell with that, Genek seethes.

'Next, please.'

A single body now separates him from the officer at the recruiting desk, from the paperwork he'll be asked to complete. He balls up his hands into fists. Beads of sweat congregate on his forehead. *That form is a deal breaker,* a voice inside declares. *It's life and death. You've been here before. Think. You haven't come this far to be turned away.*

'Next, please.'

Before the man in front of him has a chance to step away from the desk, Genek pulls his cap down low over his brow and ducks quietly out of line.

Weaving his way through the dry, crumbling town, his mind races. Mostly, he's angry. Here he is offering up his manpower, possibly even his life, to fight for Poland. How dare his country deprive him of this right because of his religion! He wouldn't be in this whole mess in the first place if he hadn't stubbornly *labelled* himself Polish. He wants to yell, to punch a wall. But then his mind flashes to his year in Altynay, and he orders himself to think clearly. *I need the army,* he reminds himself. *It is the only way out.*

He pauses at a street corner, at the entrance to a small mosque. Staring up at its stout gold dome, it hits him. Andreski.

On paper, Genek and Otto Andreski have little in common. Otto is a devout Catholic – an ex-factory worker with a perpetual scowl and a chest as big as a bass drum; Genek is a lithe, dimpled Jew who has spent his career, until recently, behind a desk at a law firm. Otto is a brute, Genek a charmer. But despite their differences, the friendship the men forged in the forests of Siberia is a solid one. Lately, in their few moments of spare time, they have taken to throwing a set of hand-carved dice, or to playing *kierki* with Genek's deck of cards, which is now in a pathetic state from overuse but somehow still complete. Herta and Julia Andreski, too, have grown close, have discovered, even, that they competed on rival ski teams at university.

'I need you to teach me to be a Roman Catholic,' Genek says later that evening. He's just finished explaining to Otto and Julia what had happened at the recruiting centre. 'From here on in,' he announces, 'Herta and I are Catholics, if anyone asks.'

Genek is a good student. Within days, Otto has taught him to recite *Our Father* and *Hail Mary*, to cross himself with his right hand, not his left, to rattle off the name of the reigning Pope, Pius XII, born Eugenio Maria Giuseppe Giovanni Pacelli. A week later, when Genek finally works up the courage to return to the recruiting centre, he greets the young officer behind the desk with a strong handshake and a confident smile. His blue eyes are steady and his hand doesn't tremble when he prints the words 'Roman Catholic' in the box marked RELIGION on the recruitment form. And when his name, along with Herta and Józef as family members, is added to the roster as an official member of Anders's Polish II Corps, he thanks the officer with a salute and a 'God bless.'

On the eve of their first official day as new recruits, Otto invites Genek and Herta to his flat to celebrate. Genek brings his playing cards. They pass Otto's secret stash of vodka, sipping from a dented tin flask between hands of the agreed-upon game, *oczko*.

'To our new Christian friends,' Otto toasts, downing a swig and passing the flask to Genek.

'To the Pope,' Genek adds, taking a sip and handing the tin to Herta.

'To a new chapter,' Herta says, glancing at Józef, asleep in a small basket beside her, and for a moment the foursome is quiet as each wonders what exactly the next several months will bring.

'To Anders,' Julia chirps, lightening the mood, reaching for the flask and holding it victoriously over her head.

'To winning this fucking war!' Otto howls, and Genek laughs, as the prospect of winning a war being fought worlds away from Wrewskoje – a dusty Central Asian town whose name he can barely pronounce – seems as unlikely as it does absurd.

The vodka makes its way again to Genek. *'Niech szczęście nam sprzyja,'* he offers, the tin raised. *May luck be on our side.* They are low, it seems, on good fortune. And something tells him they'll need it.

DECEMBER 7, 1941: *Japan bombs Pearl Harbour.*

DECEMBER 11, 1941: *Adolf Hitler declares war on the United States; on the same day, the United States declares war on Germany and Italy. A month later, the first American forces arrive in Europe, landing in Northern Ireland.*

JANUARY 20, 1942: *At the Wannsee Conference in Berlin, Reich director Reinhard Heydrich outlines a 'Final Solution' plan to deport the millions of Jews remaining in German-conquered territories to extermination camps in the east.*

CHAPTER TWENTY-EIGHT

Mila and Felicia
Outside Radom, German-Occupied Poland ~ March 1942

It's warm inside the train car, despite the cold March air whipping at their cheeks through the open window. Mila and Felicia have been standing for over an hour, packed in too tightly to sit, but the mood is bright, giddy almost with excitement. Whispers of freedom, of what it will feel like, taste like, circulate throughout the car. They are the fortunate few, the forty-odd Jews from the Wałowa ghetto who have made the list: doctors, dentists, lawyers – *Radom's most liberal and educated professionals* – selected to emigrate to America.

Mila was sceptical at first. Everyone was. America had declared war on Axis powers in December. They'd sent troops to Ireland in January. Why would Hitler offer up a band of Jews to a country that had designated itself an enemy? But he'd sent a group to Palestine the month before, and despite what everyone thought – that surely the Jews had really been shipped off not to Palestine but to their deaths – rumours had begun flying through the ghetto that they had made it safely to Tel Aviv. And so when the opportunity arose, Mila was quick to put her name on the list. She believed it: this was her chance.

Felicia stands with her arms wrapped around Mila's thigh, relying on her mother's balance to steady hers. 'What does it look like now, *Mamusiu?*' she asks – it's the same question every few minutes. She's too little to see out the window. 'Just trees, love. Apple trees. Pastures.' Occasionally Mila hoists her to her hip so Felicia can see. Mila has explained where they are going, but the word *America* has little significance in Felicia's three-and-a-half-year-old mind. 'What about Father?' she'd asked, when Mila first told her of the plan, and the sentiment had nearly broken Mila's heart. Despite having no memories of him, Felicia worried that Selim would return to Radom only to find that she and her mother had disappeared. Mila had assured her as best she could that she would send an address as soon as they arrived in America, that Selim could meet them there, or they could return to Poland once the war was over. 'It's just that right now,' Mila had said, 'staying here isn't safe.' Felicia had nodded, but Mila knew it was hard for the child to make sense of it all. Mila herself had no concept, really, of what to expect.

The one thing that *was* undeniably clear was just how dangerous it had become for Felicia in the ghetto. Hiding her in that sack of fabric scraps – and then walking away – was one of the hardest things Mila had ever done. She would never forget waiting outside the workshop as the SS conducted their raid, praying that Felicia would remain still as she'd instructed her to, praying that the Germans would pass her by, praying that she'd done the right thing in leaving her baby girl there, alone in the workshop. When the SS retreated and Mila and the others were finally allowed to return to their desks, Mila sprinted to the wall of fabric scraps, nearly hysterical, crying hot grateful tears as she pulled her daughter, shivering and wet, from the sack.

Mila vowed that day in the workshop to find a safer place for Felicia to hide – somewhere outside the ghetto, where the SS wouldn't think to look for her. A few months ago, in December, she'd tucked her daughter into a straw-filled mattress and held her breath as she dropped the mattress from the flat's second-storey window. Their building lay on the perimeter of the ghetto. Isaac waited below. As a member of the Jewish Police, he was allowed outside the ghetto walls. The plan was for him to take Felicia to the home of a Catholic family, where she could live, under their care, posing as Aryan. The terrifying two-storey drop, thankfully, was a success. The mattress broke Felicia's fall, just as planned. Mila had cried into a clenched fist at the sight of Isaac leading Felicia away by the hand, as petrified of leaving her daughter in someone else's care as she was relieved that Felicia had survived the fall. Anything had to be safer than the ghetto, though, where disease spread like wildfire, and where every day, it seemed, a Jew without the proper papers, or too old, or too sick, was discovered and killed – shot in the head or beaten and left to die in the street for everyone to see. She'd done the right thing, Mila told herself over and over again that night, unable to sleep.

The next day, however, Mila found a note from Isaac beneath the door to the flat – *Offer renounced*, it read. *Returning the parcel at 22h.* Mila would never learn what went wrong, whether the family changed their minds or whether Felicia was deemed too Jewish-looking to pass as their own. At ten that evening, she was returned to the ghetto, clinging white-knuckled to a rope of sheets dangling from the same second-storey window. To make matters worse, a week later, feverish and short of breath, Felicia was diagnosed with a severe case of pneumonia. Mila had never wished harder for Selim to return – surely he would tend to their daughter more effectively than any of the doctors at Wałowa's clinic could. Felicia's recovery was slow; twice Mila thought she might lose her. In the end, it was the steam from a boiled eucalyptus branch Isaac smuggled in that finally opened up her windpipe, allowing her to breathe again and eventually to heal.

A few days after Felicia was finally back on her feet, the SS announced they would send a select group of Jews from Wałowa to America. And now, here they are. Mila tries to imagine what it means, to be *American*, envisioning warm homes filled with well-stocked pantries and happy, healthy children and streets where, Jewish or not, you were free to walk and work and live just like everyone else. Resting a hand atop Felicia's head, she watches the leafless domes of beech trees speed by through the window of the train car. It is a thrilling prospect, the idea of a new life in the States. But of course it is also devastating, for it means leaving her family behind. Mila's throat tightens. Saying goodbye to her parents in the ghetto had nearly broken her resolve. She brings a hand to her stomach, where the pain is still sharp, like a fresh stab wound. She'd tried hard to convince her parents to put their names on the list, but they refused. 'No,' they said, 'they won't take a couple of old shopkeepers. You go,' they insisted. 'Felicia deserves a better life than this.'

In her head, Mila takes inventory of her parents' valuables. They are down to twenty zloty, and they've sold off most of their porcelain, silk, and silver. They have a bolt of lace, which they could barter if they needed to. And of course there's the amethyst – thankfully Nechuma hasn't had to part with that yet. And better than any wealth, she has Halina now. Halina and Adam had moved back to Radom not long after Jakob and Bella arrived. They live outside the ghetto walls with their false IDs, and with Isaac's help they are able to sneak an egg or a couple of zloty into the ghetto every now and then. Her parents also have Jakob nearby. His plan, he told Mila before she left, was to appeal for a job at the factory outside of town where Bella worked. He would be less than twenty kilometres away and promised to check on Sol and Nechuma often. Her parents are not alone, Mila reminds herself, and that brings her some comfort.

Outside there is hissing, brakes screaming. The train slows. Mila peers out the window, surprised to see nothing but open fields on either side of the track. *An odd place to stop.* Perhaps there is another train meeting them to take them the rest of the way to Kraków, where, they've been told, a group of Americans from the Red Cross will escort them to Naples. The door slides open and she and the others are ordered to disembark. Outside the car, Mila's eyes follow the length of the tracks splayed out before them; they are empty. Her stomach flips. And just as suddenly as she realises that something is amiss, the group is surrounded by a throng of men. She can tell right away that they are Ukrainian. Burly, dark haired, and broad chested, they look nothing like the fair-skinned, sharp-featured Germans who'd piled them into the train car hours earlier at the station in Radom. The Ukrainians shout orders, and Mila tightens her grip on Felicia's hand, her plight instantly and horrifically clear. *Of course.* How could she have been so naive? They'd *volunteered* for this, thinking it was their ticket to freedom. Felicia looks up at her, eyes wide, and it is all Mila can do to keep her knees from buckling. This was her decision. She'd brought this upon them.

The group is arranged into two lines, marched twenty metres into the field, and handed shovels. 'Dig!' one of Ukrainians yells in Russian, his hands cupped around his mouth in place of a bullhorn, the metal barrel of his rifle catching the waning rays of the afternoon sun. 'Dig or we shoot!'

As the Jews begin to dig, the Ukrainians walk circles around them, their teeth bared like wild dogs, barking orders or insults over their shoulders. 'You with the children,' one of them yells. Mila and the three others with children at their sides look up. 'Work faster. You dig two holes.'

Mila instructs Felicia to sit at her feet. She keeps her chin down, with one eye always on her daughter. Every once in a while she glances over at the others. Some are sobbing, tears rolling silently down their cheeks and onto the cold earth beneath them. Others appear dazed, their eyes glazed, defeated. No one looks up. No one talks. The only sound filling the thin March air is the scrape of steel against the cold, hard dirt. Before long, Mila's hands are cracked and bleeding, her lower back slick with sweat. She peels off her wool coat and sets it on the ground beside her; within seconds, it is snatched up and added to a mound of clothing beside the train.

The Ukrainians continue to keep a close watch, making sure that hands are moving and bodies are occupied. An officer in a captain's uniform surveys the scene from his position by the train. He appears to be German, SS. *Obersturmführer*, perhaps – Mila has begun to recognise the various Nazi military ranks by their insignia, but she's too far away to know for sure exactly what position this man holds. Whoever he is, it's obvious that he is calling the shots. What went through his mind, Mila wonders, when he was assigned this job? She grimaces as her weight on the shovel's wooden handle tears another coin-sized flap of flesh from her palm. *Ignore it*, she commands, refusing to feel the pain. Refusing to feel sorry for herself. With the ground nearly frozen, her progress is slow. *Fine.* It'll buy her some time. A few more minutes on earth to spend with her daughter.

'*Mamusiu*,' Felicia whispers, tugging at Mila's slacks. She sits cross-legged at her mother's feet. '*Mamusiu*, look.'

Mila follows Felicia's gaze. One of the Jews in the field has dropped his shovel and is walking toward the German by the train. Mila recognises him as Dr Frydman, who before the war was a prominent dentist in Radom. Selim used to see him. A couple of the Ukrainians notice, too, and cock their rifles, aiming them in his direction. Mila holds her breath. *He's going to get himself killed!* But the captain motions for his subordinates to lower their weapons.

Mila exhales.

'What happened?' Felicia whispers.

'Shh-shh, *chérie*. It's okay,' Mila breathes as she presses her foot into her shovel's blade. 'Be still, okay? Stay just here, where I can see you. I love you, my darling girl. Just stay close to me.' Mila watches as Dr Frydman converses with the German. He appears to be talking fast, touching his cheek. After a minute, the captain nods and points over his shoulder. Dr Frydman bows his chin, and then walks quickly to an empty train car and climbs inside. *He's been spared.* But why? In Radom, the Jews in the ghetto were always being called upon to help the Germans – perhaps, Mila thinks, Dr Frydman has done some dental work for the captain in the past, and the German has realised he'll need his services again.

Mila's stomach turns. She certainly hasn't done any favours. She'd be better off grabbing Felicia and running for their lives. She glances at the tree line, but it's two hundred metres beyond the tracks. No. They can't run. They'd be shot in an instant.

A sharp wind whorls a cloud of dirt across the field, and Mila leans into her shovel, her eyes gritty, blinking as she contemplates her reality: no favours to be returned. Nowhere to run. They're stuck.

As she wraps her mind around the inevitable, a gunshot rips through the air. She wheels her head around in time to see a man a row over from hers fall to the ground. *Had he tried to run?* Mila covers her mouth, and immediately looks to Felicia. 'Felicia!' But her daughter is transfixed, her eyes glued to the body lying facedown now on the dirt, to the blood rippling from the back of his skull. 'Felicia!' Mila says again.

Finally, her daughter turns. Her eyes are huge, her voice tiny. *'Mamusiu?* Why did they—'

'Darling, look at me,' Mila pleads. 'Look at me, only me. It's going to be okay.' Felicia is trembling.

'But why—'

'I don't know, love. Come. Sit closer. Just by my leg here, and watch me. Okay?' Felicia crawls closer to her mother's leg and Mila reaches quickly for her hand. Felicia gives it to her and Mila bends down quickly to kiss it. 'It's okay,' she whispers.

As she stands, the air is filled with yelling. 'Who will be the next to run?' the voices taunt. 'You see? You see what happens? Who is next?'

Felicia stares up at her mother with tear-filled eyes, and Mila bites the insides of her cheeks to keep from unravelling. She mustn't cry, not now, not in front of her daughter.

CHAPTER TWENTY-NINE

Jakob and Bella
Armee-Verpflegungs-Lager (AVL) Factory, Outside Radom,
German-Occupied Poland ~ March 1942

Jakob waves a handkerchief as he approaches the factory entrance. '*Schießen Sie nicht!* Don't shoot!' he pants, his breath coming and going in a staccato of short, shallow puffs. He's jogged nearly eighteen kilometres carrying his suitcase and his camera to get there, and he is terribly out of shape. The muscles in his right arm will be sore for a week and the soles of his feet are swollen and abscessed from the journey, but he hasn't yet noticed.

An SS guard rests a hand on his pistol and squints in Jakob's direction. 'Don't shoot,' Jakob pleads again when he's close enough to hand the guard his ID. 'Please, I'm here to see my wife. She's—' He glances at the dagger dangling by a chain from the guard's belt and suddenly he's tongue-tied. 'Shesexpectingme.' It comes out as one long word.

The guard studies Jakob's papers. They're his real ones; in the ghetto and here at the factory, there's no point in posing as someone he's not.

'From,' the guard asks, studying Jakob's ID, although it's more a statement than a question.

'Radom.'

'Age.'

'Twenty-six.'

'Date of birth.'

'First of February. 1916.'

The guard quizzes Jakob until he's certain he's the young man his papers say he is.

'Where is your ausweis?'

Jakob swallows. He doesn't have one. 'I requested one but – please, I'm here for my wife . . . it's her parents, they are very sick. She has to know.' Jakob wonders if the lie is as obvious as it feels on his tongue. The guard, surely, will see through it. 'Please,' Jakob begs. 'It is dire.' A film of sweat has collected on his brow; it glistens under the glare of the midday sun.

The guard stares hard at him for a moment. 'Stay here,' he finally grunts, pointing with his eyes at the ground before disappearing through an unmarked door.

Jakob obeys. He sets his suitcase at his feet and waits, wringing his felt cap in his hands. The last time he saw Bella was five months ago, in October, just before she was assigned to work at the Armee-Verpflegungs-Lager factory, which everyone referred to simply as AVL. Back then, they were living with her parents in the Glinice ghetto, just down the road from the factory. Bella was still a wreck. The days were long and miserable, and there was little he could do to comfort her as she descended into the depths of despair over the loss of her sister. Jakob would never forget the day she left. He'd stood at the ghetto entrance, his fingers curled around the iron bars of the gate, watching as she was escorted to a waiting truck. Bella had turned before climbing in, her expression heavy with sorrow, and Jakob had blown her a kiss and watched, through wet eyes, as she'd brought her own hand to her lips; he couldn't tell if she'd meant to return the kiss, or if her hand was there to keep from crying.

Soon after Bella left for the factory, Jakob requested to be transferred to the Wałowa ghetto, so he could live with his parents. He and Bella kept up by letter. Reading her words brought Jakob some peace – she'd barely spoken since Anna disappeared, but putting pen to paper, it seemed, was easier for her. At AVL, Bella said, she'd been allocated the job of mending leather boots and broken holsters from the German front. 'You should join me,' she coaxed in her most recent letter. 'The foreman here is tolerable. And there is far more space in the factory barracks than there is in the ghetto. I miss you. So much. Please, come.'

Jakob knew when he read those words – *I miss you* – that he would find a way to be with her. It would mean leaving his parents, but they had Halina to watch out for them. False IDs if they needed them. A small stash of potatoes, flour, and some cabbage his mother had stockpiled before winter. The amethyst.

He'd be close. Eighteen kilometres. He could write to them, visit if he needed to, he reasoned.

There was also his job, however, and the prospect of leaving it was daunting. In the ghetto, a job was a lifeline – if you were deemed skilled enough to work, you were, for the most part, worthy of living. When the Germans discovered Jakob knew how to operate a camera, they assigned him work as a photographer. Every morning, he was allowed to exit Wałowa's arched gates to take pictures of whatever it was his supervisor asked for – weapons, armories, uniforms, sometimes even women. Every so often his supervisor would recruit a couple of blonde Polish girls who for a few zloty or an evening's meal were more than willing to pose for Jakob wearing nothing but a tattered fur kept for this purpose. When he returned at the end of the day, he would hand over his film, without any idea as to who would eventually look at his photos, or why.

Today, however, would be different. He'd received his assignment as he always did, but he'd set off from his supervisor's office with a pocketful of Yunak cigarettes and an assignment he wouldn't complete. If he is forced to return to Wałowa, his roll of film still blank, his plan will likely cost him his life.

Jakob checks his watch. It's two in the afternoon. In three hours, his boss will realise he's missing.

The factory door swings open and Bella appears, clad in the same navy slacks and white collared shirt she was wearing when she left. A yellow scarf covers all but a small fraction of her hairline. She smiles when she sees him, and Jakob's heart warms. A smile.

'Hello, sunshine,' he says. They hug quickly.

'Jakob! I didn't know you were coming,' Bella says.

'I know, I'm sorry, I didn't want to –' Jakob pauses, and Bella nods, understanding. Their letters have been censored for months; it would have been foolish to write and tell her of his plans.

'I'll go talk to the foreman,' Bella says, glancing over her shoulder at the guard parked a few metres behind her. 'Did your sister make it off?'

In his last letter, Jakob had told Bella of Mila's plan to move to the States. 'She left this morning,' he says. 'She and Felicia.'

'Good. That's a relief. I'm glad you came, Kuba,' Bella says. 'Stay here.' The guard follows her back inside, and Jakob remembers a second too late about the cigarettes – he'd meant to sneak them into Bella's palm so she could use them for a bribe. He curses himself silently, left once again to wait outside in the cold, cap in hand.

Inside, Bella makes her way to the desk of the foreman, Officer Meier, a big-boned German with a broad forehead and a thick, well-kept mustache. 'My husband has come from the ghetto,' she begins, deciding it best to get straight to the point. Her German is now fluent. 'He is here, outside. He is an excellent worker, Herr Meier. He is in good health, very responsible.' Bella pauses. Jews don't ask favours of Germans, but she has no other choice. 'Please, I beg of you, can you find him a job here at the factory?'

Meier is a decent man. In the past three months he's been good to Bella – allowed her to take her meal on Yom Kippur after nightfall, to visit her parents every so often in the Glinice ghetto, a short walk from the factory. Bella is an efficient worker – nearly twice as productive as most of the others at the factory. Perhaps this is why he treats her well.

Meier runs a thumb and forefinger over his moustache. He sizes Bella up, narrowing his eyes at her, as if searching for some ulterior motive.

Bella removes the gold brooch that Jakob gave her so long ago from the chain she'd strung around her neck. 'Please,' she says, dropping the tiny rose with its inlaid pearl into her palm and offering it to Meier. 'This is all I have. Take it.' Bella waits, her arm outstretched. 'Please. You won't regret it.'

Finally, Meier leans forward, resting his forearms on his desk, his eyes meeting hers. 'Kurch,' he says, in his thick German accent. 'Keep it, Kurch.' He sighs, shakes his head. 'I'll do it for you, but I won't do it for anyone else.' He turns to the guard standing at attention by the door to his office. 'Go on. Let him in.'

CHAPTER THIRTY

Mila and Felicia
Outside Radom, German-Occupied Poland ~ March 1942

The pile of earth beside what Mila knows will be her grave has grown to half a metre high. 'Deeper,' a Ukrainian shouts as he struts by, making his rounds.

Mila's palms are caked now with blood, her entire torso drenched with sweat, despite the March cold. She takes off her sweater, drapes it over Felicia's shoulders, and wraps her scarf tightly around her right hand, the more painful of the two. Pressing the sole of her shoe to the head of her shovel, she ignores the sting and glances again toward the train tracks to survey the scene.

The captain stands with his arms folded over his chest at the front of the train. A few cars down, a dozen Ukrainians appear bored as they fiddle with their caps, twirling them around their fingers, their rifles slung to their backs. Some kick the dirt. Others converse, their shoulders rocking at a remark one of the others has made. *Barbarians.* Two more Jews have joined Dr Frydman – apparently they too have doled out special favours and have been spared. Clamping her jaw shut, Mila lifts another mound of dirt from the hole at her feet, pours it atop her pile.

'Look,' someone behind her whispers. A young blonde woman has dropped her shovel. She struts quickly toward the tracks, toward the German, her shoulders pinned back, her black overcoat cinched tightly to her waist, its tails billowing behind her. Mila's heart skips as she is reminded of her sister Halina, the only other woman she knows with that kind of bravado. As others begin to whisper and point, one of the Ukrainians beside the train raises his rifle, aims it; the others follow suit. The young fugitive raises her palms. 'Don't shoot!' she cries in Russian, picking up her pace to a trot as she approaches the men. The Ukrainians cock their weapons and Mila holds her breath. Felicia looks, too.

The gunmen glance to the German, awaiting approval, but the captain tilts his chin and fixes his gaze on the petite, fearless Jew approaching. He shakes his head and says something Mila can't decipher, and the Ukrainians slowly lower their arms.

Mila catches a glimpse of the young woman's profile when she reaches the tracks. She's pretty, with fine features and skin the colour of porcelain. Even from afar, it's easy to see that her hair is the kind of strawberry blonde that can only be real. Peroxided hair, which was common now in the ghetto – anything to look less Jewish – was easy to spot. Mila watches as the woman gestures casually with one hand, the other resting on her hip, and says something that makes the German laugh. Mila blinks. She's won him over. *Just like that.* What did she offer? Sex? Money? Mila roils with a mix of disgust with the captain and jealousy of the beautiful, unflinching blonde.

A perimeter guard shouts, and the Jews go silently back to their digging. Mila tries to imagine herself putting on a bold, provocative face and strutting across the meadow. But she's a mother, for goodness' sake – and even when she was young she never had Halina's talent for flirting. She'd be shot before she even reached the train. And on the chance she managed to make it to within earshot of the German, what could she possibly say to seduce him into saving her? *I have nothing to –*

And then an idea strikes her. Her spine snaps upright.

'Felicia!' she whispers. Felicia looks up, surprised by the intensity in her voice. Mila speaks softly, so the others won't hear. 'Watch my eyes, love – do you see that woman over there, by the train?' Mila looks toward the train car, and Felicia's gaze follows. She nods. Mila's breath is shallow. She's shaking. *No time to second-guess yourself – you got your daughter into this; you can at least try to get her out.* Mila kneels for a moment, pretending to pull a pebble from her shoe, so she and Felicia can see eye to eye. She speaks slowly. 'I want you to run to her, and pretend she's your mother.' Felicia knits her eyebrows together, confused. 'When you reach her,' Mila continues, 'hold on to her, and don't let go.'

'No, *Mamusiu* . . .'

Mila brings a finger to her daughter's lips. 'It's all right, you will be all right, just do as I say.'

Tears well in Felicia's eyes. '*Mamusiu*, you will come too?' Her voice is barely audible.

'No, darling, not right now. I need you to do this – alone. Do you understand?' Felicia nods, her eyes lowered. Mila reaches for Felicia's chin, lifting it so their eyes meet again. '*Tak?*'

'*Tak*,' Felicia whispers.

Mila can barely breathe, her lungs suffocated by the sadness in her daughter's eyes, by the plan that is about to unfold. She nods as bravely as she can. 'If the men ask, that woman is *twoja Mamusia*. Okay?'

'*Moja Mamusia*,' Felicia repeats, but the words taste strange and wrong in her mouth, like something poisonous.

Mila stands and glances again at the woman by the train, who appears now to be telling a story; the German is rapt. She lifts her sweater from Felicia's shoulders. 'Go now, love,' she whispers, nodding toward the train. Felicia scrambles to her feet, looking up at her, pleading with her eyes – *don't make me!* Mila squats, presses her lips quickly to Felicia's forehead. As she rises, she braces herself with her shovel; she can't feel her legs, and everything about the moment suddenly feels wrong. She opens her mouth, all the parts of her that are a mother clawing at her throat, begging her to change her mind. But she can't. There is no other plan. This is all she has.

'Go!' Mila orders. 'Quickly!'

Felicia turns to face the train, looks over her shoulder, and Mila nods again. 'Now!' Mila whispers.

As Felicia runs, Mila tries to resume her digging, but she's paralysed from the neck down and all she can manage is to watch, breathless, as the scene she's orchestrated transpires in slow motion before her. For a few interminable seconds, no one seems to notice the small body darting across the meadow. Felicia is a third of the way to the train when one of the Ukrainians finally spots her and points. The others look up. One of them shouts an order Mila can't understand and lifts his rifle. Suddenly, every pair of eyes in the meadow is locked on her daughter's small frame, watching as she runs, knees high, arms wide, appearing discombobulated, as if at any moment she might fall.

'*Mamusiu!*' Felicia's scream cuts through the thin air, shrill, sharp, desperate.

Despite the fact that she was expecting this, it severs Mila's heart to hear her daughter call the blonde woman *mother*. Her eyes leap between Felicia, the German, and the Ukrainian with his rifle raised, awaiting approval. '*Mamo! Mamo!*' Felicia bawls between breaths, over and over again as she nears the tracks. The German watches Felicia, shaking his head, seemingly confused. The young woman looks at Felicia and then behind her. She, too, is confused. The Ukrainians on the perimeter swivel their heads and scan the meadow, trying to decipher from where the child has come. *Don't any of you dare point,* Mila silently commands, grateful that she hadn't yet begun to dig a second hole, for Felicia. No one moves. After a few more slow seconds, Felicia reaches the train, and her cries dissipate as she flings her arms around the legs of the pretty blonde, burrowing her face into her overcoat.

Mila knows she should return to her shovelling but she can't help but stare as the young woman peers down at the feather of a child clinging to her thighs. When the woman looks up, she glances toward the meadow, in Mila's direction. *Please, please, please,* Mila mouths. *Take her. Pick her up. Please.* Another second passes, then two. Finally, the woman leans down and lifts Felicia to her hip. She says something inaudible and brings a hand to the back of Felicia's head, kisses her cheek. The Ukrainians look at one other, then snap at the Jews watching to get back to work. Mila exhales, looks down, steadies herself. *It's okay. You can breathe now,* she tells herself. When she looks up, Felicia has wrapped her arms around the woman's neck and laid her head on her shoulder, her rib cage heaving still, from the exertion of the run.

'Garments off! Everything! Now!'

The Jews look around, panic-stricken. Slowly, they set down their shovels and begin to untie their shoelaces, unbelt their trousers, unzip their skirts. Mila reaches for the top button of her blouse, her fingers shaking. A few of the others are already half naked, shivering, their pallid skin stark against the brown earth at their feet.

'Hurry up!'

The Jews stand with their hands feebly trying to cover their nakedness as the Ukrainians stoop to pick up their clothing. Mila refuses to undress. She knows there are only seconds before someone notices her, forces her to strip, but the moment her shirt comes off, it will be over. Her daughter will see her mother shot before her eyes. She twists her wedding ring around her finger, and for a brief moment allows herself the indulgence of remembering when Selim slipped the thick gold band over her knuckle, how full of hope they were – and then, she blinks.

Without hesitating, she bolts for the train, dashing along the pockmarked earth, tracing her daughter's steps. She moves as fast as her legs will carry her. Pyramids of freshly dug dirt, shadowy graves, uniformed soldiers, and white-fleshed bodies fade to a blur in her periphery as she runs, her eyes fixed not on her daughter, but on the only person who can help her – the German. At any moment, she realises, a rifle will crack, a bullet will send her careening to the ground. With tunnel vision, she counts the passing seconds to stay calm. *Just make it to the train,* she commands, the cold air searing her lungs, the exertion setting her calves ablaze. The young woman at the train, still holding Felicia, has turned so Felicia can't see Mila approaching.

And then, somehow, miraculously, the twenty metres are behind her. Mila is at the train, unscathed, standing beside the German, panting, her legs shaking as she presses her wedding ring into the meat of his palm. 'Very expensive,' she says, trying to catch her breath, willing herself not to make eye contact with Felicia, who's turned at the sound of her voice. The captain eyes Mila, turns the gold ring over in his fingers, bites it. Mila can see now from the silver stripes on his shoulders that he is *Hauptsturmführer.* She wishes she had a curvier build, or ample lips, or something funny or flirtatious to say that might persuade him to spare her. But she doesn't. All she has is the ring.

A rifle cracks. Mila's knees crumple and she covers the back of her head instinctively with her hands. From a squat, she peers through her elbows. The shot, she realises, was aimed not at her but rather at someone in the meadow. This time, a woman. Like Mila, she had tried to run. Mila stands slowly and immediately looks to Felicia. The woman she'd called 'mother' just moments before has covered Felicia's eyes with a free hand and is whispering something in her ear, and Mila's heart fills with gratitude. The Ukrainians at the perimeter shout as they swarm their latest victim, who disappears as one of the soldiers kicks her corpse into a hole.

'A damn commotion,' the German says, slipping Mila's ring into his pocket. 'Wait here,' he huffs, leaving the women alone by the train.

Mila, still breathing heavily, glances at the young blonde-haired woman. 'Thank you,' she whispers, and the woman nods. Felicia turns and locks eyes with Mila.

'*Mamusiu*,' she whispers, a tear trickling down the curve of her nose.

'Shhh, shhhh, it's okay,' Mila whispers. It's everything she can do not to reach for her daughter, to wrap her up in a hug. 'I'm here now, love. It's okay.' Felicia burrows again into the stranger's coat lapel.

In the field, the soldiers continue to yell. 'Line up!' they order. Their voices are cold, detached. As the Jews stand shivering beside their graves, the Hauptsturmführer commands the Ukrainians to form a line as well.

'Come,' Mila says, looping an arm around the woman's waist. They hurry toward the near-empty train car to join the others who have been spared. The moment they are out of view of the soldiers, Mila gathers Felicia up in her arms and holds her close, devouring her warmth, the smell of her hair, the touch of her cheek against her own. The group shuffles into the corner where they huddle together, their backs to the meadow. Outside, they can hear sobbing. Mila holds a palm to Felicia's ear, cradling her head to her chest in an attempt to block out the sound.

Felicia pinches her eyes shut, but she's figured it out. She knows what is about to ensue. And at the sound of the first muffled *crack,* something in her three-and-a-half-year-old mind realises she'll never forget this day – the smell of the cold, unforgiving earth; the way the ground had shaken beneath her when the man a row over had tried to run; the way his blood had spilt from the hole in his head like water from an overturned jug; the pain in her chest as she'd run like she'd never run before, toward a woman she'd never seen before; and now, the sound of shots being fired, one after another, over and over again.

CHAPTER THIRTY-ONE

Addy
Rio de Janeiro, Brazil ~ March 1942

Since he arrived in Brazil in August, Addy has found that the best way to avoid dwelling too much on the unknown, on the alternate universe he's left behind, is to keep moving. If he stays busy enough, he can see Rio for all that it is. He can appreciate the city's limestone and tree-lined mountains, offshoots of the Serra do Mar, that jut up from behind the beautiful coastline; the ever-present, enticing smell of fried, salted cod; the narrow, bustling cobblestoned lanes of the centro, where colourful, Portuguese colonial-era facades brush shoulders with modern, commercial high-rises; the purple jacaranda trees that bloom in what the calendar says is fall, but which is actually Brazil's spring.

Addy and Eliska have spent nearly every weekend since they arrived exploring the streets of Ipanema, Leme, Copacabana, and Urca, following their noses to the various vendors selling everything from sweet corn *pamonhas* to spiced shrimp on skewers, savory *refeição,* and grilled *queijo coalho.* When they pass a samba club, Addy jots down the address in his notebook, and they return later that evening to drink *caipirinhas* on ice with the locals, whom they've found to be quite friendly, and listen to music that feels fresh and alive, and unlike anything they've ever heard before. On most nights, Eliska foots the bill.

When Addy is on his own, his life is consumed by more practical concerns – like whether or not he can afford his next month's rent. It has taken almost seven months for his work permit to finally clear. During those months, he'd struggled, eking out a living with odd jobs that paid under the table, first at a bookbindery, and later at an advertising agency, where he was hired as a draftsman. The jobs paid poorly, but without a permit there was little he could do but wait. He slept on the floor of his twenty-five-square-metre studio in Copacabana, splayed out on a cotton rug (a gift he received after installing the electrical system in the home of a new friend) until he was finally able to save enough to buy a mattress. He bathed beneath the faucets of a public shower on Copacabana Beach until he could afford to pay his water bill. He discovered a lumberyard north of town that was willing to sell him scrap wood for next to nothing, and he was able to build a bed frame, a table, two chairs, and a set of shelves. At a flea market in São Cristóvão, he convinced a vendor to sell him a set of dishes and cutlery at a price he could afford. Last month, even though Eliska had been urging him to splurge on a proper churrascarian feast, he bought something more dear, something that would last – a Super Six Crosley tube radio. He found it used. It was broken and, to Addy's delight, underpriced. It took him twenty minutes to dismantle it and figure out the issue – a simple one, really, just a bit of charcoal built up on the resistor. An easy fix. He listens to the radio religiously. He listens to the news from Europe, and when the news grows too bleak, he spins the station selector until he finds classical music, which soothes him.

Just as he had on Ilha das Flores, Addy wakes early in Rio, and begins his days with his morning exercises, which he performs on the rug beside his bed. Today, it isn't yet seven and he's already sweating. It's the end of summer in Rio, and the heat is intense, but he's grown to like it. As he lies on his back bicycling his legs, he can hear the grate of metal gates being lifted as the cafes and newsstands three stories below open up on Avenida Atlântica. A block east, a blazing sun on the rise over the Atlantic beats down on Copacabana's white-sand beach. In a few hours, the crescent-shaped cove will be teeming with its usual Saturday crowd: bronzed women stretched out in figure-hugging suits beneath red umbrellas, and men in short swim trunks playing endless games of soccer.

'*Eins, zwei, drei* . . .' Addy counts, holding his hands behind his head as he twists his torso left to right, reaching elbows to knees. Eliska once asked him why he always counted in German. 'With everything that's happening in Europe and all . . .' she'd said, leaning over the bed to peer at him quizzically. It was the closest they'd gotten to talking about the war. Addy didn't really have an explanation, except that when he imagined a drill sergeant prodding him to complete his exercises, he always pictured a block-jawed German.

With his sit-ups complete, Addy stands and wraps his fingers around the wooden bar he's hung in the doorway, counts out ten chin-ups, and then lets himself dangle, his body limp, enjoying the sensation of his spine elongating toward the floor. Satisfied, he showers quickly, then dresses in a pair of linen shorts, a white cotton V-neck T-shirt, canvas tennis shoes, and a straw Panama hat. He slides a pair of newly purchased wire-rimmed sunglasses into the *v* of his tee, then reaches for an envelope resting on his bed, tucks it into his back pocket, and leaves the apartment, locking the door behind him.

'*Bom dia!*' Addy sings under the awning of his favourite open-air juice bar on Rua Santa Clara, his shirt already clinging to the sweat on his back. From behind the counter, Raoul beams. Addy met Raoul during a game of pickup soccer one day on the beach. 'You're not from around here, are you?' Raoul had chuckled when he caught a glimpse of Addy's pale chest. Later, when he discovered that Addy had never tasted a guava, he insisted on a visit the next day to his juice bar. Since then, Addy has made an effort to swing by the bar as often as he can. He can't get over all the different flavours on hand. Mango. Papaya. Pineapple. Passion fruit. Rio tastes nothing like Paris.

'*Bom dia! Tudo bem?*'

'*Tudo bem*,' Addy replies. He's become fluent in Portuguese. '*Você?*'

'No complaints, friend. The sun is shining, and it's hot as hell, which means it'll be a busy day. Let's see,' Raoul says to himself, looking around at the produce arranged across the counter in front of him, '– ah! Today I have a special treat for you, just in – açai. Very good for you, a Brazilian specialty. Don't let the colour scare you.'

Addy and Raoul make small talk as Raoul prepares Addy's juice.

'So where are you off to today?' Raoul asks.

'Today, I celebrate,' Addy says triumphantly.

Raoul squeezes the juice from an orange through his press, mixes it with the dark purple acai puree in Addy's cup.

'*Si?* What are you celebrating?'

'You know how my work permit finally arrived? Well, I've found a job. A real job.'

Raoul's eyebrows jump. He raises the cup in his hand. '*Felicitações!*'

'Thanks. In one week I start work in Minas Gerais. They want me to live there for a few months, so this weekend I say good-bye for now, to you, my friend, and to Rio.'

Addy had heard about the job in Brazil's interior several months ago. The project, called the Rio Doce, involved building a hospital for a small village. He'd applied right away for the position of lead electrical engineer, but when he met with the project managers, they shook their heads, claiming that without the proper paperwork, their hands were tied. 'Perfect your Portuguese, and come back when you've got a work permit,' they said. Last week, on the day his permit was cleared, Addy contacted the managers. They hired him on the spot.

'We'll miss you in Copacabana,' Raoul offers, and then reaches behind him for a banana. He tosses it to Addy. 'On me,' he winks.

Addy catches the banana and sets a coin on the counter. He tries a sip of his drink. 'Ahh,' he says, licking the purple juice from his upper lip. 'Lovely.' A line has begun to form behind him. 'You are a popular man,' Addy adds, turning to go. 'I'll see you in a few months, *amigo.*'

'*Ciao, amigo!*' Raoul calls after him as he turns to leave.

Addy slips the banana into his back pocket beside the envelope and glances at his watch as he sets off down Rua Santa Clara. The day is his to explore until three, when he's due to meet Eliska on Ipanema Beach for a swim. From there, they'll head to dinner at the home of a fellow expat they met a few weeks ago at a samba bar in Lapa. But first, he must mail his letter.

His is a familiar face at the Copacabana post office. He stops by every Monday with an envelope addressed to his parents' home on Warszawska Street, and to enquire about whether anything's come for him. So far, the answer has been a consistent and sympathetic *no*. Two and a half years have gone by since he received news from Radom. As much as he tries not to dwell on this, his trips to the post office are a constant reminder. As the weeks and the months pass, the agony of wondering what has become of his family worsens. Some days it erases his appetite and fills his gut with a dull ache that lingers through the night. Other days, it wraps around his chest like a strand of steel wire and he's sure that at any moment the flesh will sever, shredding his heart into pieces. The headlines in the *Rio Times* only heighten his anxiety: 34,000 Jews killed

217

outside Kiev, 5,000 dead in Byelorussia, and thousands more in Lithuania. These killings are massive, far bigger than any one pogrom, the numbers too wretched to fully conceive; if Addy thinks too hard about them, he will imagine his parents, his brothers and sisters, as part of the statistics.

Brazil, too, is preparing for war. Vargas, who, like Stalin, flipped his loyalty to the Allies, has battled German U-boats off the south Atlantic coast, has sent supplies of iron and rubber to the United States, and in January began allowing the construction of US air bases on its northern coasts. Brazil's involvement in the war is real, but Addy often marvels how he wouldn't know it in Rio. Just as in Paris in the days before the war, here there is life and music. The restaurants are full, the beaches packed, the samba clubs pulsing. Addy wishes sometimes that he could disconnect, as the locals seem to be able to do – to immerse himself in his surroundings and forget about the war completely, the intangible world of death and destruction that lies, crumbling, 9,000 kilometres away. But as quickly as the thought enters his consciousness, he chides himself, inundated with shame. How dare he stop paying attention? The day he disconnects – the day he lets go – is the day he resigns himself to a life without a family. To do so would mean writing them off as dead. And so, he stays busy. He distracts himself with his work and with Eliska, but he never forgets.

Addy pulls his letter from his back pocket, traces his fingers over his old address in Radom, thinking of his mother. Rather than imagine the worst, he has taken to re-creating his lost world in his mind. He thinks of how, on Sundays, the cook's day off, Nechuma would prepare a family dinner, taking great care as she crumbled caraway seeds between her fingers over a hash of red cabbage and apples. He thinks of how, when he was little, she would lift him up every time they entered and left the apartment so he could run his fingers along the mezuzah that hung in the arched doorway to his building. How she would lean over his bed and kiss his forehead in the mornings to wake him, smelling faintly of lilacs from the cold cream she'd rubbed onto her cheeks the night before. Addy wonders if his mother's knees still bother her in the cold, if the weather has warmed enough yet for her to plant her crocuses in the iron basket on the balcony – if she still has a balcony. *Where are you, Mother? Where are you?*

It's quite possible, Addy realises, that in the midst of war, his letters aren't reaching his mother. Or that they are reaching her, and it's her letters that aren't reaching *him*. Addy wishes he had a friend in a neutral country in Europe who could forward his correspondences. There is also the possibility, of course, that his letters are arriving at his old address, but the family is no longer there. It's unbearable, picturing his parents confined to a ghetto, or worse. He'd begun writing to his physician, to his old piano teacher, and to the superintendent of his parents' building, asking each to share some news, to pass his missives on if they happened to know the whereabouts of his parents and siblings. He hasn't heard back from anyone yet, but he refuses to stop writing. Putting words to paper, engaging in a form of conversation, seeing the word *Radom* scrawled across the face of an envelope – these are the things that keep him grounded.

Addy pushes open the door to the Copacabana post office, breathing in its familiar scent of paper and ink. '*Bom dia, Senhor Kurc*,' his friend Gabriela calls from her usual perch behind the counter.

'Good morning, Gabi,' Addy replies. He hands her his letter, already stamped. Gabriela shakes her head as she takes it. He no longer has to ask.

'Nothing today,' she says.

Addy nods in understanding. 'Gabi, I'm moving to the interior for a few months next week, for a job. Is it possible to hold my mail, in case anything comes while I'm away?'

'Of course,' Gabriela smiles kindly, in a way that tells him he's not the only one waiting for news from abroad.

As he leaves the post office, Addy's heart is heavy, and he realises it's not just the fate of his family that is weighing on him, but something else. Twice in the last week, Eliska has brought up the subject of a wedding; she's asked him to think about what kind of food they might serve, and later suggested they talk about a honeymoon. Both times he's changed the subject, realising it's impossible to contemplate a wedding with his family still missing.

Addy lets his mind slip back in time to the beach in Dakar, where he and Eliska had clung to each other as fiercely as they did to the idea of a life of freedom, their love swept along by a swift current of danger and uncertainty . . . Would they make it to Rio? Would they be sent back to Europe? Whatever happened, they told each other, they'd be together! Now, at long last, they are safe. There are no more fishermen to bribe, no more expired visas to agonise over, no more hour-long walks to a deserted beach to make love in privacy. But now, for the first time in their relationship, they argue. They argue about whom to include in their dinner plans – Eliska's friends are more fun, she says, his friends too intellectual. 'No one wants to sit around talking about Nietzsche,' she once groused. They butt heads about unimportant things like the fastest route to the market, and whether the espadrilles in the shop window are worth the splurge. ('I think not,' Addy will say, knowing that Eliska will inevitably show up to their next date wearing them.) They bicker over which station to tune to on the radio – 'Forget the news, Addy,' Eliska once said, exasperated. 'It's too depressing. Can we listen to some music?'

Addy sighs. What he would give to spend an hour with his mother, to get her advice about the woman he plans to marry. *Talk to her,* Nechuma would say. *If you love her, you must be honest with her. No secrets.* But they *had* talked. They *were* honest with one another. They'd talked about how things felt different between them on South American soil. Once, they'd even discussed ending their engagement. But neither is willing to give up just yet. Addy is Eliska's anchor, and Eliska, Addy's thread to the world he left behind. In her eyes, he sees Europe. He sees a reminder of his old life.

Walking instinctively toward the Teatro Municipal, Addy finds himself recalling Eliska's words from the week before, when he'd confided in her once again how anxious he felt about losing contact with his family. 'You worry too much,' she'd said. 'I hate it, Addy. I hate seeing the sadness in your eyes. We're free as birds here; let's relax, enjoy ourselves a bit.' *Free as birds.* But he cannot feel free when so much of him is missing.

CHAPTER THIRTY-TWO

Mila and Felicia
Radom, German-Occupied Poland ~ April 1942

Since the massacre, which is what everyone began calling it when Mila, Felicia, and the four others were returned to the ghetto, the SS have unleashed a beast. Perhaps they realised what they were capable of, or were holding back before. They aren't holding back any longer. The violence at Wałowa escalates by the day. There have been another four roundups in the weeks since Mila returned. In one case the Jews were marched to the train station and herded into cattle cars; in another they were simply brought to a perimeter wall and shot. There are no more lists, no more false promises of a life of freedom in Palestine or the States. Instead there are raids, there are factories searched, there are Jews lined up and counted. The Germans are always counting. And every day, a Jew in hiding or without the proper work papers is killed. Some are even gunned down at random. Last week, as Mila and her friend Antonia returned from a day's work at the factory, a pair of SS soldiers strolled by on the street, casually unholstered their pistols, knelt down, and began shooting, as if in target practice. Mila ducked silently into an alleyway, giving thanks for the fact that Felicia wasn't with her, but Antonia panicked and ran straight into their path. Mila sank to her knees and prayed as the sound of several more gunshots ricocheted off the brick walls of the two-storey apartments lining the street. When the stomp of German boots finally receded, she ventured out and found Antonia a few metres away, lying still, face down on the cobblestones with a bullet hole between her shoulder blades. *It could have been me*, she thought, sickened by the reality that what little order had existed when the ghetto was first erected had long been lost. The Germans were killing now for *sport*. Any day, she knows, could be her last.

* * *

221

'Remember, walk only in your socks, and play very quietly,' Mila instructs. She glances at her watch. She mustn't be late. Panicked over what might happen should Felicia be discovered at the factory, Mila has begun leaving her behind in the flat to fend for herself while she's at work.

'Please, *Mamusiu* – can I come with you?' Felicia begs. She wants nothing of staying home alone.

But Mila is adamant. 'I'm sorry, love. You're better off here,' she reasons. 'I've told you – you're a big girl now, and you barely fit beneath my desk at the workshop.'

'I can be small!' Felicia pleads.

Mila's eyes water. It's the same struggle every morning and it's awful, hearing the desperation in her daughter's voice, letting her down. But she mustn't relent. It's far too dangerous.

'It's not safe,' Mila explains. 'And it won't be for long. I've been thinking of a new way to get us out of here. Both of us. We must be patient. It will take some time to prepare.'

'Will we be with Father?' Felicia asks. Mila blinks. It's the third time in the past week Felicia has asked about Selim. Mila can't fault her for it. When she'd been at her most despondent, she'd indulged in hours of telling Felicia about Selim, a way of fooling herself into thinking that by talking about him, he would come back, give her some answers, some advice on how to survive, how to keep Felicia safe. She'd told Felicia countless stories of her handsome doctor father: the way he'd push his glasses up his nose, the way the corners of his mouth had crinkled when Mila first told him that she'd become pregnant within months of marriage – as if the strength of their love needed a physical manifestation – and later, after Felicia was born, the way he would make her laugh by counting her toes, by blowing kisses into her belly, by playing endless games of peek-a-boo. Felicia can recite these stories, along with the details of his face, as if recalling them from her own memory.

Mila has put so much hope into Selim's return, it is understandable that her daughter would assume that any plan for their safety would involve him. But the odds of her husband being alive have begun to feel impossibly small, and Mila knows that the longer she clings to this fantasy, the more dangerous it becomes. It's been two years of constant worry. Constant fear of the worst. Mila has had enough. She can't do it any longer. She has to let him go, to take responsibility for herself and for Felicia. It will be less harrowing, she realises, to mourn him than to worry incessantly about him. Until they are safe, she's decided, she must believe he is dead. It is the only way to keep her wits about her.

But how can she tell this to Felicia? How can she explain to her almost-four-year-old daughter that she might never know her father? 'You need to prepare her,' Nechuma has said over and over. 'You can't keep her hopes up; she'll resent you for it.' Her mother is right. But Mila isn't ready yet, for the conversation, for the heartbreak that will ensue. Instead, she will try a new tack. She will tell part of the truth. She reaches for Felicia's hands, holds them in hers.

'I want so badly to believe your father will come back to us. But I – I don't know where he is, love.'

Felicia shakes her head. 'Something happened to him?'

'No. I don't know. But what I do know is that if he is well, wherever he is, he's thinking of you. Of us.' Mila manages a smile. Her voice is soft. 'We will try to find him, I promise. It will be a lot easier to ask around once we're outside the ghetto. But until then, we must think about what's best for us. You and me. Okay?'

Felicia looks at the floor.

Mila sighs. She squats before Felicia, wraps her fingers gently around her upper arms, and waits for her to look up. When she does, there are tears in her eyes. 'I know it's awful, being alone all day,' Mila says quietly. 'But you have to know it is for the best. You are safe here. Out there . . .' Mila looks to the door, shaking her head. 'Do you understand?'

Felicia nods.

Mila glances again at her watch. She is late. She'll need to jog to the workshop. She reminds Felicia about the bread in the pantry, about walking in her socks, about the place in the cabinet, the secret spot where she's meant to hide and to stay perfectly still, like a statue, should anyone knock while Mila is at work.

'Goodbye, love,' Mila says, kissing Felicia on the cheek.

'Goodbye,' Felicia whispers.

Outside, Mila locks the door to the flat and closes her eyes for a moment, praying as she does every morning that the Germans won't raid the flat while she's gone, that she will return in nine hours to find her daughter right where she left her.

Felicia frowns. Her mind buzzes. Her father is out there somewhere, she is sure of it. He will come back to them. Her mother may not believe it, but she does. She wonders for the thousandth time what it will feel like to meet him, imagining him scooping her off her feet, magically easing her hunger, filling her up with happiness. Her mother had mentioned a way to get them out of the ghetto. Maybe this new idea of hers will lead them to her father. Felicia's shoulders sink as she remembers the two plans before it. The mattress. The list. Both were horrifying. With each, she had ended up back where she started, and worse off for it. Her mother speaks often of waiting. Of being *patient*. She hates that word.

It takes Mila several weeks to gather what she needs for her plan to work: a pair of gloves, an old blanket, scissors, two needles, several lengths of black thread, two buttons, a handful of fabric scraps, and a newspaper. What she takes from the factory she tucks discreetly into her bra or under her waistband, keenly aware that the last worker who was searched and caught with a spool of thread in the pocket of his winter coat was murdered on the spot.

Every night, from the flat's second-storey window, she presses her nose to the glass and runs her gaze along the brick apartments lining the ghetto perimeter, studying each of the three gates at the main entrance on the corner of Wałowa and Lubelska Streets – a wide arch for vehicles, flanked by two narrower openings for pedestrians. And every night it's the same: the German wives arrive just before six, dressed in their sleek overcoats and felt caps. They stroll in through the vehicle gate and congregate at the ghetto's cobblestoned entrance, waiting for their husbands, the ghetto guards, to be relieved from duty. Some cradle infants in their arms, others clasp the hands of small children. While the women mingle, the three hundred or so Jews returning from day labour camps outside the ghetto are herded back in through the two smaller pedestrian gates. At six o'clock sharp, the guards, along with their wives and children, disappear from beneath the arched vehicle entrance, and all three gates to the outside world are sealed shut, not to be reopened until morning.

Mila checks the time. Ten minutes until six. At the ghetto entrance, a little boy darts from his mother's side to wrap his arms around the leg of one of the guards. Which of these strangers, she wonders, lives in her parents' old home? Which of the wives bathes in her mother's porcelain bathtub? Which of the children practises scales on their beloved Steinway? The thought of a Nazi family making themselves comfortable at 14 Warszawska makes her sick.

She watches as the ghetto gates swing closed. Six o'clock on the dot.

This time, Mila decides, her plan will work. It has to. She and Felicia will escape. And they'll do it in plain daylight, for all of the goddamn guards to see.

It's after curfew and the ghetto is quiet. Mila and her mother stand at their small kitchen table, their supplies laid neatly in front of them. A single candle burns for light. 'Shame I left my patterns at the shop,' Nechuma says quietly, as she cuts a page of newspaper into the shape of the body of an overcoat. 'You'll have to dress warmly,' she adds. 'We have nothing for lining.' Mila nods as she kneels to pin her mother's makeshift pattern to the blanket she's spread across the floor, snipping the wool carefully along the edges of the paper. She and Nechuma trade the scissors back and forth, repeating the process for the coat's sleeves, lapels, collar, and pockets. And then, sitting on opposite sides of the table, they begin to sew.

The hours slip away as the women work. Every so often they look up at one another, their eyes glassy, and smile – it's been a long time since they've sewn together and it feels good, a distant reminder of the afternoons, long before Felicia was born, when they'd sit down to fix a hem or patch a seam – it was often during those afternoons at each other's side that their most meaningful conversations would unfold.

At around three in the morning, Nechuma tiptoes to the pantry and pulls out a drawer to reveal a safe hidden underneath. She returns with four fifty-zloty notes. 'Here,' she says. 'You will need it.' Mila takes two of the notes and slides the remaining two across the table.

'You keep these,' she says. 'I'll be fine. I'll be with Halina soon.'

Halina had left Radom three weeks earlier when Adam was assigned a job working for the railroad in Warsaw, mending tracks destroyed by the Luftwaffe before the city fell. Franka and her brother and parents had gone with her. Halina had written as soon as she was settled, urging Mila to come to Warsaw. *We found a flat in the heart of the city,* she wrote – this, Mila knew, meant they were living outside the ghetto walls, as Aryans – *I am working on getting our parents positions at the arms factory in Pionki. For you, jobs in Warsaw are plentiful. Franka has a job nearby. We have everything you need here. Please – find a way to come!*

Nechuma slides the notes back across the table. 'Here we have work, and our ration cards. You will be on your own for a while,' she says, nodding toward the window. 'You will need this more than we will.'

'Mother, it's the last—'

'No, it's not.' Nechuma taps her breastbone gently with her forefinger. Mila had nearly forgotten. The gold. Two coins, covered in ivory cotton – her mother had camouflaged them as buttons. 'And there is the amethyst,' Nechuma adds. 'If we need to, we'll use it.' What was left of the silver had bought Adam his life. Everything else they'd sold or traded for extra food rations, blankets, and medicine. Thankfully, they hadn't yet been forced to part with Nechuma's purple stone.

'All right then.' Mila tucks two bills into each side of the coat's collar before stitching it up.

When she first devised her plan, Mila had petitioned her parents to flee to Warsaw with her, but they'd insisted it was too dangerous. 'Go find your sister and Franka, get Felicia to a safe place,' they said. 'We'll only get in your way.' It was wrenching for Mila to admit it, but they were right. Her chances of a successful escape were greater without them. Her parents moved slowly now, and still carried the faint Yiddish accents of their childhoods. Posing as Aryan would be more difficult for them. Halina had mentioned in her letter a factory in Pionki, a plan to transfer Sol and Nechuma there. In the meantime, they were still employed, and everyone knew that a job was the only thing that mattered in the ghetto.

As a dull, silver light fills the room, Nechuma sets her needle down. Mila sweeps the leftover shreds of fabric from the table into her palm and hides them under the sink. Their work is complete. Mila wraps a scarf around her neck, a patchwork of SS uniform scraps, and then slides her arms into the sleeves of her new overcoat. Nechuma stands, running her fingers over the seams, feeling for loose threads on the buttonholes, eyeing the hem that hangs a centimetre off the floor. She smooths a lapel and tugs at a sleeve to make it lie perfectly flat. Finally she takes a step back, and nods.

'Yes,' she whispers. 'This is good. This will work.' She wipes a tear from the corner of her eye.

'Thank you,' Mila breathes, wrapping her arms around her mother, holding her close.

The next day, Mila hurries home from the workshop at five-thirty. She is dressing Felicia in the foyer when Nechuma returns from the cafeteria.

'Where is Father?' Mila asks, slipping a third shirt over Felicia's head. She worries when her parents are more than a few minutes late returning to the flat.

'He was put on dish washing duty today,' Nechuma says. 'Had to stay a few minutes to clean up. He'll be here.'

'Why do I need so many clothes, *Mamusiu*?' Felicia asks, looking up at her mother, her eyes curious.

'Because,' Mila whispers, squatting so her face is level with her daughter's. She brushes a few fine strands of cinnamon hair behind Felicia's ear. 'We're leaving tonight, *chérie*.' She'd purposefully waited to share the details of her plan with Felicia – she herself was nervous enough about it, and she didn't want Felicia to be nervous, too.

A flash of excitement spreads across Felicia's face. 'Leaving the ghetto?'

'*Tak*.' Mila smiles. And then her lips tighten. 'But it's very important you do exactly as I say,' she adds, even though she knows that Felicia will. Mila buttons a second pair of pants around her daughter's narrow waist, helps her into her winter coat and pulls a pair of her socks over her hands as mittens. Finally, she tugs a

227

small wool cap over Felicia's head, tucks the ends of her hair underneath it.

Nechuma hands Mila a handkerchief lumpy with her day's ration of bread. Mila slides it down her shirt. 'Thank you,' she whispers. In the kitchen, she retrieves the ID Adam made for her from the drawer with the false bottom and tucks it into her purse. Returning to the foyer, she slips into her new coat, her scarf, her hat, her gloves. Finally, instead of securing her armband around her sleeve as she normally would, she holds it between her teeth and forefingers and tears it at the seam. Felicia gasps. 'Don't worry,' Mila says. Even though she's too young to wear one, Felicia knows what happens to Jews in the ghetto if they're caught without their armbands. Mila holds the white strip of cotton to her arm so the blue Star of David faces out, and lifts her elbow. Nechuma sews the ends back together with two small stitches and snips the thread without knotting it. As Mila adjusts the band, she hears her father in the stairwell.

'There she is!' Sol beams, arms outstretched as he lumbers through the doorway. He bends to pick Felicia up, and swings her around, kissing her on the cheek. 'My goodness,' he says, 'you feel like an elephant with all of these clothes on!' Felicia giggles. She adores her *dziadek*, loves it when he hugs her so tightly she can barely breathe, when he sings her the lullaby about the kitten with the blinking eyes – the one his mother sang for him when he was a boy, he told her once – when he swings her in circles until she's dizzy, and tosses her into the air and catches her so it feels like she's flying.

'You won't need that, will you?' Sol asks as he sets Felicia down, his eyes suddenly serious, pointing at Mila's arm.

'Just until I get to the gate,' Mila says, swallowing.

'Right. Of course,' Sol nods.

Mila looks at her watch. It's a quarter to six. 'We have to go. Felicia, give your *babcia* and *dziadek* a hug.' Felicia looks up, suddenly disappointed. She hadn't realised that her grandparents would be staying behind. Nechuma kneels, pulls Felicia to her chest.

'*Do widzenia*,' Felicia mumbles, kissing her grandmother's cheek. Nechuma closes her eyes for a long moment. As she stands, Sol bends down and Felicia wraps her arms around his neck. '*Do widzenia, dziadku*,' she says, her nose tucked into the hollow over his collarbone.

'Goodbye, pumpkin,' Sol whispers. 'I love you.'

It is all Mila can do to keep from bawling. She throws her arms around her father, and then her mother, clutching them to her, hoping, praying it is not the last time they will be together.

'I love you, Myriam,' her mother whispers, calling her by her Hebrew name. 'God be with you.'

And with that, Mila and Felicia are gone.

Mila scans the street for SS. With none in sight, she takes Felicia by the hand and together they begin making their way toward the ghetto gates. They move quickly, the wind biting at their cheeks. It's nearly dark, and as they walk, their breath, translucent grey, evaporates into the night.

When they are a block away from the gates and the guards are in sight, Mila opens her coat. 'Come,' she says quietly, pointing to her shoe. 'Stand here on my foot and grab hold of my leg.' Mila can feel Felicia's tiny frame push against her, her arms wrap around her thigh. 'Now hold on.' Felicia peers up and nods, eyes wide as Mila closes her coat around her. They make their way, more slowly now, toward the gates, Mila doing her best to walk without a limp despite the extra eleven kilos she's carrying on one leg.

There are fifteen, maybe twenty guards stationed at each of the two pedestrian arches at the ghetto entrance, each with a rifle slung over his shoulder. Several of them count aloud as a throng of Jews shuffles in through the gates, blind with exhaustion from their day's work outside the ghetto. 'Hurry up!' one of the guards yells, waving a baton over his head like a lasso.

Mila cranes her neck, scanning the weary-eyed Jews moving past, as if she were there to greet one in particular – her husband, maybe, or her father. No one seems to notice as she weaves her way slowly through the crowd, toward the ghetto gates. Soon, she's but a few metres from the large vehicle gate in the centre, where, as she'd anticipated, a dozen or so German wives have begun to gather, bundled up in overcoats, their rosy-cheeked children in tow.

Her leg aches from Felicia's added weight. She stops to check her watch. Seven minutes to six. Shivering, she contemplates for the thousandth time the consequence of a failed escape. *Have I lost my mind?* she wonders. *Is this worth the risk?* And then her world goes dark and she's back at the roundup, huddled in an empty train car, her arms wrapped around Felicia's head in a futile attempt to protect her from the atrocious scene, even though they both heard the gunshots, the *thump* of frail, naked corpses collapsing to the frozen earth just twenty metres from them.

Mila's upper lip is damp with sweat. *You can do this,* she whispers, shaking off her doubt. *Just count,* she thinks. It's her father's technique, one he's used since she was a child. 'On three,' he'd say, and whatever the daunting challenge – pulling a tooth, yanking a splinter from under a fingernail, pouring peroxide over a bloodied knee – the counting somehow made it easier.

To her right, a horse and wagon carrying food from the Jewish Council clatters through the vehicle entrance and halts as half a dozen SS search the carriage contents, shouting, the entranceway din suddenly swelling. This is it, Mila realises – the distraction she needs.

On three. Mila holds her breath and counts. *One . . . two . . .* On *three,* she turns her back to the gates, opens her coat and reaches down, touching Felicia's head. In a second Felicia is by her side, holding her hand. Mila reaches up with her free hand and rips the white band off of her arm, feeling the electrifying *pop pop* of Nechuma's two stitches giving way. She crumples the band into her fist and stuffs it quickly into her pocket. *No one saw,* she tells herself. *From this point on, you are a German housewife, here to meet one of the guards. You are a free person. Think like one. Act like one.*

'Stay right by me,' Mila orders coolly. 'Look straight ahead, into the ghetto. Don't look behind you.' In her periphery, Mila can see that several of the German women to her left have found their husbands. They stand chatting in pairs, their arms folded over their chests to stay warm. She squeezes Felicia's hand. 'Slowly,' she whispers, and together they begin inching their way, backward, toward the gate, moving as if in slow motion so as to remain unnoticed. Mila tries to force some slack into the rope-tight muscles of her neck and jaw, to imitate the easy-going expressions and mannerisms of the German women around her. But as they move closer to the gates, she's thrown off by the sensation of a body too close to hers. She turns just as a young wife, her head craned in the opposite direction, knocks into her from behind.

'*Entschuldigen Sie mich*,' the woman apologises, adjusting her cap. She smells of shampoo.

Mila smiles, waves her free hand in the air. '*Es ist nichts*,' she says quietly, shaking her head. The woman peers at Mila through crystal blue eyes for a moment, glances down at Felicia. And then she's gone, lost in the crowd. Mila exhales and squeezes Felicia's hand once more. They continue on, shuffling backward toward the vehicle gate. More wives stroll in from behind them – they tilt their chins now and then in Mila's direction, but seem to look through her. *You are one of them*, Mila reminds herself. As long as they keep their backs to the entrance and move discreetly enough, she prays, they'll blend in. *Slowly, now. Right foot, left foot. Pause. Right foot, left foot. Pause. Not so tight*, she tells herself, loosening her grip on Felicia's sock-clad hand. *Right. Left. Right. Left. Steady, almost there.*

The last of the Jews has made his way into the ghetto, and Mila watches from the corner of her eye as the pedestrian gates are closed and padlocked. When a body suddenly brushes by, bumping her elbow with something hard, she presses her lips together just in time to silence a yelp that nearly escapes her throat.

'Move!' the guard yells, but marches by without stopping.

Finally, Mila senses a structure overhead. They are beneath the main entrance – the arched vehicle gate. A gust of wind lashes at their backs and Mila reaches for her hat to keep it from blowing away. She tugs its brim low over her brow and glances down at Felicia, who is white in the face but whose expression is remarkably calm. *Stay focused*, Mila reminds herself. *You're so close! Count your steps. One . . . two . . .* They creep backward. *Three . . . four . . .* On her fifth step Mila can see the outer wall of the entrance and the sign that reads DANGER OF CONTAGIOUS DISEASES: ENTRY FORBIDDEN.

She can hardly believe it. They've made it outside the ghetto walls! But these next few steps, she realises, are the most important. *This* is the moment she'd replayed, in her mind, over and over again like a scene out of a movie, until she'd convinced herself her plan could work.

Summoning the last ounce of her courage supply, Mila inhales sharply. This is it. 'Come!' she whispers. She swivels 180 degrees, pulling Felicia with her.

And then, with the ghetto behind them, they walk. *Right, left – slowly, not too fast*, Mila thinks, resisting the instinct to run. *Right, left, right, left.* She tries to pull her shoulders back, to carry her chin high, but her heart is a jackhammer, her stomach a ball of barbed wire. She waits for the shouts, the gunshots. Instead, though, all she can hear is the sound of their footfall, Felicia's three steps for her two, the heels of their shoes clicking lightly on the pavement of Lubelska Street, moving slightly faster now, away from the guards and their wives, away from the workshop and the filthy streets and the so-called contagious diseases.

Mila makes her first right onto Romualda Traugutta, and they walk in silence for another six blocks before ducking into an empty alleyway. There, in the shadows, Mila's heart begins to slow. The muscles in her neck loosen. In a moment, once she's gathered herself, she'll make her way back to Warszawska Street, to her parents' old building, where she will knock on the door of their neighbours and friends, the Sobczaks, and, if they'll let her, spend the night. Tomorrow, she will use her false ID to try to arrange travel to Warsaw. They are far from safe – if they are caught, they will be killed – but they have escaped the prison of the ghetto. Her plan, the first phase of it at least, has worked. *You can do this*, Mila tells herself. She glances behind her to be sure she hasn't been followed and then stops and bends down to cup a palm around Felicia's cheek and presses her lips against her daughter's forehead.

'Good girl,' she whispers. 'Good girl.'

CHAPTER THIRTY-THREE

Sol and Nechuma
Radom, German-Occupied Poland ~ May 1942

Nechuma and Sol lie awake on their mattress, their fingers entwined. They stare at the ceiling, too distressed to sleep. There are whispers in the ghetto that Wałowa will soon be liquidated. No one is entirely sure what this means, but the rumours, each more terrifying than the last, have recently been compounded by news of what happened in Łódź. There, according to the Underground, the Germans deported thousands of Jews from a ghetto far bigger than Radom's to a concentration camp in the nearby village of Chełmno. The Jews thought they were being sent to a labour camp. But then a few days ago a pair of escaped prisoners surfaced in Warsaw with tales so chilling that Nechuma can think of little else. There was no work at Chełmno, they reported. Instead, the Jews were piled, up to 150 at a time, into vans and asphyxiated with gas – men, women, children, babies – all within a matter of hours.

Nechuma used to reassure herself that they had lived through pogroms before, that in time, the fighting, the bloodshed would pass. But with the news from Łódź she's come to understand that the situation they are in now is something entirely different. This isn't just being subjected to profound hunger and poverty. This isn't persecution. This is extermination.

'The Nazis will not succeed in this,' she says. 'They will be stopped.' Sol doesn't answer.

Nechuma exhales slowly, and in the suffocating silence that follows she realises how entirely she aches. Even her eyelids are sore, as if begging for rest. Her own body confounds her. She often wonders how she and Sol still have the strength to go on at all. They live in a state of perpetual pain and exhaustion and hunger – depleted by their long days at the cafeteria, by their pathetic rations, by the mental tricks they play to ignore the daily horrors that surround them. They are almost numb now to the constant cracking of rifles within the ghetto walls, to stepping around the bodies of the dead and dying on the streets, to shielding their eyes when they pass the ghetto entrance, where the SS have taken to stringing up rows of Jews by their necks and hanging them slowly, prolonging their agony as long as possible so that others will see, will understand: *This is what happens when you break the rules. This is what happens to those who are insolent, defiant, or simply unlucky.* Nechuma once saw a boy as young as five or six hung up this way, minutes, it seemed, from death, and though she couldn't bring herself to look into his eyes, she did allow herself to glimpse his shoeless feet, so small and pale, his ankles flexing in pain. She wished she could reach over and touch him, to comfort him in some way, but she knew doing so would mean a bullet in her brain, or a rope around her own neck.

'At least the Americans have entered the war,' she says, repeating the shred of hope that has been circulating among the others in the ghetto – a glimmer of possibility, something to hold on to. 'Maybe the Germans can be stopped.'

'Maybe,' Sol acquiesces. 'But it will be too late for us.' His voice cracks and Nechuma can tell he is holding back tears. 'If they start in on the Radom ghettos, we will be two of the first to go. They might spare the young. And who knows, maybe not even them.'

Nechuma knows in her soul that her husband is right, but she can't bring herself to admit it, not out loud at least. She takes Sol's hand and kisses it, presses his palm to her cheek. 'My love. I don't know any longer what is going to happen, but whatever is in store for us, at least we will have each other. We will be together.'

A month ago, one of their children might have been able to help them. But they are alone now in the ghetto. Jakob is with Bella at the AVL factory near the Glinice ghetto, and Mila, Nechuma prays, is on her way to meet Halina in Warsaw. She and Felicia had not returned to Wałowa since attempting to escape, but that could mean anything. Now, with the situation growing ever more dire by the day, their only real hope is Halina. But Halina hasn't had any luck yet securing them jobs at the Pionki arms factory, and their time is running out. 'I'm still working on a transfer,' Halina promised in her last letter. 'Stay strong, do not lose faith.'

They are in contact with Halina, at least – able to communicate through letters sneaked into and out of the ghetto with Isaac's help. Nechuma can hardly bear to consider the fates of her children who are missing. She hasn't heard a word from Genek since he and Herta disappeared from Lvov two years ago, and soon it will be four years since she last saw Addy. She would give anything, even her life, to know that they were alive, and unharmed.

Nechuma brings a hand to her heart. There is nothing worse, not even the daily hell of the ghetto, than for a mother to live with such fear and uncertainty about the fates of her children. As the weeks and months and years tick by, the torment inside her builds and burns, a crescendo of misery threatening to crack her open. She's begun to wonder how much longer she can bear the pain.

Beneath her fingertips, Nechuma can feel the faint tap of her heart. She wants to cry but her eyes are dry, her throat like paper. She blinks into the darkness, her daughter's words echoing through her. *Stay strong. Do not lose faith.* 'Halina will find a way to transfer us to the factory,' she says after a long while, almost in a whisper. But Sol doesn't answer, and from the slow draws of his breath she knows he is asleep.

Our destiny, she thinks, *in Halina's hands.* Nechuma's mind darts to her youngest as a child – to how, even before she could talk, Halina would demand attention, and when she didn't get it, her solution was to find something fragile and break it. Or simply scream. To how, when Halina was at gymnasium, she would often claim she was too ill to go to school; Nechuma would hold a hand to her forehead and every now and then let Halina stay home, only to watch her trot down the hallway to the living room a few minutes later, where she would lie for hours on her stomach, flipping through one of Mila's magazines, tearing out pictures of dresses she liked.

She's grown up so much, her Halina, since the start of all this. Maybe she really *will* be the one to get them out of here. *Halina.* Nechuma closes her eyes and tries to rest. As she drifts toward sleep, she imagines herself at the window of her old home, looking out over the tops of the chestnut trees bordering Warszawska Street. The road below is empty but the sky is animated with birds.

In her half-dream, Nechuma watches them as they dip in and out of the clouds, touch down on a branch every now and then to survey their surroundings, then take off again. Her breathing slows. She falls asleep with thoughts of Halina soaring over her, arms spread wide as wings, bright eyes alert as she figures a way out for them all.

CHAPTER THIRTY-FOUR

Halina and Adam
Warsaw, German-Occupied Poland ~ May 1942

'Do you think someone's ratted us out?' Halina whispers. She and Adam are seated at a small table in the kitchen of the attic apartment they've rented in Warsaw.

Adam removes his glasses, rubs his eyes. 'We barely know anyone in Warsaw,' he says. They've been in the apartment for a month and had felt safe there at first. But then yesterday, the landlord's wife had trounced up the stairs unannounced, sniffing around like a hound onto a scent as she pelted them with questions about their families, their jobs, their upbringing. 'And our papers are flawless,' Adam adds. He'd taken extra care in making their IDs. The name they chose, Brzoza, is as Polish-Catholic as they come. Thanks to their false identities and their looks – Halina's blonde hair and green eyes and Adam's tall cheekbones and fair skin – they easily pass for Aryan. But there is no getting around the fact that they are recent arrivals in Warsaw, with no friends or family nearby, and these things alone make them suspicious.

'What do we do? Should we move?'

Adam slides his glasses back over his nose, peers at Halina through thick, round rims. 'That would be like admitting we're in the wrong. I think . . .' he pauses, tapping his forefinger on the blue-and-white checked cloth draped over the table, 'I think I have a plan.' Halina nods, waiting. They need a plan, desperately. Otherwise it's only a matter of time before the landlord's wife reports them to the police.

'Aleksandra suspects we're Jewish, despite our papers . . . I've been trying to figure out how we can explain that we're *not* – and the only way to prove it, I mean to *really* prove it . . . is for her to *see* that we're not. Well, that *I'm* not.'

Halina shakes her head. 'I don't follow.'

Adam sighs, fidgets in his seat. 'I've been experimenting with a way to . . .' He glances uncomfortably at his lap but his words are interrupted by a sound. Someone climbing the stairs to the attic. His chin snaps toward the door behind him. 'It's her,' Adam whispers, as the footsteps grow closer. He and Halina lock eyes. Adam points at the light hanging over the sink. 'The light!' he says. Halina looks at him quizzically. 'The light by the sink, turn it off.' He unbuckles his belt.

'Why?' Halina asks, hurrying to the sink. There's a knock on the door.

'Coming,' Adam calls.

Halina pulls a chain to extinguish the light. Adam's hands are in his trousers, moving quickly.

'What in God's name . . . ?' Halina breathes.

'Just trust me,' Adam whispers. The knocks grow louder. Adam stands and hurries to the sink, buckling his belt. Halina nods and makes her way to the door.

'Are you there? Let me in!' The voice on the opposite side of the door is shrill, on the verge of hysteria. Adam gives Halina a thumbs-up. A moment later, Aleksandra barrels into the apartment, glaring at them.

'Hello, Aleksandra,' Halina offers, glancing at Adam, whose hands rest nonchalantly on the porcelain sink behind him.

Aleksandra ignores the greeting and crosses the room toward Adam, trailing a cloud of dissent. 'I'll make this brief,' she says, pausing an arm's reach from him and narrowing her eyes to slits. 'Someone has led me to believe that you've been lying to us. They claim that you are *Jewish*! And you know what?' she points a long finger at Adam, 'I *defended* you – I told them your name, assured them you were good Christians like the rest of us – but now I'm not so sure.' A little white bead of saliva clings to her upper lip. 'It's true, isn't it?' she barks. 'You are Jews, aren't you?'

Adam holds up his palms. 'Please—'

'Please *what*? Please forgive you for putting our lives in danger? Don't you know we could be *arrested* and hung by our necks for harbouring *Jews*?'

Adam's spine stiffens. 'Whomever you spoke with is wrong,' he says, his voice cool. 'And to be frank, I'm offended. There's not a drop of Jewish blood in our family.'

'Why should I believe you?' Aleksandra snarls.

'Are you calling me a liar?'

'I have a source.' Aleksandra wraps her fingers around her hip bones, her arms forming triangles at her torso. 'You say you're not a Jude. But you can't prove it.'

Adam presses his lips together into a tight, thin line. 'I don't have to prove *anything* to you,' he says, willing the words to come slowly.

'You say that because you're *lying*!' Aleksandra spits.

Adam holds her glare. '*Fine.* You need proof?' He reaches for his belt. Halina hasn't moved from the door. Behind Aleksandra, she gasps, covers her mouth. As Adam wrestles with his buckle, Aleksandra makes a strange noise, like a hiccup. But before she can object, Adam, in a fit of fury, unzips his trousers, tucks his thumbs under his waistband, and in one motion pushes them, along with his underwear, down to his knees. Halina covers her eyes, unable to watch.

Aleksandra's jaw drops. She freezes.

Adam lifts his shirt. 'Is this enough *proof* for you?' he shouts as his pants fall into a heap around his ankles. He glances down, half expecting to see his camouflage gruesomely exposed. He'd attached the skin-toned bandage that morning with a solution of raw egg white and water, studying himself in the mirror. In the shadows, he hoped, it would pass as foreskin. The bandage, to his relief, has stayed put.

Halina squints through her fingers at the silhouette of her husband by the sink. In the shadows, she can just make out the shape of his genitals. She understands now why he'd asked her to extinguish the light over the sink.

'Good God almighty, enough!' Aleksandra finally huffs, turning her chin away in disgust. She slinks toward the door, looking as if she might be sick.

Halina exhales, dumbstruck that Adam's plan had worked, and wondering how long he'd been walking around with a bandage adhered to his groin. She clears her throat and opens the door, an indication that it's time for Aleksandra to leave.

'Calling us *Jewish*,' Adam mutters under his breath as he bends to pull his trousers back up over his thighs.

The landlord's wife pats nervously at her blouse, the skin on her neck smeared with hot, red blotches. She avoids eye contact with Halina as she steps through the door to the stairs without a word. Halina locks the door behind her and waits for the footsteps to recede before turning to look at Adam. She shakes her head.

Adam lifts his palms to the ceiling, shrugging his shoulders toward his ears. 'I didn't know what else to do,' he says.

Halina covers her mouth. Adam glances at his feet and up again at her, and as their eyes meet, the corners of his mouth curl into a smile and Halina laughs silently into her palm. It takes her a moment to collect herself. Wiping tears from her eyes, she makes her way across the room. 'You could have warned me,' she says, resting her forearms on Adam's chest.

'I didn't have time,' Adam whispers. He loops his arms around her waist.

'I wish I could have seen Aleksandra's face,' Halina says. 'She looked wretched on her way out.'

'Her jaw nearly touched the floor.'

'You're a brave man, Adam,' Halina says softly.

'I'm a lucky man. I'm actually surprised the bandage stuck.'

'Thank God it did! You had me nervous.'

'I'm sorry.'

'Is it still – on?' Halina glances down at the space between them.

'I slipped it off as Aleksandra was leaving. It was driving me crazy. I've been wearing it for hours – I'm surprised you didn't notice me walking strangely.'

Halina laughs again, shakes her head. 'Did it hurt coming off? Is everything all right – down there?'

'I think so.'

Halina narrows her eyes. Her adrenaline has made her skin electric to the touch and Adam's warmth against her is suddenly irresistible. 'I'd better have a look,' she says, reaching for his belt, unfastening it. She kisses him, closing her eyes as his trousers fall once again into a pile at his ankles.

AUGUST 4, 1942: *Late in the evening hours, Radom's Glinice ghetto is cordoned off by police and lit with searchlights; 100-150 children and elderly are murdered on the spot; the following day approximately 10,000 others are sent by railway to the Treblinka extermination camp.*

CHAPTER THIRTY-FIVE

Jakob and Bella
AVL Factory, Radom, German-Occupied Poland ~ August 6, 1942

Standing precariously on a toilet seat in the men's lavatory, Bella listens for Jakob's knock. She keeps one hand on the stall wall for balance, her winter coat draped over her elbow, the other hand by her side, clutching the handle of a small leather suitcase. The washroom door is small, her position excruciating: if she rights herself, her head will show over the top; if she steps down off the toilet, her feet will be visible below; if she moves at all, for that matter, she'll risk falling, or worse, slipping into the fetid hole between her feet. Thankfully, no one has come to check the lavatory in the past thirty minutes. But Bella holds her position anyway, trying her best to ignore the sweltering heat, the throb in her lower back, the overwhelming stench of faeces and stale urine. *Hurry, Jakob. What's taking so long?*

Their plan, if it works, is to escape the confines of AVL unnoticed and make their way to the nearby Glinice ghetto. A part of her still clings to the thread of hope that she'll find her parents there, alive. Spared. But she can feel it. They're gone.

The ghetto has been liquidated. Bella and Jakob had been warned that it would happen, by a friend in the Polish police force. They'd been close with Ruben in school and were hopeful when he was assigned patrol duty at AVL; perhaps, they thought, he might be of some help to them. But the two times Bella had run into him, he'd walked by without so much as a nod or a glance in her direction. It was no surprise, of course – this was common now, this new dynamic between old friends. And so it caught Bella off guard when a week ago Ruben took her by the arm, pushed her into a storage closet, and followed her inside, locking the door behind them. Bella, who by now expected the worst, had prayed that whatever he had planned for her would at least be quick. Instead, Ruben surprised her by turning to her with a look of abject sorrow. 'I'm sorry I've been ignoring you, Bella,' he said in a voice just barely above a whisper. 'They'd have my head if – anyway, you have family in the ghetto, yes?' he'd asked in the darkness. Bella had nodded yes. 'I heard today that Glinice is meant to be liquidated within a week. There will be a handful of odd jobs left, a few may be spared, sent to Wałowa, but the rest . . .' he looked at the floor. When Bella asked where the Jews would be sent, Ruben spoke so softly Bella had to strain to make out the words. 'I heard a couple of SS officers talking about a camp near Treblinka,' Ruben whispered. 'A labour camp?' Bella asked, but Ruben didn't answer, just shook his head.

With this news, Bella pleaded with Maier, the factory foreman, to allow her to bring her parents to AVL. Somehow he'd agreed, and even issued her an ausweis so she could walk the two kilometres to Glinice one night. Ruben escorted her. But her parents had refused to leave. 'If you think we can just waltz out of here, you're crazy,' her father told her. 'This Herr Maier says we can work for him, but tell that to the ghetto guards – tell them we're leaving our jobs here to work for someone else, and they'll laugh, and then put a bullet through our heads, and yours, too. We've watched it happen before.'

Bella could see the terror in her father's eyes. But she was persistent. 'Please, Father. They've already taken Anna. Don't let them take you, too – you must try, at least. Ruben can help,' she pressed, her voice unnaturally high, pinched with desperation.

'It's too dangerous for us,' her mother said, shaking her head. 'Go, Bella. Go. Save yourself.'

Bella hated her parents for dismissing her plan, for surrendering hope. She'd given them the chance to escape – to take fate into their own hands – but rather than grab the reins, they'd balked and slumped in the saddle, overcome with fear. 'Please!' Bella had finally begged, sobbing into her mother's arms, tears flooding her cheeks, but she could see it in the pitch of their shoulders, in the downward cast of their eyes – they had lost the will to fight. What strength they had left in them had been siphoned when Anna disappeared. They were shells of their old selves, empty, depleted, and afraid. When Bella and Ruben finally left Glinice without them, Bella was beside herself.

Just four days later, at midnight on the 4th of August, the Glinice ghetto liquidation began, as Ruben had predicted. Two kilometres away at the factory, Bella could hear the faint gunshots, the ensuing bone-chilling screams. Helpless, frantic, and barely functioning after days without sleep, she collapsed. Jakob found her in the factory barracks, curled into the fetal position and refusing to talk, or even to look at him. She could do nothing but sob. Without any comforting words to offer, Jakob lay down beside her, wrapped himself around her, and held her as she wept. It was hours before the pop of gunfire finally let up. When it did, Bella went silent.

At dawn the next day, Jakob helped Bella back to her bunk, and told the guard assigned to the barracks that his wife was too sick to work. 'Are you sure she's alive?' the guard asked when he leant his head into her barracks and found Bella lying motionless on her back, a wet cloth over her brow. An hour later, Maier declared over the loudspeakers that AVL would be closing, that the Jews would be sent to a different factory, and they should pack their belongings. They were to prepare to leave, Maier said, the following morning at nine o'clock sharp. But Jakob knew exactly where they'd be sent. They needed a way out. That night, Jakob forced Bella to eat a crust of bread, and begged her to gather her strength. 'I need you with me,' he said. 'We can't stay here, do you understand?' Bella had nodded, and Jakob had explained his plan, which included a pair of wire cutters, although Bella had a hard time following. Before he left, Jakob begged her to meet him in the morning at eight-thirty in the men's lavatory.

With the summer sun beating down on the corrugated metal roof overhead, the air in the washroom stall is stifling. Bella fears she might faint. It had taken all of her effort to rise that morning, and when she did it felt as if she no longer inhabited her own body, as if her muscles had surrendered. When the loudspeakers crackle, she blinks, thankful for the distraction. It's Maier's voice.

'Workers – make your way to the factory entrance for your rations. Bring your belongings.'

Bella closes her eyes. A line will soon form at the front of the factory.

She pictures the guards gathered to escort the Jews to the train station, and wonders if they were the same guards who oversaw her parents' trip toward almost certain death. Her stomach turns. *Where is Jakob?* She'd managed to arrive at the washroom at eight twenty-five, five minutes early. At least a half hour has passed. *He should be here by now. Please* – Bella prays, listening to the faint slap of sweat dripping every few seconds from her chin to the cement floor beneath her and shaking away the inclination to burst from the washroom and scream for the guards to take her, too. *Please, Jakob, hurry.*

Finally, she hears a soft *tap-tap-tap-tap* on the door. She exhales, and steps gingerly from the toilet. Her double knock is met quickly with another four. She unlocks the door. Outside, Jakob nods, looking relieved to find her there. 'Sorry I'm late,' he whispers. He takes the suitcase from her and guides her around the outside of the washroom, hugging the wall. Wiping the sweat from her face, Bella gulps the fresh air, grateful to put herself in Jakob's hands now, to simply follow.

'You see that field, just beyond the men's barracks?' Jakob asks, pointing. 'That's where we're going. But first we have to make it to the barracks.'

Bella squints at the barracks, which appear to be some thirty metres away. Beyond is a fence, a wall of chain link and barbed wire surrounding the property, and on the other side of that, their target – a field of overgrown wheat.

'We're going to have to run,' Jakob whispers. 'And hope that no one sees us.' He peers cautiously around the corner of the washroom facility toward the backside of the factory, narrating what he sees: the tail end of a line of people stretching around the building from its entrance; three guards bringing up the rear, motioning for the last few workers to join the back of the line. After a few long minutes, Jakob reaches behind him and takes Bella's hand. 'They're gone,' he says. 'Quick. Let's go!'

Bella is jerked forward and soon they are kicking up dust as they sprint toward the barracks, their backs now to the factory. Within seconds Bella's lungs begin to scream, but she is aware only of holding tight to Jakob's hand, and of the temptation to turn and look back as she runs, to see if anyone has spotted them – but she fears that if she does she might panic and stop dead in her tracks. Thirty metres shrink to twenty, then ten, then five, and then their pace slows as they duck behind the men's barracks, pressing their backs up against the weathered wood, sucking fistfuls of air into their burning lungs. Bella leans over and rests her hands on her knees, feeling her heart thrashing in her chest. The run has nearly put her over the edge, but it has also stirred something in her. For the moment at least, it has brought her back into her body.

They breathe as quietly as they can despite the exertion, listening intently for footsteps, shouts, the crack of a rifle. Nothing. Jakob waits a full minute and then nudges his nose around the corner. No one, it seems, has seen them.

'Come,' Jakob says, and they make their way, out of sight now, toward the fence. When they reach it, Jakob kneels and works quickly with the wire cutters, his forehead damp as he clips away methodically at the steel until he's cut a hole large enough for them to fit through. 'You first, love,' he says, lifting the flap of fence. Bella crawls on her stomach through the opening; Jakob passes her the suitcase and then follows, bending the chain link back down behind them as best he can. 'Stay low,' he says.

They scramble to the meadow, where they drop to hands and knees and crawl, their bodies enveloped in stalks of overripe wheat that sway beside them as they edge away from the freshly lacerated fence, from the factory and the cattle cars filling up with the men and women who the night before had slept by their sides. On all fours, Bella is reminded for a moment of the morning she'd crawled across a meadow to reach Lvov at the start of the war. There was so much at stake, it had seemed, at the time – so many unknowns. But at least then, she'd had a sister. She'd had her parents.

After a few minutes she and Jakob pause, standing on their knees so they can peer through the tips of the grass toward the factory. They've travelled quite a distance – AVL appears small, like a beige brick on the horizon.

'I think we're safe here,' Jakob says. He pats at the stalks around them, creating a lair of sorts so they can stretch out. The wheatgrass is tall; they can sit up with their heads still obscured. Bella, sticky with sweat, spreads her coat on the ground and climbs on top. Jakob glances again toward the factory. 'We should wait until dark before we press on.' Bella nods and Jakob scoots to sit beside her, reaching into his pocket for a half a boiled potato. 'Saved this from last night,' he says, unfolding his handkerchief.

Bella isn't hungry. She shakes her head and pulls her shins to her chest, rests her cheek on a knee. Beside her, Jakob frowns, bites his lip. They haven't spoken about what happened the night before at Glinice. What's there to say? Bella has thought about trying to open up, to explain what it feels like to lose a mother, a father, a sister – her whole family – what it feels like to wonder how different things would be had she and Anna been in hiding together during the pogroms in Lvov, and had she convinced her parents to come to AVL. The factory, like the ghetto, will soon be liquidated, but if her parents had taken jobs at AVL, at least they could have tried to escape together. Bella can't bring herself to talk about these things, though. Her grief is larger than words.

Around them the wheat whispers and sways in the breeze. Jakob wraps an arm around Bella's shoulders. As she closes her eyes, tears gather in her lashes. They sit in silence, the minutes stretching into hours, with nothing to do but wait as the amber light of the afternoon fades to dark.

CHAPTER THIRTY-SIX

Halina

Countryside near Radom, German-Occupied Poland ~ August 15, 1942

Her father hums as he drives, tapping his thumbs on the wooden steering wheel of the tiny black Fiat. Behind him, Halina and Nechuma sit close, their arms linked at the elbow. Thankfully, their old friends and neighbours the Sobczaks had come through for them again, and were willing to lend their car for the journey. Halina had considered travelling with her parents from Radom to Wilanów by train, but worried that they would have to cross too many checkpoints at the stations. The car, Halina hoped, would be the safer bet, even though it would mean scrounging for fuel, which was expensive and nearly impossible to come by. Halina had promised to refill the Fiat's tank upon returning it to the Sobczaks, and had insisted that Liliana hold on to the silver bowl and ladle Nechuma had left with them before they were evicted, in exchange for the loan.

From the back seat, Halina watches as her father takes in the scenery – the cerulean sky, the verdant countryside, the sun's brilliant reflection on the winding Vistula River. She had offered to drive, but Sol insisted. 'No, no. Let me,' he said, nodding as if it were his obligation, but in truth she knew he'd love nothing more than the chance to take the wheel. For fourteen months, he and Nechuma have lived in a world confined by brick walls and barbed wire, by blue-starred armbands, by the tedium and fatigue of forced labour. Halina smiles, knowing how good they must feel out here, on the open road. Together, they drink in the fleeting smell of freedom, sweet and ripe like the scent of the linden tree flowers washing over them through the open window.

Nechuma has just finished describing what it was like to live and work at the Pionki arms factory. 'We felt so *old* there,' she says. 'The others were practically children. You should have heard the gossip – *I've fallen in love . . . she isn't even pretty . . . he hasn't spoken to me in days* – the jealousy, the drama; I had forgotten how exhausting it was to be that young. Although,' she confides, lowering her voice and leaning into Halina, 'sometimes it was quite entertaining.'

Halina can't help but laugh, imagining her parents surrounded by frivolous chatter. She was happy to hear that at Pionki they were better off than they had been in the ghetto, and she would have been comfortable with them living out the war in the factory confines had Adam not warned her the week before that it was to be shut down. 'I'm sorry I didn't find out earlier,' he said. 'It could happen any day.' Halina knew she had to get her parents out before they wound up in one of the dreadful camps the Jews were being sent to when their labour was no longer needed.

Receiving permission to extract her parents from Pionki, of course, was hopeless. Halina knew she would have to work outside the system. A week ago, armed with her Aryan papers and a pocketful of zloty, she visited the factory intent on bribing a guard at the entrance to let her parents leave discreetly at the end of their workday – she would claim they were old friends, wrongly accused of being Jews. But she arrived on a Friday, and her mother had been taken along with the rest of the female laborers to the public showers; Halina had to work that evening, and couldn't afford to wait for her to return. This morning, sensing that she was short on time and that one hundred zloty might not suffice, she decided to bring along the last of her mother's jewels – the amethyst. Nechuma had slipped the necklace to Isaac on the day of their transfer from the ghetto to Pionki, begged him to bring it safely and quickly to Halina. Isaac had written to Halina in Warsaw right away, claiming that he had a special purple delivery and that she should come for it as soon as possible.

Hitler had put the price of life on any German who accepted bribes from Jews, but as Halina learnt at Adam's work camp, this didn't stop many of the Nazis from accepting them. And sure enough, when she flashed Pionki's entranceway guard the brilliant purple stone, his eyes lit up. He returned fifteen minutes later, with her parents in tow.

'Left here,' Halina directs at a wooden sign for Wilanów, a small farming village on the outskirts of Warsaw. As they veer off of the main thoroughfare, the paved road turns to dirt, and Sol glances in the rear-view mirror, smiling at the image of Halina and Nechuma beside one another, enjoying the closeness.

'Tell us about you, about the others,' Nechuma says.

Halina hesitates. Her parents haven't yet heard about Glinice, about Bella's family. She hasn't had the heart to tell them. The past hour has been so pleasant, talking with her mother about trivial things, it's felt almost normal. She's reluctant to invite the sadness of the world back in just yet. So instead she tells her parents about Adam's recent close call with the landlord's wife, telling the story for the laughs and glossing over the fact that she'd been petrified at the time; she tells them about her job in Warsaw working as a cook for a German businessman; about how Mila had recently found work, also posing as Aryan, in the home of a wealthy German family.

'And Felicia?' Sol asks over his shoulder. 'I've missed her so much.'

'Mila's landlord was suspicious of Felicia from the start,' Halina explains. 'Took one look at her sad, dark eyes and knew she was Jewish. Mila has managed to pass with her papers, but for Felicia it is much more difficult. I've found a friend willing to keep her in hiding.' Halina tries to keep her tone light, even though she knows how much Mila's decision to leave her daughter in the care of someone else had tormented her.

'She's there alone, without Mila?' Sol asks, and Halina can tell from the reflection of her father's eyes in the rear-view mirror that he's no longer smiling, that he'd intuited the parts she'd left unsaid.

'Yes. It's been hard on both of them.'

'Sweet girl,' Nechuma says softly. 'Felicia must be so lonely.'

'She is. She hates it. But it's for the best.'

'And Jakob?' Nechuma asks. 'Is he still at the AVL factory?'

Halina hesitates, looks down at her lap. 'He's still there, yes, as far as I know. I wrote to tell him you'd left Wałowa, and he asked if I could help get Bella's parents out, too, from the Glinice ghetto, but . . .' Halina swallows. It's quiet in the car. 'I tried,' Halina whispers.

Nechuma shakes her head. 'What do you mean?'

'It's . . . they've . . . Glinice has been liquidated.' Halina's voice is barely audible above the hum of the engine. 'Isaac says there are a few people still left, but the rest . . .' She can't say the words.

Nechuma brings a hand to her mouth. 'Oh, no. And Wałowa?'

'Apparently Wałowa is next.'

Halina can hear her father's breath grow heavy in the front seat. A tear rolls down her mother's cheek. What joy they'd felt at being reunited at the start of the journey has evaporated. No one speaks for several minutes. Finally, Halina breaks the silence. 'Slow down, Father – it's this next one on the left.' She points over his shoulder to a narrow drive. They follow it for two hundred metres until they reach a small, thatched-roofed farmhouse.

Nechuma dabs at her eyes, sniffs.

'Is this it?' Sol asks.

'It is,' Halina says.

'What do they go by again?' Nechuma asks. 'The owners?'

'Górski.'

Adam had found the Górskis through the Underground on a list of Poles with space to spare who would accept money in exchange for hiding Jews. Halina didn't even know if *Górski* was their real name, just that they could take her parents; and with her steady work, she could afford to pay them.

Halina is familiar with the home – she'd visited once, to introduce herself and to inspect the living conditions. The wife had been out, but Halina and Pan Górski, who hadn't yet offered up his given name, had gotten along well. He was middle-aged, with salt-and-pepper hair, a bird-like build, and kind eyes. 'And you're sure your wife is all right with this arrangement?' Halina had pressed before she left. 'Oh, yes,' he said. 'She's nervous of course, it's only normal to be, but she's on board.'

Sol slows the Fiat to a crawl as they near the house. There isn't another home in sight.

'You picked well,' Nechuma says, nodding.

Halina glances at her mother, allowing herself for a moment a childlike pride in Nechuma's approval. She follows her gaze, taking in the small cottage with its squat, square frame, cedar-planked siding, and white shutters. She'd chosen the Górskis partly because they seemed genuinely trustworthy, and because they lived an hour from Warsaw, in the country; without any neighbours nearby, Halina hoped there would be less risk of someone reporting them.

'It's nothing fancy, but it's private,' Halina says. 'Don't let yourselves get too comfortable, though. Pan Górski says the Blue Police have come knocking twice already, looking for hideaways.' A captured Jew, they've heard, can be worth as much as a bag of sugar, or a dozen eggs. The Poles take the hunt seriously. The Germans, too. They've come up with a name for it: *Judenjagd*. Jew hunt. Jews caught can be delivered dead or alive, it makes no difference. The Germans have also imposed the death penalty against any Poles found with a Jew in hiding.

'The Górskis have promised to tell no one, of course, not even their family and closest friends. But keep your false IDs on you at all times,' Halina continues. 'Just in case. We can't expect them not to have visitors.'

Nechuma squeezes Halina's elbow. 'Don't worry about us, dear. We will be fine.'

Halina nods, although she doesn't know how not to worry about her parents any more. It's become second nature, tending to them. It's all she thinks about.

Sol flips the key to the ignition; the engine burps and quiet comes over the car as he and Nechuma peer through the bug-splattered windshield at their new home. A blue-slate walkway leads to the front door, where a brass stirrup-shaped knocker glints in the sunlight.

'This works,' Sol says. He glances at Halina in the mirror. His eyes are red.

'Hope so,' Halina breathes. 'We should head inside.'

Sol pulls the driver's seat forward so Nechuma and Halina can wriggle their way out, and then opens the Fiat's trunk to gather what is left of their belongings – a small canvas satchel carrying a change of clothes each, some photographs, his Haggadah, Nechuma's handbag.

'This way,' Halina says, and her parents follow her around the house to the back, where half a dozen greying shirts hang from a length of twine strung between two maples and where there is a small vegetable garden planted with peas, cabbage, and tomatoes.

Halina knocks twice at the back door. After a minute, Pan Górski's face appears in the window, and a second later, the door opens. 'Come,' he says, motioning for them to enter. They step quietly into the shadows of a den and

Sol pulls the door closed behind them. The room is just how Halina remembers it – small, with low ceilings, a paisley armchair, a weathered sofa, a set of bookshelves on the far wall.

'You must be Pani Górski,' Halina says, smiling at the slender woman standing beside her husband. 'I am Halina. This is my mother, Nechuma, and my father, Sol.' The woman nods quickly, her hands wrung together in a ball at her waist.

Halina looks from the Górskis to her parents. Despite their time in captivity, Sol and Nechuma have figures that are still ample, soft around the edges. They make the Górskis, with their narrow waists and protruding shoulder bones, look like skeletons.

Sol sets their satchel down and steps forward to offer his hand. 'Thank you for this, Pani Górski,' he says. 'You are very generous and brave to take us in. We will do everything we can not to bother you while we are here.' Pani Górski eyes Sol for a moment before lifting a hand, which Sol envelops in his. *Be gentle*, Halina prays, *or you'll break her bones.*

'Madame,' Nechuma offers, also extending a hand, 'do let us know what we can do to help around the house.'

'That's kind of you,' Pan Górski says, glancing at his wife. 'And please – call us by our given names, Albert and Marta.' Marta nods in agreement, but her jaw is tight. Something about the woman's demeanor doesn't sit well with Halina. She wonders what conversations the Górskis have had before their arrival.

'I should be getting back soon,' Halina says. She points to the bookshelf. 'Could you explain to my parents how this works before I go?'

'Of course,' Albert says. Sol and Nechuma watch as Albert wraps his torso around the small case and slides it gently along the cedar-planked wall.

'It's on wheels,' Sol notes. 'I hadn't noticed.'

'Yes, you can't see them, but they make moving it easier – and quieter.' Albert brings a hand to the wall. 'The wall has eight planks from floor to ceiling. If you count up to the third, and press just here, by these two nails,' he says, running his fingers over a couple of iron nailheads flush to the wood, 'you will hear a clicking sound.' Sol squints at the wall as Albert presses firmly against it.

Sure enough, the wall clicks, and a small square door swings open. 'I've aligned the hinge with the seam of the planks, so unless you know it's here, the door is invisible.'

'Meticulous work,' Sol whispers, genuinely impressed, and Albert smiles, pleased.

'There are three stairs that lead to the crawl space. You won't be able to stand,' Albert says as Sol and Nechuma crane their necks, peering into the black square behind the wall, 'but we've laid down some blankets and left you a flashlight. It's dark as night down there.' Sol swings the small door open and closed a few times. 'This here,' Albert says, pointing to a metal latch, 'will let you lock it from the inside.' He pushes the door closed until it clicks again, and then rolls the bookcase back into place. 'Now, come,' Albert says, waving over his shoulder, 'let me show you to your room.' Marta steps aside and brings up the rear as her husband leads the Kurcs down a short hallway to a bedroom just off the den.

'When it's safe,' Albert says, 'you can sleep here.' Sol and Nechuma take in the room, with its white stucco walls and two single beds. A rusted mirror hangs over a simple oak dresser. 'We'll let you know when we're expecting visitors. Marta's sister Róża, she comes by twice a week. Should someone arrive unannounced, we'll delay them at the door to give you time to slip into the crawl space. You'll need to bring all of your things, of course, so perhaps it's best not to unpack.'

'You have a son?' Sol asks, eyeing a pair of boxing gloves in the corner.

Marta flinches.

'Yes. Zachariasz,' Albert says. 'He's joined the Home Army.'

'We haven't heard from him in several months, though,' Marta adds quietly, looking at the floor. They make their way back to the den in silence.

Nechuma lays her hand on Marta's shoulder. 'We have three sons,' she says.

Marta looks up. 'You do? Where – where are they?'

'One,' Nechuma explains, 'last we heard, works at a factory outside Radom. But the other two we haven't heard from since, well, the start of the war, really. One was taken by the Russians, and our middle son was in France when the war broke out. Now, we don't know . . .'

Marta shakes her head. 'I'm sorry,' she whispers. 'It's awful, not knowing where they are, whether they're okay.'

Nechuma nods and something passes between the two women that eases Halina's heart.

Albert returns to his wife's side, rests his hand on the small of her back. 'Soon,' he declares, his voice suddenly grim, 'this godforsaken war will be over. And we can all go back to life as normal.'

The Kurcs nod, praying that there is truth to his words.

'I really must go,' Halina says, fishing an envelope with 200 zloty from her purse and handing it to Albert. 'I'll be back in a month. You have my address; please, should anything happen,' she says, avoiding eye contact with her parents, 'write to me right away.'

'Certainly,' Albert says. 'We'll see you next month. Be safe.' The Górskis leave the den to give the Kurcs some privacy.

When they are alone, Sol smiles at Halina, and then at the room around him, his palms turned up to the ceiling. 'You care for us well,' he says. Crow's feet flank his eyes, and Halina's heart emanates longing for her father, for his smile that she will miss the moment she walks out the door. She reaches for him, presses her cheek into the soft barrel of his chest.

'Goodbye, Father,' she whispers, cherishing the feeling of being wrapped up in his warmth and hoping he won't be the first to let go.

'Take care of yourself,' Sol says as they part, handing her the keys to the Fiat.

With the green of her eyes amplified behind a wall of tears, Halina turns to her mother, thankful the room is dark – she promised herself she wouldn't cry. *Be strong*, she reminds herself. *They are safe here. You'll see them in a month.* 'Goodbye, Mother,' she says. They hug and exchange kisses on the cheek, and Halina can tell from the way her mother's chest rises and falls that Nechuma is doing her best to hold back tears, too.

Halina leaves her parents standing by the trick bookcase and walks to the door. 'I'll be back in September,' she says, with a hand on the knob. 'I'll try to bring some news.'

'Please do,' Sol says, taking Nechuma's hand in his.

If her parents are as nervous as she about her leaving, they've done a good job of masking it. She opens the door and squints into the afternoon light, half expecting to catch someone spying on them from behind one of Albert's laundered shirts. She steps outside and turns to look back at her parents. Their faces are obscured by the shadows. 'I love you,' she says to their silhouettes, and closes the door behind her.

AUGUST 17–18, 1942: *Radom's larger Wałowa ghetto is liquidated. Eight hundred residents, including those from the shelter for the old and disabled as well as patients at the ghetto's hospital, are murdered over the course of two days. Approximately 18,000 others are deported by train to Treblinka. Some 3,000 young, skilled Jewish workers remain in Radom for forced labour.*

CHAPTER THIRTY-SEVEN

Genek and Herta
Tehran, Persia ~ August 20, 1942

A flash of orange hurtles through the space between their shoulders. Genek flinches. Herta covers Józef's face instinctively with her hand. They are three of twenty Polish recruits wedged into the bed of an old pickup, sitting hip bone to hip bone on slabs of plywood running the length of the bed. They've all come from different camps – released as Genek and Herta had been, on amnesty – to fight for the Allies. Their bodies are in bad shape – riddled with boils, ringworm, scabies, their hair sweaty and lice-infested, pasted to their foreheads. Tattered clothes hang loosely over gaunt frames and a foul odour surrounds them, following the truck like a repulsive, malodorous shadow. A few of the sickest lay crumpled at Genek's and Herta's feet, incapable of sitting up on their own, hours, it seems, from death.

They've been driving for three days, skirting the coast of the Caspian Sea on a narrow dirt road flanked by sand dunes and the occasional palm tree. 'I suppose we've nearly reached Tehran,' Genek says. They stare wide-eyed at the Persians lining the dusty thoroughfare, who stare back at them. 'We must look pitiful,' Herta whispers.

Tehran marks the end, for now, of their 5,000-kilometre journey. It's been a year since they were released from their work camp in Altynay, nine months since they finally left Wrewskoje, Uzbekistan, where they'd been forced to spend the winter. January and February were tough on them. Subjected to a diet of eighty grams of bread and a bowl of watery soup a day, their midlines had been whittled away until they'd lost a quarter of their body weight. Were it not for the blankets Anders had issued, they'd have frozen to death.

But they were lucky. Hundreds of others who'd come to Uzbekistan as they had, to join the army, were laid to rest in Wrewskoje. Every week, a carriage would clatter through the village to collect the skeletal remains of those who had lost their battles with malaria, typhus, pneumonia, dysentery, starvation. The dead were gathered up with pitchforks and heaped into piles outside the city. When the piles rose too high, someone would smother the corpses in crude oil and burn them, causing a sickly smell that hung in the air long after the bodies had turned to ash.

By March it was clear that Stalin either wasn't able or wasn't *willing* to properly feed or equip the exiles who'd enlisted in Anders's Army. There were 44,000 recruits, according to the registrar, awaiting orders in Uzbekistan; rations issued by the Soviets, however, were maintained for 26,000. Furious, Anders pushed Stalin to allow him to evacuate his troops to Persia, where they would come under the care of the British. When Stalin finally agreed, Genek and Herta set off on another four-month exodus, traversing 2,400 kilometres of endless steppe and desert through Samarkand and Chirakchi to the port of Krasnovodsk, Turkmenistan, on the eastern shore of the Caspian Sea. There, they were surrounded by NKVD toting large canvas bags; 'Drop the belongings you can't carry,' they were told – a rather pointless order, as most had nothing more to their names than the shirts on their backs. 'Money and documents, too,' the NKVD added. They'd be searched on embarkation, they were told. 'Anyone trying to smuggle money or papers out of the country will be arrested.' Genek and Herta had used the last of their zloty months ago. Their Polish passports had been confiscated in Lvov. They said goodbye to their amnesty certificates and non-resident permits issued in Altynay, along with their foreign passports issued in Wrewskoje. Without a single coin or form of identification in their pockets, they were true nomads. But it didn't matter – whatever the requirements to get them out of the grip of the Iron Fist and into the caring hands of the British and General Anders, they were more than willing to oblige. It wasn't until they finally climbed the steep gangway to board the *Kaganovich*, the rusted-up freighter that would deliver them to the Persian port of Pahlevi, that they smelt their first hint of freedom in the hot, salty air.

After a few days at sea, however, that smell was quickly overpowered by one of vomit, faeces, and urine. For forty-eight hellish hours, they stood shoulder to shoulder with the thousands of other passengers on board, their shoes drenched in excrement, their scalps sizzling beneath the blaze of the relentless sun, their stomachs churned by the never-ending ocean swells. Every square centimetre of the ship was occupied: the hold, the deck, the staircases, even the lifeboats. Dozens died, their limp bodies held aloft by outstretched hands, passed overhead to the nearest opening on the vessel's railing to be tossed overboard, where they were swallowed by the sea.

Genek and Herta finally arrived in Pahlevi, a Persian port on the southern shore of the Caspian Sea, in August. Numbed by fatigue and dizzy with hunger, thirst, and seasickness, they learnt that the last vessel to cross the Caspian, carrying with it over a thousand souls, had sunk. They slept for two nights on the beach in Pahlevi under an open sky until a caravan of pickups arrived to take them to Tehran, where they were told a division of the Polish Army awaited.

A second sphere sails overhead, and this time Genek reflexively catches it. Why would the locals taunt such a pitiful-looking group of people, he wonders? But when he opens his hand, he finds an orange. A nice one, too. Fresh. Plump. The first piece of fruit his fingers have touched in over two years. He glances over his shoulder to see if he can spot whoever threw it, catching the eye of a young woman wearing a maroon headscarf, standing on the sidewalk with her hands on the shoulders of two young boys in front of her. She smiles, her brown eyes soft and full of pity, and suddenly it's clear: the orange wasn't hurled as a sign of disrespect – it was a gift. Sustenance. Genek's eyes well up as he rolls the fruit between his palms. A *gift*. He waves at the Persian woman, who waves back and then disappears into a cloud of dust. Genek can't remember the last time a stranger did something nice for him without expecting something in return.

He digs a dirty fingernail into the orange, peels it, and hands a wedge to Herta. She bites off a piece and holds what's left of it to Józef's lips, laughing softly as his nose crumples. 'It's an *orange*, Ze,' she offers. A new word for him. '*Pomarańcza*. Soon enough, you'll learn to like it.'

Genek peels off a wedge for himself and closes his eyes as he chews. The flavour explodes on his tongue. It's the sweetest thing he's ever tasted.

* * *

Their camp faces north, overlooking the shore of the Caspian Sea and beyond that the purple-grey of the Elburz mountains. 'Are we in heaven?' Herta whispers as they approach, reaching for Genek's hand. Two young English women nod from beneath the brims of army caps and direct them toward a series of long, narrow tents with canvas flaps rolled and tied up to allow for airflow. 'Men to the right, women to the left,' they explain, pointing at two tents marked STERILISATION.

Inside the men's tent, Genek is more than willing to undress – he'd traded what clothes he could spare for firewood and extra food rations to help get through the Siberian winter; he's been wearing the same trousers, shirt, and undergarments nearly every day since. He makes his way, naked, to a hose spraying something that burns his nostrils as he approaches. 'You'll want to close your eyes,' the recruit who is just finishing before him calls out. The sterilisation shower stings, but Genek savours the cold bite of the solution cascading over his ribs, sloughing the grime from his skin, cleansing him of his time in exile. When it's over he opens his eyes, relieved to see that his small pile of threadbare clothes has been removed, undoubtedly to be burnt. He shakes a few drops of the sharp-smelling solution from his limbs and joins the other recruit at a bucket of what appears to be seawater, where he rinses off with a sponge – a sponge! With others waiting behind him, it's everything he can do not to revel for an extra minute or two in his first real bath in months. Smelling now like a mix of chlorine and the sea, he's handed a towel and guided to another tent, this one stocked with neat piles of new clothes: underwear, undershirts, and uniforms in several shapes and sizes. He selects a pair of lightweight khaki pants and pulls a collared short-sleeved shirt over his head, the cotton luxuriously soft against his chest. In a third tent, he's handed a pair of white canvas shoes, a cork helmet, a sack of dates, six cigarettes, and a small paycheck. 'Breakfast is at seven o'clock sharp,' he's told by the quartermaster as he turns to leave.

'Breakfast?' He's so accustomed to living off of a single meal a day, the concept of putting something nourishing in his stomach at daybreak has become foreign.

'You know, bread, cheese, jam, tea.' Cheese and jam and tea! Genek nods, salivating, too elated to speak.

261

On the beach, he finds Herta sitting with Józef in her lap and a basket of oranges beside her. She's been issued the same khaki slacks and shirt, in a women's cut. Józef is naked but for a cloth diaper and a handkerchief that Herta has drenched with ocean water and draped over his head. He kicks his feet in the sand, fascinated by the feel of the tiny hot grains against his skin. A young Persian boy walks by selling grapes. They sit for a while in silence, staring at the horizon, at the shimmering surface of the Caspian Sea, and at the saw-toothed line of the Elburz range looming over it. 'I think we've come to the right place,' Genek says, smiling.

AUGUST 1942, TEHRAN: *Soon after Anders's men reach Tehran, Stalin pushes hard to send the Poles directly to battle, but Anders insists that they need more time to recuperate. Many of his men die in Tehran — some too weak and sick from the exodus, some unable to stomach the sudden intake of rich food. Others, with the care of the Persians and the supplies sent from Britain, grow stronger. When new battle attire and real leather boots arrive in October, morale at the Tehran tent camp reaches an all-time high.*

AUGUST 23, 1942: *The Battle of Stalingrad begins. Nazi Germany, supported by Axis forces, pushes the boundary of its European territories and fights for control of Stalingrad in south-western Russia in what will become one of history's bloodiest battles.*

CHAPTER THIRTY-EIGHT

Felicia
Warsaw, German-Occupied Poland ~ September 1942

Felicia sings quietly to herself – the song about the kitten that her grandfather taught her – as she squats on the kitchen's linoleum floor, balancing a nest of metal bowls one on top of another. She glances every few minutes at the round clock hanging by the stove (her mother had taught her recently how to read time), counting down the minutes to five o'clock, when Mila is meant to arrive. The apartment belongs to a friend of her aunt Halina's. It's much nicer than the flat in the ghetto, but at least in the ghetto her mother came home to her every night. Here in Warsaw, for reasons Felicia still can't understand, her mother lives in a separate apartment down the street. They spend time together on the weekends, and once a week Mila comes to the apartment to deliver money for the landlord. The couple that owns the place works, so Felicia has grown accustomed to spending her days alone. There's another stowaway, an old fellow called Karl who arrived a few weeks ago, but she doesn't interact with him much – he mostly reads, or stays in his room, which is fine with Felicia as it makes her uneasy when people she doesn't know, men especially, ask her questions.

The lock on the apartment door rattles and Felicia looks up at the clock, at the long hand. It's too early. Her mother is usually here just after five, not before, and the owners of the place don't get home until six. For a moment she imagines it to be her father. 'I found you!' he'd say as he burst through the door wearing his army uniform. But then she freezes, wonders if she should hide. She's been told to be careful about strangers. The apartment door opens and closes, and after a moment a voice calls. Felicia softens when she recognises it as her mother's cousin Franka's.

'Felicia, honey, it's me. Franka. Your mother couldn't make it,' she explains as she makes her way from the foyer into the kitchen. 'There you are,' she says, finding Felicia sitting on the floor among her bowls. 'Your mother is fine, just has to work late today.' Franka sets a box on the kitchen table and bends to give Felicia a hug.

'She has to work late?' Felicia asks, looking past Franka, as if willing her mother to appear.

'She'll try to come visit you tomorrow.' Franka stands. 'Are you all right? Is everything okay here?'

Felicia glances up at Franka. She seems nervous, like she's in a hurry.

'I'm okay. Are you going to stay with me?' she asks, although she knows what the answer will be.

'I wish I could, love. But I'm working this evening, and Sabine is waiting for me downstairs. She came with me to keep watch while I brought the money. I shouldn't be seen up here.'

Felicia sighs and stands to get a closer look at the box Franka had set on the kitchen table. 'What's that?' she asks. With her fourth birthday approaching, she's been begging her mother for a new dress. It occurs to her that perhaps Franka has brought her one.

'It's shoes. Thought it best to look like I'd come with a delivery, in case anyone asked why I was here,' Franka says.

'Oh.' Felicia's eyes are level with the box. She stands on her toes to peek under the lid, wondering what a new pair of shoes might look like, smell like. But the oxfords inside are scuffy and worn.

'Is there anything that you need?' Franka asks, pulling an envelope from inside her shirt.

Felicia looks at the floor. There's a lot she needs. She doesn't answer.

Franka tucks the envelope into the usual spot – behind a picture frame over the stove. 'Where is Mister – what's the fellow's name?' she asks, checking her watch.

Felicia is about to explain that Karl hasn't yet ventured from his room when someone knocks hard on the door. Felicia's first thought is that it must be Franka's friend Sabine. But Franka jumps. She looks at her watch, and then at

Felicia. They stare at one another, unsure of what to do. After another knock, Franka lifts the tablecloth and points.

'Hide, quickly!' she whispers.

Felicia scrambles beneath the table. There is a third knock; this time it sounds like metal smacking wood. *They're going to break the door down,* Felicia realises, *if no one answers it.*

Franka adjusts the tablecloth so it hangs a centimetre from the floor. 'Coming!' she calls, and then squats and whispers through the tablecloth: 'If they find you, you are the daughter of the concierge.'

I'm the daughter of the concierge. These are the words she's supposed to recite, should someone discover her in hiding. In the months since she moved to the apartment, she hasn't needed to use them; until today, no one but the landlord has come unannounced. 'I'm the daughter of the concierge,' she whispers, feeling out the lie.

As soon as Franka reaches the door, Felicia hears voices. Three, four maybe, yelling in a language she has learnt to recognise as German. The voices belong to men. They stomp from the foyer into the kitchen. Beneath the table, Felicia startles at the jarring clatter of her bowls scattering across the floor.

Amid the chaos, Franka's voice is there too, talking quickly – she doesn't live here, she explains, then something about the shoes – but the Germans don't seem interested. '*Halt die Schnauze!* ' one of them barks, and Felicia holds her breath as they retreat down the hallway toward the bedrooms. For a moment it's quiet. Felicia is tempted to run, or to call out for Franka, but she decides instead to count. *One, two, three.* Before she can count to four, there's more yelling, and when she hears Karl's voice, too, she shivers. Is it him they've come for?

Soon bodies are moving, boots pounding *boom boom* back up the hallway in her direction, and then there are people in the kitchen, more yelling, and Karl is crying as he begs, his voice pathetic, pleading, 'Please don't, please! I have papers!' Felicia prays for him, prays for the Germans to take his papers and leave, but it's no use. A shot is fired. Franka screams, and a moment later the linoleum floor shakes from the weight of something heavy meeting it with a disturbing *thud.*

Felicia claps her hands over her mouth, trying to muffle whatever tortured sound might slip from her. Her heart beats so hard and fast it feels as if at any moment it will bolt right up and out of her throat.

One of the intruders laughs. Felicia tries to steady her breath, her body quaking from the effort. There is rustling. More laughter. Something about zloty. 'You see?' a voice croaks in broken Polish, presumably to Franka. 'You see what happens when they try to hide? You tell who owns this place we will be back.'

Something moves in Felicia's periphery. A ribbon of crimson, snaking slowly toward her beneath the tablecloth. She nearly vomits when she realises what it is. Sliding silently to the far side of the table, she pulls her knees to her chest and squeezes her eyes closed.

'Yes, sir.' Franka's voice is barely audible.

Finally, the voices and footsteps begin to recede and the door to the apartment clicks shut. The Germans are gone.

Felicia's instinct is to move, to scramble as quickly as she can from under the table, away from the bloody scene, but she can't. She rests her head on her knees and cries. In the next moment, Franka is there, beneath the table with her, holding her balled-up frame.

'It's okay,' she whispers, her lips pressed up against Felicia's ear as she rocks her back and forth, back and forth. 'You're okay. Everything will be okay.'

CHAPTER THIRTY-NINE

Addy
Rio de Janeiro, Brazil ~ January 1943

Addy's first stop upon returning to Rio de Janeiro from Minas Gerais, his job in the interior complete, is the Copacabana post office. He had prayed every night in Minas that a letter might have arrived, but his hopes are immediately eradicated as he walks in and catches Gabriela's eye.

'I'm sorry, Addy,' Gabriela says from behind the counter. 'I was hoping I'd have something for you.' She seems genuinely sorry to deliver the news.

Addy forces a smile. 'It's okay. Wishful thinking.' He runs his hand through his hair.

'It's nice to have you back,' Gabriela calls as Addy turns to leave.

'See you next week,' Addy offers with stilted optimism.

As he exits the post office, his chin drops and his chest begins to ache. He's been a fool to hope. He sniffs, fighting tears, then squares his shoulders. *Nothing good will come of all this yearning,* he tells himself. *You must do more. Something. Anything.* This afternoon, he decides, he'll visit the library. He'll leaf through the foreign papers, search for clues. Perhaps he'll find a bit of news that will lift his spirits. What he'd read in Minas was disheartening, and at times confusing. One article called Hitler's efforts to eradicate the Jews in Europe 'premeditated mass murder' and reported an unthinkable number of deaths. Another article said that the 'Jewish situation' had been largely exaggerated, that the Jews were not being exterminated, but simply persecuted. Addy didn't know what to believe. And he found it infuriating that what little information he was able to find was usually tucked into the middle of a periodical, as if the editors themselves weren't quite sure whether the facts were true, as if the headline OVER 1,000,000 DEAD SINCE THE WAR BEGAN didn't belong on the front page. The fate of Europe's Jews, apparently, attracted little attention in Brazil. But for Addy, it was all he could think about.

He slips on his sunglasses and tucks a hand instinctively into his pocket to find his mother's handkerchief, rubbing the soft white linen between his fingers until his eyes are dry. He glances at his watch. He's due to meet Eliska for lunch in fifteen minutes.

Eliska had come to visit Minas once while he was there, but seeing her hadn't done anything to repair what's begun to feel like a broken relationship. Eliska had grown despondent when Addy told her how preoccupied he was, how he could think of nothing but his family. 'I wish I could understand what you're going through,' she'd said, and for the first time Addy had seen her cry. 'Addy . . . what if you never find your family? What then? How will you manage?' Addy had hated hearing those words and what they implied, had resented her for saying them, even though they were the same questions he asked of himself.

'I'll have you,' Addy had said softly, but his words fell flat. It was obvious now. Eliska knew as well as he did that as long as his family was missing, he would never be able to commit himself fully to building a life with her – to put his whole heart into loving her. Eliska's tears weren't for him, Addy realised; they were for herself. She'd already begun to envision a future without him.

At the end of the block, Addy approaches the outdoor tables of Café Campanha. He's early. Eliska isn't there yet. He takes a seat at an open table, wondering if the conversation that is about to ensue will lead to a called-off engagement – and if so, what that would mean for the two of them. Heavy-hearted, he pulls his leather notebook from his breast pocket. It's been months since he put notes to paper, but all the thoughts of his family and Eliska and what it meant to love and be loved have churned up a melody. He sketches a staff across the blank page before him and adds the familiar three-quarters time signature. This new piece, he decides as the first notes spill onto the paper, will be a slow waltz, in a minor key.

CHAPTER FORTY

Mila
Warsaw, German-Occupied Poland ~ January 1943

Edgar, who'd turned five the week before, skips beside Mila as she walks. His nose is running and pink from the cold. 'This is not the way to the park, Frau Kremski.' He says it like he's smarter than she.

'I know. We're making a stop on the way. It will only take a moment.' Having spent the past four months in Warsaw working for a family of Nazis, Mila has become fluent in German.

In the Bäcker home (which Mila learnt had belonged to a family of Jews who now, she presumed, lived in the Warsaw ghetto), Mila is known as Isa Kremski. Edgar's father is a high-ranking officer in the Gestapo. His mother, Gundula, is as lazy as the house cat, but what she lacks in productivity she makes up for in a hot temper and a raging sense of entitlement – a know-it-all with a propensity for slamming doors and squandering her husband's money. Mila's work is far from ideal, but it pays, and despite the fact that her heart breaks every day to be around a child that is not her own, she likes Edgar, as spoilt as he is, and the job is far better than her old one at the workshop in Wałowa. At least here in Warsaw, unlike in the ghetto, she has a small semblance of autonomy.

Mila spends her mornings wiping furniture with a damp cloth, scrubbing porcelain bathroom tiles, and preparing meals. In the afternoons she takes Edgar to the park. No matter the weather – frost or rain, sleet or snow – Gundula insists that her son spend an hour outside. And so every day, Mila and the boy walk the same route from the Bäckers' doorstep along Stępińska Street to the southern tip of Łazienki Park. Today, though, Mila has deviated a few blocks west to a street called Zbierska. It is a risk – she isn't sure yet how she'll convince Edgar to keep quiet about the detour – but Edith had told her to come during the day, and she desperately needs to see her.

Mila met Edith, a seamstress, soon after taking the job with the Bäckers. Edith visits the apartment weekly, to sew a tablecloth or tailor a dress for Frau Bäcker, a jacket for Herr Bäcker, a pair of knickers for Edgar. Yesterday when Gundula was out, Edith arrived as Mila was midway through polishing a drawerful of silver, and the pair struck up a conversation. They got on beautifully, speaking in hushed tones in their native Polish. Mila couldn't help but suspect that Edith was also a Jew posing as an Aryan, a hunch that was confirmed when Edith mentioned casually that she grew up just east of Okopowa Street – an area Mila recognised immediately as the Jewish quarter, now part of the city's ghetto. When Mila told her about Felicia, Edith mentioned a Catholic convent outside of town that might be accepting orphaned children. 'I could find out if there is room for one more,' she offered, but just as she said it, Gundula returned, and the women worked the rest of the afternoon in silence. Before she left that day, Edith slipped Mila her address, scrawled across a corner torn from one of the Bäckers' periodicals. 'I live just up the street,' she whispered, and then added, 'you'll need to visit in the early afternoon when my neighbours are at work – they are . . . watchful.'

Mila glances down at the small triangular piece of paper in her palm, checks the address: 4 ZBIERSKA.

'What kind of stop?' Edgar wants to know. 'I want to go to the park.'

'Your mother asked me to pay a visit to Edith, the seamstress,' Mila lies. 'You know her, you've seen her around the house. She measured you last week, for a shirt.'

'What for?'

'Never mind. It will only take a second.' Mila rings the button next to Edith's name, grateful that the seamstress had included a surname on the address, and after a moment Edith's voice chirps through a speaker.

'Who is there?' she asks in Polish.

Mila clears her throat. 'Edith, it is – it's Isa. I have Edgar with me. Please, could we come up for a moment?' A second later, the door buzzes and Mila and Edgar climb a narrow stairwell three floors to a door marked 3B.

Edith greets her with a smile. 'Hello, Isa. Edgar. Please, come in.' Edgar scowls as they step inside.

'I'm sorry to barge in on you unexpectedly,' Mila says. She glances at Edgar, wondering how much Polish he can understand, and looks back up at Edith. 'You mentioned a convent yesterday . . .'

Edith nods in understanding. 'Yes. It's in a town called Włocławek about eighty kilometres from here. I sent a letter today actually, to let them know there is a child in need. I'll tell you as soon as I hear back.'

'Thank you.' Mila breathes. 'I – very much appreciate the help.'

'Of course.'

Edgar tugs on Mila's skirt. 'Can we *go*? It's been a minute.'

'Yes, we can go. We're off to the park,' Mila adds, reverting to German as she turns to leave, trying to retain a semblance of levity in her voice.

'Thanks for the visit, Isa,' Edith offers. 'Stay warm out there.'

'We'll try.'

The moment she hangs her coat on the rack in the Bäckers' foyer the following day, Mila senses something is wrong. The apartment is stagnant, eerily quiet. Herr Bäcker would be at work by now, but on most days Mila arrives to Gundula puttering about, scribbling a list of chores, and to Edgar bouncing a ball or darting through the house engaged in some sort of imaginary battle, yelling, 'Pow! Pow! Pow!' his hands cocked like imaginary pistols. Today, though, the silence in the apartment sends a cold trickling through Mila's veins.

She shivers as she makes her way down a corridor to the living room. It's empty. She continues on toward the kitchen but stops short as she passes the dining room. There is a figure at the far end of the room, sitting motionless at the head of the table. Even from the hallway, Mila can see that Gundula is red in the cheeks, her eyes ablaze with anger. Fighting the instinct to leave as quickly as she'd come, Mila turns to face her but remains in the doorway.

'Frau Bäcker? Is everything all right?' she asks, her hands clasped together at her waist.

Gundula glares at her for a moment. When she speaks, her lips barely move. 'No, Isa, everything is not *all right*. Edgar told me you went to the seamstress's house yesterday, on the way to the park.'

Mila's breath catches. 'Yes, we did. I apologise, I should have told you.'

'Yes, you should have told me.' Gundula's voice is suddenly louder, and more stern than Mila has heard it before. 'What, pray tell, would prompt such a visit?'

Mila had guessed that Edgar might say something and had constructed an excuse in her mind.

'I asked her if she would come to my home later this week,' Mila begins, 'as I'm in dire need of a new skirt. I was embarrassed to tell you.' Mila looks down. 'I've been wearing this one for years, as I . . . I can't afford to buy a new one. Edith mentioned one day that she had some extra fabric she could sell for a fraction of what it would cost in a store.'

Gundula glowers at Mila, shaking her head slowly left to right. 'A *skirt*.'

'Yes, Madame.'

'Where *is* this skirt?'

'She's cutting it for me as we speak, said she would bring it next week.'

'I don't believe you.' What composure Gundula held a minute ago has begun to unravel.

'Excuse me?'

'You lie! I can see it in your eyes! You lie about the skirt, about your name, about *everything*!'

Edgar's face pokes through a doorway behind Gundula. '*Mutter?* What—'

'I told you to stay in your room,' Gundula snaps. 'Go!' Edgar disappears and Gundula's chair scrapes loudly against the wooden floor behind her as she stands. 'You take me for a fool, Isa – if that's even your name – is it?'

Mila lets her hands fall to her sides. 'Of course it's my name, Madame. And of course you are right to be angry about one thing, and that is the fact that I didn't tell you about our visit to the seamstress. For that I am truly sorry. But you are wrong to accuse me of lying about my identity. I'm offended you would say such a thing.'

As Gundula approaches, Mila notices a vein protruding like a purple snake from her neck and takes a step back, her instinct begging her once again to turn and run, to get out. But she holds her ground – running would only admit the truth.

Gundula is close enough for Mila to smell her breath, when she stops, balls up her hands into fists, and exhales, exasperated. It sounds like a growl. 'I told

Carty,' she spits. 'I told him you couldn't be trusted. Just wait until he has you arrested, just wait!'

Mila backs up slowly, into the corridor. 'Madame,' she says calmly, 'you are overreacting. Perhaps a glass of water would help. I will fetch you one.' As she turns to make her way to the kitchen, Mila catches something alarming in her periphery – the shadow of an object moving rapidly overhead. She ducks, but it's too late. The vase hits the back of her skull with the hollowed knock of two heavy objects colliding. At her feet, glass shatters.

Mila's world goes dark for a moment. The pain is searing. With her eyes closed, she reaches for the doorway, grateful when her fingers find it, catching herself. When she opens her eyes, she touches the back of her head with her free hand; a lump has formed on the spot where the vase struck her. She glances at her fingers. Amazingly, there is no blood. Just pain. *You should have run.*

'Oh my God. Oh my God.' Gundula is crying. 'Are you all right? *Ach mein Gott.*'

Regaining her balance, Mila steps gingerly from the mound of the broken glass at her feet and makes her way down the hallway to a closet to retrieve a broom. When she returns, Gundula is standing in the place where she left her, shaking her head, her eyes wild, like those of a crazed woman.

'I didn't mean to – I'm sorry,' she whimpers.

Mila doesn't reply. Instead, she sweeps. Gundula lowers herself to sit in a dining chair, muttering to herself.

When her dustpan is full, Mila carries it to the kitchen, empties the glass into a trash receptacle under the sink, and returns the dustpan to the closet. Reaching for the two empty milk jars on the counter, she holds one in each hand and retraces her steps, trying desperately to ignore the throb radiating from the back of her head to her eye sockets, the voice inside pleading with her to get out, and to get out fast. 'I'm going to the dairy,' she says, her voice calm, as she passes the doorway to the dining room. And as quietly as she'd come, she leaves, without any intention of returning.

CHAPTER FORTY-ONE

Bella
Warsaw, German-Occupied Poland ~ January 1943

They are a mother and daughter, Bella realises from behind the shop register as she studies the two German women perusing dresses. They have the same ivory skin and sharp curve to their jaws, the same way of carrying themselves, tilting their heads just so as they run their fingers along the dresses hanging in rows throughout the shop. Bella blinks away the tears filling her eyes.

'This one would look nice on you,' the girl says, holding a blue wool dress up to her mother's torso. 'The colour is just right for you. It complements your eyes.'

Bella and Jakob have been in Warsaw for six months. They'd thought for a moment about staying in Radom, but Radom was a small town compared with Warsaw, and they feared they would be recognised. There was no work to be had, anyway. Both ghettos had been liquidated, and only a few young workers remained. And Bella's parents, of course, were gone. They'd been deported with the others, as Ruben had warned, and it was no secret any more – if you were sent to Treblinka, you didn't come back.

And so, with no more guards manning the ghetto gates, Bella and Jakob had gathered up the few belongings that they could salvage from their empty flats, prayed that their IDs would serve them, and boarded a train to Warsaw, using all but a few of the zloty they'd stashed away for the fare.

At first, Bella had hoped that the change of scenery in Warsaw might help her shed some of her grief. But it seemed that everywhere she went, everywhere she looked, there were reminders. Three sisters, playing in the park. A father helping his little girl into a wagon. The mother–daughter pairs who frequented the shop where she worked. It was torture. For weeks, Bella couldn't sleep.

She couldn't think. She couldn't eat. Not that there was much to eat in the first place, but she found the thought of food repulsive and refused it. Her cheekbones grew more pronounced, and under her shirt, her ribs jutted from beneath her skin like a keyboard made up of only sharps and flats. It felt as if she were treading water with weights strapped to her wrists, as if at any moment she might drown. She was heartsick, and hated the way Jakob asked her, constantly, if she was all right, the way he was always trying to coax a bit of food into her mouth. 'Come back to me, love,' he would plead. 'You seem so far away.' But she couldn't. The only time she felt a semblance of her old self was when they made love, but even then the feeling didn't last. The touch of his skin against hers reminded her that she was alive – and the guilt that consumed her afterward was so powerful it made her sick.

Bella knew during those first few weeks in Warsaw that she couldn't live much longer chin-deep in a sea of sorrow. She wanted, badly, to feel herself again. To be a better person, a better wife. To accept what had happened. To move on. But losing her sister, and then her parents – it was crippling. Their deaths gnawed at her in her waking hours, and haunted her in her sleep. Every night, she would see her sister being dragged into the woods, she would see her parents boarding the trains that would deliver them to their deaths. Every night she dreamt of ways she could have helped them.

In November she began pinning the waistline of her skirt to keep it from falling from her hips. It was then that she realised she was in trouble, that Jakob was right. She needed to eat. To take care of herself. She needed him. She wondered, though, if it were too late. They'd been living apart for months – Jakob had said they were safer, their forged IDs more believable that way – but Bella knew there was part of him that couldn't stand by, futile, watching her deteriorate. How could she blame him? She'd been mourning so deeply she'd forgotten what it meant to love the man who, before her world came crashing down, was her everything. She vowed to try to pull herself together.

'We'll take it,' the mother says, laying the dress over the counter.

Bella takes a deep breath, willing away her tears. 'Of course,' she says.

Her German is now perfect. 'It's a nice choice.' She musters a smile. *Don't let her see that you are upset.* She hands the woman her change.

As the pair leaves, Bella closes her eyes, drained from the effort of keeping her composure. *There will always be reminders,* she thinks. *There will be days that are not so bad, and others that are unbearable.* What matters, she tells herself, is that even on the hardest days, when the grief is so heavy she can barely breathe, she must carry on. She must get up, get dressed, and go to work. She will take each day as it comes. She will keep moving.

CHAPTER FORTY-TWO

Mila and Felicia
Warsaw, German-Occupied Poland ~ February 1943

When her mother told her she had finally found a safe place for her to live – a *convent*, she called it – Felicia was dubious. 'You will have children around you,' Mila said, trying to cheer her up. 'Girls of all ages. And a nice group of nuns who will care for you. You won't have to be alone anymore.' Though Felicia was desperate for company, it was her mother's companionship she craved. She hated the fact that Mila would once again be leaving her. 'Will the others be like – like me?' she'd asked, wondering if, in fact, any of the girls in this place her mother spoke of would actually want to be her friend. They were Catholics, Mila said, explaining that while she was there, Felicia would be Catholic, too. Surely the other girls would want to be her friends. 'Just do as the nuns say, love,' she added, 'and I promise, they will take good care of you.'

On her first day at the convent, Felicia's cinnamon-red hair is dyed blonde. She is no longer Felicia Kajler; she is Barbara Cedransk. She is taught how to cross herself, and to take communion. A week into her stay, when one of the nuns notices her mouthing the words to her prayers, she drags Felicia into the office of the Mother Superior and questions her upbringing. Felicia is surprised to hear the conviction in the Mother Superior's voice as she snaps, 'I've known this child's family for a long time. We treat her like the rest.' In fact, malnourished as she is, Felicia is treated slightly *better* than the rest. The Mother Superior often sneaks Felicia a bite of cake when the others aren't watching, allows her a few extra minutes each day outdoors in the sun, and keeps a close watch during the children's free time, intervening when the older girls, who've deemed the skinny newcomer the runt of the group, hurl insults, or sticks.

* * *

Pulling her wool cap low over her brow, Mila strolls along the split-rail wooden fence of the convent's garden, trying to make out the faces of the children playing inside. She's allowed one visit per week, but this one is unscheduled. She can't help it. She hates being apart from her daughter. She scans the garden, trying to decipher which of the small bundled bodies is Felicia's. The children look alike in their dark winter coats and hats. They run and shout, their breath puffing in fleeting clouds from pink-lipped mouths as they play. Mila smiles. There's something about the sound of their laughter that fills her momentarily with hope. Finally, she notices a girl, slighter than the rest, standing still, staring in her direction.

Mila makes her way casually toward the fence, fighting the urge to wave, to jump the wooden beams, to gather her daughter up in her arms and sneak her back to Warsaw. Felicia approaches the fence, too, her chin cocked, curious as to why her mother has come – she keeps close track, and must realise it's too soon for her next scheduled visit. Mila smiles and nods gently. There's no reason to worry, she says with her eyes.

Felicia nods, too, in understanding. A stone's throw from her mother, she stops beside a bench, props her foot on it, and bends over, as if tying her shoelace. Upside down, her hat falls off and her bleached-blonde hair spills toward the earth, haloing her small, freckled face. She peers between her legs at her mother, and, knowing the others can't see, waves.

I love you, Mila mouths, and blows a kiss.

Felicia smiles, and returns the kiss. *I love you, too.*

Mila watches, blinking back tears, as Felicia stands, adjusts her hat on her head, and trots back to the other children.

CHAPTER FORTY-THREE

Genek
Tel Aviv, Palestine ~ February 1943

Genek's stomach pains are back. When they come – typically every thirty minutes or so at their worst – he doubles over, grimacing.

'What does it feel like?' Herta asked, when the pains first started, the winter before. 'Like someone's twisting up my intestines with a pitchfork,' he said. Herta had begged him to see a doctor, but Genek was reluctant to do so. He assumed that his digestive system just needed time to readjust to a somewhat normal diet. 'I'll be fine,' he insisted. And anyway, there were so many people in Tehran worse off than he, it was difficult to justify using up the one medic's precious time and resources.

But that was in Persia. Now they're in Palestine, where, under the care of the British Army, he and his Polish colleagues in Anders's Army have access to half a dozen medical tents, a host of supplies, and a team of doctors. Now, the pains are persistent – and have escalated to the degree that Genek wonders if an ulcer has eaten through his stomach lining. 'It's time,' Herta said, the day before, her tone filled less with pity than with frustration. 'Please, Genek, go see someone, before it's too late. Don't let something that could have been fixed bring you down now, after all that we've been through.'

He's seated at the edge of his cot, his toes grazing the ground beneath him, naked but for a white cotton gown that opens in the back. Behind him, a doctor presses the cool, round chest piece of a stethoscope to his ribs, making *hmm* sounds through his nose as Genek answers each of his questions.

'Lie down,' the doctor instructs. Genek swings his legs onto his cot and leans back, wincing as the doctor's fingers press into the pale flesh of his stomach.

'My guess is you've got an ulcer,' he says. 'Stay away from citrus, and anything acidic. No more oranges or lemons. Try to eat only mild foods. I have some medicine, too, to help neutralise you. Let's start there, and we'll see how you're doing in a week.'

'All right,' Genek nods.

The doctor adjusts his stethoscope around his neck and tucks his pen into the breast pocket of his lab coat. 'I'll be back,' he says. 'Stay put.'

Genek watches him disappear. The last time he was made to wear a hospital gown was at fourteen, when he had his tonsils removed. He doesn't remember much of the surgery, except for the constant supply of freshly pressed apple juice he enjoyed afterward, along with a week's worth of doting from his mother. A wave of longing. What he would do right now, to see his mother. It's been three and a half years since he left home.

Home. He thinks about how far he's travelled in the last forty-two months. About his apartment in Lvov and the night the NKVD came pounding on his door; how he'd packed a suitcase, somehow knowing when they left that they wouldn't return. He thinks of the cattle cars to which he's been confined for weeks on end – dark and dank and riddled with disease, and of his barracks in Siberia and the ice-cold night Józef was born. He thinks about all the corpses he'd seen on his exodus from Siberia, through Kazakhstan, Uzbekistan, and Turkmenistan to Persia, about the military camp he called home for four months in Tehran, and about the trip from Tehran to Tel Aviv and how, as their truck had snaked along the narrow roads of the Zagros mountain range, he'd contemplated the very real possibility of careening 1,500 metres to the valley floor. He thinks of Palestine's beautiful beaches, and of how much he will miss them when he's shipped off to battle; there has been much talk of late, of Anders's Army being sent to Europe to fight on the Italian front.

His true *home,* of course, will always be Radom. That he knows. He crosses his ankles and closes his eyes, and in an instant his mind has left the medical tent and arrived at a scene he knows well – a family gathering on Warszawska Street, in the apartment where he grew up. He's in the living room, seated on a blue velvet couch beneath the portrait of his great-grandfather Gerszon, for whom he was named. Herta nurses Józef beside him. Addy is at the Steinway playing an improvised version of Cole Porter's 'Anything Goes'. Halina and Adam dance. Mila and Nechuma chat by the walnut mantle over the fireplace, watching, laughing, as Sol twirls Felicia in the air. In the corner, Jakob stands on a chair, taking in the spectacle through the lens of his Rolleiflex.

Genek would do anything to relive an evening of dinner and music at home in prewar Radom. But as quickly as the scene in his parents' living room entered his mind, a new thought arises, another memory. His gut tightens, sending a shock of pain through his abdomen, as he recalls the conversation he'd overheard as he passed by the captain's quarters earlier that week: 'It has to be an exaggeration,' one of the captains had said. 'Over a million?' 'Someone said two,' another voice replied. 'They've liquidated hundreds of camps and ghettos.' 'What sick fucking bastards,' the first voice replied. It was quiet for a moment, and Genek had to fight the instinct to claw his way inside, to demand more information. But he knew better. The panic in his eyes might give him away – he was supposed to be Catholic, after all. But *millions*? Surely they were talking about Jews. His mother, his father, his sisters and little niece – last he knew, they were all in the ghetto. Aunts and uncles and cousins, too. He's written home a dozen times but hasn't received a reply. *Please,* he prays, *let the numbers be an exaggeration. Let the family be safe. Please.*

With a lump in his throat, Genek reminds himself that he should be grateful, he is with Herta and Józef. They are together and, for the most part, in good health. Who knows how long they'll stay, but for now he is lucky to make Tel Aviv his home. The city, perched on the white sand and palm-fringed banks of the blue-green Mediterranean, is more beautiful than any he's ever seen. Even the *air* is pleasant, somehow smelling always of sweet oranges and oleander. Herta had summed it up in one word on the day they arrived: 'Paradise.'

The din of the medical tent filters back into Genek's consciousness – the murmur of voices, the groan of canvas stretching as his neighbour rolls to his side, the clang of a chamber pot being replaced beneath a cot – and as he comes to, something draws his attention. A voice. One he recognises. One from a previous life. A voice that reminds him of home. His real home. He opens his eyes.

Most of the patients in the tent are asleep or reading. A few talk quietly with doctors beside them. Genek scans the room, listening intently. The voice is gone. He's imagined it – part of him is still stuck in his memory of Radom. But then he hears it again, and this time he sits up. *There,* he realises, looking over his shoulder – it's coming from a doctor standing with his back to him, three beds down. Genek swings his legs over his cot, intrigued. The doctor is a head shorter than Genek, with stick-straight posture and dark hair shorn close to his scalp. Genek stares until finally he turns, peering through perfectly round eyeglasses as he scribbles something on his clipboard. Genek recognises him immediately. His heart vaults into his throat as he stands.

'Hey!' Genek yells. The two dozen men, half a dozen doctors, and handful of nurses in the tent stop what they're doing for a moment to look in Genek's direction. He yells again, 'Hey, Selim!'

The doctor looks up from his clipboard, surveying the room until finally his gaze lands on Genek. He blinks, shakes his head.

'Genek?'

Genek leaps from his cot, oblivious to his half-exposed backside, and rushes toward his brother-in-law. 'Selim!'

'What . . .' Selim stammers, 'what are you doing here?'

Genek, too overcome to speak, wraps his arms around Selim's torso, nearly lifting him from the floor in his embrace. The others in the medical tent watch for a moment, smiling. A few of the nurses to Genek's exposed rear exchange glances and suppress giggles before going back to their business.

'You have no idea how happy I am to see you, brother,' Genek says, shaking his head.

Selim smiles. 'It's really good to see you, too.'

'You disappeared in Lvov. We thought we'd lost you. What happened? Wait, Selim –' Genek holds him at arm's length, studying his face. 'Tell me, have you heard from the family?' Seeing his brother-in-law has ignited something in Genek – a mix of hope and longing. Perhaps this is a good sign. Perhaps if Selim is alive, the others are, too.

Selim's shoulders drop and Genek lets his hands fall to his sides. 'I was going to ask you the same,' Selim says. 'They shipped me off to Kazakhstan, wouldn't let me write from the camp. What letters I've sent since have gone unanswered.'

Genek lowers his voice so the others in the tent won't overhear. 'Mine, too,' he says softly, deflating. 'The last I heard from anyone was just before Herta and I were arrested in Lvov. That was almost two years ago. Back then, Mila was in Radom, living in the ghetto with my parents.'

'The *ghetto*,' Selim whispers. His face has gone white.

'It's hard to imagine, I know.'

'They've – they've been liquidating the ghettos, have you heard?'

'I've heard,' Genek says. The men are quiet for a moment.

'I keep telling myself over and over they're fine,' Genek adds, looking up to the tent's rafters, as if searching for answers. 'But I wish I knew for sure.' He lowers his eyes to meet Selim's. 'It's terrible, not knowing.'

Selim nods.

'I think about Felicia often,' Genek says, realising he hasn't told his brother-in-law yet about Józef. 'She must be – three now?'

'Four.' Selim's voice is distant.

'Selim,' Genek starts. He pauses, licks his lips, embarrassed at his riches when, for all either of them knows, Selim might have lost everyone. 'Herta and I have a son. He was born in Siberia. He'll be one year old in March.'

Selim looks pleased. He smiles. 'Mazel tov, brother,' he says. 'What's his name?'

'Józef. We call him Ze for short . . .'

The two men stare at their feet for a while, unsure of what to say next. 'What was the name of your camp in Kazakhstan?' Genek finally asks.

'Dolinka. I was a medic there, and for the nearby town.'

Genek nods, struck by the notion that it took an internment camp, an amnesty, and an army to enable Selim to practise the profession he'd been denied in Radom. 'Wish we'd had a couple medics like you at our camp,' he says, shaking his head.

'Where were you?'

'I have no idea, to be honest. The nearest town to us was called Altynay. A total shitscape. Only good thing that came of it was Ze.'

Selim scans Genek's lithe frame, quizzical. 'Are you feeling all right?'

'Oh. Yes, fine – just my stomach, is all. Altynay ruined me. Goddamned Soviets. Doc thinks it's an ulcer.'

'I've been treating quite a few of those. If you're not better soon, let me know. I'll see what I can do to help.'

'Thanks.'

A patient calls from across the room, and Selim motions with his clipboard. 'I'd better get going.'

Genek nods. 'Of course.' But as Selim turns, something occurs to Genek and he reaches for his brother-in-law's shoulder again. 'Wait, Selim, before you go,' he says, 'I've been thinking I should start writing to the Red Cross, now that I'm traceable through the army.' Genek's friend Otto had just been able to connect with his brother this way, and Genek couldn't help but wonder whether he might have similar luck. 'Perhaps we could go together, fill out some forms, send some telegrams.'

Selim nods. 'It's worth a try,' he offers.

They make a plan to meet in a few days at the Red Cross office in Tel Aviv. Selim tucks his clipboard under his arm and turns once again to go.

'Selim,' Genek says, allowing a smile to stretch across his cheeks. 'It's really great to see you.'

Selim returns the smile. 'You, too, Genek. I'll see you on Sunday. I'm looking forward to meeting your son.'

Genek shakes his head as he makes his way back to his cot. *Selim – in Palestine of all places. It's a good sign, it has to be.* He won't limit his Red Cross search to Poland, Genek decides. He'll send telegrams to Red Cross offices all over Europe, to the Middle East, and to the Americas. Surely, if the others are alive, they'll have been in touch with the location services as well.

He climbs back onto his cot and lies down, resting one hand on his heart, the other on his stomach, where, for the moment, the pain has subsided.

APRIL 19-MAY 16, 1943 – WARSAW GHETTO UPRISING: *In liquidating the Warsaw ghetto, Hitler deports and exterminates some 300,000 Jews. The 50,000 who remain secretly plan an armed retaliation. The uprising begins on the eve of Passover at the outset of a final liquidation operation; ghetto residents refuse to be taken and fight off the Germans for nearly a month until defeated by the Nazis systematic destruction and burning of the ghetto. Thousands of Jews die in combat and are burnt alive or suffocated; those who survive the uprising are sent to Treblinka and other extermination camps.*

SEPTEMBER 1943: *Anders's men stationed in Tel Aviv are mobilised and sent to Europe to fight on the Italian front; wives and children stay behind in Tel Aviv.*

CHAPTER FORTY-FOUR

Halina
Warsaw, German-Occupied Poland ~ October 1943

'Sit,' the officer hisses, pointing to a metal chair opposite his desk in the small railway police office.

Halina presses her lips together into an angry line. She's more confident when she stands.

'I said, *sit.*'

Halina obeys. Seated, she's eye-to-barrel with the pistol holstered to the German's belt.

It's only a matter of time, she realises, before her luck runs out.

Leaving her apartment in Warsaw's centre that morning, she'd kissed Adam goodbye and reminded him she wouldn't be returning until late. Her plan was to make her way to the train station after work, ride to Wilanów, then walk the four kilometres from the station to the Górskis' home in the country, where she would see her parents and deliver the Górskis their payment for the month of October. She'd stay for an hour and then return to Warsaw. She's made the trip to Wilanów three times already, and until now, her false papers, required to purchase tickets and to board and disembark the train, have worked flawlessly.

Today, though, she'd barely made it through ticketing at the Warsaw station. She was waiting by the tracks when a member of the Gestapo, Hitler's secret police, approached her, demanding her papers. 'Why do you need to see them?' she asked in Polish (she's fluent now in German, but the Gestapo, she's learnt, are suspicious of German-speaking Poles).

'Routine check,' he'd replied. He studied her ID and quizzed her on her name and birth date.

'Brzoza,' Halina had recited with conviction. 'April 17, 1917.' But the officer shook his head as the train approached. 'You're coming with me,' he said, leading Halina by the arm through the station.

'Who do you work for?' the officer wants to know. He remains standing.

Halina met her new employer, Herr Den, only two weeks earlier. He'd attended a dinner party at the home of her previous boss, where she worked as a maid and kitchen helper. Den is Austrian – a successful banker, in his sixties. Halina recalls the night she first served him dinner, how he'd watched her closely as she worked. Apparently he was impressed, which was no surprise – Halina had grown up in a home with a cook and a maid; she had an appreciation for good service. Later that same night, Den had surprised her. She was at the kitchen sink when he approached; she didn't realise he was even in the room until he was beside her.

'Chopin?' he'd asked, catching her off guard.

'Excuse me?' she'd said.

'The melody you were just humming, was it Chopin?' Halina hadn't even realised she was humming. 'Yes,' she'd nodded. 'I suppose it was.'

Den had smiled. 'You have lovely taste in music,' he said, before turning to go. The next day, she received notice from her placement agency that she would begin working for Den the following week. Whether or not he suspects she is Jewish, Halina has no idea. So far, he seems to like her.

'I work for Herr Gerard Den,' Halina says, sighing as if put off by the question.

'What is his occupation?'

'Head of the Austrian Bank in Warsaw.'

'What sort of work do you do?'

'I am his housemaid.'

'What is his telephone?'

Halina recites the bank's phone number from memory and waits as the officer dials. Damn these routine checks. Damn the Gestapo. Damn the Poles, who are constantly taking it upon themselves to tip off the Germans, rat out the Jews. For what? A kilo of sugar? Friendship means nothing any more. She knew it in Radom, the day her school friend Sylvia refused to acknowledge her when she passed by on her way to the beetfarm – and she was reminded of it often here in Warsaw, where she's been accused on several occasions of being Jewish.

It wasn't just the suspicious landlady. There was the friend of her old boss, a German woman who followed her down the street one day and whispered a spiteful 'I know your secret!' as she came shoulder to shoulder with Halina on the sidewalk. Without thinking Halina had pulled her into an alleyway, stuffed a week's worth of pay into her palm, and told her through clenched teeth to keep her mouth shut – this before she realised it was safer never to confess to anyone. Shortly after, worried that if she didn't keep bribing her, the woman might reveal her identity to her boss, she found a new job.

There was also the Wehrmacht soldier who recognised Halina from Lvov, from before she'd taken on her new name. She'd opted for a softer approach to feeling him out, and invited him for an espresso at a Nazi-run cafe on Piękna Street. She'd turned up the charm as she chatted for a full hour, at the end of which the soldier seemed more smitten than curious about her previous life; she left him with a kiss on a cheek and an intuitive feeling that even if he *did* remember her true identity, he'd keep it under wraps.

Of course, there was nothing she could do about the Poles she overheard on Chłodna Street the day in May when the SS finally razed the city ghetto and liquidated the last of its inhabitants in a last-ditch effort to quell an uprising. 'Hey look, the Jews are burning,' one of the Poles had said when Halina passed. 'They had it coming,' another professed. It was all Halina could do not to seize the men by the lapels and shake them. She'd nearly forfeited her Aryan identity that day, to fight alongside the Jews in the uprising. To play a part, no matter how doomed the effort was, in standing up to the Germans. She'd reminded herself at the time that she had her parents to think of. Her sister. She had to keep herself safe in order to keep her family safe. And so she'd watched from afar as the ghetto burnt, her heart filled with sorrow and hatred but also with pride – never before had she witnessed such a valiant act of self-defence.

The officer holds the receiver to his ear and glares at her. She returns the glare, defiant, outraged. After a minute, someone at the other end answers.

'I wish to speak with a Herr Den, please,' the officer says. There is a long pause, then another voice at the other end of the line. 'Herr Den. I apologise for bothering you. I have someone here at the station who claims to work for you – and I have reason to believe she is not who she says she is.' Silence. Halina holds her breath. She focuses on her posture: shoulders down, back straight, knees and feet pressed tightly together. 'She claims her name is *Brzoza* – B-R-Z-O-Z-A.' The line is quiet. Has Den hung up? What's her backup plan? She hears a murmur, her boss's voice, but she can't make out the words. Whatever he's saying, his tone is angry.

The reception must be poor because the officer slows his speech to enunciate every word. 'Her-papers-state-she-is-a- *Christian*.' Den is talking again. Louder now. The officer holds the phone a fist-width from his ear, scowling, until the barking ceases. Halina catches a few words: 'Ashamed . . . certain . . . myself.'

'You are *sure*. All right, all right, no, don't come in. That won't be necessary. I – yes, I understand, we will, sir, right away. I apologise again for bothering you.' The officer slams the phone into its base.

Halina exhales. Standing, she thrusts a palm over the desk. 'My papers,' she says with disgust. The officer frowns as he slides her ID across the table. Halina snatches it up. 'Outrageous,' she spits softly, just loud enough for the officer to hear, before turning to leave.

JANUARY–MARCH 1944: *The Allies, in an effort to secure a route to Rome, begin a series of unsuccessful attacks on the German stronghold of Monte Cassino, located in the Lazio region of central Italy.*

CHAPTER FORTY-FIVE

Genek
River Sangro, Central Italy ~ April 1944

'This'd better be good,' Otto says, leaning back in his chair, crossing his arms over his chest. Genek nods, suppressing the urge to yawn. Between the persistent lull of rain and the pea *grochówka* filling his stomach – this particular batch was so heavy his spoon had stuck straight up in the bowl, like a flagpole – he's nearing a comatose state. At the front of the mess tent, their commanding officer, Pawlak, climbs onto a metre-high wooden platform, a podium of sorts, from which he delivers his speeches. His expression is serious.

'Looks like he means business tonight,' Genek remarks as conversation beneath the tent fades and eyes turn toward the square-shouldered captain standing before them.

'You said that last time. And the time before that,' Otto huffs, shaking his head.

Genek and Otto, along with the rest of Anders's 40,000-odd recruits, have been holed up for the month of April on the banks of Italy's River Sangro. Their position, as Pawlak showed them on the map when they arrived, is strategic – a two-day trek from Monte Cassino, a German stronghold 120 kilometres south-east of Rome. The Cassino is a 1,400-year-old rock-walled monastery towering 520 metres above sea level – but more important, it's the hub of the Nazis' line of defence. The Germans occupying it are using it as a vantage point to spot and shoot down anyone who approaches. Allied forces have made three separate attempts on it – so far, it's proved impregnable.

'Maybe tonight's news will be different,' Genek offers. Otto rolls his eyes.

Despite Otto's complaining, Genek is grateful to have his friend by his side. He's been the one constant since they left Herta, Józef, and Otto's wife, Julia, behind in Tel Aviv to travel with the army through Egypt and across the

Mediterranean by British ship to Italy. They'd only ever fired practice shots from their tommy guns, of course, but the men understood without actually verbalising it that when the orders finally came and they found themselves aiming at real targets, they'd look out for each other, and for one another's families, should anything happen to either of them in the field.

'Gentlemen!' Pawlak calls. The men of the Polish Army's First Survey Brigade sit at attention. 'Listen up! I have news. Orders. Finally, what we've all been waiting for.'

Otto's eyebrows jump. He glances at Genek. *You were right,* he mouths, and smiles. Genek uncrosses his legs, leans forward in his chair, his senses suddenly heightened.

Pawlak clears his throat. 'Allied forces and President Roosevelt have met to discuss a fourth massive offensive on Monte Cassino,' he begins. 'The first phase of the plan – code name Operation DIADEM – calls for large-scale deception, targeted at Field Marshal Kesselring. The goal: to convince Kesselring that the Allies have *abandoned* further attacks on Monastery Hill, and that our mission is now to land at Civitavecchia.'

Genek and Otto have been briefed in detail about the three previous attacks on Monte Cassino, each a bitter, bloody failure. The first came in January, when the British and the French attempted to flank the monastery from the west and the east, respectively, while the French Expeditionary Corps fought in ice and snow against the Germans of the Fifth Mountain Division in the north. But the Brits and the French met heavy mortar fire, and the frostbitten fighters in the Expeditionary Corps, though close to victory, were finally outnumbered. A second attempt came in February, when hundreds of Allied fighter planes dropped round after round of 450-kilo bombs on Cassino, reducing the monastery to rubble. The New Zealand Corps was set to occupy the ruins, but the steep terrain leading up to it was impossible to manoeuvre, and German parachuters reached the now-roofless monument first. A month later, in a third Allied attempt on Monte Cassino, the New Zealand Corps dropped 1,250 tons of explosives over Cassino, flattening the town and stretching the German defence to a breaking point. A division of Indian troops came close to securing the monastery, but after nine days of being pummelled by mortar bombs, Nebelwerfer rockets, and smoke shells, the Allies were once again forced to retreat.

Genek runs the numbers in his mind. Three failed attempts. Thousands of casualties. What makes their commanding officer believe that a fourth attempt will be successful?

'Diversionary tactics,' Pawlak shouts, 'include code messages meant to be intercepted by German intelligence, and Allied troops dispatched to Salerno and Naples to be seen "practising"' – he rabbit-ears his fingers around the word – 'amphibious landings. They also include Allied air forces making conspicuous reconnaissance flights over the beaches at Civitavecchia and false information fed to German spies. These tactics are key to the success of the mission.'

Pawlak's men nod, collectively holding their breath as they await the news that matters most: their orders. Pawlak clears his throat. Rain patters on the waxed canvas overhead.

'In this fourth attempt on Monte Cassino,' Pawlak says, his voice lower than before, 'thirteen divisions have been assigned orders, with the goal of securing Cassino's perimeter. The US II Corps will attack from the west up the coast along the line of Route 7 toward Rome; the French Expeditionary Corps will attempt to scale the Aurunci Mountains to the east; in between, the British XIII Corps will attack along the Liri valley. Anders's Army, however, has been assigned what I believe to be the most critical task of the mission.' He pauses, looks around at his men. They are silent, listening intently, their spines rifle-barrel straight, jaws locked. Pawlak enunciates each of his words carefully. 'Gentlemen, we – the men of the Polish II Corps – have been charged with the task of capturing Monastery Hill.'

The words hit Genek like a punch to the oesophagus, leaving him breathless.

'We will attempt what the Fourth Indian Division in February failed to do: to isolate the monastery and push around behind it into the Liri valley. There we will link with XIII Corps. Canadian I Corps will be held in reserve to exploit the breakthrough. If we are successful,' Pawlak adds, 'we will penetrate the Gustav line and pinch out the position of the German Tenth Army. We'll open up the road to Rome.'

A murmur fills the tent as the recruits process the momentousness of their mission. Genek and Otto look at one another.

'I have complete faith in this army,' Pawlak continues, nodding. 'This is *Anders's* moment in history. This is *Poland's* moment to shine. Together, we will make our country *proud!* ' He raises his first two fingers to his cap and the tent erupts as men leap from their chairs, cheering, pumping their fists, saluting, yelling. *'This is our time! Our moment to shine! God save Poland!'* they shout. Genek follows suit and stands, although he can't bring himself to partake in the revelry. His knees are soft and his stomach churns, threatening to disgorge his dinner.

As the men settle back into their seats, Pawlak explains that the French Expeditionary Corps has already begun secretly constructing camouflaged bridges over the River Rapido, which Anders's Army will need to cross in order to reach the monastery. 'So far, the bridges have gone unnoticed,' he explains. 'As soon as the last is complete, we'll leave our position here and move east to a location along the Rapido. To maintain secrecy, we'll travel in small units by night, under strict radio silence. Pack your things, gentlemen, and prepare yourselves for battle. Our orders to move will come at any moment.'

Sitting cross-legged in his pup tent, Genek rolls his spare socks and undershirt into tight, damp bundles and stuffs them into the bottom of his pack. He adjusts his headlamp, Pawlak's words clattering about in his mind. It's happening – he's going to battle. How will the mission unfold? There's no telling, of course – and it's the unknown that scares him the most – even more so than the thought of climbing up a 520-metre hill toward an army of Germans with weapons trained at him from behind a fortress of stone.

What Genek *does* know is that the Poles are one of some *twenty* Allied divisions, among them American, Canadian, French, British, New Zealander, South African, Moroccan, Indian, and Algerian, positioned along the thirty-kilometre stretch from Cassino to the Gulf of Gaeta. Why would the Allies assign the *Poles*, of all armies, what one might call the most daunting task of all? Why choose the men who have come not from elite training camps but from labour camps – men who required nearly a year of rest and recuperation in the Middle East before their leader deemed them fit enough to fight? It doesn't make any sense. For the world to have that much faith in Anders's Army is an aberration as much as it is an honour. And then of course there is the notion

Genek refuses to believe – that the ragtag group of Poles is so devoid of value, they're best put to use as cannon fodder on what is surely a suicide mission. No, Genek reminds himself, they have been chosen for a reason; they are Poles and what they lack in preparedness they will make up for in fervour.

He slips a pair of woollen undergarments and gloves into his pack along with a journal and his deck of cards. Eyeing a worn copy of Jasieński's *I Burn Paris* beside his mat, he pulls a spare piece of army-issued letterhead from the inside cover and reaches to his breast pocket for a pen. Taking a break from packing, he lies on his side, setting the blank page on the book's cover.

Dearest Herta, he writes, and then pauses. He'd feel better if he could tell her about his mission – his first: to capture the Cassino! The linchpin of German defence! He tries to picture himself in battle, but the image feels surreal, like a scene out of a film. Would she be impressed to learn of his orders? To know he was about to be part of something so noble? So monumental? Or at least something that had the *potential* to be monumental? Or would she be terrified, as he is, by the enormity of the task at hand – by the prospect of finding himself in the wrong place at the wrong time? She would be terrified, Genek knows. She would beg him to be safe. But Herta will never know, Genek reminds himself. He's been forbidden to put anything to paper that would, if intercepted, offer a clue of their plan. So instead he writes:

How is Tel Aviv? Sunny, I hope. We are here still on Italian soil. The rain is relentless. My tent, my clothes, everything is perpetually damp – I can't remember what it feels like to pull on a dry shirt. Without much to do but take cover and wait, I've spent hours playing cards and reading and rereading the handful of books passed around – Strug, Jasieński, Stern, Wat. There's a work of poetry by Leśmian which you would enjoy, called 'Forest Happenings'. You might look for a copy.

Genek listens to the drum of raindrops on the A-frame of his tent, thinking of the weekend in the mountains when he first laid eyes on Herta. He pictures himself in his white cable-knit sweater and English tweed pants, Herta close by his side in her smart goosedown ski jacket, her cheeks pink from the cold, her hair freshly washed and smelling of lavender. How surreal it felt now, looking back on it – as if he'd dreamt it.

Despite the rain, he continues, *morale here is surprisingly high. Even Wojtek seems to be in good spirits, lumbering happily around camp in search of handouts. You should see how big he's grown.*

Private Wojtek, the only official four-legged member of Anders's Army, is a bear. He was discovered in Iran as an orphaned cub. *Wojtek,* Polish for 'smiling warrior,' is now the unofficial mascot for the Polish II Corps. He's travelled with the army from Iran, through Iraq, Syria, Palestine, and Egypt, and finally to Italy. Along the way, he's learnt to haul ammunition and to salute when greeted; he enjoys a good boxing match, and he nods in approval when rewarded with a bottle of beer or a cigarette, both of which he eagerly devours. Understandably so, Wojtek is easily the most popular member of the Polish II Corps.

Genek rolls onto his stomach, reads what he's written. Will his wife see through it? Herta knows him well enough to sense when he's hiding something. He flips to the back of *I Burn Paris* and retrieves a photo. In it, Herta, perched on a low stone wall in Tel Aviv, wears a new grey collared dress. He's standing beside her in his army attire. He remembers when Otto took the photo. Julia had held Józef while Otto counted to three, and just before he snapped the picture, Herta had looped her arm through Genek's, leant into him, and flipped her toe playfully, like a school girl on a date.

He misses her – more than he knew was humanly possible. Józef, too.

I'm not sure when I'll be able to write next. We'll be restationed soon. I'll be in touch as soon as I can – please don't worry.

Of course Herta will worry, Genek thinks, regretting his word choice. *He's* worried. Petrified. He chews on the end of his pen. Three failures. An army of ex-prisoners. The odds aren't in the Polish II Corps's favour.

How are you? he concludes. *How is Ze? Reply soon. I love you and miss you more than you can imagine. Yours, Genek*

CHAPTER FORTY-SIX

Addy
Rio de Janeiro, Brazil ~ April 1944

On the night Addy returned from Minas Gerais, he and Eliska ended their engagement. They weren't meant to be married, they agreed. It wasn't easy – neither of them wanted to be alone, nor did they want to be seen as people who would voluntarily give up, even though they both knew that giving up, in this case, was for the best. They would remain friends, they said. And as hard as it was, Addy felt a thousand kilos lighter on his feet, once the decision was made.

Madame Lowbeer, of course, was thrilled to learn that the engagement had been called off, and shortly after, in an ironic twist, she took a new liking to Addy. Apparently with the prospect of having him as a son-in-law officially erased, the Grande Dame was capable of socialising with a Pole. She'd begun inviting Addy to her apartment on the weekends to play the piano and requesting his handyman help when her radio malfunctioned. She'd even offered to put him in touch with a contact at General Electric in the States, should he ever decide to emigrate north.

Addy spent the months following the breakup focusing on his work, on his weekly trips to the post office, and on the radio broadcasts and periodicals that brought him news of the war. None of it was encouraging. The constant battling in Anzio and Monte Cassino, Italy; the bombs dropped in the South Pacific and over Germany – Addy was sickened by all of it. The only auspicious bit of information he stumbled across was that of American president Franklin Roosevelt issuing an executive order to create a War Refugee Board, which would be responsible for 'rescuing victims of enemy oppression in imminent danger of death,' as the article phrased it. At least someone somewhere was helping, Addy thought, wondering what the chances were of his parents, brothers, and sisters being among the rescued.

Addy's spirits were particularly low when his friend Jonathan knocked on the door to his apartment in Copacabana. 'I'm throwing a party next weekend,' Jonathan said in his smart British accent. 'You're coming. If I recall, your birthday is right around the corner. You've been hibernating long enough.' Addy waved his hand in protest, but before he could decline the invitation, Jonathan added, 'I've invited the embassy girls,' flashing a smile that said, *You could use a date, brother.* Addy had heard plenty about the American embassy girls – amid Rio's small circle of expats they were rather famous for their good looks and adventurous spirits – but he'd never met any of them. 'I mean it. You should come,' Jonathan pressed. 'Just for a drink. It'll be fun.'

On Saturday evening Addy stands in the corner of Jonathan's Ipanema flat nursing a *cachaça* and water, slipping in and out of conversation. He's distracted by thoughts of home. In two days, he will turn thirty-one. Halina, wherever she is, will be twenty-seven. It will have been six years since they celebrated together. Addy recalls how, for that last birthday, his twenty-fifth, he and Halina had spent the evening at one of Radom's new clubs, where they'd drunk too much champagne and danced until their feet hurt. He's sifted through the details of the night a thousand times, rolling them over in his mind to keep them sharp: the tangy aftertaste of the lemon chiffon cake they'd shared; the way his sister's hands had felt in his as they danced; the thrilling *pop* of their second bottle of Ruinart being uncorked, how the bubbles had burnt his throat and, a few sips later, made his tongue go numb. Pesach had been the night before. The family had celebrated in the usual boisterous fashion, gathered first at the dining table and then around the piano in the living room on Warszawska Street.

Addy swirls his drink, watching a single ice cube orbit the glass, wondering if Halina is somewhere thinking about him, too.

When he looks up his eyes are drawn to a figure across the room. A brunette. She stands by the window with a wine glass in hand, listening to a friend – a single point of calm amid the cacophony. An embassy girl? Must be. Suddenly everyone else in the room is invisible. Addy studies the young woman's tall, slender frame, the graceful slope of her cheekbones, her easy smile. She wears a pale green cotton halter dress that buttons down the front and ties at the waist, a watch with a simple band, brown leather sandals with thin straps that wrap loosely around the fine bones of her ankles. Her eyes are soft, her expression open, as if she has nothing to hide. She is beautiful – strikingly so – but in an unassuming way. Even from afar he can sense her modesty.

What the hell, he decides. Maybe Jonathan was right. With a disconcerting jitter in his gut, Addy sets his glass down and makes his way across the room. As he approaches, the girl turns. He offers her his hand.

'Addy,' he says, and then in the same breath, 'Please excuse my English.'

The brunette smiles. 'Pleasure to meet you,' she says, taking his hand. Addy was right – she is definitely American. 'I'm Caroline. Don't apologise, your English is lovely.' She speaks slowly, and the way she pronounces her words, soft and round so he can't quite tell where one ends and the next begins, makes Addy feel at home beside her. This woman, Addy realises, emanates an air of acceptance and ease – she is perfectly content, it seems, to simply be. Something stirs in Addy's heart as he realises he was once that way.

Caroline is patient with Addy's broken English. When he stumbles over a word, she waits for him to gather his thoughts, to try again, and Addy is reminded that it's okay to slow down, to take his time. When he asks where in the States she is from, she tells him about the town in South Carolina where she was born. 'I loved growing up there,' Caroline says. 'Clinton was a close-knit community, and we were always very involved with the schools and the church . . . but I think I always knew I wouldn't stay. I just – I had to get out. It started to feel so small. My poor mother.' Caroline sighs, describing her mother's shock upon hearing that she and her best friend, Virginia, had made plans to travel to South America. 'She thought we were crazy to up and leave our lives in South Carolina.'

Addy nods, smiling. 'You are – how do you say . . . you have no fear.'

'I suppose you could say we were brave for coming here. I think, though, we were just after an adventure.'

'My father leave his home in Poland, too,' he says. 'For America. For adventure. When he was young man. No children. He always tell me how much I will love New York City.'

'Why did he return?' Caroline asks.

'For helping his mother,' Addy says. 'After his father die, she care for five children in the home, all alone. My father want to help.'

Caroline smiles. 'He sounds like a good man, your father.'

Their conversation ends when a friend Caroline introduces as Virginia, who goes by Ginna, finally pulls her away. They are headed to another party, Ginna says, winking a blue eye at Addy as she links elbows with Caroline. Addy watches the backs of the women's heads as they bob toward the door, wishing the conversation hadn't ended so quickly.

He leaves shortly after, offering Jonathan a friendly slap on the back on his way out. 'Thank you, *amigo*,' he says. 'I'm glad I came.'

He thinks of Caroline on his walk home, and nearly every minute for the next week. There was something about her that made him want, badly, to get to know her better. And so, after tracking down her address in Leme, he musters the courage to leave a note under her door, written with the help of a newly purchased French/English dictionary.

Dear Caroline,

I enjoyed to speak with you last weekend. If you will be so obliged it would please me to take you to dine at the restaurant Belmond, near Hotel Copacabana Palace. I proposition we meet at the Palace for an aperitif at eight o'clock this Saturday, April the 29th – I hope to see you there.

Yours, Addy Kurc

A few days later, wearing a freshly pressed shirt and carrying a purple orchid he'd picked up at a flower stand along the way, Addy arrives at the Copacabana Palace, the same flutter tickling at his insides that he'd felt when he and Caroline first met. He's checking the time – eight o'clock to the minute – when Caroline steps through the lobby's revolving glass door. She waves when she sees him, and in an instant Addy forgets to be nervous.

At the hotel bar, they talk about their days and the things they love about Rio. Addy's English has improved – never before has he been so motivated to learn – but it is still rough. Caroline, though, doesn't seem to notice.

'The first time I ate at a *churrascaria*,' she blushes, 'I ate myself sick. I felt so awful leaving any meat on the plate, so I'd force it down, and then they'd bring me *more*!'

Addy jokes about the excruciatingly slow pace at which the locals in Rio move, parading his first two fingers along the bar to demonstrate his cadence compared to that of a typical Brazilian. 'No one here is in hurry,' he says, shaking his head.

Later on at Belmond, Caroline asks Addy to order for the two of them. As they converse, this time over bowls of *moqueca de camarão,* shrimp stewed in coconut milk, Addy learns that Caroline is one of four Martin siblings, and that her three older brothers, whose names he asks her to repeat again and again – Edward, Taylor, and Venable – still live at home in Clinton.

'We had a cow in our backyard when we were children,' Caroline says, her eyes lighting up as she reminisces. Addy nearly chokes when she reveals that the cow's name was Sarah – his little sister Halina's Hebrew name, he explains. Caroline blushes. 'Oh, I hope I haven't offended you,' she says. 'Sarah was part of the family!' she adds. 'We'd milk her, and sometimes even ride her to school.'

Addy smiles. 'It sounds like your Sarah was a lot less stubborn than mine.' He goes on to tell Caroline about Halina, reminded of the time, after seeing *It Happened One Night,* that she insisted on cutting her hair short to look like Claudette Colbert, and how she'd refused to leave the apartment for days after, convinced the look didn't suit her. Laughing, Addy realises how good it feels to talk of his family, how hearing their names helps, in a way, to confirm their existence.

Caroline tells him about her family as well, about her father, a mathematics professor at Presbyterian College in Clinton, who had taught right up until his death in 1935. 'We didn't grow up with many luxuries,' she says, 'except for our schooling. You can imagine with a professor for a father how he felt about our education.'

Addy nods. His parents weren't professors, but receiving a good education was paramount in his household growing up, too. 'What did you call your father?' Addy asks, curious. 'What was his name?'

Caroline smiles. 'His name was Abram.'

Addy looks at her. 'Abram? As similar to *Abraham*?'

'Yes, Abram. Derived from Abraham. It's a family name. Passed down from my great-grandfather.'

Addy smiles, and then reaches to his pocket for his mother's handkerchief, laying it flat on the table between them. 'My mother, she . . .' he mimes the act of sewing with a needle and thread.

'She sews?'

'Yes, she sews this for me, before I leave Poland. Here,' Addy points, 'these are my – how do you call them?'

'Initials.'

'These are my initials – the *A* is for my Hebrew name, Abraham.' Caroline leans over the handkerchief, studying the embroidery. 'You are an Abraham, too?'

'*Sí.*'

'Our families have very good taste in names,' Caroline says, smiling.

Addy folds the handkerchief and slips it back into his pocket. Perhaps they are woven from the same thread, he decides.

Caroline is quiet for a moment. She looks down at her lap. 'My mother passed away three years ago,' she says. 'It's one of my biggest regrets, that I wasn't there when she died.'

It is a confession that surprises Addy, for he has just met Caroline. In the years that he was with Eliska she hardly ever spoke of her past, let alone her regrets. He nods in understanding, thinking of his own mother and wishing he could say something to comfort her. Maybe Caroline would feel less alone knowing that he, too, missed his mother terribly. He hasn't told her, of course, about losing contact with his family. He'd grown so accustomed to avoiding the subject he wasn't even sure he could bring himself to talk about it. Where would he begin?

He looks up, meeting Caroline's eyes. There is something so earnest about her, so gentle. *You can talk to her,* he realises. *Try.*

'I know how it is you feel,' he says.

Caroline looks surprised. 'You've lost your mother, too?'

'Well, not exactly. I don't know, you see. My family, I think, is still in Poland.'

'You think?'

Addy glances at his lap. 'I don't know for sure. We are Jews.'

Caroline reaches for his hand across the table with tears in her eyes, and all of a sudden the story that he hasn't told for so many years comes tumbling out.

Two weeks later, Addy and Caroline sit at a desk pushed up against an east-facing window in Caroline's apartment overlooking Leme Beach, a stack of parchment before them. They've seen each other almost every day since their first dinner at Belmond. It was Caroline's idea to contact the Red Cross for help locating his family. Addy dictates, leaning over Caroline's arm as she writes. Her optimism has energised him, and the words spill from his lips faster than she can keep up.

'Wait, wait, slow down.' Caroline laughs. 'Can you spell your mother's name for me again?' She looks up, the velvet brown of her irises catching in the light. Her fountain pen hovers over the paper. Addy clears his throat. The softness in her eyes, the soapy smell of her auburn hair, make him lose his train of thought. He spells *Nechuma,* trying not to butcher the English pronunciation of the letters, then his father's name and those of each of his siblings. Caroline's cursive, Addy notes, is effortless and elegant compared with his own.

When the letter is complete, Caroline retrieves a slip of paper from her purse. 'I asked at the embassy,' she says, setting it between them and running her finger down a list of cities, 'and it seems there are Red Crosses stationed everywhere. We should send your letter to several offices, just in case.' Addy nods, scanning the fifteen cities Caroline has compiled, ranging from Marseille, London, and Geneva, to Tel Aviv and Delhi. She's written an address next to each.

They talk quietly as Caroline carefully pens fifteen copies of Addy's letter. When she's finished, she gathers her stack of stationery and taps it gently on the table so the edges are neatly aligned, and then hands it to Addy.

'Thank you,' Addy says. 'This is so very important for me,' he adds, one hand over his heart, wishing he could better articulate how much her help means to him.

Caroline nods. 'I know. It's just awful, what's going on over there. I hope you hear back. At least for the moment you'll know you've done everything you can.' Her expression is sincere, her words comforting. He'd met her only a few weeks ago, but Addy has learnt that there's no guessing when it comes to knowing what Caroline is thinking. She simply says what she means to say, without embellishment. He finds the trait refreshing.

'You have a heart from gold,' Addy says, realising as the words leave him how cliched they sound, but he doesn't care.

Caroline's fingers are long, narrow at the tips. She waves them in front of her face, shakes her head. She's not good, Addy's also learnt, at receiving praise.

'I bring to the post office tomorrow,' he says.

'You'll let me know the moment you hear something?'

'Yes, of course.'

Through the window, Addy looks east over Leme Rock and the deep blue of the Atlantic, toward Europe. 'In time,' he says, trying to sound hopeful, 'in time I will find them.'

MAY 11, 1944: *The fourth and final battle of Monte Cassino begins. As hoped, the Allies take German forces by complete surprise. As the French Expeditionary Corps destroys the southern hinge of German defences, the XIII Corps, a formation of the British Eighth Army, moves inland, capturing the town of Cassino and striking German forces in the Liri valley. The Poles, in their first attempt to capture the Cassino, are repelled; casualties approach 4,000 as two battalions are wiped out entirely. Under continued assaults, the monastery remains impregnable.*

CHAPTER FORTY-SEVEN

Genek
Monte Cassino, Italy ~ May 17, 1944

Mortar rockets overhead. Genek cups the back of his helmet with his hands, his body pressed up against the face of the mountain. He's grown accustomed to the stabbing pain of his knees and elbows landing hard against the unforgiving rock, to the grit of dust between his teeth, to the constant clap and whir of artillery buzzing his ears at an exceedingly uncomfortable proximity. Four hundred metres above, what's left of the enemy – a regiment of what is thought to be 800 German paratroopers – fires round after round of shells from the ruins of the monastery. Genek can't help but wonder where all of their ammunition is coming from. *Surely they'll run out soon.*

The Poles have succeeded in taking the Germans by surprise, but though they far outnumber the Nazis, Anders's Army is still at a distinct disadvantage. The mountainside, after days of aerial bombardment, has been reduced to rubble, making the uphill climb extremely challenging. They can't see the enemy, and therefore they must reach the top of the monastery before having a chance at a clean shot; in the meantime, without a safe place to take cover, they are, for the most part, helplessly exposed.

With his body still hugging the side of the mountain, Genek swears through his teeth. The army was supposed to be the safe choice. The way out of Siberia. The way to keep the family together. And it was, for a while. Now, he's as safe as a bullseye in a shooting range, and his family is some 4,700 kilometres away in Palestine. Genek can't help but think about how the Poles' first attempt on Monte Cassino, five days earlier, like the three before it, had been a gut-wrenching failure. Met with mortar, small arms fire, and the devastating wrath of a 75mm panzer gun, Anders's leading infantry divisions were all but wiped out after just a few hours of fighting. As quickly as the operation began, the Polish II Corps was forced to retreat, reporting casualties of nearly 4,000 men. Genek and Otto had said thanks for the fact that they'd been assigned to an infantry division at the rear – and cursed the fact that despite the losses the enemy, too, had suffered, the monastery still lay in German hands. Thus far the only uplifting piece of news they've received in the campaign has come from General Juin, leader of the French Expeditionary Corps, who reported that his men had taken Monte Maio and were now in a position to assist the British XIII Corps stationed in the Liri valley. It was still up to the Poles, however, to capture the monastery. They'd set forth on a second attempt that morning.

More mortar. The crack of artillery overhead. The snare-drum *pop-pop-pop* of flak meeting stone. Someone down the mountain screams. Genek stays low. He thinks of Herta, of Józef, contemplates finding a rock and hiding under it until the fighting stops. But then an image flashes through his mind – his family in the hands of the Nazis, forced into a death camp. His family, part of the purported *millions* lost. A lump rises in his throat and his cheeks grow hot. He can't hide. He's here. If this mission is successful, he'll have helped to break the Germans, and to remind the world that Poland, though defeated in Europe, is still a power to be reckoned with. Swallowing the metallic tang of fear at the back of his tongue, he realises that, suicide mission or not, if there's a chance that he can help put an end to this wretched war, he sure as hell isn't giving up.

Genek waits for a lull in artillery fire and then scrambles a few metres up the mountain, keeping his body low and watching closely for mines and trip wires. In securing the stronghold, the Germans left a barrage of booby traps in their wake that had cost the lives of dozens of Genek's comrades. He's been trained to disable a mine, but he wonders if, under the circumstances, he'd have the wits about him to pull off the act should he stumble across an explosive in his path. Another thunderous *boom,* a monstrous explosion, somewhere to Genek's right. His body meets the mountain, nearly knocking the wind out of him. *What in fuck's sake was that?* His ears ring. There's been much talk among Anders's men about whether the enemy paratroopers in Cassino have access to the 28cm K5 railway gun employed at Anzio. The Germans call the gun the Leopold. The Allies refer to it as Anzio Annie. Her shells weigh a quarter of a ton, with a range of over 130 kilometres. *There's no way they could have gotten that thing up the mountain,* Genek reasons, trying to catch his breath – if they *had*, he's pretty certain he'd have been blown to bits by now. The air is alive again with submachine-gun fire. He lifts his chin, finds his breath, and scrambles another few metres up the mountain.

MAY 18, 1944: *In their second attack on Monte Cassino, the Polish II Corps meets constant artillery and mortar fire from the strongly fortified German positions above. With little natural cover for protection, the fighting is fierce and at times hand-to-hand. Thanks to the successful advance of the French Expeditionary Corps in the Liri valley, however, German paratroopers withdraw from Cassino to a new defensive position on the Hitler Line, to the north. Early in the morning of May 18, the Poles take the monastery. They are so battered, only a few have the strength to climb the last hundred metres. When they do, a Polish flag is raised over the ruins, and an anthem, 'The Red Poppies on Monte Cassino', is sung to celebrate the Polish victory. The road to Rome is open.*

JUNE 6, 1944 – D-DAY: *Code-named Operation Overlord, the Battle of Normandy begins with a massive amphibious military assault as some 156,000 Allied troops, led by General Eisenhower, storm a heavily fortified fifty-mile stretch of the Normandy coast-line. Low tide, poor weather, and an Allied deception plan allow the Allies to catch the Nazis by surprise.*

CHAPTER FORTY-EIGHT

Jakob and Bella
Warsaw, German-Occupied Poland ~ August 1, 1944

At the sound of the first explosion, Bella's blood whooshes from her head to her toes. Without thinking, she drops to all fours behind the checkout counter at the back of the dress shop. The detonation – close enough to rattle the coins in the cash register drawer – is followed by shouting, and the rapid burst of gunshots. Bella crawls to the corner of the counter, peeks around it toward the glass storefront. Outside, three uniformed men run by carrying Błyskawica submachine guns. Another bomb drops, and she covers her head instinctively with her hands. It's happening. The Home Army uprising. She has to get out. Fast.

She crawls to the small room she's rented at the back of the shop, thinking frantically of what to bring. Her purse, her hairbrush – no, not her brush, not important – her keys, although she wonders if the building will still be standing in a day. At the last second she lifts her mattress, retrieving two photographs – one of her parents, one of her and Anna as children – and slips them into the hem of her coat. She thinks about locking the shop's front door, but when four more uniformed men sprint by, she decides against it. Hurrying to the rear of the store, she exits quietly through the back door.

Outside, the street is empty. She pauses to catch her breath. Jakob's words ring in her ears. 'My building has a secure basement,' he'd told her a week ago, when the uprising seemed imminent. 'If there is fighting, meet me there.' She'll need to cross the Vistula River to reach him.

Bella sets off at a jog, headed north-east toward the bridge off of Wójtowska Boulevard, ducking into an alleyway when she hears the drone of approaching Luftwaffe aircraft. Pressing her body to the brick, she cranes her neck and counts six planes. They fly low, like vultures. She wonders if she should wait it out, make a run for it once the skies have cleared, but decides she'd better not waste any time. She needs to be with Jakob. *You've walked this route dozens of times,* she reasons – *it'll be ten minutes on the road. Just get there.*

Bella picks up her pace, trying her best to keep one eye on the sky as she runs, but the uneven cobblestones make it difficult. Twice, she catches herself a millisecond before twisting an ankle, and finally decides she's safer watching her step and listening for planes, rather than stepping blindly, her chin cocked to the sky. She's made it six blocks when the growl of a Stuka returns. She ducks into another alleyway, just as a shadow darts overhead. *Please, God, no,* she prays, squeezing her eyes shut, pressing up against the wall behind her, waiting. The growl fades. She opens her eyes and takes off again. Where is everyone? The streets are empty. They must be hiding.

The uprising is no surprise. Everyone in Warsaw had heard rumours of it happening, and everyone had a plan for when the day finally came, although no one knew exactly when it would. Bella and Jakob had been lucky to have Adam to rely on for updates through the Underground. 'It could start any day,' he said the weekend before. 'The Home Army's just waiting for the Red Army's approach.'

Axis powers, as reported in the *Biuletyn Informacyjny,* were finally beginning to falter. Allied troops were breaking through Nazi defences in Normandy, and there was talk of a massive Allied campaign in Italy. The Polish Home Army, Adam explained, hoped that with the Red Army at their backs, they could force the Germans out of their country's capital, and in turn, tip the scales toward an Allied victory in Europe.

It sounded noble. Jakob and Adam had talked about sneaking their way into the Home Army – they wanted desperately to help. Bella is grateful now that Halina had convinced them otherwise. She, too, wanted nothing more than a liberated Poland. But the Home Army, she reminded them, didn't look favorably upon Jews, and not only that, the Poles were greatly outnumbered. Warsaw was still overrun with Germans. *Look what happened,* Halina prompted, *after the ghetto uprising. And what if the Red Army doesn't cooperate?* The Home Army was counting on Stalin's help, but he'd let them down before, Halina warned, begging Jakob and Adam to keep their wits about them. *Please,* she said, *the*

Underground needs you. There is more than one way to stand up to the enemy.

Bella bears a hard right as she heads east on Wójtowska Boulevard, grateful to see river water ahead. As she nears, however, she slows. *Where is the bridge?* It's – gone. Destroyed. A pile of sizzling iron and wide-open water in its place. Picking up her pace, she veers north, hugging the curve of the Vistula, praying now for a bridge that's intact.

Ten blocks later, her lungs on fire and her blouse saturated with sweat, she is relieved to find the Toruński Bridge still standing. The sky, however, is now crawling with Junkers. Ignoring them, along with the searing pain in her chest, the burning in her quadriceps, the voice inside her screaming to find a ditch somewhere and take cover, she runs as hard as she can.

Halfway across the bridge, a dozen men appear. They rush toward her with frantic, loping strides. Bella's legs go numb until she realises from their attire that they are Poles. Civilians. Several have rifles slung around their necks. Others carry pitchforks and shovels. A few grip butcher knives. They gallop in her direction, yelling, but Bella is too exhausted, her breath too loud to make out the words. It isn't until their paths nearly intersect that she realises the men are yelling at her. 'You're running the wrong way!' they roar, holding their weapons over their heads like warriors. 'Come fight with us! For Poland and for victory!' Bella shakes her head as she sprints by, watching the ground to keep her balance. She doesn't look up until she reaches Jakob's door.

It's their eighth day in hiding; the bombing hasn't stopped. Bella and Jakob agonise incessantly about whether the others – Halina, Adam, Mila, Franka and her family – have found a safe place to take cover, about what Warsaw will look like when the bombing finally lets up.

They share the basement with a couple who had arrived toting an eighteen-month-old child, a hay bale, and, to Jakob and Bella's amazement, a dairy cow. It took some work, but they'd finally coaxed the recalcitrant animal down the stairs to the basement. The cow smells – there's nothing to do but scoop her manure into a pile in the corner – but her udders are always full. Twice a day, fresh milk is carried in a bucket upstairs to boil over the stove, 'so it's suitable for the baby to drink,' the mother of the toddler had said, although Bella was convinced that fresh cow's milk wouldn't harm the child. She'd thought of protesting – venturing upstairs was dangerous and downright foolish under the circumstances – but instead she held her tongue, not wanting to disturb the friendly dynamic of the group. Today it's Bella's turn to boil the milk.

She checks her watch. It's been nearly thirty minutes since the last explosion. A lull. Jakob, standing with her at the foot of the stairs, nods.

'Be safe,' he says.

She returns the nod and makes her way up the staircase, bucket in hand, then hurries down the hallway to the kitchen. At the stove, she pours the milk into a saucepan, lights a match, and turns the black knob under the burner to ignite a flame. As the milk begins to simmer, she tiptoes to the window. Outside, the cityscape is surreal. One of every three buildings along Danusi Street is levelled. Others are still standing but missing their roofs, as if they'd been decapitated. She scans the sky and curses as a swarm of Luftwaffe planes buzzes into view. *Dammit.* The planes are small at first, but they inch closer, and as they do, they change course and disappear. Bella steps away from the window, wishing she could keep an eye on them. She listens intently, glaring at the milk, willing it to boil. After a moment, the drone of engines overhead grows louder. She can hear Jakob knocking the floor below with a broom handle, signalling for her to return to the basement. He must hear it, too. And then, somewhere not so far away, a bomb drops and the room shakes, jostling the porcelain dishes on the shelves. Jakob knocks again, harder this time. She can hear him calling for her through the floorboards.

'Bella!'

'Coming!' she cries, cranking the stove's knob to the off position. Another bomb. This one closer. On the same block, maybe. She should drop everything and run, but first, she decides, wrapping a towel around her hand, she will retrieve the milk. As she reaches for the handle of the saucepan, her ear catches something new. It sounds like a cat at first, like a deep, feline whine. *Forget the milk,* she chides, dropping the dish towel as she turns. But she's too late. She's barely made it to the door when the window explodes. The kitchen goes black with soot and Bella can feel herself being thrown off her feet. Her arms stroke the air helplessly, moving in slow motion as if swimming under water, as if trying to escape a bad dream. Broken glass. Shrapnel. Dishes spill from shelves, shatter. Bella lands hard and lies motionless on her stomach, cradling the back of her head with her hands, trying to breathe, but the air is thick with smoke and it's difficult. Another bomb falls and the floor thrums beneath her.

Jakob is yelling now, but his voice sounds muted, far away. With her eyes pinned shut, Bella gives her body a mental scan. She moves her fingers, her toes. Her extremities are there, and they seem to work. But she's wet. Is she bleeding? She doesn't feel any pain. What's burning? Dazed, she pulls herself to a sit, coughing, and opens her eyes. The room is foggy; it's like she's looking at it through a pane of filthy glass. She blinks. As her world comes into focus she notices what appears to be a plume of grey snaking toward the ceiling from the back of the stove. Bella freezes – had she turned off the burner? She had, right? *Yes, yes, it's off.* She glances at the debris scattered across the floor: the slivers of windowpane, broken dishes, splintered wood, a dozen large, mangled hunks of shrapnel. The saucepan lies on its side in a pool of milk amid the rubble. She looks down at her clothes – she is not bleeding; she is wet from the milk.

'Bella!' Jakob cries, his voice rippling with fear. He is there suddenly, squatting next to her, his hands on her shoulders, her cheeks. 'Bella! Are you okay?'

Bella can hear him, but only faintly. She nods. 'Yes, I'm – I'm okay,' she mumbles. He helps her to her feet. Something smells as if it's burning. 'The stove?' Jakob asks. It has begun to hiss.

'It's off.'

'Let's get out of here.'

Bella's legs teeter beneath her like stilts. Jakob helps her up and throws her arm over his shoulder, half carrying her back to the basement stairs. 'Are you sure you're okay? I thought – I thought . . .'

'It's okay, love. I'm all right.'

OCTOBER 17, 1944: *'[Warsaw] must completely disappear from the surface of the earth and serve only as a transport station for the Wehrmacht. No stone can remain standing. Every building must be razed to its foundation.'*

– SS chief Heinrich Himmler, SS Officers Conference

CHAPTER FORTY-NINE

Mila
Outside Warsaw, German-Occupied Poland ~ Late September 1944

Nearly eight weeks have passed since the bombs began to fall on Warsaw in early August. When the first one dropped, Mila had considered borrowing a car to retrieve Felicia at the convent in Włocławek, but she knew she would never get there. Not alive, at least. Warsaw was a giant battlefield. Everyone was in hiding. There were Germans stationed on the outskirts of the city, holed up in bunkers, waiting to pounce the second the Home Army showed a sign of weakness. To leave would be impossible. So instead she fled to Halina's downtown apartment on Stawki Street, where she spent her days and nights huddled with her sister and Adam in the building's crawl space, listening in the dark as the city was decimated above them.

Every week or so, a friend from the Underground would bring a small parcel of food, a bit of news. None of it was promising – the Poles were outnumbered, and greatly out-armoured; 10,000 residents, apparently, had been executed in Wola, 7,000 in Old Town; tens of thousands more were transported to death camps; even the sick weren't spared – nearly all of the patients at Wolski Hospital had been murdered. As the siege dragged on, the Home Army became desperate. 'Has Stalin sent reinforcements?' Adam asked each time he received news from the Underground. The answer was always no – no sign of help from the Russians. And so the bombing persisted, and little by little, Poland's one-time thriving capital slowly disappeared. After a week, a third of the city was razed, then a half, then two thirds.

Mila is a disaster, sickened by the distance between her and Felicia. She has no way of knowing if the bombs have reached Włocławek, and she never thought to ask if the convent had a shelter. With little to eat and an even smaller appetite, her slacks have begun to hang low and loose around her waist. She is stuck. And with each passing day – she's counted fifty-two since she's been in hiding – she grows more frantic. Every few minutes, it seems, the ground shakes as another steel explosive plummets to the earth, shredding homes, shops, schools, churches, bridges, cars, and people in its wake. And there's nothing she can do but listen, and wait.

CHAPTER FIFTY

Halina
Montelupich Prison, Kraków,
German-Occupied Poland ~ October 7, 1944

Halina is jolted awake by the metallic click of a key in a lock and the grate of iron scraping cement as her cell door is wrenched open. She narrows her eye that isn't swollen shut. 'Brzoza!' Betz spits at her. 'Up. *Now.*'

She stands slowly, breathing through the stabbing pain in her back. In the four days that she's been imprisoned, she's been questioned over a dozen times. With every interrogation, she's returned to the cell with more bruises, each a deeper shade of purple than the last. She is on the brink of giving up. But she knows she must swallow the pain, the humiliation, the blood dripping from her nose, her forehead, her upper lip. She mustn't break. She's smart enough to know that the ones who break don't return. And she refuses to take her last breath in this godforsaken jail. She cannot – will not – let the Gestapo win.

Halina was incarcerated just days after General Bór waved his white flag, declaring the uprising in Warsaw over. In the end, Stalin's men, stationed on the outskirts of the city, never arrived; after sixty-three days of fighting, the Home Army was forced to surrender. On the second of October, for the first time in two months, a hush came over the city. When Halina ventured outside, shell-shocked, filthy, and half starved, Warsaw, still ablaze, was unrecognisable. Her building was one of only two still intact on Stawki Street. The others had been obliterated. Some were shorn in half, exposing their insides in an alarming state of disarray – toilets, headboards, porcelain, tea kettles, and parlour couches pushed up haphazardly against twisted metal and brick – but most were nothing more than shells, their insides hollowed out, gutted, like fish. Halina had picked her way through the rampaged city to try to find Jakob and Franka – a nearly impossible task as many of the roads were impassable.

She arrived at Franka's doorstep first, where she fell to her knees – the building was gone. Franka, her parents, and her brother were nowhere to be found. An hour later, when Halina finally reached Jakob's apartment, she discovered that his building, too, had been eviscerated. She nearly fainted when Jakob surfaced from the remains with Bella in tow. They were *safe*. But they were also starving.

By then, Halina could barely think straight. Franka and her family were missing. She knew she couldn't leave Warsaw without trying to find them. But she, Adam, Jakob, and Bella were in trouble. They were hungry and broke and soon it would be winter. Before the uprising, Halina's employer, Herr Den, had told her that he'd requested a transfer to Kraków. 'If you need anything, find me at the bank in the city centre on Rynek Kleparski,' he'd said. Halina had no other option but to call on him for help. Adam objected to the idea, of course, claiming that it wasn't safe for Halina to travel to Kraków alone. But Halina insisted. There was a pocket of the Underground that was still functioning in Warsaw and they needed Adam now more than ever. And there was also Mila, who was in a panic to reach Felicia. 'If you stay, you can help Mila find a way to Włocławek, and you can keep searching for Franka,' Halina said. 'Please, I'll be fine on my own.' She would go and return straight away, she promised, with some money – enough to get them through the winter. Finally, Adam agreed. And so, after arranging an exchange with another young Jew – her coat for a sack of potatoes to feed the others while she was away – Halina left for Kraków.

Her well-laid plan, however, came to an abrupt halt a day later at the Kraków train station when, moments after disembarking, she was arrested. The Gestapo who pulled her in showed no interest in her story, or in contacting Herr Den to validate it. 'Then let me wire my husband,' Halina said, making no attempt to mask her anger. Again, the Gestapo ignored her. Within an hour she found herself being escorted by police car through Kraków's centre to the city's infamous jail, Montelupich. As she passed through the prison's red-brick entrance, she glanced up at the barbed wire and broken glass surrounding the building and knew without a doubt she wouldn't be returning to Warsaw. At least not anytime soon. And that Adam would be a wreck. 'Brzoza!'

'Coming,' Halina grunts. She steps over legs and arms as she limps toward the door.

Of the nearly three-dozen women who share the cell, surprisingly few are Jews, at least that she knows of. She's one of four, maybe five. Most of the incarcerated in Montelupich's women's ward seem to be thieves, smugglers, spies, members of various resistance organisations. Her offense, according to the Gestapo, is her faith. But she'll never admit it. Her religion will never be a crime.

'Get your hands off me,' she growls as Betz locks the cell door behind them and wrenches one of her arms behind her back, pushing her down the hallway in front of him.

'Shut up, Goldie.'

At first, Halina thought her nickname was derived from her blonde hair, but she quickly realised it was born from the yellow stars the Jews in Europe were made to wear.

'I'm not a Jew.'

'That's not what your friend Pinkus says.'

Halina's heart wallops her rib cage. *Pinkus.* How do they know his name? Pinkus – the Jewish boy with whom she'd bartered her coat before leaving Warsaw. Pinkus must have been caught and given up her name in the hopes that it would help him somehow. She curses his stupidity. 'I don't know a Pinkus.'

'Pinkus, the Jew who took your coat. He claims he knows you. Claims you're not who you say you are.'

Pinkus, you spineless shit.

'Why would a Jew turn in another Jew?' Halina huffs.

'It happens all the time.'

'Well, I told you, I don't know this person. He's lying. He'll tell you anything to save his own life.'

In the windowless, bloodstained cell the Gestapo have designated for interrogation, she offers the same explanation, over and over again, this time to two brutes she recognises from past interrogations – one by the gruesome scar over his eye, the other by his limp.

'You gave him your coat,' the one with the scar yells. 'If you are a Pole like you say, then why were you doing business with a Jew?'

'I didn't know he was a Jew!' Halina postures. 'I hadn't eaten in weeks. He offered potatoes. What was I to do?' Suddenly she's off her feet, a fist lifting her up by her collar, slamming her ribs against the cell wall. 'I didn't know he was a Jew,' she wheezes.

Crack. Her forehead meets the wall.

'Stop lying!'

The pain is blinding. Halina's body is limp. 'Don't . . . don't you see?' she spits. 'It's revenge! The Jews . . . are trying for revenge . . . on the Poles!'

Another *crack*, a trickle down her nose, the hot, acrid taste of blood. *You must not waver.*

'He swore on his mother's grave,' one of the Gestapo hisses. 'What do you say to that?'

'The Jews . . . *hate* us.' *Whump.* She speaks through her teeth, with one cheek stamped up against the wall. 'Always have . . . it's retribution!' *Whap.* The bony, muted crunch of her jaw meeting the back of a hand.

'Look at you – you *look* like a Jew!'

Halina's breathing is wet, heavy. 'Don't . . . insult . . . me. Look at *you* . . . at *your* women. Blonde . . . with . . . blue eyes. Are *they* Jews?'

Crack. Again, her skull against the wall. Blood in her lashes now, burning her eyes.

'Why should we believe you?'

'Why *shouldn't* you? My . . . my papers don't lie! And . . . neither does my boss . . . Herr Den. Call him. He is at the bank on Rynek Kleparski. I've told you . . . I was en route to see him when you bastards arrested me.' This part of her story, of course, is true.

'Forget about Den. He's of no use to us,' the one with the limp hisses.

'Then wire my husband.'

'The only person of use to us is you, Goldie,' the scar-faced one yells. 'You say you're a Pole. Then recite the Lord's Prayer!'

Halina shakes her head, feigning annoyance and saying silent thanks for the fact that her parents had chosen to send her to Polish gymnasium rather than to one of Radom's Jewish schools. 'This again. Our Father, which art in heaven, hallowed be thy name . . .'

'All right, all right, enough.'

'Call my boss,' Halina pleads, exhausted. He's the only card she has left to play, her last hope. She wonders if the Germans have even tried to reach him. Perhaps Herr Den got caught up in the uprising in Warsaw and never made it to Kraków. Or perhaps they've called, and he's finally given up vouching for her. But he seemed so adamant: 'Come to Kraków. Find me, I will help.' She'd tried. And now she's here. It's been less than a week and already her body is in ruins. She doesn't know how many more of these interrogations she can take. She's heard from one of the new arrivals in the women's ward that Warsaw is still smouldering. She worries constantly of Adam, who would have been out of his mind when she didn't return, of Mila, who could barely function when Halina left, and of Franka, but mostly she worries about her parents. The Górskis expected money once a month to keep her parents safe, and now they haven't received anything in nearly two months. Could she count on the goodness of the Górskis for her parents' survival? She's seen their meagre home; they can barely afford to keep themselves. Halina can't help but imagine it – Albert escorting her parents out of the cottage, unable to meet their eyes: *I'm sorry, I wish you could stay, but either you go, or we all starve.* Surely, in time the Górskis will presume her dead. The family will presume her dead.

I'm coming back to you, she says silently, part to herself, and part to Adam and her parents, in case they are listening, as she's escorted, finally, back to her cell.

CHAPTER FIFTY-ONE

Mila

Outside Warsaw, German-Occupied Poland ~ October 1944

The drive to the convent takes twice as long as usual. Many of the streets are impassable, forcing Mila to veer off on painstakingly long detours. Everything that once looked familiar along the way is gone – the barrel factory in Józefina, the tannery in Mszczonów – the scenery reduced to an endless patchwork of rubble.

Mila leans forward, squinting through the windshield of the stolen V6. She and Adam had found the car lying on its side a block from Halina's apartment; it took six people to flip it back onto its wheels. Adam had helped her jump-start it. All four of its windows were missing, but it didn't matter. Its tank, in a stroke of good luck, was still a quarter full – it had just enough fuel to get her to and from the convent.

She taps her thumbs nervously on the steering wheel, scanning the wreckage before her. She must be in the wrong place, Mila thinks. Has she made a wrong turn? She's barely slept in weeks – it's certainly possible she'd lost her way. The convent should be just *there,* ahead, she could swear it . . . and then her eye catches something black, a shard of slate jutting up out of the earth. Her stomach heaves as she recognises it for the chalkboard it once was. She's in the right place. The convent is gone. Vanished. It's been blown to pieces.

Without thinking, she climbs from the car, its engine still running, and sprints across the plot of land where she'd last seen her daughter, leaping over scattered bricks and mangled fence posts in the tall grass. At the sight of a miniature desk chair lying upside down, she crumples to her knees. Her mouth is gaping, but she is breathless, faint. And then her screams slice like knives through the October sky, growing more violent with each desperate inhale.

* * *

'Miss, Miss.' Mila is being shaken by a young man. She can barely hear him, even though he's knelt down beside her. 'Miss,' he says.

She feels the weight of a hand on her shoulder. Her throat is raw, her cheeks tear-stained, the voice in her head relentless. *Look what you've done! You should have never left her here!* Her heart throbs as if someone has driven a javelin through it.

Mila looks up, blinks, a palm to her chest, another to her forehead. Someone, she realises, has turned off the engine to the V6.

'There is a basement,' the young man explains. 'I've been trying to reach them for days. My name is Tymoteusz. My daughter Emilia is down there, too. Yours is . . . ?'

'Felicia,' Mila whispers, her mind too frantic to remember that at the convent, her daughter went by Barbara.

'Come, help me, there could still be hope.'

Mila and Tymoteusz take turns lifting rubble from the place where the convent once stood.

'You see,' Tymoteusz explains, pointing, 'this appears to be a stairwell. If we can clear it perhaps we'll find a door to the bunker.'

They've been at work for nearly two hours when Tymoteusz stops, kneels, and presses his head to the earth. 'I heard something! Did you hear it, too?'

Mila drops to her knees, holding her breath as she listens. But after a few moments, she shakes her head. 'I don't hear anything. What did it sound like?'

'Like a knock.'

Mila's pulse quickens. They stand and begin slinging rubble again, this time with a renewed sense of purpose, a thread of hope. And then, as Mila bends to reach for a block of cement, she freezes. *There it is. A sound.* Yes, a *knock,* coming from beneath their feet. 'I hear it!' she gasps. She places her face to the wreckage and yells as loudly as she can, 'We hear you! We're here! We are coming for you!' Her cries are met by another knock. A muffled shout. Tears immediately spring to Mila's eyes. 'It's them.' She half sobs, half laughs, and then reminds herself that a knock could mean anything. It could mean a single survivor.

They work faster now, Mila brushing sweat and tears from her cheeks, Tymoteusz breathing heavily, his eyebrows knit together in concentration.

Their hands bleed. The muscles running the lengths of their spines spasm. When they break, they rest for a minute or two, no longer, making small talk to keep themselves from imagining the worst.

'How old is Emilia?' Mila asks.

'Seven. And Felicia?'

'She'll be six in November.'

Mila asks where Tymoteusz is from, but skirts the subject of Emilia's mother, in hopes that he won't ask about Felicia's father.

They are halfway through clearing the stairwell when the sun disappears, which means they have another hour, at most, of light. They both know, though, that they won't leave until the stairwell is cleared.

'I've brought a flashlight,' Tymoteusz says, as if reading Mila's thoughts. 'We're pulling them out of there. Tonight.'

There are stars overhead when they finally reach the bunker door. Mila had thought there would be more shouting, more communication with whoever had knocked earlier, but since they'd made initial contact, she's heard nothing, not a sound, and suddenly it's not the rubble or the dark or the task of prying open the door that terrifies her, but the quiet. Surely whoever is inside can hear them now – so why the silence? She grips the flashlight with two shaking hands as she shines it on the door's handle, watching with her face half turned away as Tymoteusz wrenches it open.

'Are you all right?' Tymoteusz asks.

Mila isn't sure if she can move. 'I think so,' she whispers.

Tymoteusz takes her arm. 'Come,' he says, and they step together into the shadows.

Mila glides a narrow beam of light a metre in front of her as they shuffle silently inside. At first they see nothing but the cement floor, its cracks and dust illuminated in the glow of light. But then the beam catches what appear to be footprints, and a second later Mila jumps at the sound of a voice, not far from them. She recognises it as that of the Mother Superior.

'We are here.'

Mila shines the flashlight in the direction of the voice. There, along the far wall of the bunker, she can begin to make out bodies, large and small. The smaller ones, for the most part, lay motionless. A few sit up, rub their eyes. *Run to them!* Mila's heart screams. *Find her! She's just there, she has to be!* But she can't. Her feet are fixed to the ground and her lungs reject the air, which suddenly smells of excrement, and something else, something horrible. *Death*, Mila realises. It smells like death. Her thoughts come and go quickly. What if Felicia isn't there? What if she had been outdoors when the bombing began? Or what if she *is* there, but she's one of the ones not moving? Too sick even to sit up, or worse . . .

'Come.' Tymoteusz nudges her and she moves alongside him, unable to breathe. Someone coughs. They shuffle toward the Mother Superior, who remains sitting, apparently unable to stand. When they reach her, Mila runs the flashlight over the others. There are a dozen bodies, at least.

'Mother Superior,' Mila whispers. 'It is Mila Kurc, Felicia . . . I mean Barbara's mother. And – and Tymoteusz . . .'

'Emilia's father,' Tymoteusz offers.

Mila directs the light at herself and at Tymoteusz for a moment. 'The children. Are they . . .'

'Papa?' Soft, scared, a voice penetrates the darkness and Tymoteusz freezes.

'Emilia!' He drops to his knees in front of his daughter, who disappears in his arms. They are both crying.

'I'm so sorry we couldn't reach you sooner,' Mila whispers to the Mother Superior. 'How – how long have—'

'*Mamusiu.*'

Felicia. Mila tracks her light swiftly along the wall of bodies until finally it lands on her daughter. She blinks, swallowing back tears. Felicia is struggling to stand. Bathed in light, the sockets of her eyes appear far too pronounced in her small face, and even from afar Mila can see that her neck and cheeks are badly blistered.

'Felicia!' Mila presses the flashlight into the Mother Superior's hand and darts across the bunker floor. 'My darling.' She kneels beside Felicia and scoops her up, cradling her with an arm under her neck and another under her legs. She weighs nothing. Her body is hot. Too hot, Mila realises. Felicia is mumbling. Something hurts, she says, but she hasn't the words or the energy to explain what. Mila rocks her gently. 'I know. I'm sorry. I'm so sorry. I'm here now, love. Shhh. I'm right here. You're all right. You're going to be all right.' She recites the words over and over again, rocking her feverish daughter in her arms like an infant.

Somewhere over her shoulder she can hear someone speaking to her. Tymoteusz. His voice is soft, but urgent. 'I know of a doctor in Warsaw. You need to get her to him,' he says. 'Right away.'

JANUARY 17, 1945: *Soviet troops capture Warsaw. That same day, the Germans retreat from Kraków.*

JANUARY 18, 1945: *With Allied forces approaching, Germany makes a last-ditch effort to evacuate Auschwitz and its surrounding camps; some 60,000 prisoners are forced to set off on foot on what will later be coined a 'death march' to the city of Wodzisław in south-western Poland. Thousands are killed before the march, and over 15,000 die en route. Those remaining are loaded onto freight trains in Wodzisław and shipped to concentration camps in Germany. In the coming weeks and months, similar marches will take place from camps like Stutthof, Buchenwald, and Dachau.*

CHAPTER FIFTY-TWO

Halina
Montelupich Prison, Kraków,
German-Occupied Poland ~ January 20, 1945

A shaft of iridescent light perforates her cell from a miniature barred window three metres overhead, illuminating a square of cement on the wall opposite her. Halina can tell from its position that it is late in the day. It will be dark soon. She closes her eyes, her lids heavy with exhaustion. She didn't sleep at all the night before. At first, she blamed her restlessness on the cold. Her blanket is threadbare, and her straw pallet does nothing to buffer the icy January chill that emanates from the floor. But even by the standards of Montelupich, the night had been a busy one. Every few minutes, it seemed, she was startled awake by the piercing screams of someone in a cell a floor above her, or by the sobs of a prisoner down the hallway. The misery is suffocating; it's as if at any moment, it will envelop her.

Halina's cellmates, who once numbered thirty-two, have been whittled down to twelve. The handful who were discovered to be Jews were taken months ago. Others come and disappear by the hour. Last week, a Polish woman arrived, accused of spying for the Home Army. Two days later, she was hustled out from the cell before dawn; as the sun began to rise, Halina heard a scream and then the pop of gunfire – the woman never returned.

Curled on her side with her hands between her knees, she teeters at the edge of sleep, half listening to the whispers of two inmates on pallets next to hers.

'Something's happening,' one of them says. 'They're acting strange.'

'They are,' the other agrees. 'What does it mean?'

Halina has noticed a change, too. The Germans are behaving differently. Some, like Betz, have vanished, which for her is a blessing – she hasn't been called into the interrogation room in weeks. The men who come to the door now to remove a prisoner or to drop off a tin of watery soup, in the brief instances that she sees them, seem rushed. Distracted. Nervous, even. Her cellmates are right. Something *is* happening. There are rumours that the Germans are losing the war. That the Red Army is entering Warsaw. Could the rumours be true? Halina thinks incessantly of her parents in hiding, of Adam, Mila, Jakob, and Bella, presumably still in Warsaw. Of Franka and her family – has Adam been able to find them, she wonders? Will Warsaw soon be liberated? Will Kraków be next?

The door slides open. 'Brzoza!'

Halina starts. She pushes herself to a seated position and then slowly to a stand, her joints stiff as she makes her way across the cell.

The German at the door reeks of stale alcohol. He grips her elbow tightly as they walk the hallway, but instead of turning right toward the interrogation room, he pushes open a door to a stairwell – the same stairwell she'd descended nearly four months ago, in October, when she was first escorted into the bowels of Montelupich's women's ward.

'*Herauf,*' the German directs, releasing her elbow. *Up.*

Halina uses the metal railing, gripping it tightly with each step for fear that her legs might give out beneath her. At the top of the stairwell, she's escorted through another door, and then down a long hallway to an office with the name HAHN printed in black letters across an opaque glass door. Inside, the man behind the desk – Herr Hahn, Halina guesses – wears a uniform bearing the double lightning insigna of the *Sicherheitspolizei.* He nods, and in an instant Halina is left standing, alone, shivering, in the doorway.

'Sit,' Hahn says in German, glancing at a wooden chair opposite his desk. His eyes are tired, his hair slightly dishevelled.

Halina lowers herself gently to sit at the edge of the chair. Her mind buckles as she contemplates how exactly the Gestapo plan to kill her, whether it will be quick, whether she will suffer. Whether her family, if they are still alive, will ever learn of her fate.

Hahn slides a piece of parchment across the desk. 'Frau Brzoza. Your discharge papers.'

Halina stares at him for a moment. And then down at the parchment. 'Frau Brzoza, it seems your arrest was invalid.'

She looks up.

'We have been trying to contact your boss, Herr Den, for months. It turns out his bank was closed. But we've finally found him, and he has stated that you are who you say you are.' Hahn laces his fingers into a tight ball. 'It appears a mistake has been made.'

Halina exhales. A smouldering rage crawls up her spine as she stares at the man opposite her. For four months, she's been locked up, starved, beaten. For four months she's worried incessantly about her family. And now this, a half-hearted apology? She opens her mouth, furious, but the words don't come. Instead she swallows. And as the relief washes over her, quelling her anger, she is dizzy. The room spins. For the first time in her life, she is speechless.

'You are free to go,' Hahn says. 'You can collect your belongings on your way out.'

Halina blinks.

'Do you understand? You're free to go.'

She presses both hands into the arms of the chair and eases herself to a stand. 'Thank you,' Halina whispers, when her balance is in check. *Thank you,* she whispers, silently this time, to Herr Den. He's done it again. Saved her life. She can't think of how she will ever repay him. She has nothing to give him. Somehow, someday, she will find a way. But first, she needs to contact Adam. *Please, just let him be alive. Let my family be alive.*

At the prison office, Halina collects her purse and the clothes she'd arrived in, and steps into a washroom to change. Her blouse and skirt feel sumptuous against her skin, but her appearance is shocking. 'Oh, my,' she whispers when she catches a glimpse of her reflection in a mirror over the sink. Her eyes are bloodshot, the skin under them eggplant purple. The bruises over her cheekbones have faded to a dull green, but the gash above her right eyebrow – thick and scabbed black, with an angry red rash around it – is lurid. Her hair is disastrous. Leaning over the sink, she cups her palms together and splashes a few handfuls of water over her face. Finally, she digs a clip from her purse and combs a lock of blonde hair with her fingers a few times before pulling it over her forehead and pinning it to the side in an attempt to cover the laceration over her brow.

Folding her tattered prison jumpsuit, she sets it on the floor, then rifles through her pocketbook, where, somewhat miraculously, she finds her watch and her wallet. The money, of course, which was intended for the Górskis, is gone. But her false ID is there. Her work permit. A card with Den's information. And – her stomach drops when she feels it still hidden in the soft lining of her purse – Adam's ID. His *real* ID. With his *real* name, Eichenwald. Halina and Adam had exchanged their old IDs at the start of the war, shortly after they were married. It was Adam's idea. 'You never know when we might need them again,' he'd said, 'until then, best not to give anyone a chance to find them on us.' Halina had cut a slit in the lining of her purse and sewn Adam's ID into it. She didn't have time to remove it after her arrest and before turning over her purse. The Germans had missed it. Breathing relief for the oversight, Halina exits the prison as quickly as her swollen joints will allow her.

Outside, the January cold slaps her hard in the face. Patches of snow and ice cover the cobblestone street. She'd arrived in early October, when the weather was still relatively mild and she'd traded Pinkus her winter coat. Her lightweight trench is no match for the winter chill. She pulls her collar up to her chin and digs her hands into her pockets, squinting uncomfortably into the glare of the sun. Ignoring the wind slicing at her cheeks and the shooting pain behind her kneecaps, she walks briskly, determined to put as much space between her and Montelupich as she can while she contemplates what to do next.

At a street called Kamienna, she pauses at a news stand, where she realises for the first time since leaving the prison that she hasn't seen any Germans on the streets. She scans the papers, elated to read that the Soviets, just three days ago, had captured Warsaw. That the Nazis had begun to retreat from Kraków. That in France, the Germans were withdrawing from the Ardennes. These are good signs! Perhaps the rumours flying around Montelupich were true – perhaps the war would soon be over.

Halina peruses the small crowd of Poles gathered at the stand for someone who might be able to direct her to the address Herr Den had left her. Hahn had said the bank was closed, but maybe with the German retreat it's been reopened.

They were able to find Herr Den, after all. If he isn't there, she decides, she'll have to track down his home address. She'll reach him. Thank him. Promise to reimburse him, then ask for a loan. Just enough to pay for some food, and for her passage back to Warsaw, where, she prays, she'll find her family intact.

CHAPTER FIFTY-THREE

Halina and Adam
Wilanów, Soviet-Occupied Poland ~ February 1945

'It's this one here, on the left,' Halina says, and Adam turns the Volkswagen down the narrow drive leading to the Górskis' home. 'Thank you for coming,' she adds.

From behind the steering wheel, Adam glances at her and nods. 'Of course.'

Halina rests a hand on Adam's knee, deeply thankful for the man at her side. She would never forget the day that she returned from Kraków to her apartment in Warsaw to find him waiting for her. Mila, Felicia, Jakob, and Bella were there, too. The feeling of seeing them together, her siblings, was indescribable. Her euphoria vanished, however, when Adam told her he had no news of Franka and her family. They were still missing. His own parents and three siblings – two brothers and a sister with a two-year-old son – had disappeared, too, not long after Halina left for Kraków. Adam had been trying desperately to find them, but without any luck, and Halina could sense how much this agonised him.

She'd felt bad at first, asking him to come along with her to Wilanów – but she knew that he would never let her travel on her own, and that if she arrived to an empty house or to bad news from the Górskis, she wouldn't have the strength to return to Warsaw alone.

Adam slows the Volkswagen to a stop and Halina peers at the Górskis' cottage through the dusty windshield. It looks tired – as if the war has given it a beating. There are a dozen shingles missing from the roof, and the white paint has begun to peel from the shutters like birch-tree bark. Weeds grow in the spaces between the blue slate walkway leading to the door. Halina's stomach turns. The house looks abandoned. Adam said he wrote to the Górskis twice over the winter to check up on them, promising to send money as soon as he could, but he never received a reply.

Halina runs her fingers along the unsightly scar over her eyebrow and then slips her hand into her pocket, where she's tucked an envelope of zloty – half of the sum Herr Den loaned her when she finally tracked him down in Kraków. It's been seven months since she has been able to deliver the Górskis their money, since she last saw her parents, and it is everything she can do not to fear that the worst of her nightmares have come true. 'Just be here,' Halina whispers, wishing away the horrific scenarios her mind has become adept at concocting: that the Górskis, destitute, had been forced to leave her parents at the train station to fend for themselves with their false IDs; that Marta's sister, nosing around, had discovered the false wall behind the bookcase and threatened to turn Albert in for harbouring a Jew unless he got rid of them; that a neighbour had spotted her parents' laundry, suspiciously larger than the Górskis', hanging to dry in the backyard, and reported the Górskis to the Blue Police; that the Gestapo had made an unexpected visit and discovered her parents before they had a chance to slip into their hiding place. The possibilities were endless.

Adam turns off the ignition. Halina takes a breath, exhales through a narrow part in her lips. 'Ready?' Adam asks. Halina nods.

She climbs out of the car and walks ahead, guiding Adam around to the back of the house. At the door, she turns, shakes her head. 'I don't know if I can,' she says.

'You can,' Adam says. 'Would you like me to knock?'

'Yes,' Halina whispers. 'Twice. Knock twice.'

As Adam reaches around her, Halina looks from the door to her feet to a line of tiny black ants marching across the stone doorstep. Adam raps his knuckles twice against the door and then reaches for her hand. Halina holds her breath, and listens. Somewhere behind her, a wood pigeon coos. A dog barks. Wind rustles the scale-like leaves of a cypress. And then finally, the sound of footsteps. If the steps belong to the Górskis, their expressions will say it all, Halina realises, staring now at the doorknob, waiting.

Albert answers the door, thinner and grayer than when she'd seen him last. His eyebrows leap at the sight of her. 'It's you!' he says, and then claps a hand over his mouth, shaking his head in disbelief. 'Halina,' he says through his fingers. 'We thought . . .'

Halina forces herself to meet his gaze. She opens her mouth but can't bring herself to speak. She hasn't the courage to ask him what she needs to know. She searches his eyes for an answer but all she can read is his surprise at finding her at his doorstep.

'Come, please,' Albert says, waving them inside. 'I've been so worried, with the news from Warsaw. Such devastation. How on earth . . .'

Adam introduces himself and in an instant they are enveloped in shadows as Albert closes the door behind them.

'Here,' Albert says, flipping on a lamp. 'It's terribly dark in here.'

Blinking, Halina scours the den for a sign, any sign, of her parents, but the room is just how she remembers it. The blue ceramic vase on the windowsill, the green paisley pattern adorning the armchair tucked into the corner, the Bible resting on a small oak side table beside the sofa – there is nothing out of the ordinary. She lets her eyes travel along the far wall to the bookshelf with the invisible wheels.

Albert clears his throat. 'Right,' he says, making his way to the shelves.

Halina swallows. A flash of hope.

'When I saw your car come up and didn't recognise it,' Albert says, sliding the shelves gently away from the cedar-planked wall, 'I thought they'd better hide. Just in case.'

They'd better hide.

Albert knocks on the wall in the place where the shelf used to be. 'Pan i Pani Kurc,' he calls quietly.

Halina's cheeks are suddenly warm. Her skin prickles in anticipation. Behind her, Adam rests his hands on her shoulders, leans in so his chin brushes her ear. 'They're here,' he whispers. Beneath the floorboards, there is movement. Halina listens intently – to the shuffle of bodies moving in her direction, the muffled sound of leather soles meeting wood, the click of a bolt sliding open.

And then, they emerge. First her father, then her mother, squinting as they climb, stooped at first, from the Górskis' crawl space into the brightly lit den. A strange sound escapes Nechuma's lips as she rights herself to find

Halina before her. Albert steps aside as the women collapse into one another.

'Halina,' Sol whispers. He wraps his arms around the union of his wife and daughter, closing his eyes as he holds them, his nose burrowed into the small space between the tops of their heads. They stand like this for a long moment, their bodies melded together as one, crying silently until finally, mother, father, and daughter part, wiping their eyes. Sol seems surprised to see Adam.

'Pan Kurc,' Adam nods, smiling. He hasn't laid eyes on his now in-laws since before he and Halina were married. Sol laughs, holds out a hand, and pulls Adam in for a hug.

'Please, my son,' he says, crow's feet flanking his eyes, 'you may call me Sol.'

Part III

MAY 8, 1945: *VE Day. Germany surrenders and Allied victory is proclaimed in Europe.*

CHAPTER FIFTY-FOUR

The Kurc Family
Łódź, Poland ~ May 8, 1945

Adam tinkers with the radio's tuning dial, adjusting it until a voice crackles through its speakers. 'In a few minutes,' an announcer says in Polish, 'we will translate a live broadcast from the White House in the United States. Please stay tuned.'

Halina slides the living-room window open. Three stories below, the boulevard is empty. Everyone, it seems, has stepped inside to gather around their receivers, to listen for the news that Łódź – that all of occupied Europe, and the world, for that matter – has been awaiting for the better part of a decade.

Halina's decision to bring the family to Łódź was a practical one. They'd managed for a while in Warsaw, but the city, what was left of it, was unlivable. They'd discussed a move back to Radom, had even ventured back for a visit and stayed the night with the Sobczaks, but they'd found that the apartment on Warszawska Street and her parents' shop were now occupied by Poles. Halina wasn't prepared for what it would feel like to be met at her old doorstep by strangers – strangers who stared at her with stubborn frowns, who claimed that they had no intention of leaving, who had the nerve to believe that what once belonged to her family was now theirs.

The encounter had infuriated Halina so much she'd flown into a rage; it was Adam who brought her back to her rational mind, reminding her that the war was not yet over, that they were still posing as Aryan and an outburst would only draw dangerous attention. She had left Radom disheartened but determined to find a city where they could settle, at least until war's end – a city with enough industry that they could find work, and with apartments to house what was left of the family, including her parents, whom she had convinced to stay in

Wilonów until the war was officially over. Łódź, Halina heard, had apartments, jobs, and a Red Cross office. And sure enough, it didn't take her long to find a place to live when they arrived. The city's ghetto had been liquidated later than most, which meant there were hundreds of vacant homes in the old Jewish Quarter and not enough Poles to fill them. It was nauseating to consider what had become of the families who had lived there before them, but Halina knew they couldn't afford to rent in the city centre. She selected two neighbouring apartments, the most spacious she could find. They were missing half of their furniture, but there were so many empty homes she was able to salvage enough pieces here and there to make them habitable.

The family is quiet as Jakob arranges five chairs in a semicircle around the fireplace, where the radio is perched like a tombstone atop the mantel. 'Sit, love,' he says, gesturing to Bella. She lowers herself gently into the chair, rests a hand on the subtle curve of her stomach. She is six months pregnant. Mila, Halina, Adam, and Jakob sit, too, while Felicia curls up on the floor, wincing as she pulls her knees to her chest. Mila combs her fingers through Felicia's hair, which has begun to grow in its natural red at the roots. It breaks her heart to see her daughter in pain. The scurvy she'd contracted in the convent bunker has cleared up for the most part, but she still complains of an ache in her joints. At least, Mila sighs, her appetite is back – Felicia had refused food for weeks when Mila first retrieved her, claiming that it hurt too much to eat.

Finally, the voice of Harry Truman, the United States' new president, spills from the radio's speakers, and the family leans in. 'This is a solemn but glorious hour,' Truman projects through a sea of static. The local broadcaster translates. 'General Eisenhower,' Truman continues, 'informs me that the forces of Germany have surrendered to the United Nations.' He pauses for effect, and then adds, 'The flags of freedom fly all over Europe!'

The words 'freedom' and 'fly' reverberate through the room, drifting overhead like confetti.

The family stares at the radio and then at one another as the president's alliteration comes to rest tentatively on their laps. Adam removes his glasses and lifts his chin toward the ceiling, pinching the bridge of his nose between his thumb and forefinger. Bella wipes a tear from her eye, and Jakob reaches for her hand. Mila bites her lip. Felicia looks around at the others and then up at her mother, her eyes inquisitive, unsure why they are crying at what she understood to be good news.

Halina tries to picture the American president seated triumphantly behind his desk some 6,000 kilometres west of them. *VE Day,* Truman called it: *Victory in Europe.* But to Halina, the word *victory* feels hollow. False, even. There's hardly anything victorious about the ruined Warsaw they left, or about the fact that so much of the family is still missing, or about how all around them in what was once Łódź's massive ghetto, they can feel the ghosts of 200,000 Jews – most of whom, it's rumoured, met their deaths in the gas vans and chambers of Chełmno and Auschwitz.

A muffled cheer trickles in from the apartment next door. Through the window, a few shouts from the street. Łódź has begun to celebrate. The world has begun to celebrate. Hitler has been defeated – the war is over. Which means, technically, they are free to be Kurcs and Eichenwalds and Kajlers again. To be Jews again. But the mood in the apartment isn't celebratory. Not while the rest of the family is unaccounted for. And not with so many dead. Every day the estimated toll rises. First it was a million, then two – numbers so large, they can't even begin to grasp the enormity of them.

When Truman's speech is over, the Polish announcer states that the Red Cross will continue to erect dozens of offices and Displaced Persons camps throughout Europe, urging survivors to register themselves. Adam switches the radio off and the living room goes quiet again. What is there to say? Finally, it is Halina who fills the silence. 'Tomorrow,' she declares, willing her voice to remain steady, 'I'll return to the Red Cross, double-check that all of our names are registered. I'll ask about the DP camps – and when exactly we will be able to access a list of names. And I'll begin making arrangements to reach Mother and Father in the countryside.'

On the street below, the cheering grows louder. Halina stands and makes her way to the window, slides it gently closed.

CHAPTER FIFTY-FIVE

The Kurc Family
Łódź, Poland ~ June, 1945

Every day, Halina walks the familiar route from the apartment in Łódź, first to the temporary Red Cross headquarters in the centre of town, then to the newly erected offices of the Hebrew Immigrant Aid Society, and finally to the American Jewish Joint Distribution Committee, or the Joint, as everyone calls it – in hopes of discovering news of missing family. When she isn't making her rounds, she scours the local daily, which has begun publishing lists of names and classified ads from survivors looking for relatives. The radio, too, has a station devoted to helping survivors reconnect; she's called in twice. Last week, Halina's hopes soared when she discovered Franka's name on a list published by the Central Committee of Jews in Poland – an organisation funded by the Joint Distribution Committee. Her cousin had been sent, along with her brother and her parents, to a camp outside of Lublin called Majdanek; by some unexplained twist of fate, she, Salek, and Terza had survived. Her father, Moshe, however, had not been so fortunate. Halina has begun trying to make arrangements for her cousins and aunt to come to Łódź, but she's been told it could take months; they are among thousands of refugees awaiting assistance at the DP camp where they've been stationed. Halina's parents, at least, are here now in Łódź; she'd managed to retrieve them at last from the country.

They must be getting bored with me, Halina reckons as she approaches the offices of the Red Cross, where the volunteers know her well. They typically greet her with a half smile, a head shake, and a doleful *Sorry, no news.* Today, though, the aluminum door has barely swung closed behind her when one of the volunteers rushes at her. 'It's for you!' the woman shrieks, waving a small white paper overhead. A dozen or so people turn. In a space usually filled with sadness, the excitement in the woman's voice is jarring.

Halina stops, looks over her shoulder and then back at the volunteer. 'For me? What – what's for me?'

'This!' The volunteer holds a telegram between thumbs and forefingers at arm's length, then reads it aloud: 'With Selim in Italy. Find us through Polish II Corps. Genek Kurc.'

At the sound of her brother's name, the room begins to spin and Halina splays her arms reflexively to keep from falling. '*What?* Where is he?' Her voice is shaky. 'Let me see that.' She reaches for the telegram, dizzy. The Polish Second Corps? Isn't that Anders's Army? With *Selim,* who they all thought was *dead?* Halina can barely breathe. General Anders is all anyone in Łódź can talk about – he and his men are *heroes.* They took Monte Cassino. Fought on the River Senio, in the Battle of Bologna. Halina shakes her head, trying to picture Genek and her brother-in-law Selim in uniform, in battle, making history. But she can't.

'See for yourself.'

Halina grips the telegram so tightly the beds of her thumbnails go white. She prays there isn't some kind of mistake.

WITH SELIM IN ITALY

FIND US THR POLISH II CORPS

GENEK KURC

Sure enough, her brother's name is spelt across the bottom. She looks up. The others watch, awaiting a reaction. Halina opens her mouth and then closes it, swallowing what might be a sob or a laugh, she can't tell which. 'Thank you!' she finally croaks, clutching the telegram to her chest. 'Thank you!'

The office swells with cheers as Halina brings the telegram to her lips, kisses it over and over again. Tears begin to spill down her cheeks, but she ignores them. A single thought fills her mind. *There is no mistake. They are alive.* She tucks the telegram into her blouse pocket, spins out of the office, and takes off running. Twelve blocks later, she scales the stairs leading to her apartment in twos and finds her parents in the kitchen, preparing dinner.

Her mother looks up as Halina peers at them through the doorway, panting, her cheeks flushed. 'Are you okay?' Nechuma asks, alarmed, her knife suspended over a carrot. 'Have you been crying?'

Halina doesn't know where to begin. 'Is Mila home?' she asks, breathless.

'She went to the market with Felicia; she'll be back in a minute. Halina, what is it?' Nechuma sets the knife down and wipes her hands on a dish towel tucked into the waistband of her skirt.

Beside her, Sol goes still. 'Halina, tell us – what's happened?' He looks at Halina closely, his brow pinched with worry.

'I – I have news,' Halina exclaims. 'How long ago did Mila—' She stops short at the sound of a door opening. 'Mila!' Racing to the foyer, she greets her sister at the door, grabbing a canvas tote from her arms. 'Thank goodness you're here! Come, hurry.'

'Why are you so out of breath?' Mila asks. 'You're soaked in sweat!'

'News! I have news!'

Mila's eyes pop, the hazel of her irises surrounded suddenly by a sea of white. 'What? What kind of news?' News could mean anything. She and Felicia follow Halina down the hallway.

At the door to the kitchen, Halina motions for her parents to join her in the living room. 'Come,' she calls. When the family is gathered, Halina takes a deep breath. She can barely contain herself. 'I've just come from the Red Cross,' she says, reaching into her blouse pocket and extracting the telegram. She wills her hands to remain steady as she holds the priceless piece of paper up for her family to see. 'It came in today, from *Italy*.' She reads the telegram aloud, enunciating every word carefully: 'With Selim. In Italy. Find us through Polish II Corps.' She looks up at her mother, her father, her sister, Felicia, her eyes dancing between them, filling up again with tears. 'Signed, Genek Kurc,' she adds, her voice cracking.

'What?' Mila pulls Felicia to her, cradling her head against her low ribs.

Nechuma reaches for Sol's arm to steady herself.

'Read that again,' Sol whispers.

Halina reads the telegram again, and once again. By the third read, Nechuma is in tears, and the small apartment is filled with the deep clap of Sol's laughter. 'That is the best news I've heard since . . . I can remember,' he says, his shoulders shaking.

They hug in pairs, Sol and Nechuma, Mila and Felicia, Mila and Halina, Halina and Nechuma, and then huddle together as one, like a giant wheel, hands wrapped around waists and foreheads pressed up against one another's, Felicia tucked somewhere in the middle. Time disappears as they hold each other, laughing and crying, Sol reciting the telegram's twelve perfect words over and over and over again.

Halina is the first to pull free from the circle. 'Jakob!' she shrieks. 'I must go tell Jakob!'

'Yes, go,' Nechuma says, drying her eyes. 'Tell him to meet us here for supper this evening.'

'I will,' Halina calls, flying down the hallway.

The door opens and then closes and soon after a hush falls over the apartment. '*Mamusiu?*' Felicia whispers, peering up at her mother as if awaiting an explanation. But Mila has gone silent. Her gaze volleys left to right, as if searching the room for something she can't see. A ghost, perhaps.

Noticing, Nechuma rests a hand on Sol's shoulder. 'Could you prepare some tea with Felicia?' she whispers. Sol glances at Mila and nods, beckoning Felicia to the kitchen.

When they are alone, Nechuma turns to Mila, reaches for her arm. 'Mila, what is it, darling?'

Mila blinks, shakes her head. 'It's nothing, Mother – I just –'

'Come,' Nechuma offers, guiding Mila to the small table in the living room where they take their meals.

Mila moves slowly, her mind elsewhere as she sits. Resting her elbows on the table, she wraps her hands together into a giant fist and leans her chin into her thumbs. For a while, neither woman speaks.

'It's not what you were expecting – to find him,' Nechuma finally says, choosing her words carefully. 'You didn't think he was still alive.'

'No.' A tear slips from the corner of Mila's eye, rolls down her cheek. Nechuma brushes it gently away.

'You must be relieved though, yes?'

Mila nods. 'Of course.' She lifts her chin, turns to face her mother. 'It's just that – I've spent the last six years thinking he was – was dead. I'd adjusted to it. Accepted it, even, as terrible as that sounds.'

'It's understandable. You had to go on for Felicia's sake. You did what any mother would do.'

'I shouldn't have given up on him. I should have been more hopeful. What kind of wife gives up on her husband?'

'Please,' Nechuma says, her voice soft, understanding. 'What were you supposed to think? You didn't hear from him. We all thought he was dead. Besides, none of that matters now.'

Mila glances over her shoulder toward the kitchen. 'I need to talk to Felicia.' Mila had spoken less and less of Selim since admitting to Felicia she was unsure of his fate – since choosing, for her own sake, to believe that he was gone. But Felicia had refused to let go. She'd spent the past year asking questions about him, begging her mother for details. 'She's built him up so much in her mind,' Mila adds. 'What if she's – disappointed? When he left, she was just a baby, healthy, pink-cheeked . . . What if—' Mila stops, unable to describe how much Felicia has changed.

Nechuma reaches for Mila's hands, lays her palms over them. 'Mila, darling, I know all of this is sudden, but think of it this way: you've been given a chance, a precious, impossible chance, to start over. And Selim is Felicia's father. She will love him. And he will love her, just the way you love her. Unconditionally.'

Mila nods. 'You're right,' she whispers. 'I just hate that he doesn't know her.'

'Give him time,' Nechuma says, 'and *yourself* time – to figure it out again – how to be a family. Be patient. Try not to worry too much about it. You've done enough worrying for a lifetime.'

Mila slips her hands from under her mother's to wipe a tear from her cheek. What does it mean, she wonders, to live a day of her life without worry? Without a plan? Every minute of every day has been orchestrated, to the best of her ability, since the start of the war. Is she even capable, Mila wonders, of letting things unfold on their own?

Later that evening, once Felicia is asleep, the family sits at the dinner table, studying a map spread out before them. Halina has sent a telegram to Genek, letting him know that for the most part, the family is alive and well. *Still no word from Addy,* she wrote. *When are you discharged? Where should we meet?*

The exercise of deciding where to go next is difficult. Because *next* most likely means a new forever. It means thinking about where to settle. Where to start over. During the war, their options were fewer, the stakes higher, their mission singular. It was simple, in a way. Keep your chin down, your guard up. Stay one step ahead. Stay alive for one more day. Don't let the enemy win. To think about a long-term plan feels complicated, and burdensome, like flexing an atrophied muscle.

'The first question,' Halina says, looking around the table, 'is do we stay in Poland?'

Sol shakes his head. His eyes are stern. Despite the news from Genek in Italy, he has found very few reasons lately to smile. Two weeks ago, not long after learning of his brother-in-law Moshe's death, he'd discovered that a sister, two brothers, four cousins, and half a dozen nieces and nephews who had been living in Kraków at the start of the war had also been killed. His extended family, once so large, has been reduced to just a few. The news had wrecked him. He presses the pad of his index finger to the table. 'Here,' he says, frowning, 'we are not safe.'

The others sit silently, considering what they do and do not know. The Germans have surrendered, yes, but for Jewish survivors, the war is far from over. Already, the Kurcs have heard stories of Jews returning to their hometowns only to be accosted, robbed, sometimes killed. In one instance, a pogrom erupted when a group of locals accused a returning Jewish man of kidnapping a Polish child – he was hung from a tree – and for days after, dozens more Jews were shot dead in the street. There is truth, it seems, to Sol's declaration.

Eyes turn to Nechuma. She nods in agreement, glancing at her husband and then down at the map. 'I agree. We should go.' The words are heavy in her lungs, leaving her breathless. It is a declaration she never thought she'd make. Six years ago, Hitler's proclamation to remove the Jews from the continent seemed absurd. No one believed such cold-blooded plans could come to fruition. But now they know. They've seen the newspapers, the photographs, they've begun to process the numbers. Now there is no denying what the enemy is capable of. 'I think it's best,' she adds, swallowing. The idea of leaving behind all that was once theirs – their home, their street, the shop, their friends – is nearly impossible to conceive. But, Nechuma reminds herself, those things are things of the past. Of a life that no longer exists. There are strangers now living in her home. Could she and Sol take it back, even if they wanted to? And who is left of their friends? The ghetto has been empty now for years. As far as they knew, there were no Jews left in Radom. Sol is right. It isn't smart to stay in Poland. History repeats itself. This is one truth of which she is certain.

'I think so, too,' Mila says. 'I want Felicia to grow up someplace she can feel safe, where she can feel – *normal*.' Mila frowns, wondering what the concept of 'normal' even means to her young daughter. The only life Felicia knows is one of being hunted. Forced into hiding. Sneaked through ghetto gates. Left in the hands of strangers. She is seven, and all but the first year of her life has been spent in war, with the sickening awareness that there are people who wish her dead just by virtue of her birth. At least Mila and her siblings have the experience to understand that it hasn't always been this way. But the war, the persecution, the daily fight to survive – *this* is Felicia's normal. Mila's eyes begin to water. 'Think of everything we've been through,' she says. 'Everything Felicia has been through. There isn't a way to erase what has happened here.' She shakes her head. 'There are too many ghosts, too many memories.'

Beside Mila, Bella nods, and Jakob's heart aches for her. Hers is an opinion that doesn't need to be spoken; they all know that for Bella, a return to Radom would be impossible. With her parents and her sister gone, there is nothing left for her there. Jakob finds Bella's hand, and as he folds his fingers around hers, he can't help but recall how, in her deepest months of despair, he'd all but lost her. How she had pushed him out of her life. It had torn him apart, to see her like that, to watch her disappear. He'd never felt so helpless. Nor had he felt such relief when she finally made the effort, little by little, to pick herself up and to carry on. He'd seen glimmers of the old Bella in Warsaw, but it is this pregnancy, this new life inside her, that seems to have helped her restore the strength she needs, at last, to heal.

Jakob glances up at his parents. He can tell from the way his mother seems to be bracing herself that she knows what he's about to say. It's old news – he's told her already that he and Bella are considering a move to the United States – but the words don't come easily. 'Bella's uncle in Illinois,' he begins quietly, 'has agreed to sponsor us. It doesn't guarantee a visa, of course, but it's a start. And it makes sense, I think, to take him up on it.' Surely the others understand that at least in the States, Bella could be surrounded by what remains of her family.

'Once we get to Chicago,' Bella says, looking from Nechuma to Sol, 'we can enquire about visas for the rest of the family. If that's something you might be interested in.'

'We'll stay in Poland for the time being,' Jakob adds, 'at least until the baby arrives.'

A sponsorship to America. The idea settles in Nechuma's heart like a lead weight. If it were up to her, she would spend every last hour she had on this earth with her children at arm's reach. But she can't argue with Jakob. It would be foolish of him not to accept help from Bella's uncle. Without a sponsorship, an American visa is nearly impossible to come by.

Jakob goes on to explain that no ships are allowed to sail from Europe to the States at the moment, but that restrictions are due to be lifted soon. 'Apparently there are passenger ships leaving from Bremerhaven,' he says, leaning over the map and pointing to a city in north-west Germany. 'Our thought, once the baby is born,' he says, 'is to make our temporary home a Displaced Persons camp here, in Stuttgart. From there we should have a better chance of securing visas.'

Halina stares at Jakob from across the table, her mouth puckered in disgust. She is appalled by the idea of her brother moving to Germany. 'Aren't there DP camps in Poland?' she snaps. 'Wouldn't you be better off here?' She shakes her head vehemently, her green eyes challenging his. 'I'd rather slit my throat than set foot into the *belly of evil.*'

Halina's tone is sharp, but though it might have bothered Jakob before, it doesn't now. It's become her job, he realises, to protect the family – she's just watching out for him. He meets her stare with a look of understanding, agreeing that the idea of a move to Germany is unnerving. 'Trust me, Halina, it won't be easy. But if it means we are one step closer to a new life in the States, then we're ready to do what it takes. At this point, I think it's safe to say we'll have been through worse.'

The room is quiet for a moment before Halina speaks up again. 'All right, then,' she declares. 'Jakob, you and Bella have reason to stay. But we don't. I think we've all agreed on that. My vote is we go to Italy. To Genek and Selim. From there, we can decide together, as a family, where to go next.' She looks to her parents.

Nechuma and Sol exchange a glance. 'I only wish we had some idea of whether Addy . . .' Nechuma says, stopping to correct her choice of words, 'of where Addy is.' The others grow silent, lost in their own fears. But Nechuma nods. 'Italy.'

'We mustn't forget that Mussolini was Hitler's ally during the war,' Sol says. 'I suggest we find a route with as few civilian checkpoints as possible.'

And so the decision is made: for Jakob and Bella to make their way in a few months from Łódź to Stuttgart and eventually, hopefully, to America, and for the others to travel to Italy.

As the family leans over the map, Adam traces his finger from Łódź south-west to Italy, listing the cities in between where he's confident there would be Red Cross offices: Katowice, Vienna, Salzburg, Innsbruck. He omits Kraków, for he's certain his wife would be better off never returning to anywhere within a fifty-kilometre radius of the Montelupich Prison. The route would require crossing through Czechoslovakia and Austria. They agree that it's their only good option.

'I will write to Terza, Franka, and Salek to let them know of our plans,' Halina says, thinking aloud. 'I will ask the Joint if they can help pay for their travel, so that they can meet us in Italy. And I'll talk to the girls at the Red Cross – perhaps they can help us plan a route, or tell us of other Red Cross locations we might not know about along the way. We'll need vodka and cigarettes. For the checkpoints.'

Nechuma looks at Sol, envisioning the journey. To get to Italy won't be easy. But if they can make it, she'll be reunited with her firstborn. And Felicia will have a father! Her mood lightens at the thought. At the start of the war, she had no idea if she and Sol would live to see the end of it, if her children would live to see the end of it, if they would ever come together again, as a cohesive whole. The day the Germans marched into Radom, her world was torn to shreds. She'd watched from then on as every basic truth of the life she once knew – her home, her family, her safety – was thrown to the wind. Now, those fragments of her past have begun to drift back down to earth, and for the first time in over half a decade she has allowed herself to believe that, with time and patience, she might just be able to stitch together a semblance of what was. It will never be the same – she's wise enough to understand that. But they are *here,* and for the most part, *together,* which has begun to feel like something of a miracle.

Of course, she can't help but fixate on the missing pieces, on Moshe and the family that Sol has lost and on Adam's relatives, who are still unaccounted for – and especially on the gaping hole that belongs to her middle son. What has become of her Addy? Nechuma's spirit plummets as she grapples with the mystery, the likelihood that she may never know – and the reality that her world, her tapestry, will never be complete without him.

CHAPTER FIFTY-SIX

Halina
Austrian Alps ~ July 1945

Through a clearing in the trees, Halina can see nothing but steel blue sky. It's past eight in the evening, yet still light enough to read a book, if she had one. Her parents, Mila, and Felicia are asleep, their sweat-caked bodies strewn across the campsite, heads propped on purses and the small leather satchels holding what's left of their belongings. Listening to the drone of a woodpecker on the trunk of a nearby aspen, Halina sighs. It'll be another hour before it's dark – another two hours, she knows, before she will surrender to sleep. She might as well take advantage of the last bit of light, she decides, retrieving a handkerchief from the inside zipper pocket of her purse. She unfolds it and arranges her remaining cigarettes into a row on the ground in front of her, counting them. There are twelve. Enough, she hopes, to bribe the guards at the next checkpoint.

Meet in Bari, Genek wrote in their last correspondence. Despite the heavy restrictions on civilian travel, Halina, Nechuma, Sol, Mila, and Felicia didn't waste much time in leaving Łódź. Adam had stayed behind. 'You go,' he told Halina. 'I'll stay, earn us some savings.' He'd found a steady job at a local cinema. 'I'll meet you in Italy when you're settled,' he said. Halina didn't argue with him. A few weeks before, Adam had found, through the International Tracing Service, the names of his parents, siblings, and nephew on a list of those confirmed dead. There was no other information, just their nine names, inked onto a page amid hundreds of others. Adam was devastated – and the fact that he'd been given no explanation of how or when they'd died was driving him mad. Halina knew it wasn't the job he was staying for. He needed answers.

And so Halina and the others had left, armed with as many cigarettes and bottles of vodka as they could carry. Halina had hired a driver to take the family to Katowice, a city 200 kilometres due south of Łódź. In Katowice, Halina, still fluent in Russian, finagled a ride in the back of a truck delivering supplies to the Red Army in Vienna. The journey took days. The Kurcs stayed hidden, tucked between crates of uniforms and tinned meat, afraid that if they were caught crossing borders in Czechoslovakia or Austria without the proper documents, they'd be turned back, or worse, incarcerated.

From Vienna, they hitchhiked to Graz, where they were dropped at the base of the Southern Limestone Alps, a towering snow-capped range that snaked south-west through Austria and into Italy. Halina wondered if her parents and Felicia, still stick-thin, would be able to make the trek – the Alps were imposing, taller than any mountains she'd seen before. But unless they wanted to face a dozen train station and border checkpoints, crossing them on foot was their best option. After a week of rest in Graz, the Kurcs shed some of their belongings, filled the remaining space in their bags with bread and water, and, using what was left of their savings (Adam had insisted they bring what little he had), they hired a guide – a young Austrian boy named Wilhelm – to show them the way over the range. 'You're lucky summer came a bit early,' Wilhelm said, the day they left. 'The Southern Alps are covered in snow ten months out of the year, and this time of year they're usually impassable.'

They walked every day from seven in the morning to seven at night. Wilhelm proved extremely helpful as a guide, until they woke up one morning to find that he'd vanished. Luckily, he'd left the remainder of the food, along with his map. Cursing the young Austrian's cowardice, Halina quickly appointed herself leader.

She wraps her handkerchief around her cigarettes and slides them back into her purse, then reaches to her breast pocket for the map and peels it open gently by the corners; with all of the use it's gotten, its edges are now velvet soft, its creases unnervingly thin. She brushes a few pebbles from the ground and lays the map down, tracing a dirt-caked fingernail between their approximate location and the nearest town at the foot of the Southern Alps, Villach – a village just north of the Italian border. She estimates another forty hours of walking, due south, which means they could be in Italy in four days. It will be a challenge. Their lungs have acclimated to the 3,000-metre altitude, but the soles of their shoes, not intended for such frequent, rugged use, have begun to disintegrate. They'll need to be exceptionally cautious, especially in their descent. Halina considers breaking up the trip to give their legs a rest. The day before, Sol had stumbled on a root along the path and nearly rolled his ankle. They are all exhausted to the bone. Twelve hours of hiking each day is a lot to ask. But they are also low on provisions, with only four to five days worth of bread and water left in their supply at most. So they'll press on, Halina decides. Best just to get to Italian soil. The others would surely agree.

A white-tailed eagle circles overhead and Halina marvels at its massive wingspan, then eyes the provisions pack she'd hung from a nearby branch, checking to be sure she'd cinched it tightly shut. *Close your eyes,* she tells herself. Slipping the map back into her shirt pocket, she laces her fingers together and leans back to rest her head in her palms. Her body is whipped from the day's exertion, but she is too wound up to sleep. Her thoughts, like the incessant drum of the resident woodpecker, come and go in triple time. What if she picks the wrong route down the mountain? They could get lost, run out of food, and never make it to Italy. What if they make it to Italy and are turned back by the authorities? It was only a month ago that the country was occupied by Nazis. What if something happens to Adam in Łódź? It will be weeks – more, possibly – before she can write to him with a return address.

Halina stares up at the darkening sky. It's not just the what-if scenarios that are keeping her awake. There is also a part of her that's too excited to sleep. She's just days from reuniting with her oldest brother! She imagines what it'll feel like to see Genek for the first time in so many years. To hear his laugh. To kiss his dimpled cheeks. To sit down together, as a family, and figure out a plan, where to go next. The idea of setting their minds to a future beyond the war is thrilling, intoxicating – it makes Halina's heart race, just thinking about it. Maybe Bella is right – maybe her relatives could sponsor the whole Kurc family, and they could move to the States. Or maybe they'll head north, to the United Kingdom, or south, to Palestine, or across the planet, to Australia. Their decision, of course, will depend on which country will be willing to open its doors.

Quit thinking and sleep, Halina tells herself. As she rolls to her side, she folds an arm into a pillow, resting her head on her elbow, and brings a hand to her low belly. She's two weeks late now. She tries to do the math, to count the days since she and Adam saw one another, but it's nearly impossible. She's spent so many years thinking ahead that her brain has forgotten how to look back in time. The days before they left Łódź are fuzzy. Could she be? Perhaps. It's possible. But also possible that she's just late. It's happened before. She didn't bleed once during the four months she was imprisoned in Kraków. Too much stress. Too little food. *You never know,* Halina allows herself, smiling. Anything is possible. *For now, just get the family safely to Italy. Focus on the task at hand. On the next four days.* At the moment, she decides, willing her mind to rest, that's all that matters.

CHAPTER FIFTY-SEVEN

The Kurc Family
Adriatic Coast of Italy ~ July 1945

Felicia sleeps curled into the fetal position on the seat next to Mila's, her cheek propped on her mother's thigh. Mila, too nervous to close her eyes, rests a hand on Felicia's shoulder and presses her forehead to the window, taking in the azure of the Adriatic as the train speeds south along the heel of Italy's boot toward Bari. She rehearses for the thousandth time what she will say to her husband when she sees him. It should be obvious – *I've missed you. I love you. So much has happened . . . where do I begin?* But even in her mind, the words feel forced.

Nechuma had told her to be patient. To try not to worry so much. But Mila can't help herself. She wonders if Selim will be the same man she knew before the war, tries to imagine falling back into the rhythm of husband and wife – Selim playing the role once again of patriarch, money earner, keeper of their fate. Could she do that? Could she learn to take a back seat, to depend on him again? It's been just her and Felicia for so long, she's not sure she's ready yet to let someone else take the reins. Even if that someone is Felicia's father.

Across the aisle, Halina fans herself with a newspaper. She'd begun the trip sitting opposite Mila, but conversing with her sister while watching the scenery stream by in reverse had made her stomach turn, so she moved to a seat where she could face forward. She's pregnant. She's sure of it now. Her stomach heaves when it's empty, her breasts are swollen and tender, and her slacks have grown snug around the waist. Pregnant! It is a truth as daunting as it is thrilling. She hasn't said a word to the family yet. She plans to tell them after they reach Bari. And she'll have to come up with a clever way to share the news with Adam back in Łódź – perhaps she'll splurge on a telephone call. *I've just walked over the Alps, and I'm pregnant,* she'll say. If someone had told her before the war that at twenty-eight she'd lead her family across a mountain range, pregnant and on foot, she'd have laughed wholeheartedly. She's not a country girl! A three-week haul over the mountains, sleeping on the dirt, with stale bread and water for sustenance? While *carrying a child?* Not a chance.

Halina replays the past few weeks of their journey in her mind, marvelling at the fact that, despite the circumstances, she hasn't heard a single complaint. Not from Mila, who trekked for hours each day with Felicia on her back; not from her parents, whose limps grew more apparent by the day; not even from Felicia, whose shoes were so small her blistered toes had finally poked a hole in one of them, and who, when her mother wasn't carrying her, had to take two strides for every one of the adults' to keep up.

Their border crossing into Italy, thankfully, had been uneventful. '*Siamo italiani,*' Halina lied to the British authorities manning the checkpoint in Tarcento. When the guards balked, Halina opened her purse. 'Returning home to our families,' she said, reaching for the remaining cigarettes.

It was a strange feeling to walk for the first time on Italian soil. Nechuma was the only one in the group who'd been before – she used to visit Milan twice a year to buy silk and linen for the shop. To pass the time and as a distraction from their aching knees on their descent through the Alps, she'd told stories of her travels – of how the vendors at the Milanese markets had nicknamed her *la tigre cieca,* 'the blind tiger,' as she would travel from stall to stall rubbing fabric swatches between thumb and forefinger, always with her eyes closed, before making an offer. There was no fooling her when it came to quality – 'I could guess the price to the nearest lira,' she said proudly.

Once in Italy, Halina asked directions to the nearest village. They then walked another six hours, depleted of their water supply; it was dusk and they were all close to delirium when they knocked on the door of a small home on the outskirts of the town. Halina could see that they were in no shape to sleep another night out in the elements, with only a crust of bread to eat and nothing to drink, and gave a silent prayer that whoever opened the door would look at their filthy, bedraggled group with sympathy and not suspicion. She breathed a sigh of relief when a kind-eyed young farmer and his wife opened the door and waved them inside. Nechuma was able to talk to them using the small bit of Italian she had, and soon they were devouring warm plates of peppery *pasta aglio e olio*. That night, all five Kurcs slept better than they had in months, on blankets the couple had spread across the floor.

The next morning, after offering up profuse thanks to their Italian hosts, the Kurcs continued on by foot toward the train station. En route, they crossed paths with a group of American soldiers who stepped out of their army-green Jeeps when Halina waved and flashed a smile at them. The Americans, one of whom fortunately spoke French, were eager to learn news of the situation in Poland. They shook their heads in disbelief when Halina told them briefly of the unfathomable devastation in Warsaw and the path that she and her family had followed in order to flee their homeland and arrive safely in Italy.

Before they parted, a young, blue-eyed sergeant with a T. O'DRISCOLL patch sewn to his fatigues reached into his pocket and squatted beside Felicia. 'Here y'are, darlin',' he said in an accent unlike any Felicia had ever heard before. She had blushed as the handsome American handed her a brown and silver foil package. 'It's a Hershey bar. I hope you like it,' Sergeant O'Driscoll said.

'Merci,' Mila said, squeezing Felicia's free hand.

'Merci,' Felicia imitated quietly.

'Where to from here?' the American had asked, patting Felicia on the head as he stood. The soldier who spoke French translated.

'To family in Bari,' Halina explained.

'You're a long way from Bari.'

'We've gotten pretty good at walking,' Halina said, smiling.

'Wait here.' Sergeant O'Driscoll left, and returned a few minutes later with a US twenty-dollar bill. 'Train's faster,' he said, handing Halina the bill, returning her smile.

* * *

Across from Halina, Nechuma and Sol drift in and out of sleep, their chins nodding as the train ricochets on its tracks. Studying them as if through Genek's eyes, Halina can see how much the war has aged them. They look twenty years older than they had before they'd been locked up in the ghetto, forced into hiding, nearly starved.

'*Bari, cinque minuti!*' the conductor calls.

Mila runs her fingertips over the scurvy scars still pockmarking Felicia's neck and cheeks. Her hair is shoulder length now, and blonde from her ears down. Beneath her eyelids, Felicia's eyes jump. Her forehead twitches. Even in her sleep, Mila realises, her daughter looks scared. The last five years have stripped her of her innocence. A tear spills from Mila's eye, down her cheek, and onto the collar of Felicia's blouse, leaving a small stain on the cotton, a perfect grey circle.

Mila wipes her eyes, her mind turning again to Selim. To the questions she can't ignore. What will he think of Felicia, the daughter he's never known? What will Felicia think of *him*? Yesterday, she had asked what to call Selim. 'How about just Father, to start,' Mila had suggested.

A few minutes later, as the train begins to slow, Mila's heart rate hastens. She pleads with herself to embrace the gift of the husband and father she and Felicia are about to receive. Heaven knows what's happened to *his* family – to his father, a watchmaker of modest means, to his eight siblings. Last she knew, a sister, Eugenia, had emigrated to Paris, a brother, David, to Palestine; the rest, she believed, had remained in Warsaw. She'd tried to locate them before the uprising, but they'd either left on their own accord or been sent away – she could find no trace of them. It's a blessing, she realises, to soon be reunited with her husband, amid the inconceivable tragedy the war has left in its wake. Most would do anything to be in her position.

Brakes squeal. The scenery outside her window slows to a crawl. Mila can see the Bari station a hundred or so metres ahead, and on the platform, people, waiting. As she rubs Felicia's shoulder gently to wake her, she makes a promise to herself: she'll embrace her husband with an open heart. She'll paint a picture of stability, no matter how hard it might be. For Felicia's sake. And what happens next – what Selim will think of the girl on her lap with unsightly hair and pink scars running down her face, whether Felicia will learn to love the man she has no recollection of ever knowing – these are things, Mila tells herself, best left in the hands of fate.

CHAPTER FIFTY-EIGHT

The Kurc Family
Bari, Italy ~ August 1945

It's chaos at the Bari station. Bodies, three rows deep, crowd the platform: men in uniform, small children gripping the hands of what appear to be grandparents, women in their best dresses, waving, standing on their toes, the backs of their calves painted with long charcoal lines to give the illusion of stockings.

As the Kurcs make their way from the train, Halina leads; Nechuma and Sol follow close behind; and Mila brings up the rear, the straps of a leather satchel looped over a shoulder, her hand holding tight to Felicia's. They shuffle their feet so as not to step on each other's heels, a body of five moving as one.

'Let's wait over here,' Halina calls over her shoulder as they make their way through the throngs to a marquee reading BARI CENTRALE, and beside it, a sign with an arrow for PIAZZA ROMA. Gathered beneath the marquee, they remain close, standing in a knot, searching the platform for familiar faces. Unaccustomed to seeing Genek and Selim in military garb, they remind themselves to look only for men in Polish uniform.

'*Kurde*,' Halina grumbles, 'I'm too damned short. Can't see a thing.'

'Listen for Polish,' Nechuma suggests.

There are several languages being spoken on the platform – Italian, of course, and some Russian, French, Hungarian. But so far no Polish. The Italians are the loudest. They move slowly, and talk with their hands, gesticulating wildly.

'Can you see anything?' Halina shouts over the din of the crowd.

Mila shakes her head. 'Not yet.' She's the tallest of the group. Pivoting in place, she scours the sea of strangers around her, letting her eyes linger occasionally on the back of a head until it turns, revealing a face that bears no resemblance at all to her husband or her brother, then jumping quickly to the next in the mob.

'*Mamusiu*,' Felicia calls, squeezing Mila's hand.

'Yes, darling.'

'Do you see him?'

Mila shakes her head and tries to smile. 'Not yet, love. But I'm sure he's here.' She bends quickly to kiss Felicia on the cheek.

As she stands, her eyes catch something in the crowd and her heart pauses. A profile. Handsome. Tall. Dark-haired, albeit with a hairline that receded farther than she remembered . . . could it be? 'Genek!' she yells, flailing an arm over her head. Behind her, Nechuma gasps. Genek turns, his eyes bright, scanning the faces in the direction from which he'd heard his name, finally meeting Mila's.

'Where? Where do you see?' Halina shouts, hopping up and down.

Genek's voice hurtles overhead, somehow audible amid the racket. 'Mila!' His arm shoots up over his head, knocking the cap from someone in front of him. He disappears for a moment to retrieve the hat, and when he surfaces again he is moving toward her. 'You stay there!' Genek shouts. 'I'll come to you!'

'It's him! It's him! It's him!' Halina, Sol, and Nechuma echo each other's elation, bouncing rapidly in place. Hearing Genek's voice is reason enough to celebrate.

Mila drops her satchel and hoists Felicia up to her waist. The child has yet to gain back the weight she'd lost in the convent bunker – Mila can easily hold her on her hip with one arm. Mila points at Genek. 'You see? Just there. Your uncle, Genek! He's the handsome one, with the big smile and the dimples. Wave!' Felicia smiles and waves along with her mother.

'And Father? Is he with him?' Felicia's voice is nearly swallowed in the cacophony.

A thought strikes Mila fast and hard like a mallet to a gong – what if Selim isn't here? What if something's happened since they last corresponded? What if he's *gone?* What if he hadn't the courage to meet them? *Where are you, Selim?* 'I don't see your father just yet,' she starts, but as her brother draws closer, she notices a body following closely behind. Dark-haired, a head shorter than Genek. She had missed him at first. 'Wait. I think I see him! He's just behind your uncle.'

Felicia cranes her neck. 'You say hello first,' she says, suddenly shy.

Mila nods, and lowers Felicia to the ground, taking her hand. 'Okay.'

'Genek – is he close?' Nechuma asks. 'Is Selim with him, too?'

Mila turns around to face her mother. 'Yes, Selim is with him. Come,' she says, reaching for Nechuma and pulling her gently to stand in front of her. 'Genek is nearly here. You should be the first to greet him.'

Genek is stuck behind a group of locals. Mila watches as he loses his patience, turns his body sideways, and pushes his way through. A couple of the men yap at him in Italian, but he is unfazed.

The tears that have welled in Nechuma's eyes stream down her cheeks like water from a broken dam when she finally sees her eldest striding toward her, even more dashing in his army attire than she remembered him. 'Genek!' is all she can manage when he sees her. His eyes are wet, too. He reaches for her and she for him, and they meld together in a long embrace, shaking with laughter and sorrow and raw, uninhibited joy. Nechuma closes her eyes, feeling her son's warmth radiate through her as he rocks her gently from side to side.

'I missed you so much, Mother.'

Nechuma is too emotional to speak. When she finally peels herself away, Genek wipes his eyes with the palms of his hands, and beams at his family. Before he can say a word, Halina jumps into his arms.

'You made it.' Genek laughs. 'I can't believe how far you've come.'

'You have no idea,' Halina says.

'And you –' Genek beams, marvelling at the sight of his niece. 'Look at you! You were no bigger than a kitten the last time I saw you!' Felicia blushes. He squats and wraps his arms around Felicia, and then around Mila, who squeezes him tight.

'Oh, Genek, it's so good to see you,' Mila cries.

When Genek finally makes his way to his father, he finds himself on the receiving end of the longest, most bearish hug of his life. 'I missed you, too, Father,' he says, his throat tight.

As father and son cling to one another, Mila turns her attention back to the crowd. Selim stands a metre away with his cap in his hands. They lock eyes for a moment and Mila lifts a hand awkwardly, as if to wave, then motions for Felicia to join her.

'I didn't want to interrupt,' Selim says, stepping toward them.

Mila barely breathes as she takes in the image of the man before her – his brown hair, cut short, his round spectacles, his perfect posture. She'd expected him to look different, but in fact he looks very much the same. She opens her mouth. 'I – Selim, I . . .' But after so many weeks of ruminating on what to say in the moment, she finds her words have left her.

'Mila,' Selim says, stepping toward her.

Mila closes her eyes as he brings her to him. He smells of soap. After a moment's embrace, she pulls away and bends down, cradling one of her daughter's hands in hers. 'Felicia, darling,' she says softly, looking from her daughter to Selim, 'this is your father.'

Felicia follows her mother's gaze, resting her eyes on her father.

Selim clears his throat, looking from Felicia to Mila. Mila stands. *Go on,* she nods. Selim lowers himself to his knee so Felicia won't have to look up to meet his eye.

'Felicia . . .' he starts, and then swallows. He takes a breath, begins again. 'Felicia, I brought something for you.' He reaches into his pocket, retrieving a minted silver coin, and hands it to Felicia. She holds it in her palm, studying it. 'A young family in Persia gave this to me,' Selim adds, 'after I helped to deliver their baby. Do you see the lion here?' He points to the embossing. 'He's carrying a sword. Up here is his crown. And on the reverse . . .' He flips the coin over gently in Felicia's palm. 'This here is a Farsi symbol for the number five. To me, though, it looks like a heart.'

Felicia rubs her thumb over the embossing.

Selim looks again to Mila, who smiles.

'What a very special gift,' Mila offers, resting a hand on Felicia's shoulder. Felicia glances up at her mother and then again at her father.

'Thank you, Papa,' Felicia says.

Selim is silent for a moment as he takes in the young girl before him. 'Would it be all right if I gave you a hug, Felicia?' he asks. Felicia nods. As Selim wraps his arms gently around his daughter's narrow frame, Felicia turns her cheek to rest it on his shoulder, and Mila has to bite her lip to keep from weeping.

CHAPTER FIFTY-NINE

Jakob and Bella
Łódź, Poland ~ October 1945

It's a German train. The letters scrawled in white paint over the splintered, rust-coloured cattle cars read KOBLEN, for Koblenz, where it originated.

A soldier in Home Army attire walks the track, sliding car doors closed as the few remaining passengers on the platform are helped inside. Jakob and Bella are two of the last to board.

'Ready?' Jakob asks.

Next to him, Bella nods. Their son, Victor, two months old, is asleep in her arms. 'You first.'

Someone has set a wooden crate by their car, making it easier to climb in. Jakob hands his suitcase up, breathing in the stale aroma of dust and decay. He shudders as he hoists himself from the crate to sit at the edge of the car, trying to push aside the image of the hundreds, thousands, maybe more, who undoubtedly boarded the same car before him, bound for places like Treblinka, Chełmno, and Auschwitz – names now synonymous with death. His chest tightens to think that Bella's parents must have been on a train just like this.

Bella peers up at him from the platform and smiles, and Jakob is nearly brought to tears. He is in awe of her strength. Two years ago, she'd nearly given up the will to live. He'd barely recognised her. Today, she reminds him of the girl he fell in love with. Except now, it's not just them. Now they are a family. Jakob extends his arms.

'Up we go,' Bella whispers. 'Got him?' she asks, before loosening her grip.

'Got him.'

Jakob kisses Victor's cheek, and then tucks him into his elbow and holds out his free hand for Bella. When all three are inside, the others in the car immediately gather around. There is something about Victor, his malted-milk scent and his satiny skin, that breathes hope into the harried survivors around him.

A whistle blares. '*Dwie minuty!*' the conductor hollers. 'Two minutes! Train departs in two minutes!'

Their car is full, but not overcrowded. Jakob and Bella know most of the faces on board – several from Łódź, a few from Radom. Most are Jews. They are destined for a Displaced Persons camp in Stuttgart, Germany. There, they've been told, the United Nations Relief and Rehabilitation Agency, which everyone refers to by its acronym, UNRRA, and the Joint have set up shop to provide the refugees with hospitable living conditions and, for the first time since most can remember, an ample food supply. At Stuttgart, Jakob and Bella hope, they'll be better able to communicate with Bella's uncle in Illinois. And if all goes well, in due time they'll be allowed to emigrate to the United States. To *America*. The word sings when they speak it – of freedom, of opportunity, of the chance to start anew. *America*. Sometimes it sounds too perfect, like the last note of a nocturne that hovers, suspended in time, before inevitably growing faint and disappearing. But it's plausible, they remind themselves. Their sponsorship, they hoped, would soon be approved, and then all that would be required were three visas.

Jakob and Bella talk frequently about the idea of their son, should their plan come to fruition, growing up American. About what it will mean to introduce Victor to a lifestyle, a language, a culture completely foreign. *Surely, he'll be better off,* they say, even though they have no concept of what growing up American entails.

A second whistle sounds, and Bella jumps.

'Oh!' Jakob cries, 'I nearly forgot!' He transfers Victor into Bella's arms, reaches for his camera, and lowers himself quickly back down to the platform.

Bella shakes her head, peering down at him from the car door. 'Where are you going? We're about to leave!'

'I meant to take a photo,' Jakob says, waving his hand. 'Here, quickly, everyone, look this way.'

'Now?' Bella asks, but she doesn't argue. She motions for the others to join her and they gather quickly at the door. Together, they stand tall and smile.

Through the lens of his Rolleiflex, Jakob studies his subjects. Adorned in collared trench coats, wool dresses that hang just below the knee, tailored blouses, and closed-toed leather shoes, the group appears, he realises as he brings it into perfect focus, much better than it should, all things considered. Exhausted. But also – Jakob glances up and smiles – proud. *Click.* He snaps the photo just as the train's wheels begin to turn.

'Hurry, love!' Bella calls, and Jakob pulls himself back up into the car.

The Home Army soldier struts by and slides the bottom door to their car closed. 'Open?' he asks, pointing to the top door.

'Open,' the passengers in the car quickly agree.

'Suit yourselves,' the soldier says.

The train begins to crawl. Jakob and Bella stand at the door, watching the world outside slide by, slowly at first, then faster as they pick up speed. Jakob grips the wooden door with one hand and wraps the other around Bella. She leans into him for balance, bending to kiss the top of Victor's head. Victor stares up at her, unblinking, holding her gaze.

'Until next time, *Polsko*,' Jakob says, although he and Bella know well there very likely won't be a next time.

As the train accelerates, Bella looks up at the fleeting Polish cityscape, taking in the seventeenth-century stone facades, the red-tiled roofs, the gilded dome of the Katedra Świętego Aleksandra Newskiego. 'Goodbye,' she whispers, but her words are lost, swallowed up by the rhythmic clack of the train rattling along its tracks, speeding west, toward Germany.

The Displaced Persons camp at Stuttgart West isn't so much a camp, but a city block. There are no fences, no boundaries, just a two-lane hilltop thoroughfare called Bismarckstrasse, lined with a row of buildings on either side, three and four stories tall. Jakob and Bella's apartment is fully furnished, thanks, they learnt, to General Dwight D. Eisenhower, who had paid a visit to the neighbouring Vaihingen an der Enz concentration camp just after VE day. Shocked and infuriated by what had occurred there, Eisenhower asked the locals in Stuttgart to provide some shelter for the Jews who'd lived to see the end of the war; when they refused, he lost his patience and demanded an evacuation. 'Take your personal belongings, but leave the furniture, the china, the silverware, and everything else,' he ordered, adding, 'You have twenty-four hours.'

Though most of the Jews who landed in Stuttgart West were left with virtually nothing – no home, no family, not a possession to their names – the camp embodies a welcome sense of renewal. It helps that Bismarckstrasse is home to a handful of survivors from Radom, including Dr Baum, whom Bella had seen for tonsillitis as a child and who now performs check-ups for Victor every month. It also helps that the DPs are able, finally, to honour the traditions and holidays that for so long they were banned from celebrating. At the end of November, when they were invited by the Jewish chaplains of the US Army to a celebration in honour of the first night of Hanukkah at Stuttgart's opera house, they were elated. Jakob and Bella, along with hundreds of other DPs, had ridden by trolley car to the city centre for the standing-room-only service. When they left, they were struck, for the first time since they could remember, with an overwhelming feeling of belonging.

No one in the camp talked about the war. It was as if the DPs were in a hurry to forget about lost years, to start fresh. And that they did. In the spring, romances at the DP camp popped up with the fire lilies. There were weddings to attend on the weekends, and each month, half a dozen babies were born. There was also a push to create an educational system – another luxury that had for the most part been discarded during the war – for the camp's youth. Apartments were converted into classrooms where the children took classes in everything from Zionism to mathematics, music, drawing, and dressmaking. There were classes for adults, too, in dental mechanics, metalwork, leatherwork, goldsmithery, and needlework. Bella led a class in undergarment, corset, and hat making.

Jakob and Bella spent most of their days those first few months in Stuttgart hopping between the UNRRA's office, where a group of Americans rationed out food, clothing, and supplies, and the US Consulate General's office, where they checked daily on the status of their emigration papers. 'Anything from my uncle, Fred Tatar?' Bella asked, at each visit. They'd received just one telegram so far, back when they first arrived at the camp: *Working on sponsorship,* Bella's uncle wrote. But they hadn't heard from him since.

On a warm Saturday afternoon, Bella and Victor sit on a blanket at the edge of a makeshift soccer field a short walk from Bismarckstrasse.

'See your Papa over there?' Bella asks, leaning her head close to Victor's and pointing. Jakob stands with his hands propped on his waist near the opponent's goal. He glances in their direction and waves. Jakob had helped create the camp's soccer league; it was good exercise, and it offered the perfect distraction from the emigration paperwork waiting game. He and his teammates practise daily and compete twice a week, mostly against teams of other Jewish DPs but occasionally against one of Stuttgart's local squads. The matches against the Germans are held on a much nicer field than those of the Jewish league, but Jakob is used to that from his days playing against the Polish leagues in Radom. He's also aware of how quickly a match can turn sour, and he can pick out the Germans who are in it for the fun of it and those who still harbour an obvious sense of resentment toward the Jews, from the moment they step onto the pitch. When he faces off against the latter, it's usually a matter of minutes before the insults are hurled – *dirty Jews, conniving thieves, pigs, you deserved what you got.* The men on Jakob's team have grown used to the hostility, and though often fully capable of beating their opponents, they inevitably decide at the half-time huddle that it's in their best interest to go ahead and let the bastards win, for there is no denying what a group of enraged Germans is capable of, on or off the field.

A whistle blows. The match is over. One of Jakob's knees is skinned and his shirt is streaked brown with dirt, but he is beaming. He shakes hands with the opposing team (a friendly one – Bella attends only the matches played among the Jewish teams), and trots over to the sideline.

'Hello, sunshine!' he says, planting a sweaty kiss on Bella's lips, and then reaching for Victor. 'Did you see my goal, big boy? Shall we have a victory lap?' He trots off with Victor in his arms.

'Be careful, darling!' Bella cries after him. 'He can barely hold his head up!'

'He's fine!' Jakob calls over his shoulder, laughing. 'He loves it!'

Bella sighs, watching Victor's near-bald head bobble as Jakob jogs a circle before returning to the blanket. Victor is grinning so widely that Bella can see all four of his teeth.

'When do you think he'll be old enough to kick a ball?' Jakob asks, once his victory lap is complete. He sets Victor gently back down beside Bella on the blanket.

'Soon enough, love,' she replies, laughing. 'Soon enough.'

CHAPTER SIXTY

Addy
Rio de Janeiro, Brazil ~ February 1946

Addy walks the black-and-white mosaic promenade of Copacabana's Avenida Atlântica, chatting with one of the few Poles he's kept up with from the *Alsina* – Sebastian, a writer, originally from Kraków. Sebastian, like Addy, had managed to hitch a ride across the Strait of Gibraltar and onto the *Cabo do Hornos* – 'by selling my grandfather's gold cufflinks off my wrist,' he said. He and Addy don't see each other often in Rio, but when they do, they enjoy the chance to slip back into their native tongue. Speaking the language they grew up with is comforting, in a way – a nod to a chapter of their lives, a time and a place that exists now only in their memories. Inevitably, their get-togethers lead to discussions of the trivial things they miss the most about Poland: for Sebastian, the smell of poppies in the springtime, the sweet, rose-petal-jam-filled goodness of a *pączki z różą* pastry, the thrill of travelling to Warsaw to take in a new opera at the Teatr Wielki; and for Addy, the pleasure of walking to the movie house on a summer night to catch the latest Charlie Chaplin film, pausing along the way to listen to the melodic rifts of Roman Totenberg's Stradivarius floating from the open windows above, the irresistible taste of his mother's star-shaped biscuits dipped in a hot mug of thick, sweet cocoa after a day spent ice skating the pond at Stary Ogród park.

Of course, more than missing *pączki* and pond skating, Addy and Sebastian miss their families. For a while, they spoke at length about their parents and siblings, comparing endless scenarios of who may have ended up where; but as the months and then the years passed with no news from the relatives they'd left behind, wondering aloud about their fate became too difficult, and they kept family talk to a minimum.

'Heard anything from Kraków?' Addy asks.

Sebastian shakes his head no. 'You, from Radom?'

'No,' Addy says, clearing his throat, trying not to sound deflated. Since VE day, as American president Harry Truman called it, Addy has doubled his efforts in communicating with the Red Cross, hoping, dreaming, praying that with the war finally over, his family would surface. But so far, the only news he's learnt is of the staggering number of concentration camps discovered throughout Europe, in Poland especially. Every day, it seems, Allied forces stumble across another camp, another handful of near-death survivors. The newspapers have begun publishing photos. The images are horrifying. In them, survivors appear more dead than alive. Their complexions are practically translucent, their cheeks and eyes and spaces over their collarbones hollow. Most wear prison-striped pyjamas that hang pitifully from too-sharp shoulder blades. They are barefoot, their heads bald. Those without shirts are so emaciated their ribs and hip bones jut out a fist-width from their waistlines. When Addy comes across a photo, he can't help but stare, boiling with anger and despair, terrified of finding a familiar face.

The possibility of his family perishing in one of Hitler's camps is all too real. His brothers in stripes. His beautiful sisters laid low, shorn of their hair. His mother and father, holding each other as they take their last breaths, their lungs choked with toxic fumes. When the images creep into his mind, he refuses them, thinking instead of his parents and siblings just the way he'd left them – of Genek reaching for a cigarette from his silver case, of Jakob smiling with his arm looped snug around Bella's shoulder, of Mila at the keys of the baby grand, of Halina throwing her blonde head back in a fit of laughter, of his mother with a pen in her hand at her writing table, of his father at the window, watching the doves as he hums a piece from Różycki's 'Casanova', the opera he and Addy saw together in Warsaw for Addy's twentieth birthday. He refuses to remember them any other way.

Sebastian changes the subject and the men walk on, squinting into the reflection of the afternoon sun boring into Copacabana's frothy surf.

'Shall we sit for a snack?' Addy asks as they approach Leme Rock at the north end of the beach.

'Absolutely. All this talk of *pączki* has made me hungry.'

At the rock, they turn left on Rua Anchieta, and Addy points out Caroline's apartment overlooking Leme Beach.

'How *is* Caroline?' Sebastian asks.

'She's well. Although talking more and more about returning to the States.'

'She'd bring you along, I presume?' Sebastian asks, smiling.

Addy grins sheepishly. 'That's the plan.' Addy had decided over the summer that he couldn't wait any longer to ask Caroline to be his wife. They were married in July, with Sebastian and Caroline's friend Ginna by their sides. Addy's smile fades as he imagines what it will feel like for Caroline to return to the States without her parents to welcome her. Her father, she'd told him, had passed before the war. Her mother had died not long after Caroline moved to Brazil. *Which is worse?* Addy wonders – *losing your parents without saying goodbye, or losing touch with your parents without any indication if – when – you'll see them next?* He digests the quandary as he walks. Caroline, at least, has answers. He doesn't. What if he never does? What if he's left, for the rest of his life, wondering what happened to his family? Or worse – what *could* have happened, had he stayed in France and found a way to return to Poland.

Addy's memory jogs to the day he last saw his mother, at the Radom train station. It was in 1938. Nearly a decade ago. He was twenty-five. He'd been home for Rosh Hashanah, and she'd accompanied him to the station on the morning he left. Reaching a hand into his pocket, he runs his fingers over the handkerchief she'd given him on that visit, remembering how she had held him close as they awaited his train, her elbow tucked into his; how she'd told him to be safe, and kissed his cheeks, hugged him tight as she'd said goodbye, then waved her own handkerchief overhead as the train departed – waved and waved until she was just a speck on the platform, a tiny silhouette, unwilling to leave until the train was out of sight.

'Let's sit at Porcão,' Sebastian suggests, and Addy blinks as he's brought back to the present. He nods.

It isn't yet five and the plastic tables scattered outside Porcão are already full of Brazilians chatting and having a smoke over plates of flash-fried cod croquettes and bottles of Brahma Chopp. Addy glances at a table of three attractive couples.

The women, gathered at one end, appear engrossed in riveting conversation; they talk quickly, their eyebrows bouncing and dipping to the rhythm of their banter, while opposite them, their dark-haired counterparts lean back in their chairs, taking in the scenery, their jaws slack, cigarettes dangling from between their first two fingers. One of the men appears so relaxed Addy wonders if he might fall asleep and topple over.

Addy and Sebastian motion to a server, who indicates with fingers spread wide that it would be another five minutes for a table outside. As they wait, they talk about their plans for the weekend. Sebastian is leaving that evening to visit a friend in São Paulo. Addy's only plan is to spend time with Caroline. He checks his watch – it's nearly five. She'll be home from the embassy soon. Addy is about to ask Sebastian of his impression of São Paulo – he's never been – when he feels a tap on his shoulder and turns. The young man beside him looks to be in his mid twenties, clean-cut with pale green eyes that remind him immediately of his sister Halina's.

'Excuse me, sir?' the stranger offers.

Addy glances at Sebastian and smiles. 'A Pole! How about that!'

The young man looks embarrassed. 'I'm sorry to bother you. I couldn't help but overhear the two of you speaking Polish, and I have to ask . . .' He looks first to Addy and then to Sebastian. 'Do either of you by chance know of a gentleman called *Addy Kurc*?'

Addy tilts his head back and emits a *Ha!* that sounds more like a yell than a laugh, startling the people sitting at the tables closest to them. The young man glances at his feet.

'I know, unlikely,' he says, shaking his head. 'But there aren't so many Poles in Rio, and I've been having trouble tracking down this Mister Kurc, is all. Seems the address we have on file is an old one.'

Addy had moved into a new apartment on Carvalho Mendonca three weeks earlier. He holds out his hand. 'It's nice to meet you.'

The young man blinks. 'You – *you* are Addy?'

'What kind of trouble have you gotten yourself into?' Sebastian asks with mock concern.

'I'm not sure,' Addy quips, his hazel eyes sparkling. He glances at Sebastian, winks, and then turns his attention back to the young Pole before them. 'You tell me.'

'Oh, there's no trouble at all, sir,' the young man says, still pumping Addy's hand. 'I work for the Polish consulate. We've received a telegram for you.'

Addy buckles at the word 'telegram.' The young man grips his hand tightly to keep him from falling. 'A telegram from *whom*?' Addy is suddenly serious. His eyes scour the stranger's face, as if straining to solve a puzzle.

The young Pole explains that he can't divulge any information until Addy comes to the embassy, which is a half hour walk from Leme. 'The office will close in ten minutes,' he adds. 'Best to come on . . .' But before he can say 'Monday,' Addy is gone.

'Thank you!' Addy cries over his shoulder as he runs. 'Sebastian, I owe you a beer!' he yells.

'Go!' Sebastian calls, although Addy is already too far gone to hear him, the top of his head dipping and weaving as he darts between the tanned bodies on the promenade moving at a much more leisurely pace than his.

When Addy arrives at the embassy he is sweat soaked, down to his white cotton undershirt. It's ten minutes past five. The door to the building is locked. He raps his knuckles against the wood until someone finally answers. 'Please!' he begs, panting, when he's told the embassy is closed. 'I've received a telegram. It's very important.'

The embassy worker looks at his watch. 'I'm sorry, sir, but –' he begins, but Addy interrupts.

'Please,' he stammers. 'I'll do anything.'

It's obvious to both men that 'the embassy is closed' isn't an answer Addy will settle for. The gentleman at the door finally nods, loosening his tie. 'Fine.' He sighs, indicating for Addy to follow him.

They stop at a small office with a plaque beside it reading M. SANTOS.

'You are Santos?' Addy asks.

The gentleman shakes his head as Addy follows him into the office. 'I'm Roberto. Santos is in charge of incoming telegrams. He keeps the ones he hasn't filed here.' Roberto walks around the desk. 'Have a seat,' he says, gesturing to a chair as he retrieves his glasses from a shirt pocket, slides them on, and peers down at a six-inch stack of what appears to be freshly inked paper.

Addy is too nervous to sit. 'I'm Addy,' he says. 'Addy Kurc.'

'Spell your name for me,' Roberto says. 'Surname first.' He licks his thumb, pushes his glasses up his nose.

Addy spells his name and then paces, biting his tongue. It's all he can do to keep quiet. Finally, Roberto pauses, pulls a paper from the stack.

'Addy Kurc,' he reads, and then looks up. 'This is you?'

'Yes! Yes!' Addy reaches for his wallet.

'No ID,' Roberto says, waving his hand. 'I believe you are who you say you are.' He glances at the telegram and then passes it over the desk to Addy. 'Looks like it came in two weeks ago, from the Red Cross.'

Addy takes the paper and braces himself. Bad news would come from the newspaper, from the lists of the dead, but a telegram . . . He tells himself that a telegram can't be bad news. Gripping the thin paper with both hands, he holds it just under his nose, and reads.

DEAR BROTHER – OVERJOYED TO FIND YOU ON RED CROSS LIST
I AM WITH SISTERS AND PARENTS IN ITALY – JAKOB WAITING FOR
VISA TO US
SEND NEWS – LOVE GENEK

Addy devours the words on the page. The letters Caroline had written to the Red Cross offices around the world – nearly two years ago – one of them, somehow, must have found his brother. He shakes his head, blinks, and suddenly it's as if he is floating in a realm that doesn't belong to his body. From somewhere just shy of the embassy ceiling, he stares down at the room, at Roberto, at himself, still holding the telegram, at the tiny black letters strewn across the paper. It is only by the sound of his own laughter that he is brought back to earth.

'Do me a favour, sir,' Addy says, handing the telegram back over the desk to Roberto. 'Would you read this to me? I want to be sure I'm not dreaming.'

As Roberto reads the message aloud, Addy's laughter fades and his head grows light. He props himself on the desk with one hand, cups the other over his mouth.

'Are you okay?' Roberto suddenly looks worried.

'They're alive,' Addy whispers into his fingers. The words lodge in his heart and he snaps upright, bringing his palms to his temples. 'They are *alive*. May I – may I see that again?'

'It's yours,' Roberto says, returning the telegram to Addy's hands. Addy holds the paper to his chest for a moment and closes his eyes. When he looks up, tears spill from the corners of his eyes, gathering up beads of sweat as they tumble down his cheeks. 'Thank you!' he says. '*Thank* you!'

MARCH 29, 1946: *A group of 250 German police armed with US Army rifles enter the Stuttgart DP camp, claiming they've been authorised by the US military to search the buildings. A fight ensues and several Jews are injured. Samuel Danziger, from Radom, is murdered. His death, along with the attack, is widely reported in the American press; soon after, the United States imparts a more liberal policy on opening its doors to Jewish refugees.*

CHAPTER SIXTY-ONE

Jakob and Bella
The North Sea ~ May 13, 1946

Standing on the bow of the SS *Marine Perch,* Jakob lifts his Rolleiflex and tinkers with its aperture as he gazes down through the lens at his wife and son. A steady breeze rolls off of the sea, salty and cool, carrying with it a breath of spring. Bella cradles Victor in her arms, smiling as the *click* of Jakob's shutter fills the space between them.

They'd set sail from Bremerhaven that morning, following the Weser River toward the North Sea. By evening, the *Perch,* as she was affectionately called, will turn her bow west as they prepare to cross the Atlantic.

Three weeks earlier, they'd received confirmation from the US Consulate General in Stuttgart that – pending a physical exam (refugees with serious conditions weren't permitted to enter the United States) – their sponsorship would be approved, and their visas would await them in Bremerhaven. Dr Baum had administered the exam and passed Jakob, Bella, and Victor with perfect marks. They were photographed and issued certificates of identification. Two weeks later, they bade their friends at Stuttgart farewell and boarded an overnight train. In Bremerhaven they slept for a week on the floor beneath a sign reading EMIGRANT STAGING AREA until the *Marine Perch* sailed into the port and they were allowed to board.

The *Perch* is an old, 1,000-passenger troop vessel – one of the first of its kind to bring refugees to America from Europe. A Liberty Ship. Without any savings to their names, Jakob and Bella relied on the Joint to pay their combined $142 fare; it had also doled out $5 in pocket money to each of the refugees on board. Before leaving Stuttgart, Jakob and Bella had saved up their UNRRA coffee rations, trading their sought-after grinds for a pair of clean shirts – a crisp blue shirt for Jakob and a white blouse with a scalloped collar for Bella – and for a new white cotton bonnet for Victor. They wanted to look their best when Bella's uncle Fred greeted them on US soil.

A young woman approaches, cooing. Since they boarded the ship, hardly a minute has passed without someone stopping to ask Victor's age, where he was born, or simply to congratulate Bella and Jakob on the young traveller accompanying them on their journey to the States.

'*Quel âge a t'il?*' the young woman asks, peering over Bella's arm.

'He'll be one in August,' Bella replies in French.

The young woman smiles. 'His name?'

'We call him Victor.' Bella touches the back of her index finger to the soft skin of Victor's cheek. It hadn't taken her and Jakob long to decide what to call their firstborn. *Victor* summed up the elation they'd felt when the war finally ended and they came to grips with the notion that, despite the seemingly insurmountable challenges they'd faced along the way, they'd not only survived, but they'd managed to bring new life into the world. Someday when he's old enough, Jakob and Bella often mused, their son would understand the significance of his name.

The woman tilts her head and nods, her eyes fixed on Victor's pink, heart-shaped lips, parted slightly as he sleeps.

'He's beautiful.'

Bella stares, too. 'Thank you.'

'Such a peaceful sleeper.'

Bella nods, smiling. 'Yes, seems he hasn't a care in the world.'

CHAPTER SIXTY-TWO

The Kurc Family
Rio de Janeiro, Brazil ~ June 30, 1946

'You'd better hurry,' Caroline says, smiling up at Addy from her bed in Hospital Samaritano's maternity ward. 'Go,' she adds, in her best schoolteacher voice, indicating that she won't take no for an answer. 'We'll be fine.' With her southern American accent, the word *fine* is long and loose around its edges.

Addy looks at her, and then at Kathleen, asleep at the foot of the bed in an incubator. She was born two days earlier, three weeks premature, weighing in at a mere two kilos. She's healthy, the doctors assure them, but she'll need the warmth and oxygen of the incubator for at least a week before she can leave the hospital. Addy kisses his wife. 'Caroline,' he says, his eyes wet, 'thank you.'

Not only had Caroline helped him find his family through the Red Cross, she'd also cashed in her American war bonds, the only savings to her name, to help pay for the family's passage from Italy. Addy had begged her not to – had sworn he would work out a way to pay for the tickets himself – but she had insisted.

Caroline shakes her head. 'Please, Addy. I'm so happy for you. Now go!' she urges, squeezing his hand. 'Before you're late.'

'I love you!' Addy beams, then bolts for the door.

His parents' ship is due into Rio at eleven. On board with Nechuma and Sol are his sister Halina and brother-in-law Adam, along with a cousin Ala, who had lost touch with the family at the start of the war but survived in hiding, Nechuma wrote, and Herta's brother Zigmund, whom Addy had met only once before the war. Genek, Herta, and a son, Józef; Mila, Selim, and Felicia; and Addy's cousins Franka and Salek and aunt Terza are scheduled to sail for Rio on the next ship from Naples. *Fifteen* relatives. Addy can't quite digest the reality of it all. It's been his singular dream since he arrived in Brazil: to find his family alive and well, to bring them to Rio, to start over together. He'd told himself over and over that the scenario was plausible, but there was always the very real possibility that it wasn't – that his dream was just that, a dream, one that would eventually slip into the realm of nightmare and haunt him for the rest of his years.

And then the telegram came, and Addy spent weeks laughing and crying, suddenly unsure of how to conduct himself without the weight of the guilt and the worry that had bonded like a barnacle to his insides for the better part of a decade. He was lighter now, and unencumbered – 'I'm *free*,' he told Caroline once, when she'd asked him how he felt. It was the only way he could describe the sensation. Free, finally, to believe with all of his heart that he wasn't alone.

Addy had replied immediately to Genek's telegram, imploring him to come to Rio – Vargas had, for the time being, opened Brazil's doors again to refugees. The family in Italy readily agreed. They would apply for visas right away, Genek wrote. The process of acquiring the paperwork and the passage to South America would be slow, of course, but it would give Addy time to prepare for their arrival.

As soon as the decision was made, Addy got to work pulling together living arrangements: for his parents, an apartment on Avenida Atlântica; for Halina and Adam, a one-bedroom studio just down the street from his on Carvalho Mendonca; for his cousins, and Aunt Terza, a two-bedroom flat on Rua Belfort Roxo. He's furnished each space with a handful of essentials he's built by hand – bed frames, a desk, two sets of shelves. With Caroline's help, he's collected a hodgepodge set of plates, silverware, and a few pots and pans, along with a couple of sarongs and canvases of inexpensive art to hang on the walls from the São Cristóvão flea market. The apartments are sparse; they pale in comparison to the beautiful home on Warszawska Street where he spent his youth, but they are the best he can do.

'I hope they don't mind living like university students for a while,' Addy had said with a sigh before Kathleen was born, looking around the apartment his parents would soon inhabit. The simple plywood desk he'd built the week before suddenly looked comical compared with the beautiful satinwood writing table he remembered from his mother's living room in Radom.

'Oh, Addy,' Caroline assured him, 'I can't imagine they'll be anything but grateful.'

The palm trees flanking Rua Bambina are a streak of green in Addy's periphery as he speeds along in the Chevrolet he'd borrowed from Sebastian for the occasion. He shakes his head. Part of him still feels as if he's living some kind of fantasy. Two days ago, he'd felt, for the first time, the tiny hand of his firstborn wrapped around his little finger – and soon he'll feel the touch of his mother, his father, his sisters, brother, and cousins, the niece he has yet to meet, a new nephew. He's imagined the reunion over and over again. But nothing – nothing at all in the world, he realises – can prepare him for what it will be like to see his family in the flesh. To feel the warmth of their cheeks against his. To hear the sound of their voices.

As Addy drives his mind flips back in time to the morning in Toulouse, in March of 1939, when he'd opened his mother's letter telling him how things had begun to change in Radom. He thinks about his stint in the French Army, about how he'd forged his demobilisation papers, which he still carries in his snakeskin wallet. He pictures himself arm in arm with Eliska aboard the *Alsina*, bartering with the locals in Dakar, talking his way out of the Kasha Tadla tent camp in Casablanca and onto the *Cabo do Hornos*. He recalls his journey across the Atlantic, his weeks of incarceration on Ilha das Flores, his first job at a bookbindery in Rio, his innumerable visits to the Copacabana post office and the offices of the Red Cross. He thinks of Jonathan's party, of how fast and hard his heart had drummed in his chest as he'd summoned the courage to introduce himself to Caroline. He thinks of the green-eyed consulate worker who'd introduced himself outside of Porcão, of the words stamped onto the tissue-thin telegram he'd received – words that, in one swift swoop, changed everything. It's been seven and a half years since he's seen his family. Seven and a half! They have nearly a decade of catching up to do. Where will they even begin? There is so much to learn, and he has so much to tell.

Addy reaches the port at eleven on the dot. He parks hastily, nearly yanking the Chevrolet's emergency brake from its console, and jogs toward the white brick customs building separating him from Guanabara Bay. He's been to the building four times already – twice when he first arrived in Rio, and twice in the past month to confirm the details of what, exactly, will happen when his family arrives. They'll be escorted from the ship to a passport control office, he's been told, and then to another office where they will be asked a series of questions before their visas are confirmed and stamped. He won't be allowed to greet them until the process is complete.

Too excited to wait indoors, Addy skirts the customs building, stopping short as the bay suddenly comes into view. There are dozens of small fishing crafts in the harbour, and a couple of freight boats, but only one that could be carrying his family. Less than five hundred metres away, a transport vessel floats in his direction, billowing steam from a pair of massive turbines into the cloudless sky. She is huge. The *Duque de Caxias*. It has to be!

As the ship approaches, Addy can make out the tiny silhouettes of passengers lining her bow, but it's impossible to distinguish one figure from the next. He shields his eyes from the sun and squints over the horizon as he walks the dock, threading between the dozens of others who have gathered to greet the ship. The *Duque* moves unbearably slowly. Addy paces at the end of the dock. Finally, he can't stand it any longer.

'*Olá!!*' he hollers, waving at a fisherman rowing by in his dinghy. The old man looks up. Addy digs five cruzeiros out of his pocket. 'Can I borrow your boat?'

Seated on the dinghy's wooden bench, Addy rows with his back to the *Duque*, watching the white bricks of the customs building grow smaller with each stroke. He glides past a buoy marking the end of the bay's no-wake zone, and a captain heading in toward the shore whistles in his direction – *Perigoso*! – but Addy only paddles harder, into the deeper water, glancing every now and then behind him at his progress.

When the greeters gathered on the dock are but specks on the horizon, Addy sets down his oars, his heart thumping like a metronome at 120 beats per minute beneath his shirt. Panting, he throws his feet over the bench, turning to face the *Duque*. Shielding his eyes again from the sun, he stands slowly, feet spread wide for balance, scouring the ship's bow. What he would do to catch a glimpse of a familiar face! No luck. He's still too far away. He lowers himself to sit, turns so his back is once again to the boat, and rows closer.

He's thirty metres from the *Duque* when his eardrums spring to life, sending a shock of energy through his body. He recognises the voice – the voice that, for the better part of a decade, he's heard only in his dreams.

'Aaaa – dy!'

He drops his oars into the dinghy and staggers to his feet – too fast – nearly capsizing before catching his balance. And then he sees her, waving a handkerchief over her head, just as she had the day he left her at the train station: his mother. And next to her, his father, pumping a cane up and down as if poking holes in the sky, and next to him, his sister, waving frantically with one arm, holding a large parcel in the other – a baby, perhaps. It would be just like his little sister to want to surprise him with this news. Addy cranes his neck and peers up at his family, his arms stretched wide overhead in a giant *V* – if he could reach just a little farther he'd touch them. He yells their names and they yell back, and he is crying now, and they are too, even his father.

CHAPTER SIXTY-THREE

The Kurc Family
Rio de Janeiro, Brazil ~ April 6, 1947

Addy and Caroline have squeezed eighteen chairs, two high chairs, and a bassinet around three card tables pushed together in their living room. Most of the furniture is borrowed. The oven has been on for most of the day, churning out heat that has turned their small apartment into a sauna of sorts, but no one seems to notice, or if they do, they don't care. Chatter, clinking china, and the smell of freshly baked matzah fill the flat as the family puts the finishing touches on a much-anticipated meal – the first Pesach they've celebrated together since before the war. Six months ago a ship called the *Campana* had brought the remainder of the family to Rio. The only people missing are Jakob, Bella, and Victor. Jakob writes often. He has found a job in the States as a photographer, he said in his most recent letter. Typically, he includes a photograph or two in his correspondence, most often of Victor, who will be two years old in a few months. On special occasions he sends a telegram. They had received one earlier that day:

THINKING OF YOU FROM ILLINOIS. L'CHAIM. J

They'll telephone him from a neighbour's apartment after dinner, Addy's decided.

Sol arranges the table, humming as he smooths the tablecloth Nechuma sewed from a small bolt of lace they'd bought in Naples. He sets his Haggadah by his seat at one end of the table and the prayer books they'd managed to collect at each of the chairs.

In the kitchen, Nechuma and Mila dole out bowls of salt water, peel eggs, and check the oven every few minutes to be sure not to overbake the matzah. Mila dips a wooden spoon into a pot of soup and blows on the clear broth before extending the spoon for her mother to taste.

'What is it missing?'

Nechuma wipes her hands on her apron, and guides the spoon to her mouth. She smiles. 'Just what I swallowed!'

Mila laughs. It's been years since she heard her mother use the expression.

At the table, Genek pours generous portions of wine, glancing now and then at Józef, who's just celebrated his sixth birthday, as he plays with his older cousin Felicia, who will be nine in November. They sit on the floor by the window, engrossed in a game of pick-up sticks, arguing in Portuguese about whether or not Józef nudged a blue stick with his little finger on his last move.

'You did, I saw it move!' Felicia says, exasperated.

'Did not,' Józef persists.

Adam sits on the floor as well, beside his one-year-old son, Ricardo, who seems perfectly content to watch his ten-month-old cousin Kathleen crawl circles around him.

'She's going to be running before you learn to stand,' Adam teases, squeezing one of Ricardo's doughy thighs.

Ricardo was born on the first of February at the Federico II Hospital in Naples. In September, however, a few months after the family arrived in Rio, Halina conveniently 'lost' his Italian birth certificate and applied for a new one. When Brazilian naturalisation officials asked her son's age, Halina lied and said he'd been born in August, on Brazilian soil. Halina and Adam had agreed – Ricardo would be better off leaving his European identity behind. With Adam's family gone – he'd learnt, finally, that they'd perished at Auschwitz – and with Halina's family now in Brazil and the States, they had no ties any more to their homeland. Had the Brazilian officials taken a closer look at Ricardo's ample jowls, they'd have undoubtedly deduced that he was far too large to have been born just a month before. But Ricardo was asleep, concealed beneath a mound of blankets in his carriage, and the officials didn't pay him much attention. Within a month, he was issued his *second* birth certificate, this one Brazilian, with a birth date of August 15,

1946. Ricardo's real birthday, it was decided, was to be kept a secret.

Next to Adam, Caroline kneels on the floor showing Herta how to swaddle her second-born, Michel, just two weeks old. 'Nechuma taught me how to do this for Kathleen,' she says quietly, adjusting the soft muslin cloth beneath Michel. Caroline had worried before their arrival about what Addy's family might think of her – the American their son invited into his life, who knew nothing of the suffering and hardships they'd endured. Addy had assured her again and again that they would adore her. 'They already do,' he'd said. 'You are the reason they are here, remember?'

Herta nods appreciatively and Caroline smiles, grateful that, despite the language barrier, she can be helpful. 'The trick is to pin down the arms,' she adds, demonstrating as she talks.

In the corner of the room where Addy keeps his turntable – a last-minute splurge before the family arrived – he and Halina flip through a small record collection, discussing what to play next. Addy suggests Ellington, but Halina objects. 'Let's listen to something local,' she says. They agree on the young Brazilian composer and violinist Cláudio Santoro. Addy adjusts the volume as the first piece begins – a piano solo with a modern, jazzy melody – and watches, smiling, as across the room, his father reaches for his mother, loops a hand around her waist, and sways with her to the rhythm, his eyes closed.

It is just before six o'clock when dinner is ready. Outside, the sky has begun to darken. It's the tail end of fall in Rio, and the days are short, the nights cool. Addy lowers the volume on the turntable before removing the needle; the room grows quiet as the others make their way to their seats. Caroline and Halina prop Ricardo and Kathleen in high chairs and tuck cotton napkins into their collars. Across from them, Genek pats the chair next to his and sneaks a pinch to Józef's ribs as his eldest slides into his place. Józef bats Genek's hand away, narrowing his blue eyes and flashing a dimpled smile. Herta sets Józef's baby brother, Michel, cocooned comfortably in his swaddle, gently into Kathleen's old bassinet.

Across from Genek, Mila and Selim sit with Felicia between them.

'You look pretty,' Selim whispers to Felicia. 'I like your bow,' he adds.

Felicia brings her hand to the navy blue ribbon – a gift from Caroline –

that holds her ponytail in place. She smiles shyly, still unsure of how exactly to accept a compliment from her father, but relishing his words; they have a way of filling her with happiness.

Terza, Franka, Salek, Ala, and Zigmund sit in the remaining chairs.

As Sol takes his seat at the head of the table, Nechuma offers Caroline a box of matches. Normally Nechuma would do the lighting – it's tradition at Pesach for the eldest woman of the house to light the candles – but Nechuma had insisted. 'It's your home,' she'd said, when Addy asked if she would like to do the honour. 'I can say the blessing, but it would please me very much if Caroline would light the candles.'

Caroline had been hesitant at first to accept the responsibility. Not only was this her first Passover, but it was the first holiday spent with her new family – she would do anything to help, she said, but would prefer to do so quietly. 'This isn't about me,' she insisted. Addy had coaxed her into it by telling her how much it would mean to him – and to his mother.

Caroline strikes a match and brings the flame to the two wicks. Beside her, Nechuma recites an opening prayer. When the prayer is complete, the women take their seats, Caroline beside Addy and Nechuma at the head of the table opposite her husband, and attention is turned to Sol.

Sol looks around, silently greeting everyone at the table, his eyes glistening in the candlelight. Finally, he rests his gaze on Nechuma. Nechuma takes a deep breath, pulls her shoulders back, and dips her chin in a gesture to begin. Sol returns the gesture. Nechuma watches his shoulders rise and fall, wondering for a moment if her husband might cry. If he does, she realises, a lump climbing up her throat, she certainly will, too. But after a moment, Sol smiles. Opening his Haggadah, he raises his glass.

'*Barukh atah Adonai eloheinu* . . .' he baritones, and immediately goose bumps spring to life on the arms of each of the adults in the small room.

Sol's blessing is short:

'Blessed art thou, Lord our God, Master of the universe,
Who has kept us alive and sustained us,
And has brought us to this special time.'

The words rest delicately in the humid air as the family takes in the depth of Sol's voice, the significance of his prayer. *Kept us alive. Sustained us. Brought us to this special time.*

'Today,' Sol adds, 'we celebrate the Festival of Matzahs, the time of our liberation. Amen.'

'Amen,' the others echo with glasses raised.

Sol recites the blessing of the karpas and the family dips sprigs of parsley into small bowls of salt water.

Across from him, Nechuma takes in the beautiful faces looking on – her children, their spouses, five grandchildren, her cousins, and in-laws, resting her gaze for a moment on the chair left empty for Jakob. She glances at her watch, a gift from Addy ('For all of the birthdays I missed,' he'd said); Jakob, far away in Illinois, was no doubt sitting at his own Pesach dinner at the very same moment, celebrating with Bella's family.

When Nechuma looks up, tears fill her eyes, and the faces around her grow blurry. Her children. All of them. Healthy. Living. Thriving. She'd spent so many years fearing the worst, imagining the unimaginable, her heart hollow with dread. It's surreal to think back on it now, to consider all of the places they'd been, the chaos and death and destruction that had followed a half step behind their every move, the decisions they'd made and plans they'd orchestrated, without her knowing if she would live to see her family again, or if they would live to see her. They'd done what they could, then waited, prayed. But now – now there is no more waiting. They are here. Her family. Finally, miraculously, complete. Tears roll down Nechuma's cheeks as she says a silent thanks.

A moment later, she senses warmth. A hand on her elbow. Addy's. Nechuma smiles and signals with a nod that she's fine. He grins, his own eyes wet, and slips her his handkerchief. When she's patted away her tears, she spreads the handkerchief over her thigh, running her fingers over the white threaded AAIK, remembering the afternoon she'd embroidered it.

Opposite her, Sol makes a to-do over breaking a piece of matzah to set aside for the afikomen. Mila whispers something in Felicia's ear. Halina bounces Ricardo on her knee, keeping him content by dipping her fingertip into a bowl of salt water beside her plate and offering him tastes. Genek wraps an arm each around Józef and Herta, resting his hands on their shoulders. Herta smiles and they glance together at Michel, sleeping peacefully in his bassinet.

Herta had discovered she was pregnant not long after learning that her parents, her sister Lola, her brother-in-law, and her niece – all but her brother Zigmund – had been killed at a concentration camp near Bielsko. The news had crushed her, and she'd wondered how she might carry on knowing she was an aunt to a little girl she would never meet, knowing Józef would recognise his maternal grandparents only by name. For months, she was blind with sorrow and anger and remorse as she lay awake at night, questioning – was there something she could have done to help them? Her pregnancy had helped her to see straight again, to draw upon the resilience that had gotten her through her years as an exile in Siberia, as a new mother alone in Palestine, awaiting news from the front. And when their second son was born in March, she and Genek readily agreed – he would be named Michel, after her father.

A plate of matzah is passed around the table and Felicia fidgets in her seat. As the youngest in the room who is able to read, her grandfather has asked her to recite the Four Questions. They'd practised together every day for weeks, with Felicia asking the questions and Sol singing the answers.

'Are you ready?' Sol's tone is gentle.

Felicia nods, takes a deep breath, and begins. '*Mah nishtanah halaila hazeh* . . .' she sings. Her voice, soft and pure as honey, casts a spell over the room. The others are rapt.

At the end of the *maggid,* Sol recites a blessing over a second cup of wine, and then over the matzah, a corner of which he breaks off and eats. Bowls of horseradish and charoset are passed for the blessings of the *maror* and the *korekh.*

When it is finally time to feast, conversation erupts as bowls of matzah ball soup are doled and platters of salted gefilte, thyme-roasted chicken, and savory beef brisket are passed.

'*L'chaim!*' Addy calls, as plates are piled high.

'*L'chaim,*' the others chime.

With full stomachs, the family clears the table, and Sol slips out of his chair. He's spent weeks plotting the perfect place to hide the afikomen, and since it would be the first traditional Pesach Józef and Felicia would remember, he'd made a point earlier in the day to explain the significance of the ritual. He tucks the matzah behind a row of books on a low shelf in Addy and Caroline's bedroom – not too difficult for Józef to find, and not too easy for Felicia. When he returns, the children tear off down the small hallway, and the adults smile at the sound of their quick, receding footsteps. Sol beams, and Nechuma shakes her head. Finally, his wish has been granted – to celebrate among children old enough to enjoy the hunt. She can only imagine the thought that will go into a hiding place next year, when Ricardo and Kathleen are able to partake.

Felicia returns a few minutes later, carrying the napkin.

'That was too easy!' Sol bellows as she presents him the matzah. 'Come,' he says, motioning for Felicia and Józef to join him at the head of the table. With a grandchild on either side, Sol wraps his arms around each. 'Now tell me, Mademoiselle Kajler,' he says, suddenly serious, lowering his voice a few octaves, 'how much are you asking for this afikomen?'

Felicia doesn't know what to say.

'How about a cruzeiro?' Sol offers, digging a coin from his pocket and laying it on the table. Felicia's eyes widen and she stares, eventually reaching for the coin. 'That's all?' Sol teases, before she picks it up. Felicia is confused. She looks up at her grandfather, her fingers still hovering above the cruzeiro. 'Don't you think you deserve more?' Sol asks, winking at the others looking on. Felicia has never haggled before. This is her first lesson. She pauses and then pulls her fingers away, smiling.

'*Mais!* It's worth more!' she declares and then blushes as the table erupts in laughter.

'Well, if you insist.' Sol sighs, setting a second cruzeiro on the table.

Felicia again reaches, instinctively, but pauses this time, catches Sol's eye. She lets her hand drop to her side, shakes her head, proud of herself for resisting.

'You drive a tough bargain,' Sol says, puffing out his cheeks as he exhales loudly, digging once again into his pocket. 'What do you think, young man; should we offer her some more?' he asks, turning to Józef, who's been following along, transfixed.

'*Si, dziadek, si!*' he exclaims, nodding enthusiastically.

When Sol's pocket is empty, he lifts his hands overhead in defeat.

'You've taken everything I have!' he declares. 'But, young lady,' he adds, resting a palm atop Felicia's red head, 'you've earned it.' Felicia smiles, kisses her *dziadek* on the cheek. 'And you, sir,' Sol says, turning his attention to Józef. 'You worked very hard as well, I'm sure of it. Next year maybe it will be *you* who steals the afikomen!' He pulls a final coin from his shirt pocket and slips it into Józef's palm. 'Now go on, you two. Find your seats. We are nearly through with our Pesach.'

The children make their way back to their spots at the table, Józef beaming, Felicia gripping her collection of cruzeiros tightly in her fist, opening it ever so slightly to show her father. Selim *oohs* silently, his eyes wide.

Wine glasses are filled for a third and then a fourth time as Sol recites a prayer to the prophet Elijah, for whom they've left the door to the apartment open. They sing '*Eliyahu HaNavi,*' and Addy, Genek, Mila, and Halina take turns reciting psalms.

As Sol sets down an empty glass, he looks once again around the table, smiling. 'Our Seder is complete!' he says, his voice thick with pride and loose from the wine. Without hesitation, he breaks into song – '*Adir Hu*' – and the others join in, their voices growing louder and more emphatic with each refrain.

Yivneh veito b'karov,
Bim'heirah, bim'heirah, b'yameinu b'karov.
Ei-l b'neihl Ei-l b'neih!
B'neih veit'kha b'karov!

May He soon rebuild His house,
Speedily, speedily and in our days, soon.
God, rebuild! God, rebuild!
Rebuild your house soon!

'Is it time, at last?' Halina sings. 'Can we dance?' On cue, her brothers jump from their seats, and the tables are pushed aside, the windows shimmied open as wide as their small frames will allow. Outside, darkness has fallen.

Addy leans his head out of a window to breathe in the night. Above him, a quarter moon beams its cockeyed grin across the velvet sky, casting a silver-blue light over the cobblestone street below. Addy returns the grin and ducks back inside.

'Mila first,' Genek charges.

'I'm out of practice,' Mila says as she takes a seat at the piano stool, 'but I'll do my best.' She plays Chopin's 'Mazurka in B-flat major' – a popular, upbeat piece with an energy that is so intrinsically Polish the Kurcs are still for a moment as the notes flood their hearts with memories of home. Despite her years away from the keys, Mila's rendition is flawless. Halina plays next, and then finally it's Addy's turn. He brings the family to their feet with a lively rendition of Gershwin's 'Strike Up the Band.' On the street, passersby crane their necks, smiling at the laughter and melodies drifting from the Kurcs' open windows four stories above.

It's after midnight. They are sprawled around the living room, draped over chairs, stretched out across the floor. The children are asleep. Louis Armstrong's 'Shine' floats from the record player.

Addy sits beside Caroline on the couch. Her head is propped against a back cushion, her eyes closed. 'You are a saint,' Addy whispers, interlacing his fingers with hers, and Caroline smiles, her eyes still closed. Not only had she orchestrated the call to the States to reach Jakob – the whole family had piled into the neighbour's living room to voice their hellos – she'd also proven a courteous, patient host, catering in her calm, quiet manner to the boisterous polyglots who'd swarmed her small home. There must have been three languages spoken at any given moment throughout the evening – Polish, Portuguese, and Yiddish – not one of them English. But if Caroline was at all fazed, she never let on.

Caroline opens her eyes, turns her head to meet Addy's gaze. Her voice is soft, sincere. 'You have a beautiful family,' she says.

Addy squeezes her hand and leans back to rest his own head against the couch cushion, tapping his toe gently to the music.

Just because I always wear a smile
Like to dress up in the latest style
'Cause I'm glad I'm livin'
I take these troubles all with a smile

Addy hums the tune, wishing the night would never end.

AUTHOR'S NOTE

When I was growing up, my grandfather Eddy (the Addy Kurc of my story) was, for all I could tell, American through and through. He was a successful businessman. His English, to my ear, was perfect. He lived in a big, modern house up the road from ours, with floor-to-ceiling picture windows, a porch perfect for entertaining, and a Ford in the driveway. I thought little of the fact that the only children's songs he ever taught me were in French, that ketchup (*un produit chimique*, as he called it) was strictly banned from his pantry, or that he'd made half of the things in his home himself (the contraption that dangled his soap by a magnet over the bathroom sink to keep it dry; the clay busts of his children in the stairwell; the cedar sauna in his basement; the living room drapes, woven on his handmade loom). I found it curious when he'd say things like 'Don't parachute on your peas' at the dinner table (What did that even mean?), and mildly annoying when he'd pretend not to hear me if I answered one of his questions with a 'yeah' or 'uh-huh' – 'yes' was the only affirmative answer that met his grammatical standards. Looking back, I suppose others might have labelled these habits as unusual. But I, an only child with a single living grandfather, knew nothing different. Just as I was deaf to the slight inflection my mother now tells me he carried in his English diction, I was blind to his quirks. I loved my Papa dearly; he simply was who he was.

Of course, there were things about my grandfather that impressed me greatly. His music, to start. I'd never met a person as devoted to his art. His shelves overflowed with 33-rpm records, alphabetically arranged by composer, and with books of repertory for the piano. There was always music playing in his home – jazz, blues, classical, sometimes an album of his own. Often I would arrive to find him at the keys of his Steinway, a no. 2 pencil tucked behind his ear as he plotted melodies for a new composition, which he'd practise and tweak and practise some more until he was happy with it. Every now and then he would ask me to sit beside him as he played, and my heart would race as I'd watch him closely, waiting for the subtle nod that meant it was time to flip to the next page of his sheet music. 'Merci, Georgie,' he'd say as we reached the end of the piece, and I'd beam up at him, proud to have been helpful. On most days, once my grandfather was finished with his own work, he would ask if I'd like a lesson, and I would always say yes – not because I shared his affinity for the piano (I was never very good at it), but because I knew how happy it made him to teach me. He'd pull a beginner's book from the shelf and I would rest my fingers tentatively on the keys, feeling the warmth of his thigh against mine, and I would try my hardest not to make any mistakes as he walked me patiently through a few bars of the theme to Haydn's 'Surprise Symphony'. I wanted badly to impress him.

Along with my grandfather's musical prowess, his ability to speak seven languages left me in awe. I attributed his fluency to the fact that he had offices around the world and family in Brazil and in France, although the only relative of his generation that I knew by name was Halina, a sister with whom he was especially close. She visited a few times, from São Paulo, and occasionally a cousin my age would come from Paris to stay with us for a few weeks in the summertime to learn English. Everyone in his family, it seemed, had to speak at least two languages.

What I *didn't* know about my grandfather when I was a kid was that he was born in Poland, in a town once home to more than 30,000 Jews; that his birth name wasn't actually Eddy (as he later renamed himself) but Adolf, though when he was growing up everyone called him Addy. I didn't know he was the middle of five children, or that he spent nearly a decade of his life not knowing whether his family had survived the war, or whether they'd perished in concentration camps or been among the thousands executed in the ghettos of Poland.

My grandfather didn't keep these truths from me intentionally – they were simply pieces of a former life he'd chosen to leave behind. In America he had reinvented himself, devoting his considerable energy and creativity entirely to the present and future. He was not one to dwell on the past, and I never thought to ask him about it.

My grandfather died of Parkinson's disease in 1993, when I was fourteen. A year later, a high school English teacher assigned our class an 'I-Search' project intended to teach us research skills while we dug up pieces of our ancestral pasts. With my grandfather's memory so fresh, I decided to sit down for an interview with my grandmother, Caroline, his wife of nearly fifty years, to learn more about his story.

It was during this interview that I first learnt of Radom, although at the time I had no concept of how significant this place once was to my grandfather, or how important it would become to me – so much so that twenty years later, I would be drawn to visit the city, to walk the cobblestone streets, imagining what it might have been like to grow up there. My grandmother pointed to Radom on a map, and I wondered aloud whether, after the war, my grandfather ever returned to his old hometown. *No,* my grandmother said. *Eddy never had any interest in going back.* She went on to explain that Eddy was lucky enough to be living in France when the Nazis invaded Poland in 1939 and that he was the only member of his family to escape from Europe at the start of the war. She told me he was once engaged to a Czech woman he met aboard a ship called the *Alsina;* that she herself first laid eyes on him in Rio de Janeiro, at a party in Ipanema; that their first child, Kathleen, was born in Rio just a few days before he reunited with his family – parents and siblings, aunts and uncles and cousins he hadn't seen or heard from for nearly a decade. Somehow, they'd all miraculously survived a war that annihilated over ninety per cent of Poland's

Jews and (I would later discover) all but about 300 of the 30,000 Jews from Radom.

Once his family was settled in Brazil, my grandmother explained, she and my grandfather moved to the United States, where my mother, Isabelle, and my uncle Tim were born. My grandfather didn't waste any time in changing his name from Adolf Kurc (pronounced 'Koortz' in Polish) to Eddy Courts or in taking the oath of American citizenship. *It was a new chapter for him,* my grandmother said. When I asked if he maintained any of his customs from the Old World, she nodded. *He barely spoke of his Jewish upbringing, and no one knew he was born in Poland – but he had his ways about him.* Just as the piano was an integral part of his own upbringing, my grandfather insisted that his children practise an instrument every day. Conversation at the dinner table had to be in French. He made espresso long before most of his neighbours had ever heard of it, and he loved haggling with the open-air vendors at Boston's Haymarket Square (from which he would often return with a paper-wrapped beef tongue, insisting that it was a delicacy). The only candy he allowed in the house was dark chocolate, brought back from his travels to Switzerland.

My interview with my grandmother left my head spinning. It was as if a veil had been lifted, and I could see my grandfather clearly for the first time. Those oddities, those traits that I'd chalked up as quirks – many of them, I realised, could be attributed to his European roots. The interview also sparked an array of questions. *What happened to his parents? His siblings? How did* they *survive the war?* I pressed my grandmother for details, but she was able to share only a few sparse facts about her in-laws. *I met his family after the war,* she said. *They hardly spoke of their experiences.* At home, I asked my mother to tell me all that she knew. *Did Papa ever talk to you about growing up in Radom? Did he tell you about the war?* The answer was always no.

And then in the summer of 2000, a few weeks after I'd graduated from college, my mother offered to host a Kurc family gathering at our house on Martha's Vineyard. Her cousins agreed – they didn't see each other nearly enough, and many of their children had never even met. It was time for a reunion. As soon as the idea was seeded, the cousins (there are ten in all) began arranging their travel, and when July rolled around, family flew in from Miami,

Oakland, Seattle, and Chicago, and from as far away as Rio de Janeiro, Paris, and Tel Aviv. With children and spouses included, we numbered thirty-two in total.

Each night of our reunion, my mother's generation, along with my grandmother, would gather on the back porch after dinner and talk. Most nights I'd hang out with my cousins, draped over the living room sofas, comparing hobbies and tastes in music and movies. (How was it that my Brazilian and French cousins knew American pop culture better than I did?) On the last evening, however, I wandered outside, settled down on a picnic bench next to my aunt Kath, and listened.

My mother's cousins conversed with a sense of ease, despite their distinctly different upbringings and native tongues and the fact that many hadn't seen each other in decades. There was laughter, a song – a Polish lullaby that Ricardo and his younger sister Anna recalled from their childhoods, taught to them by their grandparents, they said – a joke, more laughter, a toast to my grandmother, the lone representative of my grandfather's generation. Languages often alternated mid sentence between English, French, and Portuguese; it was all I could do to keep up. But I managed, and when conversation shifted to my grandfather and then to the war, I leant in.

My grandmother's eyes brightened as she recounted meeting my grandfather for the first time in Rio. *It took me years to learn Portuguese,* she said. *Eddy learnt English in weeks.* She spoke of how obsessed my grandfather was with American idioms and how she didn't have the heart to correct him when he botched one in conversation. My aunt Kath shook her head as she recalled my grandfather's habit of showering in his undergarments – a means of bathing and laundering his clothes simultaneously when he was on the road; *he would do just about anything,* she said, *in the name of efficiency.* My uncle Tim remembered how my grandfather would embarrass him when he was a kid by striking up conversations with everyone, from waiters to passersby on the street. *He could talk to anyone,* he said, and the others laughed, nodded, and from the way their eyes shined I could tell how adored my grandfather was by his nieces and nephews.

I laughed along with the others, wishing I'd known my grandfather as a young man, and then grew quiet when a Brazilian cousin, Józef, began telling stories of his father – my grandfather's older brother. Genek and his wife, Herta, I learnt, had been exiled during the war to a Siberian gulag. Goose bumps sprang to my arms as Józef told of how he was born in the barracks, in the thick of winter, how it was so cold his eyes would freeze shut at night and his mother would use the warmth of her breast milk each morning to gently pry them open.

Hearing this, it was all I could do not to shout, *She what?* But as shocking as the revelation was, others soon followed, each somehow as astounding as the last. There was the story of Halina's hike over the Austrian Alps – while pregnant; of a forbidden wedding in a blacked-out house; of false IDs and a last-ditch attempt to disguise a circumcision; of a daring breakout from a ghetto; of a harrowing escape from a killing field. My first thought was, *why am I just learning these things now?* And then: *someone needs to write these stories down.*

At the time, I had no idea that *someone* would be me. I didn't go to bed that night thinking I should write a book about my family history. I was twenty-one, with a freshly minted degree under my arm, focused on finding a job, an apartment, my place in the 'real world.' Nearly a decade would pass before I'd set off for Europe with a digital voice recorder and an empty notebook to begin interviewing relatives about the family's experiences during the war. What I fell asleep with that evening was a stirring sensation in my gut. I was inspired. Intrigued. I had a boatload of questions, and I craved answers.

I have no idea what time it was when we all finally meandered back to our rooms from the porch – I just recall that it was Felicia, the oldest of my mother's cousins, who was the last to speak. She was a bit more reserved than the others, I'd noticed. While her cousins were gregarious and uninhibited, Felicia was serious, guarded. When she spoke, there was sadness in her eyes. I'd learnt that night that she was a year old at the start of the war, eight at its end. Her memory was still sharp, it seemed, but sharing her experiences made her uneasy. It would be years before I would gently uncover her story, but I remember thinking that whatever memories she harboured must have been painful.

'Our family,' Felicia said in her thick French accent, her tone sober, 'we shouldn't have survived. Not so many of us, at least.' She paused, listening to the breeze rattling the leaves in the scrub oak trees beside the house. The rest of us were silent. I held my breath, waiting for her to go on, to offer up some sort of explanation. Felicia sighed and brought a hand to the place on her neck where her skin was still pockmarked, I would later learn, by a near-fatal case of scurvy she'd contracted during the war. 'It's a miracle in many ways,' she finally said, looking out toward the tree line. 'We were the lucky ones.'

These words would stay with me until the burn to understand how, exactly, my relatives could have defied such odds finally overcame me and I couldn't help but start digging for answers. *We Were the Lucky Ones* is the story of my family's survival.

SINCE THEN

By the time I walked the streets of Radom while writing this book, the Kurcs' hometown had been rebuilt and felt friendly, quaint; but knowing what I now know about its devastating Holocaust history, it comes as no surprise that at war's end, returning to Poland, for my relatives, was never a consideration. Below is a brief explanation of where the Kurcs decided to settle once they made it safely to the shores of the Americas. (Note that I've used Bella's real name, Maryla, here. I changed it in the book as I felt Maryla was too close phonetically to Mila and could be confusing to readers.)

'Home' for the Kurcs after the war became Brazil, the United States, and later France. The family kept in close contact, mostly by letter, and visited each other whenever they could, often for Passover.

Mila and Selim remained in Rio de Janeiro, where Felicia attended medical school. Upon graduating, she met a Frenchman and a few years later moved to Paris to start a family. After Selim passed away, Mila followed her daughter to France. Today, Mila's grandson lives in her old home in the Sixteenth Arrondissement, just blocks from Felicia and her husband, Louis, whose elegant apartment looks out on the Eiffel Tower. Mila kept in close touch with the nun who took Felicia in during the war. In 1985, thanks to Mila's nomination, Sister Zygmunta was honoured posthumously as a Righteous Among the Nations.

Halina and Adam put down roots in São Paulo, where Ricardo's sister, Anna, was born in 1948. They shared a house with Nechuma and Sol, and Genek and Herta lived close by with their two sons, Józef and Michel. To repay Herr Den for saving her life during the war, Halina sent regular checks to him in Vienna. She and Adam never told their firstborn of his real birthday; Ricardo was in his forties and living in Miami when he discovered that he was born on Italian soil and not in Brazil as his birth certificate indicated.

In the States, Jakob and Maryla landed in Skokie, Illinois, where Victor's younger brother, Gary, was born and where Jakob (Jack, to his American friends and relatives) kept up his career in photography. They remained close with Addy (who changed his name to Eddy) and Caroline, who settled in 1947 in Massachusetts, where Kathleen's sister (my mother), Isabelle, and their brother, Timothy, were born. Eddy travelled often to visit the family in Illinois, Brazil, and France, and continued to make music; he produced a number of recordings, both popular and classical, composing up until his death.

As of 2017, Nechuma and Sol's grandchildren, along with their spouses and progeny, number more than one hundred. We are scattered now throughout Brazil, the United States, France, Switzerland, and Israel; our family reunions are truly global affairs. Among us are pianists, violinists, cellists, and flautists; engineers, architects, lawyers, doctors, and bankers; carpenters, motorcyclists, filmmakers, and photographers; naval officers, event planners, restaurateurs, DJs, teachers, entrepreneurs, and writers. When we come together our gatherings are loud and chaotic. There are few of us who look the same or dress the same or even grew up speaking the same languages. But there is a shared sense of gratitude, for the simple fact that we are together. There is love. And always, there is music.

ACKNOWLEDGEMENTS

This book began as a simple promise to record my family's story, something I needed to do for myself, for the Kurcs, for my son, and for his children and their great-grandchildren and so on – I had little concept, however, of what exactly the project would entail, or of just how many people I would rely upon for help along the way.

The bones of *We Were the Lucky Ones* came together, first and foremost, with oral histories passed down to me by family. I've collected hours (and hours) of digital voice recordings and filled dozens of notebooks with names and dates and personal narratives, thanks to the stories and memories my relatives so readily shared. I am especially indebted to my late grandmother, Caroline, for quietly safeguarding the seeds of my grandfather's story until the time was right to pass them along, and to Felicia, Michel, Anna, Ricardo, Victor, Kath, and Tim for welcoming me into their homes, showing me around their beautiful cities, and patiently answering my endless barrage of questions. Thank you as well to Eliska, who opened a window into what it was like to be a refugee in those harrowing first months of 1940, and whose description of my young grandfather made her blue eyes, even at eighty-eight, sparkle.

For years I flew around the world to meet with family and close friends of the Kurcs – anyone with a connection to my story. Where there were gaps in my research, I located survivors with similar backgrounds and reached out to scholars who specialised in the Holocaust and World War II. I read books, watched films, and mined archives, libraries, ministries, and magistrates, following just about any lead, no matter how far-fetched it seemed, for details of the family's journey. I was continuously amazed at the records that could be found with enough digging, and at the willingness of people and organisations around the world to offer assistance. Although there are far too many cooperating sources to mention by name, I'd like to express my gratitude to a few of them here.

Thank you to Jakub Mitek of the Resursa Obywatelska cultural centre in Radom, who so graciously spent a day guiding me through the streets of my grandfather's hometown and whose encyclopedic knowledge of the city and its history added layers of depth and colour to my story; to Susan Weinberg for her work with the Radom KehilaLinks, and to Dora Zaidenweber, for sharing with me what it was like to grow up in prewar Radom; to Fábio Koifman, whose book about Ambassador Souza Dantas and whose assistance in retrieving records at the Brazilian National Archives were invaluable; to Irena Czernichowska at the Hoover Institution, who helped me uncover (among other things) my great-uncle Genek's nine-page handwritten account of his years in exile and in the army; to Barbara Kroll at the UK Ministry of Defence, who sent me stacks of military records and helped me retrieve unclaimed medals of honour for relatives who fought for the Allies; to Jan Radke of the International Red Cross, who hand delivered dozens of relevant documents; to the librarians and archivists at the US Holocaust Memorial Museum, who fielded my many questions; to the USC Shoah Foundation for recording interviews with thousands of Holocaust survivors (these video narratives, for me, are like gold); to the members of the Kresy-Siberia Yahoo group who shared their first-hand accounts and pointed me down the proper paths to understanding Stalin's World War II; to the Seattle Polish Home Association, through which I was connected to a handful of gulag survivors and to a translator-turned-friend, Aleksandra, with whom I worked closely in my research; to Hank Greenspan, Carl Shulkin, and Boaz Tal, historical readers who so generously offered their time and their tremendous expertise; and to the innumerable individuals who have helped catalogue and digitise the extensive databases of organisations such as JewishGen, Yad Vashem, the American Jewish Joint Distribution Committee, the International Tracing Service, the US Holocaust Memorial Museum, the Polish Institute and Sikorski Museum, and the Holocaust and War Victims Tracing Centre. The vast amount of searchable information available today, thanks to these resources, is mind-boggling.

Long before my book remotely resembled a book, Kristina, Alicia, Chad, John, and Janet of my writing group in Seattle were among my earliest supporters; they offered thoughtful feedback and, perhaps most important, the encouragement I needed to keep writing month after month. Conversations with Janna Cawrse Esarey inspired my own list of Big Hairy Audacious Goals (including that of completing this book). The nonprofit 826 Seattle believed enough in my work to include a sample of it in its 2014 anthology, *What to Read in the Rain;* the invitation to contribute was an honour, and just the motivation I needed to hone my work.

John Sherman, dear friend and fellow author, was one of the first few people to read my book from front to back; his unwavering endorsement and keen insights over the years have helped buoy my confidence and take my work to another, better level.

Jane Fransson's editing prowess did wonders for my book. Her genuine excitement around my family's story and belief in me as a writer lit a fuse in me, and helped propel my project into the next phase of its life.

Thank you to Sarah Dawkins, for her friendship and her sound advice in navigating the path to publication, and to my girlfriends near and far, who for the past decade have fervently anticipated the release of this book (I pray that it's been worth the wait!) and have filled me with morale-boosting love and support in the times I needed it most.

If books could have soul mates, that person for *We Were the Lucky Ones* would be my agent, Brettne Bloom of The Book Group. Brettne's connection with my story was immediate and heartfelt. Her brilliant mind and gentle yet discerning eye have guided my thought process and my prose through countless collaborations and revisions. I am grateful every day for Brettne's friendship, for her extraordinary talent, and for the volumes of energy and TLC she has poured into the success of this project.

When my manuscript fell into the nurturing hands of my editor at Viking, Sarah Stein, I knew the book had found its home. Sarah embraced my story and my vision with unchecked enthusiasm and enduring patience, offering round after round of rich and remarkably spot-on feedback. Our partnership has pushed my story, along with my capability as a writer, to heights I'd never have reached on my own.

A huge thanks to the entire team at Viking, and to the creative minds that have been so integral in bringing this book to fruition: Andrea Shultz, Brian Tart, Kate Stark, Lindsay Prevette, Mary Stone, Shannon Twomey, Olivia

Taussig, Lydia Hirt, Shannon Kelly, Ryan Boyle, Nayon Cho, and Jason Ramirez. My gratitude as well to Alyssa Zelman and Ryan Mitchell for their artistic design contributions.

Many thanks, also, to my colleagues at Allison & Busby, for their belief in this novel, and for their help in shepherding it into the hands of a UK audience. I am especially thankful to Lesley Crooks, Sophie Robinson, and Kelly Smith for their sharp editorial eyes, to Christina Griffiths for her gorgeously designed cover, and to Emma Finnigan for her publicity efforts.

On the days over the past decade when I wondered if all of the research and writing was worth the effort, it was my husband who kept me inching toward the finish line. A heartfelt thank you to Robert Farinholt – for his unswerving faith in me and in my project (there is no greater champion of *We Were the Lucky Ones*), for his infinite optimism (it was Robert who made certain that we celebrated each of the book's major milestones), and for his insistence on spending our recent summer vacations not relaxing with our toes in the sand but retracing the footsteps of the Kurc family through Poland, Austria, and Italy. There isn't a soul on this planet I would have rather traversed those 1,100 miles with.

I must thank our son, Wyatt, as well, who has grown alongside this project (he will be five years old upon publication) and who carries himself with a fierce and familiar sense of determination – a trait I'd like to think his great-grandfather would be proud of, and one I hope he will continue to rely upon, as I have, to persevere through life's highs and lows. Wyatt has grounded me, humbled me, and brought me more joy and perspective than I could have ever thought possible.

I can't thank my son, of course, without also thanking 'his Liz,' as he calls her – our beloved nanny who quietly kept our family afloat when I was buried in my work.

Finally, I would like to offer special thanks to my parents. First, to my father, Thomas Hunter, who penned his debut novel (after a long and successful career in acting and screenwriting) when I was three – I'll never forget the sound of his Olivetti banging away upstairs in our small home deep in the woods of Massachusetts, or how thrilling it felt to hold a newly minted copy of his *Softly*

Walks the Beast in my hands. From the time I scrawled my own first work (I was four; I called my 'novel' *Charlie Walks the Beast),* my father has been an avid believer in my writing. He is a constant, energising source of inspiration.

And at last, to the person who seeded the idea for this project many, many years ago and who has been with me every single step of the way since: my mother, Isabelle Hunter. It is impossible to thank her enough for what she has done to help bring *We Were the Lucky Ones* to life. Having grown up surrounded by several of the characters in the book, my mother has shared priceless personal stories illuminating the Kurcs' unique family dynamic. She has read and reread my manuscript, and offered meticulous editorial feedback; she has fact-checked and sleuthed for details on my behalf, and dropped everything on multiple occasions to read a chapter, often sending me comments at an ungodly hour in order to meet a deadline. My mother's passion for this project, like mine, runs deep. She has been a steady, indefatigable presence from start to finish, and I am exceedingly grateful not only for her time and her thoughtful perspective, but for the abundance of love she has infused in me, and into the pages of this book.